W9-BMA-450

The Kingdom
Where
Nobody Dies

Books by Kathleen Hills

Past Imperfect
Hunter's Dance
Witch Cradle
The Kingdom Where Nobody Dies

The Kingdom Where Nobody Dies

Kathleen Hills

Poisoned Pen Press

Copyright © 2007 by Kathleen Hills

First Edition 2007

10 9 8 7 6 5 4 3 2 1

Library of Congress Catalog Card Number: 2007927881

ISBN: 978-1-59058-476-7 Hardcover

Poisoned Pen Press
6962 E. First Ave., Ste. 103
Scottsdale, AZ 85251
www.poisonedpenpress.com
info@poisonedpenpress.com

Printed in the United States of America

for Eric Robert

"Childhood is the kingdom where nobody dies.
Nobody that matters that is."
—Edna St. Vincent Millay, 1934

Chapter One

The thing about protecting yourself is knowing what your enemies are up to. Claire figured that as long as she could hear the tractor she was safe. When she got high enough she'd be able to see it, too; then she could keep an eye on the old bastard. She put one foot on the ladder and whispered, "bastard," then tried it aloud, but low and under her breath. "Bastard."

"Old son-of a bitch," she added in her every-day voice, and felt a thrill of guilt and daring. Spike stopped snuffling around the foundation and looked up at her, whining way down in his throat "Lay down. Stay!" She said it like she meant business, for all the good it would do. The minute she was out of his sight he'd be off like a shot, getting in to who knows what kind of trouble. She could tie him up, but then he'd start howling, and Ma would wonder what was going on.

The rungs of the ladder were rotten and cracked, and Claire kept her feet far to the sides and was careful to never put both feet on the same rung. Once she got onto the hen house roof, she ran as fast as she dared, both on the chance that Ma might be looking out the window and because the corrugated metal was blistering hot on the bottoms of her feet.

The big pine tree grew against the building, so close that the edge of the roof cut right into its bark. When she stretched up, she could just reach the lowest branch. She tucked her skirt into her underpants, dug her toes into the rough bark, held on tight, and scrambled, until there she was, sweaty and scraped, straddling the branch. From here on it was easy, just climbing up until she got to her spot.

The branches grew in a curve to make a perfect chair; one to sit on and another to brace her feet against in case of a sudden gust of wind. What if a tornado came? Would she go flying off above the barn and swoop over the chicken coop like she sometimes did in her dreams? It wasn't such a scary thought now. There wasn't a cloud in sight. Thinking about climbing back down *was* kind of scary. She didn't need to worry about that until the time came.

She leaned her shoulder into the trunk and lifted her butt enough to pull her skirt back down around her legs. Then she settled back and looked up into the green needles and blue sky. The tree swayed just enough to make it creak where it scraped against the roof, and the breeze made a whooshing through the needles. If she shut her eyes she could imagine herself perched in the crow's nest of a ship on the sea, hearing the ocean's roar and the grate of ropes against wood as she sailed over endless green waves.

In books, running away to sea was an adventure and the best way ever to escape. No one ever found you. Years later you'd come back home grown up and rich. At first people wouldn't know it was you, but when they figured it out, they were sorry they'd been so mean. But that was only if you were a boy; girls couldn't run away. It wasn't fair. When boys got big enough, they just did as they darn pleased, anyway, so they didn't really have to bother to run away. They only did it for fun. Girls had to stay at home and put up with things no matter what.

Claire wasn't sure she was brave enough to run away even if she could. Go off by herself? Leave Ma and Joey? If she just stayed in the tree, how long would it take for them to find her? They'd hunt everywhere, for days on end, but never think of looking up. And all the time she'd be watching them.

She undid the rusty safety pin that held the pocket of her dress closed and brought out an apple—hard, green, and no bigger than a chicken egg. She rubbed it on her dress, polishing it, screwing up her courage, and then nibbled off a tiny piece of the skin, and spit it out quick before it had a chance to touch her tongue. A crack in the tree where her backrest met the trunk made a hiding place where she kept her salt, a solid chunk chipped from the block in the barnyard and wrapped in a scrap of oilcloth to keep it dry. She rubbed the salt into the white flesh of the apple and sank her teeth into it. Pa'd skin her alive if he knew she had either the salt or the green apples. Well, he didn't know. She ate all five of them, salting before each bite, loving the crisp sour taste, until her gums felt fuzzy and her stomach queasy, all the while keeping her ears open for the rumble of the tractor. As long as she could hear it, it meant Pa was a half mile away, raking hay. He wouldn't waste gas by driving the tractor back to the house until he'd raked the whole field. She'd have to take his dinner out to him. If he needed to come back for something else, he'd walk. She could shinny down out of that tree and be pulling weeds in the garden long before he'd make it home.

If she leaned around the tree and looked behind her, she could see the tractor, a bright orange speck in the green field, inching along, like a ladybug crawling across a leaf. It was all that moved or made any noise. Otherwise everything was hot and lazy and still.

Until the crack of a gunshot broke the spell. People were always shooting at something around here, crows, tin cans... chicken-killing fox terriers. She hung over the branch to look down. Spike wasn't there. Her stomach felt even queasier. She said a little prayer and crossed herself.

Pa didn't like guns. He might stop mowing to see what was going on. But no, the tractor had just turned around and was heading for the other side of the field, not orange now, but a black shadow against the narrow blue band on the edge of the world that was the lake.

Lake Superior was almost like the ocean, probably. You couldn't see across to the other side. Claire'd never heard of anybody running away to spend their life sailing on it, though, but maybe sometimes people did.

Once, right after they moved here, Pa went to Gibb's Bay. He said he'd be gone for the whole day, so after they'd done the chores, Ma let them go to the lake. They took peanut butter sandwiches and a jar of cottage cheese, and walked through the pasture and along the railroad tracks.

The lake was bigger that she ever thought a lake could be. The water was clear as glass, not greenish like the lakes back home, and it didn't have any lily pads or weeds around the edges. Claire waded in and squealed when she felt its icy grab on her ankles. She hadn't been in for even a minute before she had to scramble out and wiggle her feet into the warm sand. Jake and Sam took off their clothes and dived right in just wearing their undershorts. Maybe boys were tougher and braver, or maybe they were just ornerier. Jake and Sam wouldn't admit they were cold even if they turned into icicles. Joey had tried to follow them, but he was still little enough to be smart, and pretty soon he came out, too, and spent the rest of the afternoon helping Claire build a sand fort.

Jake said he could tell time by the sun, but he was just bragging, because when they got back six o'clock had come and gone and they weren't at the supper table. Pa was. He threw their food to the chickens, and they ended up planting beans until two o'clock the next morning. Even Joey had to come out and hold the lantern.

Still, that lake was worth seeing, and that cold water would feel good today. She'd go again, next time the old son-of-a-bitch got out of the way.

She was jolted out of her daydream by a screechy twanging sound. She swung around again to see the tractor struggling along by the fence at the edge of the field.

"Claire! It's almost eleven-thirty!" Ma yelled out the window, and Claire didn't get the chance to see what happened next. Maybe he'd sink into the ditch and drown.

Hurrying down didn't give her enough time to be scared.

It was cooler in the house, but not much. Ma had the fan on low and the radio loud. *Our Gal Sunday* was just starting, so Claire had plenty of time to get Pa's dinner out to him. She put the bread and butter on the table and went to the cellar for salad dressing and cream for the coffee. When she got back up, Our Gal was having trouble with her wealthy and titled Englishman again, and Ma had laid out the slices of bread and started spreading on the butter. "We're almost out of cheese. Who do you suppose I should give it to?"

"How about we eat it ourselves? That'll take care of the problem."

Claire hadn't meant it as a joke, exactly, but Ma laughed and said, "Oh well, I'll give some to Pa and save the rest for Joey. Where is he?" She folded a piece of the buttered bread and put it in her mouth.

"He's upstairs. I'll get him." Joey probably didn't want to come down. He was up sick in the night, and went out to the garden to pick the last of the peas before the rest of them were done eating breakfast. After that he'd stayed out of sight, so Ma wouldn't see that he wasn't feeling well. He wasn't going to want to take Sam and Jake's dinner out to them either, because it was the fight that Jake had with Pa that scared him so bad, and that was probably what made him sick, too. And boys were supposed to be so tough.

"Get him to dig up a few potatoes to go with the peas for supper."

They put potted meat on the rest of the sandwiches. Claire twisted salt and pepper into wax paper for the boiled eggs and cut three pieces of yesterday's spice cake. She scraped the crusty parts from the corners of the pan and popped them into her mouth. Then she cut a small extra piece for herself, and poured coffee into the thermos jugs.

She yelled up the stairs for Joey, but he didn't answer, so he must have gone back outside.

He was coming out of the can, looking green around the gills.

"Are you still sick?"

"I puked again."

"You shouldn't have eaten all those fried potatoes. They're too rich for you." He never listened to her, anyway. "It's almost a quarter past."

Joey looked so scared, and so white, that Claire gave in. "Oh, all right. I'll do it." It meant she'd have to make two trips. One for Sam and Jake and one for Pa. And *that* meant it'd be past twelve-thirty when Pa got his dinner and he'd be mad. She'd have to think up some kind of story. Lying was bad, but Claire would sooner have God mad at her than Pa. If you went to confession, God would forgive you. Pa wouldn't.

"Go on inside. Ma's got some cheese for you." He looked like he might puke again, and Claire took off. She ran all the way to the potato field with the dinner pails bumping against her legs. She couldn't even see the boys; they'd sneaked off somewhere. Smoking, probably. She left the lunch bucket and thermos in the pickup and honked the horn so they'd know it was there.

She trotted back to the house for Pa's lunch, and after that her side hurt too bad to run anymore. She'd just have to be late. Most of the time, she liked going to the fields. She could hurry there and take her time walking back through the woods, or along the river. It was a cheat. She hollered back to Joey, "You have to take my turn pumping water!"

She could fake that she'd sprained her ankle, but then she'd have to remember to limp for a couple of days. Better to just leave the dinner pail and high-tail it back to the house before he had a chance to say anything.

She couldn't hear the tractor anymore, so he was either waiting, or he'd dropped dead of starvation. Too bad. She looked down at Spike, "Wouldn't that be too damn bad?"

Chapter Two

It wasn't just in the house. Even the outdoors felt empty. The horses' heads jerked up at the slamming of the screen door. After a bug-eyed stare at McIntire standing on the porch, they went back to twitching and stamping at flies. Did horses really care? Wasn't the occasional bucket of grain all it took to keep them happy? Did it matter who brought it? McIntire wasn't sure, and he didn't have a bucket of grain handy to test the hypothesis.

Kelpie, he was sure about. He knelt and pulled the spaniel's floppy ears around her chin. "It'll only be another month." He tried to raise the pitch of his voice and imitate Leonie's London accent. Kelpie wasn't fooled. McIntire picked her up in his arms. She felt boney.

A grinding of gears announced a car navigating the corner a half mile away. McIntire sank to the steps and settled the dog onto his knees. "Who do you reckon that is?" Judging from the roar of the accelerating engine, it was not someone out to take in the view. "Driving a B-52, you think?" McIntire leaned back into the railing. "What have we come to? Two old codgers sitting in the shade watching the world pass by."

The car didn't pass by. Gears screeched again, and tires spit sand, as it slowed just enough to swing into the driveway. A dark maroon Buick headed straight for McIntire and stopped with its blinding shark's maw grill two yards from his feet. The man who leapt gracefully out was slim and dark, with a later-than-five-o'clock shadow. He was the last person McIntire expected to see and one of the last he wanted to see. Father Adrien Doucet leaned on his open car door and demanded, "Don't you answer your phone?"

"No." McIntire considered standing up, but sitting on the steps kept him at about the same level as the diminutive priest. Besides, it was too hot to make any unnecessary moves. "Have you come to chastise me for my backsliding ways? Somebody spill the beans that my wife's not around to protect me?"

Doucet didn't smile or turn off his car's engine. "Maybe you can give me a rain check. There's been an accident. A death, near as I can see."

McIntire couldn't bring himself to respond. He couldn't bring himself to think. *A death.* The words meant that he needed to get into that Buick and let himself be driven somewhere. Further than that, his brain refused to take him. He got to his feet and carried Kelpie into the kitchen. Struggling to keep his hand steady, he slopped a dipperful of fresh water into her bowl and reached for his hat. This time when the door whacked shut the horses didn't look up.

The Buick was a flashy but comfortable vehicle, or would have been if the seat wasn't pulled so far forward that McIntire's knees bumped his chest, and if it hadn't reeked of cigarette smoke.

He braced himself as they careened down the driveway and asked the question that would set in motion a ritual with which he'd become far too familiar, "Who?"

Doucet's flock was small. Outside of McIntire's own family, all either moved away or dead, and Nick Thorsen, fellow back-slider, the only Catholics around that he could think of were Indians. The only Indians he knew personally were the Walls. Twila Wall was older than Methusela, but her death shouldn't require the constable's presence.

The father pulled out onto the road and hit the gas pedal. Hard. "Reuben Hofer."

McIntire didn't even try to quell the relief. The man had only been around since late spring, when he'd moved his family into the old Black Creek schoolhouse and set to farming the land around it. Unlike most newcomers to St. Adele, the Hofers really were newly come, not 'returners' or shirt-tail relatives of some current resident. McIntire wasn't acquainted with him, but he'd heard enough gossip to know Hofer wasn't Catholic.

"His wife is." Doucet steered with his elbow as he stuck a filtered cigarette between his lips. "And the children." His priestly vocation must extend into even the most mundane facets of his life; the man drove like he was in a race with Satan. Maybe he figured he had divine protection. Or possibly it was a plan calculated to urge McIntire into a desperate plea to his maker and thus back into the fold. Mercifully the ride was short, and the flirting with deep ditches and fishtailing around corners kept McIntire's mind off its conclusion.

They turned into a narrow side-road, not much more than a strip of weeds and grass between two sandy tracks that went nowhere. The sawmill it once led to had been abandoned years before when its young owner was drafted into the war, not to return.

The road was bordered on one side by a wide hayfield and the other by swamp thick with alder. They rounded a bend and skidded to a stop inches in back of Doctor Marc Guibard's Plymouth coupe.

A side-delivery rake blocked the way. The tractor that had pulled it there rested at a forty-five degree angle, nose in the roadside bushes, its front wheels sunk in the mire.

Guibard emerged from the brush, soaked to the knees of his impeccably creased trousers. He sagged against the fender of his car and wiped his sleeve across his brow, chalk white despite the heat. His words, "We'll need the sheriff," crushed McIntire's hopes that Hofer's premature death had been the result of a simple stroke or heart attack.

Father Doucet re-started the Buick.

"Call from my place." Guibard had the luxury of a private phone line and his home was also miles nearer than the priest's house in Aura.

Doucet gave a quick nod and drove off in reverse at approximately the same speed he'd come.

McIntire let the buzzing flies lead him to Reuben Hofer. The man hung, solid denim covered rump in the air and head—or what was left of it—down, wedged between the tractor's seat and steering wheel. Blood ran thick and black down the tangled beard, onto the crumpled hat and bright orange machine. Blood dripped over the leaves, disappearing into the surface of the murky water, and blood filled the hand that rested, palm upward, on the clutch. The hand was long fingered, elegant in its offering; not the hand of a farmer.

McIntire stood at the edge of the road, unable to force himself to move nearer, equally unable to take his eyes from the grisly scene. A crow perched on the top of a nearby tamarac in a similar attitude. McIntire turned back to the doctor. "Have you got something we can cover him with?"

Guibard shrugged and opened the Plymouth's door. He pulled a plaid flannel shirt from the back seat. "Koski won't like it."

McIntire waded into the muck, each step sending up the sulphurous odor of rotted vegetation to mingle with the smell of blood and heat. He flicked the shirt to discourage the sluggish blue flies. The silent crow hopped to a higher perch. McIntire averted his gaze as he spread the fabric over the head and shoulders. The flies settled onto it, probing in frustration.

As he turned away, McIntire felt himself overwhelmed with anger. Pure, unmitigated ice-cold rage pounded in his skull. A life ended and how many more altered, devastated, or destroyed? It was those lives that made him the most infuriated. Which was worse, to die, or to be left behind to suffer the loss forever? The dead were dead. Past pain. Out of the line of fire.

Perhaps that was not quite true. Reuben Hofer would now be fair game, powerless to defend himself or his dignity. McIntire hadn't been acquainted with the living Reuben Hofer. He'd come to know him now, all too well. He'd pry into the most intimate details his life, question and probe and listen until a Reuben Hofer would materialize, moulded from all the snippets of perception and prejudice of those around him. Would it be a more honest depiction than his own narrow view might have been? Whatever the truth of it, the man himself would provide no information. The Hofer McIntire would come to know would be only a reflection.

He stumbled back onto the road. "Who found him?"

"The good father. He was on his way to pay a good-fatherly visit to Mrs. Hofer." Guibard had never been in the habit of referring to Adrien Doucet with the respect that might be expected. Probably because the two of them were far too much alike.

"Sort of an indirect route, ain't it?" McIntire asked. The road didn't go to the schoolhouse. Doucet would have had to leave his car at the old sawmill and walk the rest of the way through the fields. He didn't seem like the kind of man who'd want to slow himself down that much.

"Apparently Father's a birdwatcher." Guibard said it with the expression he might have used for "pick-pocket."

"Did you know this man?"

"Not really. I've met him, but not to get to know. I've seen the wife a couple of times. She…" Guibard hesitated, perhaps on the brink of a further disclosure, but discretion won out.

"Is she sick? Maybe that's something we should know about. She's going to have to be told what's happened before much longer."

"She has a few medical problems." That could mean anything, but the doctor apparently wasn't going to say more.

McIntire had run into Reuben Hofer once in Karvonen's store and had introduced himself. Hofer seemed a pleasant enough person, if a bit…intense. His piercing *I-know-what-you've-been-up-to* eyes, combined with a full beard, put McIntire in mind of old illustrations of the John Brown whose body had lain mouldering in the grave for the past ninety or so years. He'd given the impression of someone who wasted no movement, no words.

When the family first moved in, Leonie had paid a duty call, but only saw a young girl who'd taken her rhubarb tart and said her mother was lying down. There were a pair of older boys, too. Potential hell-raisers if rumor proved correct. Maybe even more so with their father dead of…what? "A gunshot?" McIntire asked.

"That or a hand grenade."

"Any idea of how close? What direction? What sort of gun?"

"Not a shotgun. Not pellets anyway. I shouldn't have said that about the hand grenade, it was most likely a single projectile. Possibly a deer rifle. In which case it could have come from quite a distance. Christ, I hate this heat." Guibard opened the buttons on his shirt and waved the sweat-sogged fabric away from his skin. McIntire wasn't sure if he was more shocked—not too strong a word—at the dignified doctor's unexpected behavior or at the hint of suntan on the sunken hairless chest. "On the other hand," he continued to fan himself, "it could have been fairly close. As long as the bullet hit its mark, the wound would look pretty much the same regardless of how far it had traveled, I guess, but what the hell would I know? I've never seen a gunshot wound to the head outside of on a deer. If we can figure out the angle it hit at, that might give some idea of the distance it came." He shook his head. "I'm way out of my league here. I think I can safely say that it came from directly behind, though, but I can't be positive until I get the wound cleaned up a little." He leaned back against the car and closed his eyes, for a moment resembling the old man he was, then straightened and began doing up his buttons. "Like I said, I'm no expert. I'll leave most of that sort of thing to my friends in Lansing."

"Think it could have been an accident?"

"Hell, no."

"He hasn't been here long enough to build up a stockpile of enemies."

"It only took one."

McIntire left the doctor decently clothed, wiping at the mud on his shoes, and walked into the field steaming with the cloying scent of sun baked alfalfa. The aroma of new-mown hay was not all it was cracked up to be. It was a big field, ten or twelve acres. He followed the course of the tractor and rake. Guibard thought the shot had come from behind, which seemed obvious even to McIntire. The far edge of the field was marked by a line of trees, maple and beech. They were spindly and widely spaced, but the patchy underbrush of hazel and dogwood might provide adequate cover for an assassin. If he even needed cover. There'd be no one around to see the attacker except Reuben, and if he was on a noisy tractor with his back turned…

The final row of cut hay was only slightly skewed. A bird's eye view might show up the point at which the tractor became driverless, but from his earthbound point, McIntire couldn't guess.

A patch of white flickered in the bushes, and a dog, one of the ugliest animals he had ever seen, skittered out of the tall grass. It stopped short at the sight of McIntire, gave a strangled yip, and darted back through the trees to a small girl standing in the shadows, not twenty yards from him. Thin and dark, with a mass of tangled hair stuck with some gluey substance and the odd cockleburr, she resembled an upended dust mop. She stared at him from wide, dark-circled eyes as she deliberately set down her syrup pail. Then she snatched up the dog and tore off, on toothpick legs, like a scared rabbit

She'd tell her mother. McIntire only hoped that Sheriff Koski made it here before Mrs. Hofer showed up. He strode back through the stubble and said as much to Guibard.

"She won't come."

He seemed confident about it. The medical problems must be something fairly serious.

A fast moving cloud of dust presaged the return of the Reverend Doucet. There was no emergency now, if there ever had been. His courting of disaster must be habit.

"The sheriff will be here in a few minutes." He rummaged in the back seat of the car and stood erect, placing a stole about his neck.

McIntire was confused. "I thought Reuben wasn't Catholic."

"That doesn't make him unworthy of our prayers."

McIntire supposed that it didn't.

For the next few minutes there was nothing to be heard but the priest's low murmur, rising and falling in harmony with the buzz of the thwarted flies. Sound that had no beginning and no end, a consistent drone that just *was*. Like the glare of the sun and the weight of the air.

Did the dead man's spirit, that soul of which the priest was seeking redemption, still linger nearby? Did it hover at treetop height, reluctant to say goodbye, angry at being taken in the middle of its earthly task. Did the spirit know, or care, who the agent of its bodily death had been? Had Reuben Hofer realized, in the instant before he died, who had killed him?

In the stillness, the approach of Sheriff Pete Koski's Power Wagon could be heard a mile away.

Father Doucet stood up, brushed ineffectually at his knees, and turned to McIntire. "We'd better go inform the widow." He pulled the cigarette pack from his pocket.

"Shouldn't we wait a while longer? We don't want her to insist on coming out here."

"She won't."

Chapter Three

The hay rake in the road, left there under Pete Koski's orders, prevented them from driving closer to Hofer's homestead, something for which McIntire was grateful, and not only because it kept him out of Father Hot Rod's car. The walk across the fields would give him time to think, to calm the beating of his heart and the pounding in his head. At the current temperatures his profuse sweating would go unnoticed, but the catch in his voice was there when he asked, "He had three kids?"

"Four. The youngest is only eight."

"Guibard says the wife is not in good health."

Doucet nodded.

"They can't be making much of a living on this place, and with her husband dead...."

"God will provide."

God wasn't likely to finish putting up that hay, but McIntire didn't pursue it.

They set off through into the sun, the priest puffing his Viceroy and apparently having no trouble matching McIntire's stride. He was slender and supple, almost girlish, the sort who might be called "wiry." Despite being dressed in black everywhere below the Roman collar, he showed not one drop of perspiration.

"Shouldn't we have Guibard with us?" McIntire asked. "Regardless of their financial condition, this is going to be a terrible shock, and if she's already not well...."

"It'll be all right."

Was the father expressing faith in God again, or in himself? McIntire persisted. "The little girl was here earlier, bringing her father's dinner pail, I think. When she saw me, she took off like a scalded dog. She was too far away to have seen anything, but she's probably already told her mother that something was going on."

Doucet only nodded. His complacency, rather than being reassuring, was building up to aggravation. McIntire half expected to be patted on his shoulder—if the priest could reach it—and addressed as "my son."

Outside of being non-Irish, chain smoking, driving like a bat out of hell, and looking like a member of *Ballet Russe*, Adrien Doucet was all priest: A selfless caring facade masking a man judgmental, dogmatic, and exasperatingly sure of his own righteousness. That was only McIntire's opinion, of course—an opinion admittedly based more on prejudice than direct observation.

McIntire was still enough of his father's guilt-driven son to give the man a wide berth when they happened to be in the same room, which wasn't often. Right now he felt a prick of envy for the priest's faith. Doucet vaulted over the barbed wire fence and struck out across the pasture on the other side, pausing now and then for scrutiny of some feathered creature, a portrait of serenity. His face would not have told if he was the bearer of bad news, good news, or a dozen eggs.

They opened the barnyard gate and walked toward the building in which McIntire had made his first acquaintance with the tortures of formal education. That had been back in the days when St. Adele township had been an up and coming settlement of half its present area with three time its present population. The heyday ended when the last white pine was cut, and two schools soon became an expensive luxury. This one had long since been converted into a home, but still looked like a schoolhouse from the outside—white and square, a pump in the front yard and two privies in the back.

The yard was rigidly tidy, with nothing to indicate that four children lived here. No bikes, no tree forts, no swings tied to the maple limbs. But the Hofers hadn't been here long.

In the distance, beyond the barn, McIntire spotted what he took to be the older boys, plying hoes in a garden plot. Two stocky silhouettes bent to their work with concentration. They gave no sign that they noticed their visitors.

The little girl and the youngest child—and the dog—he didn't see.

At McIntire's knock the blaring of the radio abruptly ceased, followed by a low "come on in," and they entered a cramped landing with stairs descending into a pit that McIntire recalled as being full of coal, and three steps up to what had been the cloakroom. But for the washing machine and the waiting pile of dirty laundry, it was little changed; jackets hung on hooks, milk buckets and rubber boots cluttered the benches that ran around three walls. Cardboard boxes were stacked high under the smudged window. The neatness of the yard and farm buildings had stopped at the door. They passed through into the kitchen.

Mrs. Hofer sat next to a heavy wooden table heaped with the peas she was shelling into an enamel basin that rested on a chair beside her. McIntire hoped that the humming of the electric fan in the window disguised his gasp.

She was a lady of freak-show proportions. Larger than McIntire would have supposed a woman could grow without bursting the translucent ivory skin. Only the wisps of lank sooty hair lessened her resemblance to a giant albino toad. Somewhere under that pile of flesh there had to be a chair, but how could it support such weight? How had she folded herself to sit down? Could she stand up? Could she walk? Only her hands, extending from doughnuts of fat at the wrists as from a heavy overcoat, looked human. Delicate nimble fingers didn't stop in stripping the peas from their pods, even as she nodded to the two men.

Despite the open window and the fan, the cluttered room was stifling, humid, and redolent with a medley of odors McIntire didn't want to know the source of.

Father Doucet stepped forward. "Hello, Mary Frances. How are you feeling today?"

"Much better, thank you." McIntire somehow expected the words, squeezed out through the bulk as they were, to be a thin, reedy croak. In fact, the voice was gentle and low pitched. "You're late." Her gaze dropped to their trouser legs. "Is wallowing in the mud as a good way to cool off as it's advertized?"

The priest smiled and introduced McIntire. "I'm afraid we've come with bad news."

McIntire could have sworn that the tears that sprang into the raisins-in-dough eyes when Mrs. Hofer learned of her husband's death were those of relief, if not joy. She looked down at the peas and murmured something that sounded like, "God's will."

God was definitely having his way with them today, but wasn't he supposed to be four-square against murder?

The resident authority seemed to back him up on that. "It might not have been an accident, Mary Frances." Doucet transferred the basin from the chair to the flamboyant oilcloth of the table and sat with his bony knees aimed toward her considerably more imposing ones. "There'll be an investigation. You and your children may be in for an unpleasant time."

It was an odd way of addressing the situation. Losing their husband and father would presumably override any accompanying unpleasantness.

Mrs. Hofer let a half opened peapod drop onto her stomach and watched it slide to the floor. She wiped her fingertips on her striped apron. "When did this happen?"

"Sometime before noon. I was on my way here when I found him."

The chins bobbled as she made an audible gulp. "Claire went with his dinner."

"She only got as far as the edge of the field before she spotted me and took off." McIntire reassured her. "She didn't see anything. The sheriff is there now." He added, "They'll take your husband's body to Chandler. You can see him there."

Would they let her? Would she want to view her husband's mutilated body. Someone would have to make a formal identification.

"I can bring my car around and take you into town, if you wish." Doucet was hesitant in his offer.

The widow was confident in her refusal. "I don't think I'm well enough for that. My husband's sister will come to take care of things. Maybe you would contact her for me? A telegram. And would you be so good as to tell my sons to come inside? They're in the potato field."

It was a dismissal. She hadn't asked any questions, not even how her husband had died. She might not be thinking clearly, and was probably in shock. Doucet was already standing up to leave. He didn't seem worried about leaving her, and the sheriff should be there in a few minutes. But it wouldn't hurt for McIntire to stick around.

Mary Frances exhaled with a grunt as she shifted enough to reach a writing tablet resting on the window sill. For a time there was no sound but the scratching of pen on paper.

She finished writing her message and the particulars of reaching her sister-in-law and handed the note to Father Doucet. Only her trembling hands betrayed any emotion.

McIntire stayed in his chair. Through the window he could see the priest stride off past the barn, presumably headed for the potato patch and the sons.

"Mrs. Hofer, do you have any idea who might have wanted to harm your husband?" It was blunt, but there was no glossing over what had happened.

"No, of course not." Amazingly, her denial was punctuated by a low, dry, chuckle. "People here have not been terribly outgoing, but no one has…." She paused for a moment, and her hand flitted to her throat. "I don't suppose it was done on purpose. We don't even know anybody around here. Surely this was an accident?"

The arrival of Pete Koski saved McIntire from the necessity of responding. The astonishment on the sheriff's face at meeting Mrs. Hofer might have been construed as distress over the purpose of his visit, but McIntire didn't think the lady was fooled. She was probably used to it.

Koski took the priest's vacated chair. "We won't stay long. I know this has been a terrible blow, and the worst of it hasn't hit yet. That's why I'd like to ask you a few questions right now, if I may. Before shock sets in and your brain starts shutting things out. Forgetting."

Her chins wobbled in a nod.

"Do you know of anybody who'd want to harm your husband?"

"No. I told...this gentleman. We only just moved in and don't really know anybody here. We've got no enemies...or friends."

"Has anything else happened recently? Anything out of the ordinary? Dealings with the neighbors that seemed odd?"

She shook her head and stated again, "Outside of the people we bought this place from, we don't know the neighbors."

"Maki?"

She nodded.

Koski half pulled the cigarette pack from his shirt pocket, then shoved it back. "I'd like you to just give me a quick rundown on the day. What time did your husband get up this morning, go out to the field, that sort of thing."

She reclaimed the ball point pen and began running it between her fingers. "He was up just about sunrise, as usual. He had breakfast. He talked some about waiting until later in the day before raking the hay, to make sure it was dry. But he said there wasn't any dew to speak of last night, so he'd go out to take a look and maybe could get at it in the morning."

"So he went out right away?"

The pen stayed poised over the paper for a long moment. "No, first he went to get some gas for the tractor."

"To Karvonen's?"

"I couldn't say."

"What time did he get back?"

"I'm not exactly sure. He went for the gas, and was outside a while—I wouldn't know what he was doing—then came in for coffee, I'd say a few minutes after nine. He'd gone to the hayfield by the time Arthur Godfrey came on at half past."

"Did you expect him to come back to the house to eat dinner?"

"No. When they're working, we take it out to them."

"Them? He wasn't alone?"

"He was doing the raking by himself. My two older boys are working in the potato field. Claire fixed dinner and took my husband's out to the hayfield. My youngest son went with Sam and Jake's."

"What time was that?"

"About a quarter past twelve. The news was just finishing up. My husband liked his dinner at twelve-thirty, sharp." Did she always keep time by the radio? She rubbed at a smear of ink on the oilcloth and replaced the cap on the pen. "I need to talk to my children now."

And they weren't likely to come in with the sheriff still there. Koski stood up. "I'll leave you for now and come back this evening. Is there anybody we can call? You don't want to be alone right now."

"I'm hardly alone, not with four children." The suppressed laugh came again, almost a giggle. She made as if to stand, then sat back. Her feet were bare, and surprisingly clean, considering that she must not have seen them in years, let alone be able to reach them.

Chapter Four

The third time the rooster crowed, Claire opened her eyes. The sun was coming up, making a pink stripe on the wallpaper. It seemed like she'd been awake for hours, maybe hadn't gone to sleep at all. A mosquito buzzed around her head and she lay quiet, barely breathing, sneaking her hand up to get ready to slap when it landed, a stealthy hunter, lying in wait for her prey. Joey twitched and the mosquito took off. Phooey! It would be back again, and she'd have to start all over.

She stretched her legs and yanked them back quick. Not again! The bottom of her nightgown was warm and soggier than it would be from just sweat. Joey hadn't peed the bed for a long time, not since winter. Not once after they moved into this house. She couldn't bear it if he started again. It was so embarrassing. He smelled like pee at school, and sometimes she did, too.

Joey hated school, and he didn't care if the other kids stayed away from him or teased him. Claire didn't like school either, but she didn't hate it as bad as Joey did, and she hated being teased.

He always looked happy when he was asleep. He shouldn't be sleeping now, and he wouldn't be happy for long; the sun was up, they weren't, and there was going to be trouble. He'd gotten out of bed in the night to go outside again, but being sick wasn't going to help him.

"Joey, wake up!"

He didn't make a move, and she rolled over, careful not to get into the wet spot. He was lying still as a mouse, but his eyes were wide open. That was when she remembered that Pa was dead. Somebody shot him. Ma said it was probably an accident. Somebody shooting at a deer, but they didn't dare say so, because it wasn't deer season.

It had been strange, sitting at the supper table with just Ma and the boys, like after Grandpa died and before Pa came back to live with them. Strange to be able to leave the radio on, and to talk if they wanted to. Mostly Ma and Jake did all the talking, though. About the creamed peas and new potatoes, and getting enough potatoes from only two plants, and what time Sister's train would get there, because Jake would have to pick her up from the depot. Nobody said anything about Pa.

Joey whispered, "Are you sad?"

He was too little to have to lie to. "No," she told him. "Not very much. Not now, anyway."

"Is that a sin?"

"I guess so. You don't have to worry about sins." He was too little for that, too.

"I know. I don't care if he's dead, either." It sounded louder and braver, but he whispered again when he asked, "Where will we go when Ma dies?"

"We'll be grown up by then."

"What if we ain't?"

His chin started to quiver, and Claire felt her face get hot with shame. Boys shouldn't cry. "I'll be grown up," she told him. "I'll take care of us."

"Maybe we'll go live with Sister."

"Don't be dumb, Joey. Ma's not going to die." Where did he get these ideas, anyway?

He turned his back and snuffled into the pillow.

Claire didn't feel like crying, so she supposed she really wasn't sad, like she'd told him. She was sort of scared. Pa was shot when he was raking hay, and when she went over with his dinner pail there was that skinny man walking around in the field. He wasn't carrying a gun, though. Maybe she should have told the sheriff about it when he came after supper, but Ma just had her make the coffee and shooed her outside. The sheriff was kind of cute for an old guy. He was very tall, and wore cowboy boots, and he had a star on his chest, like a sheriff in a movie. There was a big police dog in his car, but Claire couldn't get a close up look, because Spike would have been scared out of his hide.

The sheriff stayed for a long time, talking to Ma and some to Sam and Jake, but he didn't say anything to her and Joey, or ask them anything. After he left, Father Doucet came. Claire didn't know when he went away; he was still there when her and Joey went to bed. Claire was glad, because she could turn out the light and go to sleep. Nothing could hurt her with a priest in the house.

Ma didn't act sad, either, but then she was grown up so she wouldn't cry or anything. She never used to be sad when Pa was gone for a long time, more than a year even, but maybe his being dead and not ever coming back made it different.

Claire thought about how she could get her nightgown off without the peed-on part touching her hair or maybe her face.

She shoved the sheet back and sat up. Her brother raised his head. His eyes were all red and bleary. "Can we go to the lake?"

Chapter Five

The knock at the door took McIntire unawares. He'd heard no car, so whoever it was had come on foot, bicycle, or horseback. Leonie was the only person he knew who traveled on either two wheels or four legs, so that left two legs, which meant Mia Thorsen. He'd not seen much of Mia that summer, and a visit at this hour meant that she must have run into some sort of crisis.

The floors were filthy, but at least he'd done his weekly dish washing. He buttoned his shirt as he peered between the curtains.

It wasn't Mia. A stocky woman in a kerchief and a dark blue dress, long sleeves and long stockings despite the heat, had retreated to the bottom of the steps and stood staring at the door. Ready to take off if the wrong person answered it? Somebody with car trouble, most likely. A lone female finding any port in a storm.

She showed no sign of bolting when McIntire stepped out, nor any damsel in distress hesitation.

"Mr. McIntire, how do you do? I'm Jane Hofer. I hope I'm not disturbing you. May I have a few minutes of your time?" The head scarf didn't quite manage to hide movie-star blond hair that made a flagrant contrast with her otherwise matronly appearance.

The victim's sister, then. She must have broken the land speed record making the trip to St. Adele. According to her sister-in-law, she lived in Iowa or somewhere pretty far off. Maybe it was Wisconsin. McIntire swung the door wider, murmured an inane apology for the state of the house, and led his visitor to the living room, which had cooled to a bearable level during the night. Leonie's pretentiously-called library, being on the north side of the house and shaded by spruce trees, was cooler still, but he'd been sleeping there, and it wasn't in a fit state for receiving female visitors. Or any visitors for that matter.

His offer of coffee or tea was met with a grateful smile and "No, thank you." She smoothed the back of her skirt and sank into the spot he'd indicated on the sofa. "I don't take stimulants."

She didn't look like the stimulant type for sure. She'd even managed to make that hair, which must be exactly the shade Leonie spent so many hours trying to glean from a bottle, look, not dowdy, but…business-like. McIntire said, "Please accept my condolences for the loss of your brother."

"Thank you. The circumstances of his death make it especially difficult to accept." Her speech was heavily tinged with German.

"Yes, it must be awful."

"Particularly for his wife."

"Of course."

"And for the children."

They were beginning to sound like a pair of wind-up dolls. McIntire asked, "Is there something I can help you with?"

"You're an officer of the law. It is possible that my brother was murdered. I should think that helping in this instance goes with the job." The soft rebuke was accompanied by a beatific smile that would have done Father Doucet proud.

"I'm only a town constable, Miss Hofer. But I'll certainly do what I can to bring your brother's killer to justice." Talk about wind-up dolls.

"May I have a glass of water, Mr. McIntire?"

"Of course. Forgive me for not offering it."

When he came back, she'd moved from the sofa to a stiff backed chair. She touched the glass to her lips, then placed it on the coffee table. Maybe the ice he'd put in was too decadent.

Maybe physical discomfort was the price of mental loosening-up. Miss Hofer sat in the chair like she was strapped to it, but spoke in a gossipy tone, "Constable McIntire, my sister-in-law is not a well woman."

"I could see that." The words slipped out before McIntire could stop them, but they brought a twitch to the corners of Jane Hofer's lips.

"Her weight is only one aspect of her health problems."

She didn't expand, and McIntire didn't like to ask, just said, "She'll have a difficult time without her husband."

The woman nodded. "Perhaps."

Perhaps? Was there some doubt? "She must not be able get around much, and the children can't be expected to run a farm."

"Jacob and Samuel are almost grown men. They've been working harder than most grown men for years. Ever since my brother returned home."

The tone was sharp. McIntire waited.

She sighed and a smidgeon more of the starch went out of her shoulders. "My brother was an idealist, but when it came to his own family…." She shook her head. "He was a firm man. Every member of a family should contribute what they can, and it's up to the parents to see that they do, but Reuben went much too far. During the war and for a few years afterwards, he was only home for a few short visits. His family lived with Mary Frances' father in Iowa. After he died they survived on letting his land out to be farmed on shares and what they got from the county. When Reuben came back, he was a stranger to the children, and he felt like he had to make up for lost time. He worked his father-in-law's farm for a year, until they lost it when the estate was settled. Then he rented a smaller farm and saved every penny, and somehow he was able to buy the place here. He worked night and day to do it, and saw to it that everybody else did, too. He made the children slaves, beasts of burden. Up before dawn so they could get a couple of hours work in before school. Even his youngest. I doubt any of them have had more than five or six hours of sleep a night in the past three years. Sometimes a whole lot less."

It was making McIntire's childhood sound positively rosy.

Miss Hofer smoothed her skirt again and went on, "Mary Frances, as you say, has not been able to do much. She has no choice but to rely on Claire's help, and it's good for a girl to learn to keep house, but it was only her influence that kept those boys from being worked right into the grave." She picked up the glass. "Reuben made their lives a misery, but he made them self-sufficient." The ice clinked. "They'll manage."

What was she saying? That Reuben Hofer's family was better off without him? It sounded like she might not be far wrong. She also might be the person, outside Reuben Hofer's immediate household, who knew the most about him. McIntire asked, "Do you have any idea who might have killed your brother?"

"No, certainly not. I expect it was an accident. Mary Frances says there's a great deal of shooting going on around here."

"Not so much this time of year."

"But it *could* have been an accident."

"Anything's possible, I guess." Why did people always say such a stupid thing? There were any number of things that were absolutely, irrefutably, beyond a shred of doubt, impossible. But Hofer's death being accidental wasn't one of them. It could have been accidental, but it sure as hell wasn't likely.

"It would be much less...harrowing for his widow and children if this were an accident."

"A murder investigation won't be pleasant for them," McIntire agreed.

"Mr. McIntire, may I speak frankly?"

McIntire doubted Jane Hofer could speak any other way. "Most certainly."

She folded her hands in her lap and fixed her eyes on his. "Mary Frances will, in all likelihood, not live to see her children grown."

"But surely—"

"She knows that. She may have another year or two. No more. Possibly much less. Her greatest fear has been what would happen to her children without her protection."

"From your brother?"

She nodded.

"That's not a concern now." There'd be no lack of other fears to step up to take its place.

"No," Jane Hofer agreed. "Now all she has to worry about is leaving behind four orphans condemned to living with the knowledge that their father was murdered. Live with everyone else knowing it, too. Memories are long, and people, children in particular, are not always kind."

It would be ugly, there was no doubt about that.

"I think it was an accident. Someone getting in some target practice, or shooting to frighten raccoons from the corn, perhaps." Her gaze remained unflinchingly direct, as she went on. "When Reuben said he'd decided to go to college, we were all astounded. He'd never shown any sign of having such ideas. He didn't ask permission, he just left. We thought that he'd come back when he'd seen enough of the world, but by the time he'd finished sowing his wild oats, he'd met Mary Frances and she was.... They were married." She took another sip from the glass and stood up. "Mary Frances is a good person. She's borne a great deal. I don't know how she manages to get through every day, sick as she is, knowing she's going to be leaving her children forever. Nothing can bring my brother back. I don't want to see his widow's suffering in her final months of life made any worse than it has to be."

Was she actually telling him to forget it? Write it off as an accident? God's will, perhaps? What did she think a township constable could do about it? He didn't even try to keep the incredulity out of his voice. "The county sheriff and the state police will be in charge of this investigation, and they are *not* going to see it as an accident."

"Yes," she said. "I'll be speaking to the sheriff soon. He's asked me to identify Reuben's body." The prospect didn't ruffle her outward placidity.

McIntire's offer of a ride home was turned down. "God saw fit to bestow two good legs upon me, I'll rely on them." She thanked him for the refreshment and walked briskly down the drive.

McIntire had heard God invoked more in the past 24 hours than any time since the short trip he'd made to Monte Carlo in 1936.

Chapter Six

It could have been an accident. If it had happened in October, McIntire would hardly have thought twice about it. But, despite Mary Frances Hofer's claims, and the fact that the odd woodchuck or two might be dispatched, bullets didn't generally fly in July the way they did during hunting season. But the wound, according to Guibard, might have been the result of a bullet fired from some distance. He wasn't sure. An accident would seem far fetched on the face of it, but why? It would hardly be the first time. If a stray bullet hit a tree, there wouldn't be a crowd of gawkers standing around marveling at the improbability of it all. Of course if the tree had been hit dead-on In the place that was sure to kill it instantly, while it was chugging through a hayfield, it might be a different story.

It did seem unlikely that, in the short time he'd been in St. Adele township, Reuben Hofer could have managed to provoke enough animosity to get himself killed. His German roots might possibly have resulted in a problem or two during the war, but nothing extreme, and that was past. Outside of those whiskers, he'd done nothing to create much of a stir.

"A firm man," his sister had called him. McIntire knew what it was like to have only your mother to provide a shield from your father. Still, Colin McIntire had been considered an All Around Great Guy by everyone *but* his son, and, so far as McIntire could see, that included his wife. It might be worth finding out if the same was true of Mrs. Reuben. Her reaction to the news of his death might be an indication that it was not.

Great guy or no, it was a relatively safe bet that somebody had wanted him dead and had seen to it. McIntire was in no position to write it off as an accident even if he wanted to. Did the woman truly think he would, or that he had that kind of influence?

She was right about one thing, murder was never pleasant for those left behind, and was going to be particularly tough for a family whose remaining parent was essentially immobile. He could at least go over and see if there was anything he might do to help out. A ride to town, phone calls. It sounded like the kids could handle the chores okay.

He dawdled long enough over his late breakfast, or early lunch, to give Koski a chance to pick up the sister and cart her off to town. But not long enough to wash the frying pan. There seemed to be no point in bothering. You washed the dishes and hardly turned your back before they were piling up again.

He took Leonie's car. Mrs. Hofer might need a lift somewhere, and the Nash was bigger than his Studebaker. Probably not big enough, but bigger.

The girl sat on the front steps, peeling potatoes. In the brief glimpse before she snatched up the pot in one arm and the dog under the other and scampered inside, McIntire could see that she was older than the seven or eight he'd first guessed. Despite her small size, her disappearing act had more intent than startled doe reflex, and there was a hint of curiosity in her aspect that you didn't see in a kid.

Not, for instance, in the tow-headed boy who knelt in the dirt at the side of the house, pushing a wooden-block bulldozer through sand moistened by water trickling out of a pipe that protruded from the foundation. A drain for the kitchen sink. It couldn't have been the most hygienic place to play.

Around his scabby knees was spread a lilliputian landscape, a masterpiece of creativity and ingenuity. Trickling streams skirted miniature hillsides covered with spruce twig forests. Stick and string fences enclosed pebble livestock. A pea pod canoe floated on a hubcap lake.

The small overlord of this universe looked briefly in McIntire's direction, then turned his back and went back to grading a road to the front door of a rusty syrup can cabin.

McIntire knocked at the door his sister had escaped through.

Her mother was in the same spot. The peas had been replaced with a heap of string beans next to an open magazine. The room's stale odors were overlain with the ghost of fried fish. Mrs. Hofer inclined her head toward a chair and reached to switch off the radio, mercifully quashing Art Linkletter's chat with a troop of saccharine four-year-olds.

McIntire accepted the offer of coffee. At temperatures already in the high eighties, he couldn't manage to convince himself that it was not only to see her stand up. The ploy didn't work. Mary Frances Hofer, without turning her head, called out, "Claire, come heat up the coffee!"

No child appeared. McIntire heard a sound from the back of the house—the creak of a screen door inching open and just as stealthily closing.

"Claire!" She called again. Her shoulders jiggled. There must have been a shrug in there somewhere. "I guess she's gone outdoors." The nervous chuckle came once more, a peculiarity that could rapidly turn irritating.

"Never mind," McIntire reassured her. "It's getting too hot for coffee. I only came to see if there's anything I can do for you."

"That's very kind. My sister-in-law is here. She's taking care of things."

"Yes. She came by this morning. I was amazed to see her here so soon."

The woman nodded, forcing several more chins to the fore. Her hands fluttered about as she talked, from her mouth to her chest, to the table, giving an impression of ditheriness at odds with both her size and the situation. "Jane's a wonder. She didn't even stop to pack a bag. Spent all night getting here, turned up about nine, raring to go. I guess she slept on the train. Not something I could ever do, all that rattling and bumping around. She's gone with the sheriff now." There was a slight hesitation, maybe simply to draw breath, before she added, "To identify my husband's body."

"Mrs.—"

"She'll take him back to be buried in South Dakota, with his family at the colony. My two boys will go with her. I'm afraid I'm not well enough to travel. I'll stay behind with my younger children."

"Colony?"

"Prairie Oak. It's a farming community."

It must be some religious organization. Quakers? Amish? It explained the sister's unconventional manner and dress as well as the family's consternation at Reuben's going off to seek his fortune in the big world and winding up married to a Catholic.

"They wouldn't let him come home when he was alive, but they will now."

"Mrs. Hofer," McIntire was not sure how to approach it. "Mrs. Hofer," he began again, "I know this is distressful for you, but…do you mind answering some questions?"

"I guess I'd have to hear the questions before I can tell you that." This utterance ended, not in a giggle, but a whistling gasp.

"Is something wrong?" What a stupid question. McIntire rephrased it, "Are you feeling ill?"

"I'm quite all right. Only a little out of breath. What is it you want to know?"

There was no point in beating about the bush. Mrs. Hofer was well aware that her husband had been murdered. "Did you hear a gunshot yesterday morning?"

"The sheriff asked me that already. No. I didn't hear it, or if I did, I didn't pay any attention. I'd have had the radio on, and the fan, too."

"What about your children?"

"What about them?"

"Did they hear anything?"

"I wouldn't know."

"Did Mr. Koski talk to them?"

"He talked to Jake and Sam for a few minutes. He didn't question them about…He just asked if they'd be able to handle the farm chores, that kind of thing." She added, "I think Mr. Koski has two very big fans. The sheriff seems to be their new hero."

This time the concluding chuckle was accompanied by a smile that said Pete probably had acquired at least three new fans.

Kids have good hearing, and they were most likely out of doors when the murder took place.

"At least one of your children could have heard the shot," McIntire said. "They might be able to say what time it was or what direction it came from, maybe even how close it sounded. We have nothing else to go on."

"You want to ask, go ahead."

It was a challenge McIntire wasn't sure he was up to. "Where can I find them?"

"My older boys are still hilling the potatoes. I don't know where Claire could have got off to. She was here getting dinner ready a few minutes ago. She must have gone to the garden for something. Joey's out there somewhere. They can't be far away."

The young lady might not be far off now, but McIntire would bet that she'd maintain a safe distance if she saw him coming, and he wasn't likely to be able to sneak up on her. The little boy, he wasn't about to tackle.

"Perhaps it might be best if you asked your youngest son."

She nodded. "I guess I could, but I don't want to worry him. He's hardly more than a baby, and he gets upset easy. He might be more likely to tell Father Doucet. He's coming over this afternoon."

McIntire set off past the barn. The occasional shout and slamming car door came from the direction of the hayfield where Reuben Hofer died. Koski's crew would be searching the area within rifle-range.

The two older boys were—suspiciously un-boylike, to McIntire's way of thinking—in the potato field, shirts off, bristly sun-bleached hair contrasting with lean muscular backs burned to a roast beef mahogany. Sons Colin McIntire would have sold his soul to have. Sons McIntire might have been proud to have himself. Curious that the idea of rearing offspring that resembled himself was as distasteful to McIntire as it had been to his father. He reflected on this epiphany as he stood in the shade of a scrawny beech and beckoned them over.

He was rarely at ease with adolescent boys. Never having been one himself, he had no idea what went on in their self-destructive little minds.

The young men put their heinie-trimmed heads together for a short conference, then trudged between the rows to present themselves. They didn't look either curious or apprehensive. They didn't even look glad for the excuse to rest in their labors, just stood, glistening with sweat, waiting. McIntire once again felt out of his depth.

His introduction—"I'm the constable here."—brought blank stares followed by, "The sheriff told us not to talk to anybody but him."

"I didn't come to question you. I just wanted to see if you could use some help."

They looked at each other, then turned their twin befuddled gazes back to him. "You wanna hill spuds?" McIntire hoped they didn't have a third hoe waiting in the wings. Thankfully the thinner of the pair, who also might have been the stupider of the pair, said, "We're almost done."

Stupid and an optimist. They were barely a third of the way into it.

"Which one of you is the older?"

The stockier boy gave a grunt, and McIntire turned to the other. "You can go back to work."

That got a reaction, one of disappointment. The kid trekked back into the field, dragging his hoe through the sandy soil.

His brother dug a finger into his left ear and squinted into the sun. "Sheriff Koski said we weren't supposed to talk to—"

McIntire wasn't interested in arguing over the heroic Koski's instructions. "I'm sorry about your father," he said. "It's going to put some heavy of responsibilities onto you."

"I guess."

What was he doing here, badgering these two children whose life was making a rapid transition from misery they would have been able to escape in a couple of years, to a hell that would be with them for a long, long time? "I just need to ask one thing, then you can get to back to work."

"The sheriff said—"

"I know what he said, but if you don't talk about things soon, you'll forget. You were in this field when your father died. Did you hear anything?"

"Like what?"

The kid wasn't making this easy. "Like a shot. Or anything that might sound like a gunshot." If it had been at close range, they couldn't have helped but hear it. The hayfield was less than a half mile away.

"No. I didn't hear nothing."

McIntire let him go and tackled the younger brother. He hadn't asked the older boy's name. He tried to be more courteous to this one. After determining that he was speaking to Sam, and that the other one was Jacob, McIntire said, "I was saying to your brother that you boys will have a lot of responsibility now."

"We can handle things. We're used to it. We work hard." His gaze darted everywhere except in McIntire's direction, belying his confident words.

"There'll only be the two of you to do everything. Your father worked hard, too."

"We got along fine without him before. For a long time. We just had Grandpa, and he was too old to do much of anything." He looked toward the house and barn. "We might have to cut back some."

"Be sure you ask for help if you need it."

Sam hefted his hoe and stepped away.

"I also need to ask you, before you forget, if you heard anything yesterday—anything that might have been a gunshot."

For the first time the boy focused his eyes directly on something, regarding the naked toe that thrust itself through the hole in his tennis shoe, almost as black as the shoe itself. "I might have heard something. It wasn't very loud."

"What did it sound like?"

"Far away. I just thought it was a car back-firing." He repeated, "It wasn't very loud."

A car. Not his father's tractor back-firing. "Could you tell the direction?"

"I wasn't paying that much attention. It was just a noise." He coughed and waved without looking up. "I think that way maybe." McIntire turned in the direction he'd indicated. Toward the main road. South. The shot that killed Reuben Hofer would almost certainly have come from the north.

"But maybe not." The choke in the young man's voice, almost a sob, brought McIntire around.

"I hated the son-of-a-bitch." It was low but emphatic.

McIntire struggled. He, of all people, should know what to say. "Sometimes that can make it even harder."

"Who's that?" Jacob had come up behind him and was looking across the pasture and barnyard toward the dark blue car chugging up the driveway.

It stopped close to the house. A man in a white shirt and brown pants that looked rumpled even from this distance got out and stood facing the porch.

"That," said McIntire, "is who the sheriff doesn't want you talking to."

A reporter. He could try to send the guy on his way, but he'd be back, and there'd be plenty more of them. And once they got a look at the widow.... He abandoned the young men to their potatoes and headed for the house.

It wasn't a reporter. By the time McIntire reached the yard, the man was on his way back to his car. No news-hunter would give up that easily. He wasn't a reporter, and he wasn't a spiffy enough dresser to be selling anything.

His gaze rested on McIntire's official tan shirt. "Doesn't seem to be anyone home."

"There might be." McIntire hesitated. "What is it you want
to see them about?"

"I heard on the radio what happened to Reuben. I didn't realize he lived around here. I just came to see if there is anything I
can—"

"You knew Reuben Hofer?"

"I haven't seen him for a few years, but I knew him during
the war."

"Where were you stationed?"

"Stationed? I was right here."

"Here?" What the hell was the guy talking about?

"In Michigan, I mean. I was a work supervisor at the camp
in Gibb's Bay."

There had been several POW camps in the area. Populated
by German prisoners commandeered to do the work that the
local boys would have been taking care of if they hadn't been so
ruthlessly wrested away from their shovels, saws, and axes. Most
of the prisoners were put to work logging or building roads. So
Hofer had gotten in some practical experience before he'd turned
to cracking the whip over his sons' backs.

"I see," McIntire said. "From what I've been told, Reuben
Hofer would have been a born overseer."

"Overseer? Oh, Reuben wasn't a guard. He was one of our
'guests.'"

"Hofer was a POW?" It was confusing. The man was definitely
of German persuasion, but he had to have married and fathered
those children before the war, and the home his sister was taking
him back to was in one of the Dakotas. South Dakota.

The man's look was wary. "You new around here?"

"Sort of."

"The camp at Gibb's Bay wasn't POWs. It was a CO camp.
Conscientious Objectors."

So the "community" did have a religious bent. And Mr. Hofer
was not such a recent arrival to this particular community as
they'd assumed. McIntire put out his hand. "John McIntire. Can
I buy you something to wet your whistle?"

Chapter Seven

Both of the men got in their cars and drove away. The skinny one with the glasses and funny hat and the new one. The skinny man had hung around the boys for ages, and he had on a brown shirt like the sheriff's, so he must be one of them and not the man who shot her father. Claire backed away from the window and put Spike on the floor. "Now behave!"

When she turned around in the dark barn, she could still see, purplish in front of her eyes, the back of the house with the porch sticking out, and the shape of Joey where he played in the sand.

It wasn't so hot inside the barn as it was out in the sun. It was a good place to hide out. They didn't keep any animals in the barn because it was summertime, only brought Opal in to milk her and give her some grain, so it didn't smell bad.

Claire kicked at the old straw in one of the horse stalls. Maybe now they could have a horse. Pa said horses were a waste of money. You only had to feed a tractor when you wanted to use it. But now…. Claire wouldn't want a fiery stallion like Tamburlain or the Red Stallion. A nice gentle pony would do. Gentle with her, but one that wouldn't let anyone else ride him. If Jake or Sam came near him, he'd kick them to kingdom come. A pinto would be nice, like an Indian pony, or maybe a golden palomino. There was a lady in the neighborhood that had a horse. Claire had seen her ride by a few times. She was sort of chubby and looked way too old for it, but the horse was pretty. Claire would have died to go riding down the road like that, sitting in the saddle on her very own horse.

Spike barked again, outside, and Claire made a dash for the door.

A lady in a blue dress stood by the porch, holding a cake pan with a lid on it. Spike was running in circles around her, jumping and yipping. She came once before, when they first moved in, but Claire had been in the garden planting corn and didn't get a good look at her. She brought a cake that time, too, and they still had the pan. Claire couldn't remember her name. Ma said her husband used to be the mailman, but now he was sick. Claire ran across the yard to grab up the dog.

The lady smiled a little bit. "He sounds pretty vicious. I hope his bark is worse than his bite."

She was the tallest woman Claire had ever seen, and she was skinnier than that man, even. Maybe she was his sister. Her hair was braided. It was pure white, so she had to be old, way too old for a pigtail, and her face was almost as white as her hair. She had light blue eyes and eyelashes so pale you could hardly see them. She looked like she wasn't finished yet. Like you had to get out some Crayolas and color her in.

"He doesn't bite." Claire said it, but she wasn't sure it was true. She hoped he wouldn't. There would be big trouble if Spike ever bit anybody.

"I bet he'd like to, though." The lady smiled more. Maybe she was making a joke. Then she asked, "Is your mother at home?"

It would probably be okay; Ma had her shoes on. Besides, they could use the cake. Claire nodded and went ahead of her up the steps to hold the door open. She went inside, too. Ma would want her to make the coffee.

Ma was writing a letter. She started to ask Claire something, then she looked up and noticed that they had company. She put her pen down and turned off the radio. "Hello, Mrs. Thorsen, how nice of you to come."

Mrs. Thorsen handed the cake to Claire. "I won't bother you for long. I just wanted to let you know how terrible my husband

and I feel about what's happened. If there's anything we can do, you know you only have to ask."

"Thank you. It's difficult being so far from family at a time like this. Please sit down. Would you care for something to drink? It might be too warm for coffee. I believe my sister-in-law made some nectar." Ma was using her polite, company voice. It made Claire feel sort of embarrassed, and stupid, too. Like one of those grown-up things she was left out of, but would have to learn to do herself someday. She didn't want to ever have to talk like that. Sometimes she hummed to herself, to drown out Ma talking that way.

Mrs. Thorsen didn't look like she really wanted nectar very much, but she said, "That would be nice," anyway.

Claire wanted nectar. Sister put a cut-up orange in it to give it some extra zip. Claire brought the pitcher from the cellar and poured three glasses.

"How are you all doing, Mrs. Hofer? Is there anything I can help you with right now?"

"It's very kind of you to offer," Ma told her. Then she said, "Claire you can take the rest of the nectar out to the boys."

If the boys got thirsty they could darn well get a drink for themselves. Ma only wanted to get rid of her. Claire took her time pouring what was left of the nectar into a jar and hunting for a lid. She left the door open a crack and hung around in the porch until Ma called, "Did you forget something?" and she had to leave. She went around and stood by the window, but the fan was going and it made too much noise to hear anything.

It was still hot as Hades. But no where near as hot as Iowa. Claire laughed to herself when she thought of Iowa being hotter than Hell. She planned to dig round in Sam's old clothes for some bluejeans, so she could get rid of the stupid dresses Pa made her wear. But when it was this hot, a dress didn't feel so bad. Maybe it would work to cut the legs off the jeans and make shorts.

She yelled to Jake and Sam and left the jar balanced on a fence post, but first she fished out the orange quarters. They were bright red from being in the nectar and had most of the juice squeezed out, but they were still good. She scraped the insides out with her bottom teeth, and licked the sticky nectar from her fingers. Spike ran after the peels when she threw them in the grass. He even picked one up in his mouth, but spit it back out.

A car was making a cloud of dust, far down the road, so she headed back to the house. It might be the sheriff bringing Sister back. When he came to get her that morning, he'd smiled at Claire and pinched her nose. He smelled like cigarettes, same as Father Doucet.

Father Doucet was nice; more friendly than Father Ryan in Iowa. Sometimes he hardly seemed like a priest at all. He was going to teach Joey to play the fiddle when he was big enough. Claire would like to play the fiddle, and she was big enough now. Maybe she'd rather play the guitar. Then she could sing and play at the same time. Someday maybe she'd be a famous singer, like Peggy Lee. Peggy Lee didn't play a guitar, though.

It turned out it wasn't the sheriff's car. It was a whole lot smaller and it was pink, of all things. Claire had never seen a pink car before. The person that got out of the car was another lady. Pink must have been her favorite color; her blouse was pale pink, and she had a bright pink silk neckerchief. She walked around to the other side of her car and took out a big casserole dish, then she looked at the house for a while like she was thinking things over. Maybe she was trying to figure how she could get up the steps in her high heels and her tight skirt. She had to wiggle herself around and go up sideways, like Ma did, but she made it. She carried the dish in both hands and bumped it against the door instead of knocking. Her fingernails were long and red. Mrs. Thorsen came out.

Claire hung on to the squirmy dog and went closer.

"Mrs. Hofer isn't up to having company right now," Mrs. Thorsen took the lady's hotdish. "If you give me your name, I can let her know you were here. I'm sure she'll appreciate it."

The lady said her name was Wanda Something or Other. "But Mrs. Hofer doesn't know me. I knew Reuben when he was here during the war. I'd like to see her, to tell her how sorry I am about what happened."

Claire had never heard that Pa was here when he was in the war. He never said anything about where he was, and Ma didn't tell them.

Mrs. Thorsen kept the door shut. "She's not well right now. I'm sure she'll appreciate your coming." She didn't sound like she was lying. Maybe Ma really was sick. Or maybe she was feeling sad about Pa being dead, after all.

Wanda had red hair that made a wave over one eye and pink spots on her cheeks the same color as her lipstick and her scarf. She looked kind of mad. "Maybe you could let her know right now, and—" Joey came from behind the house and she quit talking and stared at him. Then her mouth went all prissy, and she stuck the dish in Mrs. Thorsen's hands, "Please give the family my sympathy. I'll come back another time."

She went back to her car. She had to sit on edge of the seat and twist around to get in.

Mrs. Thorsen sat down on the steps. She pulled her long braid over her shoulder and stared at Claire until she felt like a fool. It was probably the stupid dress.

But a grown up lady with a braid looked silly too, especially the way she twisted the end of it like she was going to yank it right off. She said, "Claire is a very pretty name."

Claire thought it was an awful name. Like Clara—or Clarabelle. She wrinkled her nose.

"I guess lots of people don't like their own name," Mrs. Thorsen said. "Too bad we don't get to choose our own."

That would be good, but, "We'd be too little," Claire told her. "We'd be just born."

"Not always," Mrs. Thorsen said. "I was five."

"You got to pick your own name?"

"No, my mother did it. But I was five."

Claire thought she might be making it up, just kidding her along. "How could you go without a name for all that time? They couldn't just call you Little Girl."

"Why not? I was little once." She looked serious, and Claire didn't know what to say. Then she smiled. "I'm sorry, I'm teasing you. They called me Ramona. But when I was five, I got a new name."

"What is it?" Ramona sounded like a nice name.

She smiled more. "Are you ready?"

Claire nodded.

"It's...." She said a long funny word that sounded like she was coughing.

"What?"

"Me-o-go-kwa," Mrs. Thorsen said. She spelled it, "M-E-O-G-O-K-W-E. It's an Indian name. It was my grandmother's. When I was five years old, she died, and I got her name."

Was Mrs. Thorsen a real Indian? Claire couldn't ask. It wouldn't be polite. She had the pigtail, all right, but she was way too white. Claire looked more like an Indian than Mrs. Thorsen did. Maybe Claire *was* an Indian, wandered away from her tribe and adopted, or maybe kidnapped by the Hofers to do the cooking. The boys all had blond hair, like Pa.

"Do you know where your younger brother is?" Mrs. Thorsen stood up. It was hard to believe a woman could be so tall, or that she'd ever been very little.

Claire shook her head. Joey was probably still hiding in back of the house. The other time Mrs. Thorsen came over, to pay a visit when they first moved in, he thought she might be a witch. She did look something like a witch. She had a pointy nose—no wart—but she looked more like a ghost. Joey might be even more scared if he knew she was an Indian.

Mrs. Thorsen went indoors with the hotdish, but she came right back out. She had her cake pan. The one she left before. "I'm going home now. Your aunt will probably be back soon. Do you know where I live?"

Claire didn't.

"It's not far, that way, and you can take a short cut through the woods." She pointed past the barn to the trees. "It's the way I used to come when I went to school here. When I was a not-so-very-little girl." She was teasing again. "I'll come back in a day or two and show you the way. Then if you ever need help, or want to use the telephone, you'll know where to go."

She patted Spike's head. Claire felt queasy in her stomach. One of Mrs. Thorsen's fingers was chopped right off.

Chapter Eight

Blinds were pulled against the windows that would have let in the sun. It rendered the room dim—dark to McIntire who had spent several minutes gazing over the brilliant waters of the bay before entering—but blessedly cool. From what he could see there was no one else taking advantage of the refuge from the sweltering heat.

"Hi there. Haven't seen you in a coon's age. Hot enough for ya?" Hilda Ellman spoke from the gloom behind the bar, but, thankfully, didn't wait for an answer. "Isn't this just ghastly?" She slapped her newspaper. A photo of the Black Creek schoolhouse filled half the page. A smaller one of Reuban Hofer's tractor was wedged in below it. "Did you...? Were you...?" she went on, with hesitation in her words but hunger in her eyes, "at the scene? It must have been ghastly."

When McIntire volunteered no ghastly details, she contented herself with, "Any idea whodunnit?"

"Not so much as the slightest." McIntire ordered a couple of Pabsts and ushered his guest into his favorite of the four booths—the one farthest from the door.

The man's name was Bruno Nickerson, and he lived across the bay in Benton. He tipped up the bottle and poured about three quarters of its contents down his throat. "That hit the spot." When he removed his hat, the band of sweat that encircled his head coincided precisely with his band of remaining hair. "To what do I owe this kind invitation? I take it I'm being plied for information. Well, I can be bought. Go ahead and ply." There was definitely a sneer lurking beneath the jocular smile.

McIntire waved to Hilda for two more. "We don't know much about Reuben Hofer. I had no idea he'd been anywhere near here before he moved in at the end of May. How long was he at the camp?"

"The whole time it was open."

"Which was?"

"Not all that long. It started up some time in 1944. Toward the end of the war, they closed it down and shipped everybody out to California to fight forest fires. And good riddance it was." He took an only sightly less eager gulp from the second bottle and wiped his lips on his sleeve. "Even if it did put me out of a government job."

"Weren't the COs free to go at the end of the war?"

"Some were, maybe. Most were in until forty-six or forty-seven, I think. Hell, the government was getting a lot of work out of most of them. Reuben Hofer took off from the camp in California and ended up spending some time in federal prison, Milan, I think. I don't know when he got out. I didn't even know for sure he *was* out, until I heard he was murdered."

"You say you were out of a government job?"

"Well, ya, ain't that what we been talking about?" Nickerson sipped more judiciously at his remaining beer.

McIntire reached for his own. "I thought the CPS camps were run by churches."

"Not Gibb's Bay. Not all the Conchies objected for religious reasons. Some were more political, Socialists, mostly. They didn't go to the church camps. There were a few places run by Selective Service. The one in Gibb's Bay—it was an old CCC camp—was where they stuck the COs that the rest of them couldn't handle. The dyed-in-the-wool trouble-makers."

"Pacifist trouble-makers?"

He gave a derisive, hops-laden snort. "They had their ways, and they weren't always that goddamn peaceful. They were dif-

ferent from the ordinary bible toting objectors. A bunch of them
had college educations. We had doctors, college professors, 'intel-
lectuals,' people who knew how to get around the system. Quite
a few were Jehovah's Witnesses, but they weren't any of them
particularly religious, not your Quaker and Amish types."

"But Reuben Hofer was one of those Quaker and Amish
types."

"He might have started out all peace and brotherly love, but
by the time he got to Gibb's Bay, he was one ornery son-of-a-
bitch."

And seemed to have stayed that way, if his son's opinion was
anything to go by. If the inmates had been allowed to leave the
camp at all, go into town, Hofer might have spread that orneri-
ness around. Enough to bring on that urge to kill? A grudge that
reached fruition when the injured party discovered the grudgee
was back in town?

"What sort of trouble did these trouble makers make?"

"About any damn thing they could come up with. A few
times they ripped the place up, broke into the storeroom and
dumped everything onto the floor, smashed eggs, made a mess
generally. Most of the time, they just refused to do anything we
told them, or they'd scratch their heads and pretend they didn't
know how. So they'd spend all day chopping down a sapling or
sweeping out a truck. They were supposed to be doing work of
'national importance.' In Gibb's Bay that was building dikes
and shit like that for the game refuge, which they didn't see
as all that important, so mostly they just laid around. Called
themselves the 'Tobacco Road Gang.' Asshole Gang, more like.
They got a big write up in *Time* magazine, so they were really
swell-headed after that."

It begged a question, and McIntire asked, "So why'd they
get away with it?"

The roll of his eyes said it sure as hell wasn't through any
fault of Bruno's. "We didn't have any real authority over them,
weren't allowed to use force with the little darlings. They weren't
subject to military law, and we weren't military anyway. We were

just supervisors. Mamas to feed them and tuck them in at night. We could yell orders 'til we were blue in the face, but if they didn't do what they were told, there wasn't a Goddamn thing we could do about it. They could leave on Sundays and would go into Benton and generally raise hell. Some of them were well off; they'd get money sent from relatives."

"Hofer?"

"No. Reuben didn't have a rich daddy. But he was one hell of a card player. What didn't get blown on booze and women mostly ended up Reuben's. Or a good percent of it anyway. The other guys would stake him."

"Is that why you remembered him?'

"What?" It hadn't seemed like an offensive question, but Nickerson looked up with a stare half bewildered and half angry, like McIntire had asked if he'd stopped beating his wife.

"Would you remember all the inmates at the camp, or is Reuben Hofer a special case?" McIntire asked. "Did you strike up a friendship with him that brings you here to express your sympathy?"

"No!" The emphatic response was followed by a short embarrassed silence before he went on, without exactly answering McIntire's question, "Reuben didn't have friends, particularly. Not that the other men disliked him. He just wasn't one of the guys, if you know what I mean. He wasn't such a loudmouth as some of the rest, but now and then I got the feeling he was a ringleader, putting the other guys up to the shit they got into." He held the sweating bottle to his temple with the faraway gaze of a moonstruck teenager. "The guy had a sense of humor though, believe it or not. He went around with this big ball chained to his leg. It was just a hunk of pine, carved round and painted black, so it wasn't heavy, but he dragged it around like it weighed a ton. He shoulda been on the stage."

Hilda approached with a rag to wipe the wet rings from their table. "Need anything?"

McIntire shook his head before Nickerson had a chance to say otherwise. Both men sat silently while Hilda busied herself, lurking at the adjoining booth, straightening menus and tidying the ketchup bottle. When she eventually gave up and retreated to the bar, McIntire asked, "So what did make you decide to call on Mrs. Hofer?"

"Why not? It seemed like the polite thing to do."

Maybe, but why should Nickerson assume that Mrs. Hofer would have any interest in meeting her late husband's prison guard? Wouldn't a nice card be more appropriate? McIntire waited.

"Anyway, I have something that belonged to Reuben. I wanted to give it to the widow."

McIntire didn't comment, just continued to sit with what he hoped was an expectant look on his face, *ala* Pete Koski. Obviously his technique needed work. Nickerson dropped his gaze to his bottle, but only volunteered, "It might have sentimental value."

"Would you like me to deliver it for you?"

"Oh, I don't think so. I'd like to speak to her in person anyway. I'll wait for the funeral."

"I don't think there's going to be one," McIntire said. "Not around here."

Seeming to belie his resounding denial of friendship with Hofer, Nickerson's disappointment was evident. "Are they leaving? Pulling up stakes already?"

"I wouldn't know about that, but Reuben will be buried back where he came from."

Nickerson nodded in understanding, and swigged down the last of his beer.

Chapter Nine

When Sheriff Koski brought Sister back, he came into the house to talk to Ma. Since Sister was there to make coffee and put out Mrs. Thorsen's cake, Claire didn't have any excuse to hang around, but nobody told her to leave. Which was good, except that the kitchen was getting crowded, and she couldn't think of anything to do with herself. It wasn't like she could just pull up a chair and have a seat next to the sheriff! She went into the front room and sat on the davenport where she'd be out of sight, but could hear what they said. In case anybody came in, she faked that she was looking at the *Saturday Evening Post*.

Sheriff Koski gave a big huff and a groan when he sat down, just like Ma did. He said, "Your husband's body will be released to you by tomorrow."

"Thank you."

"There'll be an autopsy report by then, too. So we should know more about what happened."

Ma just said, "Thank you," again, and the sheriff gave another cough in his throat. "Mrs. Hofer, did your husband own a gun?"

Claire felt her stomach go queasy and stared at the page, trying not to listen. There was an advertisement with a picture of a bathroom with a great big tub. That would be heaven. A real bathtub. Someday, if she got some privacy, she was going to fill up the copper boiler and take a bath in that. If she fit.

"My husband was a pacifist," Ma said. She sort of laughed even though it wasn't funny, like she did when she didn't have the money for the Electrolux man. "Reuben hated guns. He would never own one."

That was true. Ma hadn't lied, but she hadn't exactly told the truth; Pa didn't have a gun, but *they* had one. Grandpa gave it to Ma. He showed the boys how to shoot it and made them practice. He also showed them how to take it apart so they could clean it, and so Ma could hide it from Pa. It was in the chest of drawers where they kept the sheets and pillow cases and stuff they weren't using, like winter clothes in summertime and things that were too small for Sam but didn't fit Joey yet. Pa never looked there.

The sheriff's chair creaked, and Claire hoped it wasn't the shaky one. "Your sister-in-law mentioned that, and she said that your husband spent some time in a CPS camp near here. It's possible that something happened there that…led to his death. What do you know about the other men he met in the camp?"

So it was true what the pink lady said. In the war, Pa was right here in Michigan.

"Not a thing," Ma said. "Once in a while Reuben mentioned a few things that happened, but no one by name, far as I remember. It wouldn't have meant anything to me, if he had."

"What about afterwards, when he was in…."

"Prison? No. He hardly ever talked about that."

He did talk about it sometimes. Once he said to Jake and Sam they didn't realize how good they had it, to be free to come and go as they pleased. When Jake said, "Good, I'll go right now," Pa looked really mad and told Jake he'd go, all right. He'd go out and paint the barn like he was told. Jake did.

Sheriff Koski asked again, "Are you sure? It must have been a disagreeable experience. I'd think he'd at least do a little griping."

"No," Ma said. "He just wanted to forget about it. He'd chosen to go to the CPS camp of his own free will. He was true to his convictions. He felt like he accomplished something there, but when it started it was only supposed to be for six months. It ended up dragging on for years. And he didn't think they'd any right to expect him to risk his neck jumping out of planes into forest fires for no pay, or to lock him up for refusing to do it."

"He might have told your sons a few stories. Maybe—"

"Reuben wasn't a big talker, especially about himself," Sister butted in. "You're looking pale, Mary Frances. Do you need to lie down?"

Ma always looked pale, and she didn't ever need to lie down in the daytime anymore.

Sheriff Koski's chair scraped on the floor. He was standing up. He didn't stay much longer, just told Ma to let him know if she thought of anybody Pa might have been on the outs with, and that he'd be back soon. When he went outside, Sister went with him. They stood by his car talking for so long that Claire gave up watching.

The front room was like an oven. Claire went to the chest and got down on her knees to open the bottom drawer. When she was younger, about four, she liked to lie on her back and draw pictures on the underneath side of the chest. She must have been puny; she would hardly be able to get her head under there now, but her drawing would still be there. Maybe some day people would look at it and know that a girl had made the pictures years ago. By then she might be a famous artist and the chest would be worth a thousand dollars. She should write her name on the bottom so people would know it was her.

The drawer was stuck tight. She gave a mighty tug. It came shooting out, and she landed on her butt on the linoleum. She sat still. Ma didn't yell, and no snoopy brother showed up.

It was gone. Claire dug under the wool socks and long johns. Her stomach began to hurt. It just wasn't there. Her father had been killed with a gun, and their gun was gone.

The floor squeaked, and Claire stood up fast. How could Ma sneak up on her like that?

"What are you looking for?"

"Oh, nothing."

"That's down in the cellar, in an empty jar." Ma's lips sort of twitched when she said something she thought was funny, but it wasn't polite to laugh at your own jokes.

"I was just seeing if there are some blue jeans. Maybe some of Sam's old ones will fit me."

"They'll fit you like a potato sack. You'll have to tie a piece of baling twine around your middle and look like Huckleberry Finn. Anyway, they're in the next drawer."

"Oh, that's right." Claire shoved the bottom drawer in quick.

"While you're at it, get out the good sheets. We'll need to get the bed on the porch ready for Jane."

"Sister might like the white ones better."

"She's company."

The drawer with the sheets wasn't pushed in so far, and it was easier to open. The sheets with the roses were folded underneath the plain white set. Claire reached in to take them out. The brown wood of the gun peeked through. She'd been so stupid. She thought it was in the bottom. She didn't even think of it being in another drawer.

"Maybe you're right after all," Ma said. "Take the white ones. Jane doesn't like anything too fancy."

Chapter Ten

What a strange little girl. And she *was* little—no bigger than her younger brother. Mary Frances had said that her daughter was eleven years old. She'd looked more like eight or nine to Mia, until she got close enough to see her eyes and those huge dark circles under them. Mostly she looked uncared for. Mia would have given her right arm to take a brush to that hair. And the boy was scratches and dirt from top to bottom. Poor ragamuffins. What would become of them now?

But right now Mary Frances Hofer's children weren't nearly so interesting as her visitor. Or potential visitor. Mia wasn't surprised that Mrs. Hofer had shown no wish to talk to just any flashy-looking woman who came waltzing in claiming to be an old friend of her late husband's.

"I've no idea who she could be, and I'm not up to chatting with strangers, now," was all Mary Frances said.

Mia hadn't liked to ask how her husband might have come to know Wanda Greely, but if Reuben Hofer hadn't been so much the stranger here as everyone thought he was, the sheriff should know about it. She dropped the dish towel and stepped out onto the porch.

Nick sat at the wicker table, wiring a new cord onto the toaster. She touched his shoulder, "I think I'll go out for a short walk."

He nodded. "When you get back, I'll make you a piece of toast."

She struck out on the same path she'd taken that morning to the Hofers', turning off where it skirted the fence that kept Leonie McIntire's horses in their pasture.

When she got to the point where she had to cross that fence, she hesitated. She hadn't seen John McIntire in weeks. The easy relationship they'd formed in the months following his return to St. Adele had, by increments, fizzled since the previous fall. She once again felt as awkward in his presence as she had when he'd first come back, a virtual stranger, a ghost of her past that she hardly recognized. Now, with his wife away, she was even more reluctant to knock at his door. Maybe she'd get lucky and he'd be outdoors. Or gone off somewhere.

She held the strand of barbed wire tight against the woven fencing and swung her leg over. Being tall had definite advantages.

The quarterhorses stood on the shady side of the barn, nose to tail, twitching at flies and stomping their feet.

Leonie had only been gone a couple of weeks, but her absence was already taking its toll. The lawn mower sat abandoned at the side of the yard, grass growing up through its blades. A few red colored hens lay half-upended close to the foundation of the pump house, dug into the dry soil of one of Leonie's many flower beds. Nearby, the infamous leghorn rooster stood guard but gave only a slight raising of his hackles and a couple of half-hearted scratchings as Mia passed by. In the stillness, the place had an air of desertion, but John's car, and Leonie's as well, were in the driveway. No chance of just leaving a note.

Maybe he was asleep—taking a siesta to avoid the heat of the afternoon. Hot weather didn't bother Mia the way it did most other people. Ninety-five degrees every day of her life would get no complaints from her. But John had spent most of his life in England, where seventy was a sweltering heatwave. He was probably suffering. She hoped he'd be decently dressed. Not lazing around in his undershorts or less.

He appeared behind the screen. "Are you just here to admire the paint job on my door, or are you planning to knock on it?" He looked happy to see her. Maybe he was getting lonely.

"I thought you might not be home. It's so quiet."

"I haven't reached the point of talking to myself yet." He held the door open. "At least not too much. Come on in."

"I just stopped for a minute."

"Well, if you stopped to see me, it will have to be in out of the sun."

It wasn't a whole lot cooler inside. The shades were pulled, the kitchen almost dark, but it only made things seem more closed in and stifling. Dirty dishes were piled in the sink, and a black skillet on the stove contained a quarter inch of grease.

"Would you like a drink?"

"Water?"

"I think I could rustle up some gin if you'd prefer that."

"No thanks, I'm not thirsty." Before he could respond, she began. "I went to see Mary Frances Hofer."

"Did she stand up?" He didn't even smile when he said it.

"No."

"Do you think she can?"

"Of course she can! She'd have to be able to get up. But I can't figure how she manages to…." Mia didn't like to think about all the things Mary Frances would have trouble doing. "It must be awful. How could a person get to such a state? She must not always have been like that. I mean, she's got the four kids…." It was time to change the subject. "But that's not what I came to tell you. While I was there, somebody else came over."

That at least brought a spark of curiosity, but John only said, "Nothing like a murder to bring out the visitors, even total strangers."

"She wasn't a stranger exactly. I don't know her personally, but I recognized her name. It was Wanda Greely."

"Should I recognize it, too?"

"I don't think so, but Leonie might. She's a beautician. She's got a shop in Benton. Wanda's Cut'n Curl."

"She cuts 'n curls Mrs. Hofer's hair?" John moved from the door toward the table like he was intending to offer her a place to sit. Sitting might have been less awkward than standing facing him in the small kitchen, but he didn't go farther than his hand on the back of a chair. "Can't say I think much of her handiwork, but it's nice of her to call."

"No, she's not responsible for Mrs. Hofer's coiffure. She doesn't know Mrs. Hofer. She said she was an old friend of Reuben's."

"Another one?"

"I wouldn't know about that. Are there more?"

"They seem to be coming out of the woodwork." Despite his obvious interest, he sounded tired. "Did Wanda say how they happened to meet?"

"No, but I doubt it was in her professional capacity. I just thought you—or the sheriff—should know that Reuben must have been here before. Not that I think Wanda Greely is a murderer. Although if looks could kill, I'd have been flat out on Hofers' doorstep when I wouldn't let her in."

"It turns out that Reuben *was* here before, incarcerated in the Gibb's Bay CPS camp. If he got chummy with people outside the camp too, that puts things in a different light. I'll let Koski know." He pulled out the chair. "You sure you won't sit down? Have something to drink?"

"I better get back. I've left Nick alone long enough."

"Mia—"

"Say hello to your wife."

He looked into her eyes, long and hard enough to make her feel like squirming, or screaming.

"I'll be sure to do that," he finally said.

If she left on that note, the stiffness between them would go on, get worse. Before she went out the door, Mia found the courage to turn back and ask, "Have your heard anything about what the family will do? The kids are a pair of lost waifs, and up until now they've had two parents. That woman can't possibly take care of them on her own."

"Reuben's sister was here. According to her, they managed to get along just fine without him for years."

"That girl is hardly more than a skeleton."

"Mia...," he said again, this time with a smile.

"Oh. I know I wasn't a *robust* child, but at least somebody combed my hair now and then."

"The mother's not very well. I expect they'll end up with the aunt."

Mary Frances had mentioned her sister-in-law, what a great help she was. She wasn't married and probably had no children of her own. Mia also gathered that she was a member of a strict religious community—the one that had produced her late brother. It might not be the best solution.

Chapter Eleven

The day began as the last one had ended and as the night separating them had been. Hot. Ugly, sultry, sticky, blistering, sweltering, hot. Maddeningly hot.

Maybe that was it. Some poor soul had been driven mad by the heat and blasted his neighbor off a tractor. Wasn't that what happened with Lizzie Borden, it was the heat that compelled her to administer those whacks?

Why did Reuben Hofer die? All through the night, McIntire had been over and over it in his head. Even the short snatches of sleep had seen Kelpie's snoring transpose itself into a rumbling chant that dominated his dreams, "*Who killed Cock Reuben?*"

It shouldn't be that difficult. Once they found the bullet, they might even be able to stick it under a microscope and match it up to the very weapon it was fired from. They'd at least know what sort of gun it was. In this neck of the woods people knew the guns at least as intimately as they knew their owners. They'd easily find out who owned the right kind of firearm, and, among those, who had the wrong sort of alibi. They could figure out what direction the shot came from and from how far away. It would then be a simple matter of matching up all the information and, bingo! Easy as the Sunday crossword.

That was if the killer was somebody from the neighborhood, which McIntire didn't believe for a minute. Unless it was an accident and the perpetrator was afraid to come forward, it was simply not credible that Reuben Hofer had antagonized one of his neighbors to the point of premeditated murder. Unless that neighbor was among those who had known him during his earlier sojourn here.

Bruno Nickerson denied knowing Reuben was back in Michigan until he heard about his being killed. What about Wanda? That made two possibilities, and there were certainly this more. His widow might know some of them. He probably should make it a practice to check in on her, every day or so.

The pup ran yipping around McIntire in ever shrinking circles, made a quick dash to nip at his pants cuff, but disappeared with a whimper at his, "Beat it!" Feeling satisfied with himself, McIntire knocked at the door.

The garden produce was gone, and the table was piled with worn clothing, most of which seemed to be of a size to have belonged to the late Mr. Hofer. Mary Frances sat in her designated spot, attacking the shirts and overalls with a scissors, cutting out the useful pieces, discarding the remaining shreds in a heap on the floor beside her. It seemed rather early to be ridding herself of her husband's belongings, but there was probably little enough she could do to keep herself occupied, trapped in her body as she was.

She switched off the radio and called to her daughter. This time the girl came down the stairs and tiptoed into the kitchen. Without a word she picked up the coffee pot, sloshed in a dipper of water, swirled it around and dumped the resulting slurry into a slop bucket by the door.

McIntire waited until the fresh coffee was poured, a plate of brownies was on the table, and the unkempt sprite had gone out of the room. The whisper of her footsteps ended just beyond the doorway, but a thin shadow stayed on the floor. McIntire didn't suppose he was going to say anything she shouldn't hear anyway.

Why hadn't Jane Hofer taken over the hostess duties?

Reading his mind, Mary Frances said, "Jane has gone into Chandler on the train, to take care of the arrangements." A lank strand of hair dropped over one eye. She blew at it ineffectually. "I don't know what I'd do without her."

"You have neighbors, Mrs. Hofer, ready to help. Your sister-in-law didn't need to take the train to town. I'd have been happy to give her a ride."

"Jane would never ask for help."

Except when it came to sidetracking the investigation of her brother's murder. "Well, I hope if you need anything, you won't hesitate to ask me or most anybody else." McIntire picked up one of the brownies with its signature pecan embedded in gooey frosting. "Lucy Delaney for instance."

"You are quite the detective!" Mary Frances laughed, then sobered quickly. "I expect that's why you're here."

"Only partly. I was thinking, wondering if your husband had looked up anybody he knew from the camp here?"

"No. Not a soul. He did go to have a look at the old camp once."

"Did he ever mention anyone? The guy that was here yesterday, maybe, Bruno Nickerson?"

"No, I've haven't heard that name before. I'm sure Reuben never brought him up or that woman that turned up in the afternoon."

"Was there anybody else?"

Mary Frances snipped thoughtfully. "I thought about it after the sheriff asked, but no, Reuben didn't talk about anybody in particular, not by name."

"Would he have said anything to your sons? Would they be likely to remember?"

"Mr. Koski asked that, too. I doubt it, but you can ask."

"Did he never talk about the past at all?"

"He talked about it incessantly. The distant past. Growing up in Prairie Oak. Paradise on earth, to hear him tell it. But he didn't want to think about all that came after he left."

Mary Frances was part of what came next. A big part. McIntire cringed at his mental pun. "Why did you decide to move here? Your husband must have found something he liked."

"He would rather have gone back to *Californ-i-ay*." McIntire was learning to distinguish genuine laughter from the self-conscious chuckle by the amount of jiggle in her chins. "But farmland there is far from cheap. I'm not sure why he picked here. He knew something about the area, I suppose, after being in Gibb's Bay. The federal prison was in Michigan, too. Reuben had some money saved up, and we bought this place for next to nothing."

She gripped the tails of a threadbare shirt, bit her lip, and pulled. The stubborn seam gave with a resounding rip, "No!" It was triumphant. "There *was* somebody I know about. Gary Cooper. That's why I remember, who could forget that name? His name…and because of what happened."

"Which was?"

She picked up the scissors and smoothed the fabric on the table. "One of the ways you could get out of going into combat service was to volunteer to be a guinea pig for medical experiments. Reuben was furious because Gary Cooper gave in, as he saw it, and tried to get into some sort of starvation experiment. He was turned down, but later, when they'd been in Gibb's Bay for a few weeks, they took him after all. Reuben said he hoped they'd starve him to death."

She shook her head and peered into McIntire's eyes, like the rest of her story lay there. "But I don't think I knew that then. I couldn't have, could I? I didn't hear anything much from Reuben when he was in Gibb's Bay."

"Did he tell you about it later then?" That was about all the help McIntire could give, and it didn't seem so hard to figure out.

"No. He never talked about any of that stuff." She squinted and snipped at some loose threads. The wheels were turning agonizingly slow, but at last she nodded. "It was when they took me to the hospital. I'd been getting sick for a long time, and I couldn't afford to see a doctor."

8 **The Kingdom Where Nobody Dies** 65

McIntire tried to look pointedly toward the slim shadow visible through the living room doorway.

Mrs. Hofer glanced briefly ceilingward and went on, "No, that's not strictly true. I did go to the doctor in Waverly. He more or less said I was imagining things, that my hair falling out was just nerves, and that if I lost weight I wouldn't be so tired all the time. Things got worse and worse, and eventually I just collapsed, couldn't do anything. They took me to the hospital at the University of Minnesota."

"That's right," McIntire said. "That's where the starvation studies were done." Had they tried cutting off Mary Frances Hofer's meals? Is that how she came to meet Mr. Cooper?

"Gary Cooper worked there. I think he was some sort of nurse. A male nurse."

Some of the conscientious objectors had ended up as attendants in psychiatric wards. Is that what Mary Frances' tee-heeing meant? But Cooper probably hadn't done both starvation and mental hospitals.

"Anyway, when Reuben came to take me home, they met in the hallway, and that was how it all came out."

"How long ago was this?"

"A couple of years. Not quite that."

So Mr. Cooper could still be working there, and if he wasn't, somebody could probably tell them where he'd gone.

McIntire stood to take his leave, and, to his great shock, Mary Frances gripped the edge of the heavy table and heaved herself to her feet in a single movement that, far from being the awkward walrus-struggle that McIntire would have expected, was almost graceful.

She moved a pan of boiled potatoes from the stove to the table. "Would you like to stay to dinner? I'm going to fry some potatoes." She didn't make any inane remarks about his wife not being around to feed him, for which McIntire was grateful.

"Another time, perhaps. Right now, I think I'll try to track down your Nurse Cooper."

As McIntire went out the door, he heard her raspy whine, "Claire, where's the black skillet?"

Getting through to the University of Minnesota Hospital and finding out that Gary Cooper was still employed there was a breeze. He was not any a nurse of any sort, but an X-ray technician. Talking to Cooper himself was another matter.

"He comes on duty at four. I'll let him know you called."

"It is urgent. Can you give me Mr. Cooper's home phone number?"

It turned out that Mr. Cooper didn't have a telephone, but his aunt, who lived across the street, did. The protocol was to leave a message with Aunt Julia, and Cooper would call back when, and, most likely, if, he happened to feel like it.

McIntire left his message. Despite tossing in the carrot that his call concerned a homicide investigation, he had time to sweep the floor and write a three page letter to Leonie before the phone rang.

"I take it this is about Reuben Hofer?"

Murder wasn't something that happened every day, but, still, McIntire was surprised that news of the shooting of an obscure farmer in St. Adele had already made it across two states.

"I understand you knew him when you were both in the CPS camp in Gibb's Bay."

"I did know him then, and for a few years before that." A door slammed in the background, and a female voice announced that it was "like the Congo out there."

"Here too," McIntire volunteered.

"That right? I thought the lake would cool you off."

"That's only in theory. You didn't spend the summer here, I take it?"

"Yes, I did, and you Yoopers don't know nothing about heat, but, no, I wasn't in Gibb's Bay very long."

"I understand that you got out by volunteering for a medical experiment?"

"That I did."

"And then you just stayed on at the hospital?"

"They owe me." The tone changed from passing-the-time-of-day to curious. "What did you want to know about Reuben? I doubt that I can tell you much that will help you find your murderer. I didn't sneak up there and kill him."

"What sort of person was he? Easy going? Hard to get along with?"

"I got along with him fine, if that's what you mean, until I volunteered to get starved. He thought I was taking the coward's way out." Cooper's laugh had a bitter edge. "I was naive enough to think so too. If I'd had any idea what hunger was going to be like, I'd have gladly had done my time in Alcatraz."

McIntire had heard that the food in Alcatraz was almost worth getting sent up for. "Reuben must have been different from the other men in the camp."

"Not really. His background was less affluent than some, and he wasn't well educated. Neither was I for that matter, but it seemed to bother him more. But we all had the same outlook, you might say—political and social leanings. I first met up with him when we were in Patapsco. We got to be pretty good friends."

He was the first person to admit to a friendship with Hofer, with the possible exception of the hairdresser. McIntire asked, "One of the old supervisors told me he wasn't so 'ornery' as the rest, but he figured him to be an instigator. Do you think that's true?"

"Instigator? Not from what I knew of him. He just more or less went along with things as they came. He did what he felt had to be done, but he took his licks, accepted his punishment, too." A smile was apparent in his voice, "But now that you mention it, he had some downright ingenious ways of turning things to his advantage."

"Was there much of any punishment? The supervisor I spoke with said they didn't have any real authority."

"That didn't stop them trying, and Reuben never put up a fuss. If they told him to scrub the floor, he'd get a bucket and a toothbrush and spend the rest of the day sitting with his back against the wall, brushing away. After one of the major…revolts, you might call it, they put us to work filling in a swampy spot by the barracks, shoveling sand from a big dune and carting it across in a wheel barrow. It would have taken ten years to do what they could have done in a day with a back hoe and a dump truck. After the first couple of days, most of the other guys refused to go, me included. There wasn't anything they could do to force us. But every day Reuben got sent out to dig that dirt, and every day he went, dragging—He'd made this ball and chain, and—"

"Yes, I heard about that," McIntire said.

"Anyway he'd head out first thing in the morning, dragging that damn ball and chain. He fiddled around out there forever, sitting on the ground, digging with a teaspoon. He never hauled more than a half a wheel barrow load in a day, but he kept at it. Just to be stubborn." He gave a grunt. "And it got him out of doing his share of any real work."

"Meaning that the real work got left for the rest of you? Did that cause some aggravation?"

"Only for the supervisors. The rest of us were as bad, if not worse."

Cooper was right. This was all interesting, but not likely to be of much help in finding Hofer's killer, and the call was getting expensive. "What about any other disagreements? Did Reuben get into personal conflicts with the supervisors or maybe other inmates? Can you think of anybody who might have had a grudge against him?"

"Anybody or nobody. There were the usual squabbles, one after another, but nothing out of the ordinary. Of course he got some grief because of the German accent. Nothing much though. Once in a while when he'd had one too many, he'd start singing German songs. That didn't go over so big with some of the staff."

One too many? Reuben Hofer? "Were you allowed liquor at the camps?" It was a dumb question. If the men had stuck to doing what they were "allowed" they wouldn't have ended up in Gibb's Bay.

"We could leave the camp on Sundays. Somebody generally managed to bring back a supply. Reuben hadn't been a drinker, of course, and he couldn't hold his liquor worth a damn."

Maybe McIntire was barking up the wrong tree. Murder was hardly ever the work of declared enemies. He asked, "Did Reuben have any particular friends?"

"Not that I knew of. Well, like I said, we were friendly, until I knuckled under."

"What about outside the camp?" Like Wanda Hair-lady, for instance. "Did you ever go into town with him, yourself?"

"Once or twice. I got made *persona non grata* right off the bat. Reuben was better behaved."

"On those trips did you ever meet a woman called Wanda Greely?" McIntire asked. "She's a beautician."

"I don't think so. Are you telling me Reuben got mixed up with some woman? I guess I didn't know him all that well, after all."

"I don't know if they were mixed up. She claims she knew him."

Cooper didn't seem to be able to tell him anymore. He did add, before hanging up, "I saw Reuben again not so long ago. His wife was in the hospital here. He was still mad as hell about my 'defecting.'"

"I heard."

"How is she?"

"Getting along, but not well, as you can imagine."

"Give her my best." He didn't express sympathy for her loss.

Chapter Twelve

The hearse drove right through the yard, around to the back of the house, and up to the door. Claire watched from the barn while two men in black suits got out, and Jake and Sam helped them carry the coffin with Pa in it up the back steps and into the house. It seemed like a long time before the men came back out and went away, leaving Pa there.

"Come on, Boy, want to stretch your legs a little?" Spike trotted to the door ahead of her. He seemed to understand everything she said.

They only got to the edge of the barnyard before the Sister came out and yelled for her, but Claire acted like she didn't hear. She walked quick and stayed behind the trees so they couldn't see her from the house.

They didn't have woods by their house in Iowa, only willow trees along the river, and it was too muddy to walk there much. The trees here in Michigan were big; it was like being in a deep forest from long ago. She broke a leafy branch off a maple tree to swish away the mosquitoes, and walked along the path that went to the river.

"Claire! Come here!" It was Joey yelling now. Sister must have sent him to find her, but he wouldn't come all the way out here looking. Claire knew she couldn't stay in the woods forever, but she didn't want to go inside with Pa there. The longer she stayed away, the harder it would be to go back, and everybody would know she was just chicken. Putting things off only made them worse and made her look stupid.

Still, she kept going until she couldn't hear him anymore. She didn't have to go back just because Joey said. It was good to be away by herself. She stole swiftly and silently through the forest, like an Indian scout. She needed moccasins. Maybe Jake would go deer hunting this year, and she could use the hide to make some.

The path started to go downhill toward the river. Claire liked the green, cool river almost as much as the lake. She was close enough to catch the sound of water bubbling over stones when she heard voices. Men talking. "Here Spike!" She squatted down and said it low, but he stopped and looked at her. She patted her knees, and he came running. It might be somebody fishing. Or it might be murderers. An Indian scout would sneak close to listen. Claire took Spike in her arms and stood up. She took one baby step forward.

"Over here!" One of the men shouted, and Claire ran back down the path.

She only ran a little ways, then she put Spike down and walked. When she got almost back to the barnyard, Sam came through the gate, looking grumpy. "Where have you been? You better get back before Sister busts a gut."

"Spike got scared by the hearse and ran away. I had to go find him."

"Like hell."

Claire didn't give a darn if Sam believed her or not. "There were some men, down by the river."

"Sheriff Koski?" Sam sounded excited.

She hadn't thought of that. It must been the sheriff or some policemen.

"Did you talk to him?"

"Not very much," she told him. "He was otherwise occupied." Sam probably didn't even know what that meant.

Sister met her at the door and handed her a bucket of water. "You can wash the porch windows." Then she said, "It's best to keep busy." She didn't seem too mad.

There were only two windows in the porch, so washing them didn't keep Claire busy for long. After she was done, Ma put both her and Joey to work scrubbing the front steps.

Then she told them that there'd be company coming, and they should go put on their good clothes. It meant they had to pass through the front room, where Pa's coffin was, with him in it. They walked fast, and Claire tried to keep her eyes straight ahead so she wouldn't see it, but she couldn't help herself. After she actually looked, it wasn't so bad. She stopped. It was a big wooden box, she'd seen that much when they took it out of the hearse. Now it was sitting on a sort of cart, all covered with a white sheet.

She took a step toward it. Then Spike trotted in and practically went berserk. The hair stood up on his back and he whined and barked and ran in circles around the coffin.

"Get that animal out of here, and keep him locked up somewhere!" Sister came barreling in from the kitchen, and Claire caught Spike and took him upstairs.

She put on her Sunday dress and found a barrette for her hair. Joey had grown in the summer, so his school clothes didn't fit very well, but there wasn't anything they could do about that. His new white suit was hanging in the closet, but it was only for when he made his First Communion.

He sat on the floor and tugged to squeeze into his shoes. "They're getting way too small."

"Don't be silly," Claire kidded him. "They're the same size they always were."

He stuck out his tongue at her.

Joking gave Claire the courage to say, "I wonder what he's wearing."

"Who?"

"Pa. I wonder what he has on."

Joey knew the answer to that. "Sister bought a suit for him in town. Tie this." He stuck his foot up.

"If I do it, you'll never learn to do it yourself." Claire said, but she got down and did it anyway.

"He's wearing a black suit." Joey said. "Double-breasted."

"What's that?" Once when Jake didn't know she was listening, Claire heard him say that he wanted to head west where men were men and women were double-breasted. She knew it was a joke.

"I don't know. But it is. Double breasted."

Claire had never seen Pa with a suit on. "Nobody will see him wearing it," she said. "Except maybe God."

"Do you think he's in heaven?"

Was he? Up there looking down at them. Would he be even better at knowing every move they made than he was when he was alive? "How would I know? You need to get downstairs and wash your face."

"He wasn't good. He got put in jail." Sometimes Joey just wouldn't give up. "How bad do you have to be to go to Hell? Pa wasn't Catholic, so he couldn't go to confession and get the priest to forgive him. Do you have to be Catholic to go to Purgatory?"

"Probably not," Claire said. "And, on second thought, there aren't all that many sins for people who aren't Catholic, so Pa is probably in Heaven already." Joey didn't look like he believed her.

When they went back down, Claire looked straight at the coffin when she walked past.

They hardly had time to wash and comb their hair before Mrs. Maki showed up. She brought a cake and some teensy-weensy sandwiches an a plate. They moved Ma's chair into the front room so she could sit by the coffin.

After a while some other people came—Father Doucet, and Mia Thorsen. Her husband, Nick, came, too. He wasn't tall like she was, and he had dimples in his cheeks, which looked funny on somebody so old. The lady from the store was there and some others that Claire didn't know. One of them was a bent-over woman with a cane that Mrs. Thorsen said used to be her teacher when she was Claire's age. She looked exactly like a mean old maid teacher, but she wasn't one; her husband was there, too.

Claire said, "I wouldn't want her to be my teacher."

They were in the kitchen, so Mrs. Thorsen could laugh out loud. "Well, you'd better mind your Ps and Qs, because now Mrs. Van Opelt is a judge!"

Everybody that came went in and looked at Pa's coffin and talked to Ma for a few minutes. Then they had coffee and food and talked to each other.

Claire stood between Joey and Sam by the windows. The sun was going down and it shone on the coffin under the sheet, like a skinny bed. It was strange to think of Pa sleeping forever in that box, in his new black double-breasted suit, not being able to see or hear all the people around, not knowing that people had come to visit, because he was dead. Unless he was looking down from heaven, or up from some place else.

Once Claire picked up a dead baby rabbit. It was newborn and didn't have any hair. It was the coldest thing she ever touched in her whole life. Colder than an icicle. She wondered if Pa would feel that way if she touched him.

Father Doucet bent down to talk to Ma. "Would you like me to say a few words?"

Ma shook her head. "I don't think so. Thank you all the same." When he started to walk away, she touched his sleeve. "Have you got your violin with you?"

He got it from his car and stood by the end of the coffin. Everybody got quiet, and he started to play. It was soft, quiet music that made you think of butterflies and raindrops; not unhappy, except if you remembered that Pa wouldn't see those things ever again. At Grandpa's funeral, the church choir sang, and it sounded sad and mysterious. But this wasn't Pa's funeral. That was going to be at Prairie Oak, and they'd sing there, probably.

Beside her, Sam started to snuffle, and Father Doucet looked at Ma. Then his mouth made the smallest smile, and he bent forward so his hair bounced onto his forehead. He started to play again, music that gave Claire goose pimples, wild, like crashing waves or a hurricane—like crashing waves *in* a hurricane! A beam of red sunshine glinted off the fiddle and made

Claire think of witches and devils with pitchforks dancing in the firelight, screaming and crying and laughing all at the same time. Jake put his hand over his ear.

Sister looked in from the kitchen. Then she left again, and, under the music, Claire heard the door slam.

Father Doucet didn't go on playing very long, but the music stayed in Claire's brain.

A short, wide lady with kinky black hair went up to Father and hugged him. She had tears in her eyes. It was funny that a woman they didn't even know was the only person crying. Except for Sam sniffling.

After that everybody went home. Jake and Sam did the chores. Mrs. Thorsen and Mrs. Maki offered to stay and help do the dishes, but Sister said her and Claire could handle it.

When they were done, Sister sat down in Ma's chair by the coffin, and the rest of them went to bed. For once Claire fell asleep right away, still feeling that wild fiddle music thumping through her chest.

But it was the thumping from downstairs that woke her up. Joey was standing by the window, looking out. He looked skinny in just his undershorts. "They're taking him away."

Claire pushed back the sheet and got up.

There was a black car in the yard, a big one, and the hearse was there, too, with its wide doors opened like wings. The same two men, with Sam and Jake helping again, brought the coffin out again and slid it inside. The men stood, one on each side, and closed up the wings with Pa inside. Sister came out of the house with her carpet bag suitcase and got into the car. Sam and Jake got in, too, and they all drove away.

"He's gone," Joey said.

Chapter Thirteen

Fifteen buckets of water and she hadn't even started on the corn yet. There had to be a better way. Mia switched off the pump and stooped to pick up the pails. The jangle of the telephone erupted through the kitchen window, and she stood erect. A short reprieve, maybe, if Nick could get to it in time. It stopped after three rings. Either he'd been in the kitchen already, or he was feeling better. Getting around better, anyway.

The shade on the open window popped up, and he called to her.

Mia squished her toes in her wet tennis shoes. "What's up?"

"Guibard. He wants to talk to you."

Any excuse for a break in the one-woman bucket brigade was a good one, but what could the doctor want with her? Maybe he had in mind to convince Nick to try some kind of treatment. Or maybe he had some bad news.

"You coming in?"

"I'm on my way." She set down the pails. "Moving in this heat is like swimming upstream."

For Nick, moving was always like swimming upstream. For the thousandth time at least, Mia wished with every smidgeon of her being that she'd never pushed her husband into facing up to his illness. From the day, less than a year before, that he'd admitted to the Parkinson's, he'd gone downhill. As long as he'd been able to deny being sick, let people think he was just a drunk, he'd gotten along fairly well. He'd at least had his pride—odd as that might seem.

Mia wiped her hands on a kitchen towel, leaving a grey smudge, before taking the earpiece.

"I'm calling to ask a rather large favor." Guibard sounded tired, and he was generally in the habit of telling, not asking. He didn't proceed until Mia said, "Go ahead."

"I'm putting Mrs. Hofer into the hospital for a couple of days. What with everything that's happened and the heat, she's worn out, and I don't want it to get worse. We were hoping you might keep an eye on the kids. It's only the two young ones, the older boys have gone with the aunt to bury their father. The girl is reasonably responsible, but after what's happened it's not a good idea to leave them alone at the mercy of reporters and gawkers."

Claire might be responsible, but she was still only a child. Surely their mother would never consider leaving them to take care of themselves for days, even without the gawkers. She asked, "You mean bring them here?"

"I'll understand if you'd rather not. I know you have your hands full. We can maybe get—"

"No! Of course I'll do it."

"You sure? You need to check with Nick?"

"It'll be fine." Mia felt a flush of elation. It was a pity the new bath wasn't ready, but she'd fire up the sauna. Take some soap and water to that hair. "No problem at all. I'll get a room ready now."

"I can't thank you enough. Should we drop them off on the way, or do you want to come and get them?"

It would take some preparation, getting beds ready, and getting Nick ready, despite her assurances to the contrary. "I'll walk over and get them," Mia said. "How soon you going?"

"Soon as I can get back over there. But don't rush. The kids are used to taking care of themselves. They'll be okay for an hour or two as long as nobody shows up to bother them."

They were going through a terrible time. Getting away from the house where they'd lived with their father might do the children good. Take their mind off things. As Mia hung up the earpiece she realized she hadn't expressed any concern for Mary Frances. She hadn't even asked about her.

She'd seemed well enough at the impromptu wake, but it was hard to tell. She was subdued, but it wasn't like she was ever exactly vivacious, and under the circumstances you wouldn't expect her to be dancing around with a feather boa.

It had been an unconventional gathering. Not a wake, exactly. Most of the people hadn't known either Reuben or his family. The only tears to be shed were brought on by the effect of Father Doucet's fiddling on Lucy Delany. Where had he learned to play like that? Someplace familiar to Lucy, obviously. The music hadn't seemed to please the aunt much.

Nick had gone with the newspaper into the darkened living room. He only nodded when Mia told him they were to have company for a few days. It was impossible to read his thoughts; his face showed so little expression these days. Mia wasn't sure he'd understood, or even been listening, but she didn't explain further.

She bounded up the stairs with an armload of sun-dried sheets and entered the bedroom that might be the least stifling. It was the room she'd slept in from infancy, first sharing with John McIntire and Wylie Petworth, then had all to herself. It hadn't been slept in since she married Nick and they moved into her parents' old room. It was a child's bedroom, and their rare overnight guests had never included children.

Mia flung open the windows to let the sun drive out some of the closed-in smell.

The other spare room was in better shape. Nick's brother and his wife had used it only a few weeks before. Now that word had gotten out about Nick's illness, his family was turning up, one or two at a time. Mia liked Tony and Carol; they ought to have kept in touch better over the years.

Making up the beds and wiping away dust took the better part of an hour.

She gave a final pat to the spread and pictured the dark tousled head on the pillow. How lovely it would be…. She caught sight of her face, naked in its euphoria, in the foggy mirror and felt a sickening jolt. That little girl—those children—would be here because their mother was seriously ill and their father had gotten his head shot off, and here she was, flitting around like some giddy Mary Poppins.

She went downstairs sobered and tried to stay that way as she strode along the path she'd first taken when she was six years old, holding tight to Johnny McIntire's hand, through the pastures to the Black Creek schoolhouse.

Mark Guibard's gray car was parked in the shade of the spruce trees, but he and Mary Hofer hadn't waited around; the big Oldsmobile was gone. The two children sat on the steps with a cardboard box between them, eyes like sheep headed for slaughter. Maybe Mary Poppins was what they needed, after all.

"They took Pa's car," Claire explained. She didn't have to explain why. "Doctor Guibard said you could use his car if you wanted."

"We can walk. It's not very far." Mia had driven their own dilapidated Dodge a few times that summer, but she wasn't about to risk crashing the doctor's jaunty coupe into a tree, or worse. The kids looked so disappointed she almost relented. "I'll bring you back in our car. Are you all set? Toothbrushes? Pajamas?"

It wasn't until Claire stood up and called out, "Here, Spike!" That Mia remembered about the dog. Nick might not object to the children, but Nick and dogs hadn't been on good terms since his days delivering the mail on a motorcycle. And a yappy little thing like this…. Mia made the timid suggestion, "Maybe he'd be better off at home."

"He's just a pup." The animal leapt into Claire's arms and she bent her cheek to his head. "He's housebroken." She looked up. "We could stay here until night. I have to milk Opal, anyway, and feed the chickens."

That wouldn't have been such a bad idea; sitting around passing the time of day with her, and Nick wasn't going to be the most fun those kids had ever had, but as Guibard had said, it wasn't a good time to leave the children alone, even in the middle of the afternoon. There was no telling who might turn up.

Claire stood on one foot, clutching the dog to her chest, rubbing the heel of her bare foot over a mosquito-bitten ankle. Her hair was a mass of knots again, her pink barrette askew. The shorts that ballooned over her toothpick legs had obviously been created with a scissors. Inspiration struck and Mia asked, "How would you like to go to the lake?"

Chapter Fourteen

It was the best day of Claire's life. The water was way warmer than it had been the day they walked there with Sam and Jake, and so blue that it hurt your eyes to look at it. They fixed a picnic—lunchmeat sandwiches, and deviled eggs, and peanut butter cookies. Mrs. Thorsen didn't put on her swimming suit because Claire and Joey didn't have any, but she rolled up her pants legs and went in anyway. She said the water was warm because the sun heated the top couple of inches and the breeze blew it into shore.

"It only happens about twice in a century, so we'd better make the most of it." She was joking, but it probably didn't happen very often.

When she was done, she sat in the sun to dry off and read a book, while Claire and Joey threw sticks for Spike and waded in to collect rocks. After a while she got out a bottle of shampoo and a comb and washed her hair in the lake. When she unbraided her hair it hung in long strings down her back, and she looked more like a witch than ever.

Claire washed her hair, too, and Mrs. Thorsen let her borrow the comb to get the tangles out. Then she braided Claire's hair.

"It's not the best job," she said, "I guess it's easier to braid your own hair. I never tried doing it on anybody else before."

Claire couldn't see it for herself, of course. She could feel that the part wasn't exactly in the middle, and some hair in back of her ear was pulled too tight and hurt, but she didn't like to say so. Anyway it was a heck of a lot cooler.

On the way home, Joey fell asleep in the back seat. He didn't wake up, even though it was a jerky ride; Mrs. Thorsen was not a very good driver. Worse than Sam, even. When they got to the yard she drove the car so close to some trees that the branches poked in through the windows, and Claire was afraid she was going to crash right into one, but she slammed on the brakes and the car stopped in the nick of time. With the trees in the way, Claire had to slide across the seat and get out on Mrs. Thorsen's side.

Joey didn't budge, even when Mrs. Thorsen tickled his feet. "We might as well just leave him to sleep awhile," she said. "He'll be okay here in the shade."

It was supper time, but they were still full from the picnic, and it was too hot to cook. Mrs. Thorsen's husband, Nick, was out pulling weeds in the garden. There were sure plenty of them. Mrs. Thorsen said that Nick was the mailman for a long time, since he was Sam's age, but he couldn't work anymore because he was sick.

She showed Claire the bedroom she could sleep in. It was a beautiful room, like a picture in a magazine. There was a soft bedspread the same color blue as the birds on the wallpaper, and, kitty-corner from the bed, a fancy little dresser with a mirror and a stool, so you could sit in front of it.

"My father made it when I was just a little girl." Mrs. Thorsen ran her hand along the frame of the mirror. "I outgrew it by the time I was ten, but I kept it anyway because I liked it," she smiled into the mirror. "And I liked my—"

She stopped, but Claire knew she was going to say "my father." She probably didn't want to mention fathers. Claire had a hard time thinking that a father could be somebody you would like, in the way you would like a friend or a dog or something. Fathers just *were*. Some might be nicer than others, she supposed. Grandpa was a father, too—Ma's father—and he was okay most of the time, but Claire had never thought about whether she liked him or not. Mrs. Thorsen's father was probably nice, and it was a pretty dresser. It didn't look homemade.

"He was very good at woodworking," Claire said.

Mrs. Thorsen sat down on the edge of the bed. "I'm very good at woodworking, too."

Claire wasn't sure what she meant. How could an old lady be doing woodworking? How would she know how, and when would she have time?

"My father taught me, and now I'm a better cabinet maker than he was. Come on, I'll show you my workshop."

The workshop was a concrete block building with just two little bitty windows, so it was practically pitch dark until Mrs. Thorsen turned on the light. There was a big wood stove in the middle and work benches with tools all around the sides. It smelled good.

Mrs. Thorsen turned on a lamp over one of the benches and picked up a piece of wood. It was about as long as a yardstick, and had a carved design, triangles and funny shapes. "It's going to go on a china cabinet," she said. "I'm making it for a man in Chicago. He's giving it to his wife for their twenty-fifth anniversary."

"Is he paying you for it?" Claire couldn't figure if the man was somebody Mrs. Thorsen knew, or if he hired her to make the carving.

"You bet he is! He's paying me a whole lot for it."

Mrs. Thorsen was an old lady, but she could do something people thought was only for men. She turned off the lamp and they went out into the bright sun. "Would you like to come over and make something one of these days? Maybe a toy truck or a tractor for Joey?"

Claire nodded. Jake would die of jealousy.

Joey was still asleep when it was time to go do the chores.

"We can wake him up. Then I'll walk over with you." Mrs. Thorsen went to the car and dragged Joey out. He stumbled when he walked to the house and hardly had his eyes open. When she left him in her front room so she could go tell Nick that they were leaving, he laid down on the davenport and was out like a rock again.

Claire didn't want to wake him up; she knew just how he felt. She'd give anything to be able to go to sleep herself, and sleep for hours, maybe even for days. Maybe until Ma and the boys got home and the sadness was over. But she didn't want to go back to do the chores without him. He was going to be scared when he woke up if he was alone with Mrs. Thorsen and Nick. He saw that long white hair swishing in the water, and probably still thought Mia might be a witch. Besides, Claire didn't want to go alone, either. If somebody came, she wouldn't know what to say without Ma there.

Annie Oakley wouldn't have been scared. Besides, Claire had Spike. "I can go by myself," she said. "It's just milking and feeding the chickens. I do it every day. It won't take any time at all."

Mrs. Thorsen pulled on her braid for a long time, but finally said, "Come straight back. It's starting to look like rain."

It was nice under the shady trees, but pretty soon the mosquitos found her, and Claire ran until she got out of the woods and back in the sunshine.

It was strange to get home and be all by herself, kind of scary and kind of exciting. It was so very quiet. Pa's car was back, and the doctor's funny little one was gone. The hens were having dust baths by the side of the barn. Claire pulled the lid off the chicken waterer and took it to the pump. By the time she'd pumped it full, she was sweating, and the water was icy cold. She yanked the pump handle down and quickly pressed her hand onto the spout to stop the water coming out. Then she leaned over, moved her hand just enough to let water bubble up, and slurped up a long drink. The icy water made her teeth ache and ran down her arms.

She lugged the waterer back to the chickens and pumped two more pails to fill up Opal's tank. After she filled the feeders with laying mash for the hens, she went to the house for the milk pail.

She stopped in front of the sink and stretched up to look at herself in the mirror. Her hair was coming loose from the braid, and her bangs were way too long. When she pushed them back it didn't look so bad. She picked the comb up from the shelf and pulled Ma's hairs from it. When she combed her bangs to the side they made a wave over her forehead, kind of like the pink lady's. She fastened it with one of Ma's bobby pins. It made her look older. Thirteen, maybe.

There was a rumble. Spike gave a whimper. "Don't worry Boy." She patted his head. "It's just thunder. When you hear it, it's too late for the lightning to hurt you." Spike wasn't scared of much, but he was a real chicken when it came to thunder. Claire left him inside where he could hide under Ma's bed and wouldn't be trying to crawl into her lap while she was milking.

The sun was still shining, but far away, in the direction of the lake, she could see a dark greenish line of clouds.

Opal was waiting by the barn door. Claire told Mrs Thorsen that she did the milking every day. In fact it was Sam's job. Claire had only tried it a couple of times, and she hoped she remembered how.

Opal went into the barn and put her head into the stanchion without any pushing. Claire pulled up the stool and sat down. The cow stamped, and her tail whacked Claire in the shoulder. There was some hay piled in the calf pen. It was from last year and dusty, and Opal didn't really need it, she had plenty of grass, but it might keep her mind off the flies and her tail off Claire's face. She got up to dump an armload in the manger and sat back down.

Claire got her bare toes as far as she could from the twitchy hooves and grabbed the tits. She gave a pull and a squeeze. Nothing happened. On the second try a couple of drops came. Next time nothing again. Tears came into Claire's eyes. It had to be easy. Maybe her hands were too small. Maybe Opal missed Sam singing. Claire leaned her head against the cow's warm side and tried to make her voice deeper. "*When the sun in the morning peeks over the hill....*" A little more milk squirted out. Claire sang and pulled and squeezed. The spot of sunshine on the floor blinked out and thunder crashed again. She milked faster until her hands started to ache. Finally, the pail was almost full. Over half, anyway. She pinched the tits at the top and ran her fingers down like she'd seen Sam do to strip them dry.

The next rumble was closer, and it didn't exactly sound like thunder. Claire lifted the pail onto the shelf and went past the horse stalls to the window.

It was already starting to get dark. The sun was just about ready to set, and it shone from behind the trees and glinted off the back end of a car sticking out from around the corner of the house. The car looked dark red, but the sun was so bright Claire couldn't tell for sure if it really was, or if it just looked that way from the sun. It was smaller than Pa's car.

The front screen door skreeked open, and Spike started barking his head off. Claire felt herself go stiff.

Maybe it was a reporter. If she stayed put, they wouldn't know she was here. They wouldn't know anybody was home.

She heard the inside door open and Spike barking like he was going mad. Somebody had gone into the house. Then Spike gave a yelp and everything was quiet, but only for a minute. A door slammed inside the house, and there was another noise, like something falling.

Would a reporter walk right in without asking? Maybe it was the murderer, back for the rest of them.

The light came on in the cellar window. There were more noises, bumps and crashes. Her stomach started to hurt. After a long time the light went out again.

Should she sneak outside? Run back to Thorsen's and tell them there was a burglar—or a murderer—in the house? To do that, she'd have to go right past the house, and she'd have to leave Spike all alone. He wasn't barking anymore.

There was a giant thump that sounded like it might be in Ma's bedroom.

All the time she was watching and listening, it was getting darker fast. The sky behind the house was almost black. Lightning went streaking across it, but it was a long time before the thunder came, and then it was low and far away.

If she was going to sneak back to Thorsens', she had to do it now, and she had to do it quick. She started to back away from the window, to head for the outside and the path through the woods, when she heard the back door open. There was a shadow behind the screen; somebody had come out onto the porch. They were standing by the door looking straight at the barn. Straight at her.

The screen door pushed open, and Claire ran for the haymow ladder.

Chapter Fifteen

"John?"

Mia coughed. McIntire waited.

"I don't like to bother you...."

It was followed by silence. She most likely hadn't called to inform him of her admirable thoughtfulness. "I'm not busy," McIntire told her. "What's the problem?"

"I'm probably being a worry wart, but...."

"But?"

"I can't go myself, because I don't want to get Joey upset..."

Joey? The Hofer kid? "Mia, what is it? Spit it out."

"Guibard took Mary Frances to the hospital. He didn't say exactly why, just that she was played out. Maybe she's on the verge of a breakdown, or something. I said I'd look after Claire and Joey. So I brought them here, but tonight Claire went home to do the chores. I didn't like to let her go by herself, but I don't know how to milk a cow, and Joey was so sound asleep—"

"What's happened?"

"I don't know that anything's happened. She just hasn't come back."

"How long has she been gone?"

"She left about eight, so it's been over two hours. All she had to do was milk the cow and feed some chickens. It's a ten minute walk. She said she'd come straight back."

So, figuring around an hour to do her chores, she was about a half hour late. Wasn't that the normal thing for a kid? "Maybe she's scared of walking back in the dark, and it looks like a thunderstorm rolling up. She could be waiting for it to be over."

"You're not going to make me feel better by telling me there's a storm coming. Could you check? Please. I don't like to leave Joey here with just Nick. In case he wakes up and is scared—not that there seems to be much chance of that. Him waking up, I mean. He must have been completely exhausted. But if he does wake up he might be scared, and Nick's not been having such a good day. I could go myself and take him along, but that might not be a good idea in case...in case something *has* happened.... Could you just go?"

"Take it easy. I'll go. And don't worry, Mia. She's most likely been fiddling around and lost track of time, and now, like I said, is afraid to walk back by herself in the dark with a storm on the way. I'm sure nothing's happened."

"Something happened to her father." Mia's voice sounded calmer, calm enough to be forced. "I have a feeling...." The sound of a great sucking in of breath came over the wires. "Just go check on her. Please."

McIntire had learned long ago to trust Mia Thorsen's feelings. "I'm on my way."

McIntire might trust Mia's premonitions, but he couldn't say the same for her judgement. What on earth had made her let that child go off by herself? Anybody might show up, including, conceivably, her father's murderer. It was a short walk, but Claire couldn't know the way all that well.

Outdoors the air was still and warm as bathwater. A half moon floated behind thin cloud, but the sky to the northwest was black, except during the brief flashes of lightning. The storm was creeping in, gathering strength.

McIntire made the mile and a half to Hofers' in time that would have tempted Father Doucet to one of those deadly sins—envy.

There might have been a light on in the barn, or it could have been reflected moonlight. Outside of that, everything was dark and quiet. Far too much so. No lights in the house. No yippy mongrel nipping at his ankles.

McIntire bounded up the steps and flung open the door. It was the smell that struck him first, the dank and musty odor that rose up from the open cellar, bringing with it the image of a slight girl lying at the bottom of the steps in a pool of milk.

"Claire!" His call sounded hollow in the dark cavern.

McIntire turned to locate a light and got nothing for his trouble but a stubbed toe. Despite the dimness, it was apparent that the old cloakroom was in even more than its customary shambles. He scuffled through a gantlet of rubber overshoes and manure scented jackets and stepped over an upended bench to reach the kitchen door. It was swollen and wedged tight from the recent humidity, but gave way with a thwack when he put his shoulder to it. He slid his hand along the wall to find the light switch and felt his blood stop in his veins.

The brewing tempest might have already struck. Cupboard doors hung open, drawers were yanked out. The floor was a mangled mess of rice, cornflakes, flour, sugar, and smashed crackers, mingled with cutlery and tin cans. Even the curtains were ripped from the window and lay crumpled, along with the gaudy oilcloth, among torn magazines.

"Claire!" The answering silence was heartbreaking. A mouse ran across his shoe and skittered under a cabinet.

He skirted a pool of syrup to reach the living room. The destruction here was not so ugly, but only by virtue of having less material to work with. The five drawers of an upright chest were dumped in a heap of clothing and papers. A slashed sofa vomited brown stuffing.

The bedroom was the same; the dresser had been emptied of its pitifully scant contents; the few articles of clothing were wrenched from their hooks on the wall. The bed—a home made frame of two by six lumber—was stripped, and the naked mattress dragged half onto the floor.

A photograph in a plain oak frame still stood on the dresser. An only plumpish Mary Frances Hofer in a pale lace-trimmed suit, holding a bouquet of roses. The short veil didn't obscure the shoulder length mane of glossy dark—"Claire!" McIntire called for a third time. "Are you here?"

A soft mewling led him to a door set into the side of the narrow stairway. The space behind it contained only a vacuum cleaner and a quivering terrier with an oddly limp front leg. He stooped to pick up the animal and was rewarded with a snarl and a nip that drew blood.

"Suit yourself." He left the pup cowering in the corner, and went up the stairs.

There were two rooms, behind opposing curtained doorways. One—the one that McIntire let the aroma of sweat and stale cigarette smoke tell him was the lair of Sam and Jake—contained only an iron bedstead and a dented metal cabinet. It was impossible to determine if the chaos that reigned was vandalism or the ordinary slovenliness of adolescent boys.

He ducked into the other room and fumbled for the light string, finally discovering that it was tied, with a series of rags, to the iron bedpost. Here, too, sheets had been pulled from the bed, exposing a stained double mattress, and the closet door—a real door with real hinges, if only four feet high—stood open. McIntire squatted down and pulled on the light. A small boy's suit, pure white, was all that hung there; everything else was on the floor. The closet extended along the wall, under the eaves, beyond the reach of the light. As far as McIntire could see, it was empty.

A great clap of thunder rattled the window, which was wide open and unscreened, accounting for the bountiful crop of mosquitoes and the moths already circling around the ceiling light. McIntire lowered the sash just as the first drops of rain struck the glass.

The room contained no other furniture other than a dressing table fashioned from two peach crates and a warped board, which was left intact and upright. A motley collection of books was strewn across the bed. From McIntire's cursory glance it seemed an odd library. The boys' adventure type stories were not so strange, although Joey was probably still too young to read them. Maybe his sister read them to him. The rest were old and heavy looking, not children's books. McIntire picked up a green leather-bound volume: *Foundation Stones, Vol. 1*. A treatise on child rearing from the Daughters of the American Revolution, 1910. Good lord. How entertaining, or enlightening, could that be for a child? The magazines, too, were mainly of the women's home making variety.

Where was that child? McIntire resisted the urge to call to her again. She wasn't going to answer.

The house had been torn apart from cellar to attic. Someone either hated Reuben Hofer's entire family or was hunting for something. If the latter, they must not have found it. It was unlikely that what they sought had been in the very last place they looked, hence they'd have left a couple of stones unturned, or a cupboard un-searched. Unless what they sought was a child with a deep closet in her room.

McIntire left by the back door. He hadn't been in the house more than a few minutes, ten at most, but it felt like a hundred years had passed. In that slender span of time, his world had changed from one disordered, but rational, to a place of insidious, senseless evil.

The transformation of spirit was reflected in the physical. The balmy summer night was gone. Wind stirred the sultry air, the sky hung low and black as ink, and thunder, grumbling for hours in the west, was now a deafening accompaniment to jagged streaks of lightening. The yellow glow still showed in the window at the side of the barn. As McIntire walked through the dark toward it, the rain began to fall in earnest.

The barn was small. A single space separated by a five foot wall that formed the end of a couple of horse stalls. The Guernsey cow lay with her tail in the gutter and her neck stretched and pinned in the stanchion. McIntire prodded her rump with his toe and was relieved when she opened soft brown eyes. The milking stool stood against the wall, and a pail half-filled with milk, a few flies floating on its surface, rested on a shelf. The child must have finished the milking, or at least got a good start.

McIntire climbed the few steps up the ladder necessary for him to poke his head into the haymow. It was pitch black and stifling. There was probably no light, at least there was no switch that he could see.

"Claire!" The call was obliterated by the cacophony of rain beating on the roof; even had she been there she'd never have heard him.

He fetched his flashlight from the Studebaker and remounted the ladder.

The batteries were dying, and the light from the torch was feeble at best. But there wasn't much to see. A tall space half filled with loose hay. He prodded at its edges, plunging his arms into the prickly stems, flinging hay across the floorboards, until the light faded and went out.

There was a sudden cessation in the drumming on the roof. He stood still. "Claire, I've come to get you." In the brief interval, his words sounded muffled and dismal. He felt no living presence. No panicked breath, no rustling. "Mia's worried about you," he added, but by that time the rain had swept in again and drowned his words, leaving him with only the sweet odor of new cut alfalfa and the beating of his own heart in the darkness.

Someone had murdered Ruben Hofer, and someone had torn apart his home, either on a search or on a malice-induced spree. The little girl had been here. She wasn't here now.

"Claire!" He called one last time.

Chapter Sixteen

Pete Koski didn't speak until after he'd made a quick survey of the kitchen, barely moving from the doorway. "I radio'd for an APB. Won't do a hell of a lot of good without a car description. Cecil and Adam Wall are out looking around. They got Geronimo, but his nose ain't gonna be worth shit in this downpour. There ain't much more we can do now. The state police will get here in the morning, and if she still hasn't turned up we can get more people out looking." He removed his hat and used it to swat ineffectually at the hordes of mosquitos that appeared to be coming in to get out of the rain. "Who knew Mrs. Hofer was in the hospital? That the house would be empty?"

"Hardly anybody, so far as I know." McIntire told him. "But the obituary was in the paper, and on the radio. It mentioned that Reuben was going to be buried in South Dakota. Most people would have assumed that the whole family would be away."

"So it could have been just a simple burglary."

"For what? The Hofer family jewels? Has there ever been a burglary in St. Adele?"

"Not that I know of." Koski didn't sound as happy about that as might have been expected.

"A young girl is missing," McIntire said. "Nothing simple about that." He didn't add that it was a situation that had happened before in St. Adele or remind Koski of its outcome.

"The kid probably took off and is hiding in the woods somewhere, maybe lost, or slightly lost."

That was possible. Even under normal conditions, Claire Hofer seemed scared of her own shadow and headed for cover at the first sight of a stranger—but wouldn't she have been more scared of running off into the dark? Of course it might not have been dark at the time. "Hadn't we better get out and start looking for her now?"

"If she's out there, Wall or Cecil will find her, if she wants to be found. Otherwise, she'll be okay once it's daylight. Getting a bunch of people out might just scare her more. The last thing we want is to get her panicked into running in the dark. With this rain the river's gonna be way up in short order, if it ain't already."

Being out in a storm would be frightening, but nothing compared to the terror she would be feeling if she was in the company of.... "Maybe we'd better get Father Doucet over here," McIntire said.

"What the hell for?" Koski asked. "He's a priest, not a magician."

"The boy was asleep when his sister left the Thorsens'. That's why Mia didn't go with her. He's going to be frantic when he wakes up and finds himself alone with her and Nick. Doucet might come in handy."

Mia herself had already gone well beyond frantic. Doucet's smug serenity might keep her from going completely off her rocker. And there was the child's mother to consider. Doucet would be the person to tell her.

Koski's head was still planted firmly in the sand. "Maybe she left before any of this happened and got lost walking back to Thorsens'. She probably didn't know the way very well, and it might have been after dark. "

"She wouldn't have left the cow locked in the stanchion and the milk sitting in the barn."

"No, I guess not," the sheriff admitted. "But she did milk the cow. So whoever ransacked the house either did it earlier, before she got back here, or turned up while she was milking." He flicked his burning cigarette butt out the door. "I'll go talk to the neighbors. See if they noticed a strange car—or any car—heading this way." His words were swallowed in a volley of thunder. "I expect they'll be awake."

Rain on the Studebaker's roof created a steady deafening roar. The windshield wipers did next to nothing, and McIntire crept along, watching the road's edge, both to stay out of the ditch and to keep his eyes peeled for a small rain-soaked sprite. He was in no hurry. He'd never felt so helpless.

Koski was probably right. Sending Claire off and running through the dark could be dangerous, and it was true that lost children often ran away from their rescuers rather than to them. But leaving her in this deluge seemed cruel. If she *was* out there, which McIntire doubted. If she'd taken off, it would have been to go back to Mia, and she wouldn't have lost her way.

Lights blazed from the Thorsens' house. As always when he came into the yard, McIntire's gaze was drawn to the window of the room he'd slept in for the first five years of his life. Now Mia stood there, framed by the light at her back, a narrow shadow distorted by the water that sheeted down the glass, crowned with a silvery halo. When McIntire stepped out into the downpour, she turned away.

She burst out the kitchen door as he got to it. Her only questions were in her eyes, and he was sure she could read the reply in his.

He shook his head. "Pete's gone to check with the Makis and Touminen. Anybody who drove in would have had to pass by one or the other of their places. They might have noticed."

"I let her go back by herself. I didn't feel right about it, but I let her go alone. I can't believe I was so stupid."

Aided by hindsight, McIntire couldn't believe it either, but what did he know? He might have done the same thing. He said, "It's not your fault, Mia. You couldn't have known."

"Couldn't I?" It sounded like more than a rhetorical question, but one only she could answer.

While they talked, she fidgeted, shifting from one foot to the other, folding and unfolding her arms, turning to look into the shadows, her body seeming to move on its own, like there was something inside struggling to get out.

"Get inside. You'll be drenched."

"I can't. I have to *do* something."

"If Leonie was here," McIntire told her, "she'd make a pot of tea."

"You want tea?"

"No."

She clutched at his arm with the grip of an alligator's jaws. "Please, John, you have to tell me. Did somebody take her? It's not going to do any good to keep it from me."

Water ran down her cheeks; rain, tears, or both, he couldn't tell. He steered her into the house. Nick was in the kitchen, lifting the coffee pot from the stove. A full bottle of whisky along with two glasses sat on the table. The single form of spirits never known to pass Nick Thorsen's lips was whisky. He pulled out a chair, which his wife ignored, continuing her restless movements. She thrust her hands in her pockets and pulled them out again. "Tell me."

"I don't know what could have happened, Mia. It's like I told you, she wasn't there, that's all. The cow and the milk were in the barn, the dog was locked in the closet, and the house was torn apart, but she wasn't—"

"Torn apart?"

McIntire hadn't mentioned that when he'd come back to give Mia the news and call the sheriff. He wished he hadn't now.

"The house was searched."

"For what?"

"How do I know?"

"Yes, how do you know? That it was searched?"

"Well," McIntire admitted, "*searched* might not be precisely the right word. It was ransacked from top to bottom. Like someone looking for something specific."

"Oh, God!"

"So she might have gotten scared and run away."

"Then why isn't somebody out looking for her?"

"People are out looking for her. Cecil Newman—"

"Cecil Newman is a first class idiot!"

"He's out with Adam Wall and Pete's dog. Pete's going out himself as soon as he checks with the neighbors. He thought it was best not to have a whole gang tramping through the woods, in case she panicked into running again and got hurt. If she's in the woods, she's hiding. She won't be wandering around in the rain, lost. And if she is, she won't stay lost for long. It's not the Amazon out there. She couldn't get far without coming out into the open and seeing somebody's house. She couldn't get into any deep woods without crossing a road."

Mia moved to the window, still at last, staring out for a long time, like she expected to see Claire Hofer strolling up the driveway through the rain. "Do you want me to tell you about today? Before she left?"

McIntire didn't know what Mia could tell him that would help in locating the girl, but if it would keep her, and himself, sane for a few minutes longer, he was all for it.

"What am I going to say to that little boy?" She remained motionless, her back to the room. Her anguish was all in her voice now. "How can he be sleeping through all this?" She turned and demanded again, "How can I tell him? What will I say? 'Your mother is sick, and your sister is....' What will I say to *her*? She trusted me. She trusted me to take care of her children. Me, of all people!"

"Mia...," Nick sighed.

McIntire took her arm. "Sit! Tell me about this afternoon." He sat down himself and poured a half inch of whisky into a glass.

Mia lowered herself into the chair like every movement hurt. Her husband added cream to a cup of coffee and shoved it her way.

"Dr. Guibard called and said he was going to hospitalize Mary Frances for a day or two. He said she was suffering from the heat and the stress of all that's happened and he didn't want her to get worse. He asked if the children could come here. He didn't think they should be left alone, even during the day, after what happened, especially if news reporters showed up, but I let her go back. Alone. At night."

"Mia...." Nick made another half-hearted protest.

McIntire said, "Keep going."

"I walked over and got them about one o'clock. They're very shy, especially Joey. He hardly makes a peep. I figured I should have some way to keep them entertained, so I decided to take them to the lake. We fixed a picnic. Claire made some deviled eggs all by herself.

"The surface water had blown in, and was, believe it or not, warm-ish. The kids said they'd only been to the lake once before, and then it was too cold to go into the water. We stayed a long time.

"It was getting late when we came back, close to seven. Joey was exhausted and fell asleep in the back seat, and we didn't want to wake him up. Claire said she could go do the chores by herself. She said she always did the milking and could do it quick. She left about seven-thirty, maybe later, and she didn't come back."

"What about before?" McIntire asked. "Did you talk about her family? Her father?"

"Not much. I asked if she knew Wanda Greely. She said she'd never seen her before, and that she hadn't come back again."

"Did she mention anyone else coming around?"

"No. I think a few news reporters maybe, but only local, and that was when her aunt was there to put the run on them. People have gone over with food, but Claire didn't say anything about anybody in particular. Father Doucet goes over most every day. Maybe we should try to get hold of him now. Somebody will have to tell Mary Frances what's happened. I don't know if he even knows that she's in the hospital."

Nick got to his feet and shuffled to the phone.

"I can't bear it, John. I just can't." Mia spoke into her cup.

"It'll be daylight soon. We'll find her." That was safe to say. They would find her eventually, but in what circumstances? McIntire didn't want to think about it.

"Somebody murdered her father. If this was the same person what might they do to her?"

"The dog's still alive. That's a good sign." He might have a broken leg, though, but McIntire thought it best not to mention that.

"The dog!" Mia looked up with a start and a splash of coffee. "I forgot about Spike! Where is he?"

"They locked him in a closet. He's still there, far as I know."

"You left him locked up?"

"No. I opened the door. He could come out if he wanted to, but the last I saw of him, he wasn't budging. He's huddled in a closet, nursing an injured leg. When I tried to pick him up, the miserable mutt almost ripped my thumb off." McIntire displayed the purplish tooth marks.

Mia went to the metal cabinet over the sink and took out a small bottle. "Do you want me to do it?"

It would sting less if he did it himself, but he nodded, "Go ahead."

She held the thumb still and brushed on the burning mercurochrome.

"Maybe you could go get the dog. It would be something—*someone*—to be here when Joey wakes up." Her hands shook, and a russet blob landed on the table. "Maybe Spike can lead you to Claire."

McIntire stood. He'd go fetch the pup if that's what Mia wanted, but he had no illusions about a heroic canine rescue. "The little mongrel ain't Rin Tin Tin."

Chapter Seventeen

The thunder was over, and it wasn't raining any more. It was so quiet that she could hear Opal huffing and snuffling below. The men must be gone by now; she hadn't heard any cars for a long time. Still Claire didn't move. Her eyes hurt from the dust, straws poked and scratched her everywhere, and her legs stung because she was wet. She'd been afraid to go out when she had to pee.

She went back to praying again.

On the fifth *Hail Mary*, it worked; the rooster crowed. In the night she had prayed for the thunder to stop, and it did. Now she prayed for morning, and it was coming. Maybe it was already light. Under the hay, she couldn't see a thing but black and the moving colored spots you can always see in the dark.

She had to go out sooner or later. Mrs. Thorsen would be mad that she didn't come back to her house. Opal was still locked in the stanchion and Spike.... He had yelped and then not made another sound, so he was hurt for sure, and she'd been a coward and deserted him.

The rooster crowed again, and Claire pushed at the hay to get it away from her face. She slid along, feeling the boards of the wall, until she came out from behind the stack. She sat back against the wall and took a long breath with no hayseeds in it. It was still dark, but she could see a grey square up high where the window was. Morning was here, and she was still alive.

A thump came from below, and she felt her stomach flip over. *Hail Mary, full of grace.* A splat hit the floor. Opal.

Claire crept forward, not making a sound, stealthy and careful, feeling in front of her for the opening in the floor. Her head hit the wall. She felt all around herself and sat up. Across the floor she could see more gray light and the ladder sticking up through the hole. She was going exactly the wrong way.

She crawled over on her hands and knees and peeked down. There was the dark shape of Opal, looking up at her. She grabbed the ladder and felt for the rungs with her toes.

Outside it was still almost dark, but a few birds were starting to sing. The air felt fresh and cool and smelled like rain. A deer stood by the block of salt, huge ears perked up, looking at her with round gentle eyes. Claire held her breath. She could see whiskers on the doe's soft brown muzzle. Then Opal coughed, and it turned and sailed over the fence without even taking a run at it.

Claire pushed the barndoor wide and opened the cow's stanchion. It would be time to milk her again in a little while. Last night's milk might be spoiled. She'd have to give it to the chickens, if they still had any chickens. She hadn't closed them in to keep out the foxes and weasels—or the dogs. If she still had a dog.

She slapped Opal on the butt and followed her through the door into a magic world.

Claire was used to getting up early. She was always out of bed when it was still dark in the winter time, but she hadn't ever in her life been outdoors before the sun came up in the summer. It was silvery and misty, and even though it seemed like it was still night, she could see everything.

The only car in the yard was Pa's. Her shorts rubbed against the hay scratches on her legs and burned like mad. She took baby steps and kept her feet apart as she walked around the puddles to the back door.

When she opened it, Spike jumped into her arms, licking her face and squirming. She wrapped her arms around him and hugged him tight, and he gave a squeal and went still.

"What's the matter, Boy?" She sat on the step and put him down next to her. He kept one paw up while he sniffed around at her damp shorts.

She took his face in her hands and kissed the top of his head. "You'll be all right, Boy. I'm here now. Come on, let's go inside. I need some different clothes." She felt sorry for him.

The front room and Ma's bedroom were in an awful mess. Things were dumped and thrown around, so it must have been burglars that came in.

Claire went straight upstairs to her bedroom. The first thing she saw was her books and magazines flung all over the bed, and the first thing she thought was that Pa would see them, and she'd be in awful trouble. Then she remembered that Pa was gone, and she could read if she wanted to.

Their clothes were on the floor, and the sheets were pulled off the mattress. The burglars saw that the mattress had holes in it.

She looked around for something to put on. Her blue and white dress was at the Thorsens', and her other underpants were in the wash. She dug in the pile of clothes and pulled out her old yellow jumper. She put it on with no blouse under it, and settled for wearing a pair of Joey's undershorts.

She gathered up the books. *Baree, Son of Kazan* was ripped almost in two. Why would burglars want to wreck her books? It didn't make sense. Then it hit her. Burglars! Thieves! What else would they take?

Claire went to the closet, opening the door as far as she could and dragging the blanket against it to keep it that way. She hated that closet. It was long and dark, like a cave, and smelled old and dirty. The thought of the door swinging shut and trapping her inside gave her shivers. She pulled the light string. The bulb flashed and sizzled and went out.

She could see fairly good without it, but not good enough to see if there were spiders in the corners. She got down on her knees and pulled up the board where it was cut out in a small rectangle. Underneath there were electric wires, and Claire held her breath as she reached past them into the dark. It was there. The wooden cheese box that held her treasures. The burglar hadn't found it. She slid it out and carried it to the window sill.

Everything was still there. The scapular from her first communion. The stone with the wolf shape on it. The silver dollar from Grandpa. Her feather collection. And her magic charm. She didn't know what it was, exactly. Probably a wheel from an old toy truck. It was kind of beat up, but was a pretty greenish color and had some fancy designs around the edges. It was the only thing Pa ever gave her.

It happened a short while after they moved here. He got a letter in the mail with a snapshot in it. Pa didn't believe in taking pictures of people, and he threw it and the letter in the stove. Then he looked kind of funny at Claire and said, "Come with me." He opened a drawer in the bedroom and took out the wheel and gave it to her. He said, "This is just between you and me. Don't lose it." He sounded different, and Claire had gotten a lump in her throat and felt stupid, so she took it and walked away quick.

She picked the charm up and rubbed it between her hands.

All of a sudden, thinking about it, tears came in her eyes again, and before she knew what was happening, she started to bawl like crazy. She laid on the floor and she sobbed and sobbed, and she couldn't stop. Spike whined and stuck his nose under her arm to lick at her face, begging her to quit, but it was a long time before she stopped crying.

Finally she sat up. She'd be sure not to lose the wheel. A pair of Sam's old shoes was in the closet waiting for Joey to grow into them. Claire took the lace from one and put it through the wheel. She tied it in a loop and hung it around her neck under her jumper. It scratched against her chest.

She put the lid on the box and shoved it back under the floor and shut the closet door. It was getting lighter by the minute, and she had to get back to Thorsen's. Joey would be scared if he woke up and she wasn't there. He'd probably think that Mrs. Thorsen had her for breakfast or something. Mrs. Thorsen might not eat her or turn her into a toad, but she was going to be really mad. Claire didn't want to face her, but she felt better now that she was dry and the sky was getting pink. And she was hungry. She didn't have anything to eat since the picnic.

The kitchen was a fright. Everything was yanked out and food was spilled all over the floor. Ma would have a conniption if she saw it.

Claire picked up the box of Cheerios and emptied the last of them into a bowl. Then she went to get the milk, but one look down the cellar stairs made her change her mind. She put the bowl on the floor for Spike and cut a piece of bread. There wasn't anything except peanut butter to put on it. She didn't like peanut butter much without butter under it, but the butter was in the cellar, too.

She went for the broom and began to sweep with one hand and eat with the other.

She felt sorry for herself. Ma had been in the hospital before, first in Iowa, and then they took her away to Minneapolis. She came home in a few days. Maybe this time she wouldn't. Maybe Joey was right and Ma would die, too. Maybe she'd die in the hospital, or she'd come home, and somebody would shoot her, like they did Pa. The peanut butter stuck in her throat, and tears made everything blurry. Maybe it wasn't a burglar in the house; it might have been a murderer who wanted to kill them all. Shoot them all. She wiped her eyes and looked through the doorway to the living room, to the chest with its drawers pulled out, to the clothes dumped all over the floor.

She went in, shoved the empty drawers to the side, and gave a few pokes under the clothes with the broom. It didn't hit anything hard. She pulled up the flowered sheets. There was nothing underneath. Getting more panicky every minute, she dug and kicked through the pile, throwing sweaters and long johns and pillow cases around the room. It wasn't there. The gun was gone.

Spike gave a squeaky whimper. A long shadow fell across the floor and words came from behind her, "So there you are. I've come to get you."

Claire forgot about the gun. She dropped the broom and ran for the door.

Chapter Eighteen

At McIntire's words the dog gave a yip, which was followed by a squeak from its owner. Claire Hofer stared terrified from a tear-blotched face, broom dangling from her hand. In a flash, she dropped it and sprinted for the outdoors.

In three steps McIntire beat her to the door. She shrank back against the screen, eyes like saucers. McIntire dropped down to her level, close enough to detect the odor of cow manure. "I'm not here to hurt you. I've come to take you back to Mrs. Thorsen. She's very worried."

The pulse pounded visibly and rapidly in her throat. McIntire didn't know what he'd do if she started screaming. He tried to speak calmly. "We've been searching for you all night."

Her words came out hoarse, unchildlike. "There's a big mess."

"The police will be here soon. We need to leave things as they are until after they see it." He didn't want to have to carry her off bodily. He added, "Your brother needs you."

That seemed to do the trick. She relinquished her grip on the doorknob and spoke in a strangled whisper, "I'll walk over."

"You'll ride."

She didn't put up a fight.

The look on Mia's face when they drove into the yard was worth any number of dog bites.

Claire dawdled over getting out of the car, carefully lifting the pup in her arms. She faced Mia and the priest standing next to her as if they were executioners. "I couldn't come back. There were people in the house. Burglars. I had to hide in the barn."

"You were very brave." Mia was being very brave, too. She smiled and calmly put a trembling hand on the girl's shoulder. "Did you sleep?"

"I don't think so."

"Maybe you should go back to bed for a while."

"Koski's going to want to talk to her," McIntire reminded her.

"For cripe's sake, John! She can sleep 'til he gets here."

While McIntire telephoned the sheriff, Mia led her small guest up the stairs. She was back in minutes.

"She insisted on sleeping next to her brother, to be there when he wakes up." She smiled. "Anybody here know how to milk a cow?"

Father Adrien Doucet was apparently a regular Renaissance Man. "I'll go," he said.

As terrified as Claire Hofer was at the mere sight of McIntire, she seemed to have no such fear of the significantly more formidable Pete Koski. She had brushed most of the hay and knots out of her hair, and Mia had fed her bacon along with at least a half dozen slices of buttered toast. Now she sat the table with a cup of Carnation-diluted coffee between her hands, giggling when Koski flicked a crumb from the tip of her nose.

Her brother, too, had awakened at last, and had gone off with Nick to see his latest acquisition, a pair of angora rabbits.

Father Doucet had not returned from his errand to milk the cow. He may have gone into town to see Mrs. Hofer, or Opal might have been more of a handful than he'd anticipated.

"Cigarette?" Koski extended a pack of Camels. Claire tittered again and shook her head.

"Good. You're much too attractive to be hiding behind a cloud of smoke."

The child blushed to the roots of her hair. She put down the cup and patted the dog in her lap.

"How old are you, Claire? About sixteen?" He was laying it on pretty thick.

She looked about to own up to sweet sixteen, but relented. "Eleven. Eleven and a half."

"Tell me about what happened yesterday and last night. Everything you can remember."

She stroked the dogs ears. "The doctor came to see my mother and said she should go to the hospital for a couple of days. He didn't think me and Joey should stay home alone, so we came here. Mrs. Thorsen took us to the lake. When we got back Joey fell asleep, and I went home to do the chores."

"What time was that?"

"I don't know. Early. It wasn't dark yet."

Mia began to speak, but Koski shushed her with a raised hand.

"It's okay. Tell me about it."

Claire went on. She'd fed the chickens and was milking the cow when she heard Spike barking like mad.

"Where was he?"

"In the house. I left him inside so he wouldn't bother me while I was milking—or chase the chickens when they were eating." The wariness returned. "He wouldn't really hurt them. He's just a puppy."

Koski nodded. "They can be a little playful. What did you do when you heard him bark?"

"I got up to take a look out the window."

"And...?"

"There was a car. I could see part of it sticking out from the side of the house."

"Which part?"

"The back end."

"Do you remember what color it was?"

"I'm not exactly sure. The sun was shining on it, so it made a bright reflection. Mostly I could just see the outline." She shut one eye and screwed up her mouth. "I think it was maybe black or blue."

"Would you know what sort of make or model?"

She stopped in her fiddling with the dog's ears. "You mean what *kind* of car it was?"

At Koski's "That's right," she pinkened again, but after some thought answered confidently. "I think it might have been a Plymouth."

"Recent model?" Needling people was one of Pete Koski's favorite pre-occupations, but badgering an exhausted and frightened child?

The thin shoulders lifted in a defeated shrug, and the sheriff favored her with a self-satisfied smile. "We'll show you some pictures later, see if you can pick it out. Did you hear it drive in?"

Her shake of the head dripped with disappointment. Then she brightened and added, "Well, I might have. I might have thought it was thunder."

"How long had the thunder been going on by that time? What were you doing when it started?"

This time the long period of concentration seemed genuine. "I remember now. I was in the house getting the milk pail. It wasn't very loud, just rumbling, far away. It was why I left Spike inside—that and the chickens. He's kind of scared of thunder."

"Good! So what did you do when you looked out and saw the car?"

Confidence regained, she went back to the dog's ears, and cocked her head in deep thought. "I just kept watching. Spike was barking like all get out, and then he stopped. I think somebody must have kicked him. His foot is hurt. It might be broken."

Koski leaned forward to peer at the paw she held for his inspection, nodded, and went on, "Tell me everything you can remember."

"It was getting dark. The light came on in the cellar for a little while, and then went out again. Then it came on in the

living room. I heard noises. Crashing and slamming around. I
wanted to go rescue Spike and tell whoever it was to get out of
my house, but I thought I'd better wait. In a little while the lights
came on upstairs. I was ready to sneak past the house and make
a run for it, but then…." Her bravado failed, and she seemed
to shrink. "I saw somebody inside the door."

"A man or a woman?"

"I don't know. It was like a shadow. I think he was looking
right at me. The door started to open, and I took off for the
haymow and crawled back under the hay."

"That was smart."

She blushed again and hid her face in the dog's neck.

"Then what?"

The response was barely a squeak. "Somebody came into
the barn."

"What exactly did you hear?"

"Footsteps walking around. He opened the cupboard door.
Then he came up the ladder."

Mia had sat silent and unmoving throughout the conversation, now her hand went to her mouth.

"Could you see him?" Koski asked.

"No. I was way back under the hay, in the corner. Anyway
the haymow doesn't have any light."

"So he couldn't see either?"

"I don't think so. Not very well. Not unless he had a flashlight."

"Did you see any light? Like from a flashlight?"

"I couldn't see anything. I could just hear walking around."

"So he might have had a flashlight?" Why was Koski going
on about a damned flashlight? What difference did it make?

Claire might have been wondering the same thing. "Maybe,"
she said. "I wasn't thinking about that. I was sort of scared."

"But you didn't make a sound. You were brave." He reached
to pat her hand, but drew back at the dog's bared teeth. After a
space of time in which the child volunteered nothing, he asked,
"Then what happened?"

"He went back down the ladder."

"What did you do after that?"

"Nothing. I just stayed way back under the hay." The stimulation of the excitement, and the caffeine, might have been wearing off. She yawned and sagged back into the chair. "After a while I heard a car. I thought maybe it was him driving away, but it wasn't."

"How do you know? Did you look out?"

"No! The haymow only has one window way up high. You can't see out of it." She sat up straight again. "Anyway, it wasn't the burglar driving away. It was the burglar *coming back*. I thought I heard somebody say my name, but I wasn't sure. The rain started all of a sudden and was making a racket on the roof so you couldn't hear anything. Then," her eyes widened in their black circles and she whispered, "the rain stopped for just a minute or two and it was very quiet, and I heard some one right close to me say my name and that they were going to get me."

Mia turned away, and Koski swallowed and asked, "A man?"

"Yes," Claire whispered.

McIntire coughed, and Koski raised his hand again.

"I stayed quiet, and he went away. After that it started raining cats and dogs. It was so loud I couldn't hear anything else. I just stayed where I was. It was dark and scratchy, and I got hayseeds in my eyes, but I didn't dare to come out." She reddened again with no prompting from the charming Sheriff Koski.

"What made you decide it was okay to come out?"

"It was morning. The rooster was crowing." She looked at Mia. "The house is an awful mess."

Koski pushed his chair back. "Thank you, Miss Hofer. You are a very brave young lady. Now I'm going to ask for your help again."

Earlier she might have betrayed some pride at the sheriff's request, now she only nodded.

"I hear you help your mother a lot."

"Sometimes she's sick. She doesn't get around so well. I do some of the work around the house."

"Cleaning up, putting things away?"

"And cooking."

"So you would know what's in your house? Where your family keeps things."

"I know where everything is."

"Good girl. I thought you would. After you've had forty winks, I want you to come back to your house with me. I want you to see if you can tell me if anything is missing."

The terror that McIntire had seen in the dark eyes when they stared at him over the broom returned.

Chapter Nineteen

"Well, well, well, don't you know how to get around the ladies?"

Koski gave his badge a quick polish. "Listen. I got four sisters, three daughters, and a very happy wife. You want lessons, just come to me."

Maybe he should take advantage of the offer. Marian Koski waited on the sheriff hand and foot, and McIntire's own wife was known to come close to swooning at the sight of Pete in his pointy-toed western boots.

Mia had taken the child upstairs and tucked her in again. The clock on the wall read 7:48.

McIntire rested his head in his hand. "Did you find out anything from Nickerson and Wanda What's-her-name?"

Koski shook his head. "Nothing that was worth driving all the way to Benton to get. They both claimed they got to know Hofer while he was in the CO camp, and both of them said they didn't realize he lived around here until they heard he'd been killed."

"Alibis?"

"Nickerson works Saturdays, so he takes a day off during the week, and, yes indeedy, this week he had Monday off, the day Reuben Hofer died. He said he was at home. His wife takes over for him on his days off, so he doesn't have any collaboration. Wanda claimed to be at her mother-in-law's, but I haven't checked."

"Nickerson said he had something that belonged to Reuben—something he wanted to give his widow. He wouldn't say what it was."

"Hmmmph. That sounds fishy, in itself. Why didn't he just leave it? It's always possible that it was the other way 'round, that he was after something he figured Reuben had."

The thought had crossed McIntire's mind. "Somebody tore that house apart, and if they were looking for something, I'd bet they didn't find it."

"In which case, they might try again."

There didn't seem to have been any closets not searched or drawers undumped. "Anything new from the autopsy?" McIntire asked.

"Hofer had eggs and fried potatoes for breakfast, and he hadn't eaten dinner yet. That part we knew." He turned to Mia. "I don't suppose you heard a shot?"

"No. If I did, I didn't notice, and I'm glad of it. Can you imagine hearing a shot, not paying any attention, and finding out later that…. Anyway I'd have had all the windows closed and the radio on."

"That's what everybody says. They were inside having dinner, with the radio or the fan going or both. Anyway, there's not anybody close enough to have heard it for sure except the Hofers themselves. Most people I talked to never heard of Hofers until Reuben made the news. Sulo Touminen says he didn't even know they existed until Sunday night when he came across one of the kids in that Oldsmobile, up to his hubcaps in sand. He had to get a tractor to pull him out."

"You know that he was shot." The grogginess in her voice said that the long night was catching up with Mia, too. "What difference does it make if somebody heard it?"

"None, except to establish the time."

"Doucet came for me around noon," McIntire offered. "It couldn't have happened very long before that. Things were still…not dried up."

Koski stirred a third spoon of sugar into a fourth cup of coffee. "And you wouldn't have got there until ten past or so?"

"I'd say that's about right, even with the padre driving at the speed of light."

"How long were you there before the girl showed up?"

"Thirty-five minutes, or about that, maybe less." Now it was McIntire's turn to wonder, "Why?"

"Her ma says she left about a quarter past. Would it take her that long to get to the field? Half an hour or better?"

"She's a kid. Kids are dawdlers."

"Claire Hofer does not seem the dawdling type to me."

McIntire had to agree with that. "Maybe Mrs. Hofer got the time wrong. I haven't seen a clock anywhere in the house."

"You don't need a clock when you got Arthur Godfrey and Helen Trent."

It beat telling time by the sun.

Koski drained the cup in one gulp and wiped his sleeve across his mouth. "There's a deer stand at the edge of the field. A cigarette butt under it. Filtered." He smiled. "No lipstick."

Maybe it was the Reverend Doucet, catching up on his bird-watching. "Recent?" McIntire asked.

"It'd have to be fairly recent. Since the last time it rained for sure, but, until last night, that was what? Two or three weeks? But anybody laying for Reuben would hardly be sending up smoke signals to advertise his presence."

"Maybe it was after the fact. You know...."

"You have got a sick mind." Koski groaned his way to his feet. "We'll let you get some rest, Mrs. Thorsen. I'll be back for the girl this afternoon."

"Are you sure that's a good idea?" Mia asked. "Making her go through the house? She looked on the verge of panic when you mentioned it."

The sheriff kneaded his lower back. "You think so? I thought she was holding up good for a kid. She has to go back sometime."

McIntire stood up, too. "She was in the house, busy sweeping things up when I got there last night—this morning."

Mia wasn't ready to give in. "Maybe it could wait until tomorrow. She's worn out."

"The rest of the bunch might be home by then. I'll be back for her about one." He added, "You can come along if you want."

That seemed agreeable to Mia. McIntire followed the sheriff out the door. He could use some sleep himself. With the cool front moved in, he just might manage more than an hour or two. He'd sleep until noon. Have some lunch. Write a letter to Leonie.

When he got to the car, he turned to look back at the house, still in the long shadows of morning. It needed painting. Not something Nick would be up to. A round face appeared at an upstairs window; Joey had returned from his excursion to see the rabbits. McIntire waved, and the little boy vanished.

Chapter Twenty

Exhausted as McIntire was, his brain refused to turn off. Someone had sneaked up behind Reuben Hofer—not difficult to do with the noise of the tractor—and let him have it. Someone had ransacked his house. Not necessarily the same person, but there was a relatively good chance that it was. There was an even better chance that the culprit was not a brand new enemy. It was absolutely not credible that Reuben could have incited homicide so quickly. Members of his family had all been spoken for when the place was searched, and wouldn't have had to break in and rip the house apart anyway. Two people had turned up who'd known Hofer from his not-so-good old days. Three, counting Gary Cooper, and there was sure to be plenty more; according to Nickerson, there'd been upwards of a hundred men in that camp. Reuben had gotten around some on his "days off," as evidenced by his friendship—if that's what it was—with Wanda Greely.

How difficult would it be to get hold of people who knew Reuben from the camp and ask what they were doing after dinner last night? Easy enough to find out who, among those who'd worked at the camp as cooks or supervisors or guards, were still around. A damn sight trickier to track down former inmates and people Hofer had met in town, but worth a shot. McIntire would suggest it to Pete Koski.

The intruder was taking a definite risk that he might be seen; the Black Creek schoolhouse was less than twenty yards off the road. Not a very busy road, to be sure, but there was a damn sight more activity on it now than there had been before the murder. And no one would be passing by without giving the place a thorough looking over. Even parked alongside the house, the car would have been partially visible from the road, and the obvious attempt to conceal it might arouse suspicion. Unless it was someone whose presence wouldn't be considered odd. A neighbor bringing condolences and a casserole, or a regular visitor? The Hofers had no social life so far as McIntire knew, and Mary Frances had said as much. Outside of the priest and possibly Mark Guibard, no one went to their house.

The storm had dropped the temperature in McIntire's kitchen by about thirty-five degrees, but the second floor still felt like a potter's kiln. He opened every window that wasn't stuck tight with paint or humidity and went back downstairs to move the bubbling pot of coffee off the burner. He'd already had way too much coffee at Mia's, but nothing was going to keep him awake for long.

He took Leonie's letter from under the butter dish and flipped open the tablet of writing paper next to it. He'd never written to Leonie before this summer. Since they met, this was their first time apart. He'd use the fountain pen.

He'd never written any sort of romantic letter before. Neither had Leonie, at least not to him. Her letter began "Dear John," which gave a brief twinge, and ended with all her love. In between, she asked after the horses and her garden, and said she missed him, but only indulged in passionate detail when discussing her grandchildren, of which there appeared to be a fourth whose entry into the world had escaped McIntire's notice.

Leonie had gone away with a pile of unanswered questions hanging over their heads, and the fear that she might not come back lurked in the back of McIntire's mind. Maybe he had no need to worry; besides himself, she'd left behind a new car and those two beloved quarter-horses.

If he searched deep, he'd have to admit that a small part of him had looked forward to being on his own again. Not that he was given to looking back on his nearly half century of bachelorhood with fondness, but the prospect of a few weeks having to answer to no one couldn't be all bad. As it turned out, while not exactly bad, there hadn't been much good about it, so far. Leaving the dishes in the sink only meant there was an ugly mess to look at, and they were that much harder to get clean when he finally got to it. At least she'd left in the middle of a heat wave; he didn't need her to keep him warm at night. Maybe that had been in her mind. She'd said she planned the trip for the summer because she'd have more reason to return, or less reason not to.

The biggest disappointment was the realization that it was Leonie who made them a part of life in this community—*his* home. Without her, the phone didn't ring, invitations didn't come, and no one dropped by, except, of course, to let him know about the latest murder.

He'd have to tell her about Reuben Hofer, if someone else hadn't already done it. He was not her only correspondent in St. Adele.

McIntire pulled the paper closer and nibbled the end of the pen.

He would be the last person to say that murder didn't happen in places like St. Adele. Murder happened everywhere, and there had always been sufficient crime in this idyllic hamlet to satisfy the sheriff and the state police. But burglary, now that was one thing that *didn't* happen in places like this. People here didn't enter other people's houses and tear them apart, looking for something or not. Pete Koski had said he'd never heard of a burglary in St. Adele.

On reflection, the mess in Hofer's house didn't appear to be the work of someone only searching. There was malice in the ruined foods and slashed upholstery. A floor fouled with syrup and rice wasn't the work of some opportunist burglar looking for whatever he could find. Whoever had ransacked Reuben Hofer's house must have been acquainted with him or some member of his family and hated him enough to want to cause his family pain, maybe enough to kill Reuben himself. If Reuben was murdered by someone who despised him, simply because they despised him, ripping up his home afterwards must have been anti-climactic, not to mention carrying an incredible risk of calling attention to himself. Was it some lunatic who had it in for the whole family?

If it wasn't a random burglar or a frenzied psychotic, had the intruder been a crafty thief looking for something specific? Who knew the Hofers well enough to know, or think, that they had something of value hidden away? Who knew them well enough to want to make a rubbish heap of their house? Outside of Reuben's own family—and that was out—the most likely candidates were those he might possibly have offended when he was in Gibb's Bay. The COs wouldn't have been the most popular folks around. Surely Reuben wouldn't have been welcomed at Karvonen's Store if they'd been aware of his background. There could be any number of people who *were* aware. So far they knew of two. Add—according to Claire—those driving dark colored cars. Not much to go on.

The paper was still blank. This letter might be best composed by a brain that was awake. Maybe the bedroom had cooled down. McIntire staggered from the chair to the bottom of the stairs. Mount Everest. The living room sofa beckoned.

Chapter Twenty-one

The ride in Pete Koski's Power Wagon was undoubtedly the most excitement that Joey Hofer had ever experienced. His eyes glowed like Christmas bulbs over flushed cheeks as he gripped the edge of the seat with both hands and gazed alternately out the window and down at the German shepherd under his feet.

His sister didn't show quite the same reaction. Claire's face—her entire body—was a mixture of fear, sadness, and resolution, overlaid with resentment over the presence of that massive dog, which necessitated the leaving of her pup in the dubious care of Nick.

A state police car was waiting in the drive, and a uniformed officer sat on the front steps. His ears stuck out at least two inches beyond his hat. He nodded when Pete Koski asked him if he'd finished taking prints and gave a huff when the sheriff said he could leave, but didn't protest.

They started in the kitchen. It was far worse than Mia had anticipated. John figured that the burglar might have been looking for something in particular. In a bag of flour? A bottle of syrup? It looked more like meanness, pure and simple. But then who knew where the Hofers might have hidden the family heirlooms, if they had any?

Mia sat near the table with Joey standing between her knees. Pete Koski leaned against the door jamb, arms folded across his ample chest, while Claire sifted through the room with a thoroughness that would have put Sherlock Holmes to shame. She picked up knives, forks, and egg beaters and returned each one to its proper spot. She scrutinized every re-filled drawer and cabinet. After each, she shook her head and spoke brightly, "Nope, everything is here."

Koski shifted from one foot to the other, and from one side of the door to the other, but didn't interfere. Why didn't he stop her? Tell her to get a move on? It was hardly likely that the burglar had been on the hunt for a second-hand can opener. They could put the stuff away later.

Joey snatched a cereal box from the table and gave it a triumphant shake. "Somebody ate all the Cheerios!"

"It was me." Clair squatted and began plucking toothpicks from the linoleum.

Koski coughed. "Do your parents keep money anywhere in the house?"

"In my mother's purse. She's got it with her." She popped the toothpicks one at a time into a jelly glass.

Koski touched her shoulder. "You can leave that for now. Let's have a look at the rest of the house."

The child paled, and Mia stood up.

"Maybe you can stay here with the young man."

Mia nodded. It was not as if he was giving her a real choice.

Claire disappeared into the living room. Koski's broad figure blocked Mia's view through the doorway.

"Have a seat." Mia pulled out a chair, onto which Joey obediently hoisted his thin backside. "Who made this mess?" he asked.

"We don't know." There was no way to protect the boy. After having his father murdered, burglary was small potatoes, anyway. "Somebody came in last night."

"Who?"

"We don't know."

"Did they steal things?" He rested his elbows on the table and his chin in his hand.

"We don't know that either. That's why Sheriff Koski wants your sister to look around. So she can try to see if there's anything that used to be here but is gone now."

"Ma's gonna be mad."

"We can get it cleaned up before she comes home." The fuzzy head bobbed, and Mia went on, "So how do you like living here?" It was an inane question, but beat, "What do you want to be when you grow up?"

His inquisitive demeanor faded to guarded, and he gave the usual child's non-commital, "It's okay."

"There's nobody around for you to play with."

He nodded again.

"School will start before you know it. Then you'll have some playmates."

"I hate school." That was unequivocal.

Mia had hated school, too. She admitted as much.

Recovering from his initial astonishment, he asked tentatively, "What part did you hate the most?"

It didn't take any thought at all. "Having to go whether I wanted to or not and having to stay indoors."

"I hate being the littlest."

"I hated being the biggest," Mia remembered. She still hated it sometimes.

"Did the other kids like you?"

Mia shook her head. "No. Not really. Mostly only one other kid liked me." She stopped herself on the brink of saying she was sure they'd like Joey. With a murdered father and a mother the sort people buy tickets to see, she was positive that, if his family stayed in St. Adele, school for Joey Hofer would be hell.

"Father Doucet likes me. He's going to teach me how to play the fiddle."

"That should be fun. Does he come to see you often?"

"Every Thursday to teach me my catechism. About God and praying and sin and that stuff."

"Sin?"

"That's for when I'm more grown up. Sometimes he comes on other days, too, because Ma can't go to church, so us kids don't go either." Once he got going, Joey could be a chatty little guy. "We used to go. When we were in Iowa, Grandpa took us. Jake could take us now if Pa'd.... Maybe we'll have to go now."

Until that "have to" Mia was beginning to wonder if Joey Hofer might be a forty year old religious fanatic midget. "Father Doucet comes to see Nick, now and then, too," she told him. She didn't add that Father didn't exactly get a rousing welcome from her husband.

"Can't Nick go to church?"

"No." Not that he'd gone when he was healthy. "Nick is sick. You probably saw that he can't always walk very well, and sometimes he shakes. He has what's called Parkinson's Disease."

"Ma's sick, too. She's got *compelcations.*"

Where on earth had he gotten that word? An apt one. Mrs. Hofer had a serious case of compelcations if anybody did.

Mia wasn't sure if she should say anything to Joey about his father. How did one express condolences to an eight year old? "It's very sad about your father," was the best she could do.

His ears reddened and he studied the empty cereal box. A shadow crossed over his face as the sheriff blocked the light from the tall schoolroom windows.

"That's it then," he was saying. "Thank you very much, Miss Hofer. Your carriage awaits."

"It's okay," Mia told him. "We can walk back." Joey looked like a hand had wiped down his face, pulling his features with it. She relented. "You two go ahead. *I'll* walk back."

"I think this should be straightened up before my mother gets home." Claire's soft words were timid, but the hands on hips stance was adamant.

Mia looked to the sheriff.

"Go ahead. There's nothing more we can do with it."

Chapter Twenty-two

The thunderous pounding ceased, and McIntire let his head sink back into the cushion. Too soon. The kitchen door creaked open, and footsteps that could only belong to Sheriff Pete Koski clomped across the floor.

"Mac! You still alive?"

"No."

The scrape of chair feet on the floor was followed by the thud of Koski's bottom hitting the seat. McIntire opened one eye enough to make out the sheriff's splayed knees. He rolled onto his back. "Go away."

"The kid didn't figure anything was missing."

McIntire heard himself say, "If it was something small and possibly valuable, like, for instance, money, she might not have known about it." He wasn't sure if he was awake or just an exceptionally lucid sleep-talker.

"Maybe not." The chair groaned, a lighter zipped, and the air was filled with a waft of cigarette smoke. "We found the bullet."

McIntire opened both eyes and fumbled for his glasses.

"A slug from a twenty gauge."

"Where?"

"In the field. Right about in the middle."

"You sure it's the one?" There was that deer stand, and a shotgun slug would lay there for a long time.

"It's the one went through Reuben Hofer's brain. No doubt about that."

Not a rifle, but a smallish shotgun. "Close range then?"

"Most likely. Well, put it this way, if it was an accident, it could have come from a ways away, and it would still have had enough power to kill him. But the accuracy over any distance at all wouldn't be shit. So if Reuben was deliberately shot, the killer would have had to be pretty close to be reasonably sure of hitting him where it would do the most good, or bad. We haven't found any shell casings, but that ain't surprising. They'd be taken away."

"Or tossed in the river."

"Speaking of which," Koski's eyes bored into McIntire's, "we also found a fish trap."

"Don't look at me!"

"No, I didn't figure you'd turned to a life of crime the minute your wife turns her back, but somebody has, so keep your eyes peeled."

McIntire assured the sheriff that he'd do just that. He leaned back against the sofa's arm. "Well, you've narrowed things down at least a little."

"Damn little."

"Can't you sometimes tell if a bullet came from a specific gun?"

The sheriff's characteristic response to McIntire's naivete was a disparaging humph. This time he laughed out loud. "You been reading again, haven't you? Listening to those radio detectives? What we found is a lump of lead that came from a smooth bar-reled shotgun and got severely squashed up on a trip through Reuben Hofer's skull. We're reasonably sure of its size and that's it. Twenty gauge shotguns are a dime a dozen. Anybody who didn't have his own wouldn't have had much trouble getting hold of one for an hour or so."

"Did Hofer have his own?"

"What are you thinking? The little woman concealed herself behind a popple tree and let him have it with both barrels? Nah, Hofer didn't have any guns. He was dead set against violence."

"He wasn't always such a stickler," McIntire told him, "even in the cause of peace."

"So I've heard."

"Might not hurt to round up some of his compadres from the bad old days."

"Question is, where do you start. You can't just go knocking on doors."

McIntire swung his feet to the floor and sat up. "Sure you can. It would only take a few doors. Reuben is a celebrity now. Once the word gets out that you're looking, anybody who knew him when he was a good-for-nothing Conchie will be falling all over himself to brag about it."

"Unless they killed him."

"Maybe. But those who admit to knowing him might also have an idea of who else he hung around with."

"Could be. You might wanna give it a try."

"Not me. This is your job."

"I need to get over to the hospital to see the widow. You could at least go talk to the lovely Wanda. Find out how she got acquainted with Hofer and who else was in that bunch."

Did Koski know something McIntire didn't? He asked, "What bunch would that be?"

The sheriff shrugged. "There was some talk that Wanda had a small side business going."

"A 'bunch' side business?"

"No, not that! Get your mind out of the gutter. It was cards. Poker in the back room, or upstairs, maybe."

"And you didn't put a stop to it?"

He shrugged again. "I didn't get no complaints. It was probably just gossip. But you could go see her."

McIntire said, "I'll think about it." To be perverse, he didn't mention that, according to Gary Cooper, Reuben had the reputation of being something of a card shark.

He was glad he hadn't when Koski responded, "What the hell else you got to do?"

McIntire would have liked to ask if the sheriff thought he just sat on his ass all day, but knew what the answer to that would be. He stood up quickly. Too quickly, all his blood was obviously in his feet. He gripped the back of the davenport.

Koski remained sitting. "What do you know about that priest?"

What did anybody ever know about a priest? "Not a hell of a lot. Why?"

"You sure he really *is* one?"

"Oh, I'd say so. It doesn't seem to be the sort of life anybody would choose to live under false pretenses."

"He doesn't act very priestish."

"That's only on the outside," McIntire said. "He just wants to lure you into thinking he's a regular guy. Then when you least expect it, wham! He's got you by the...soul."

"I don't think he wants me."

"He wants me."

"Ain't you the lucky one?" The sheriff stared up into his smoke rings. "He seems to have got pretty chummy with Mrs. Hofer in the short time they've been here."

"He has to. Visiting the sick, comforting the poor..." or was it vice versa? "It's his job."

"I guess it is." Koski stretched his legs and drummed his fingers on his thighs. "She might have told him things that we ought to know."

"And you think he'd pass it on to you? Good lord, Pete, sometimes you are every damn bit as dumb as you look!"

The sheriff was unperturbed. "I don't mean things he heard in confession or anything like that. Just normal, everyday stuff. We got a dead guy here, after all."

"Go ahead and ask him. I don't think you'll get very far."

"I plan to." He stood up with a grunt. "I'll be on my way and let you get over to Benton."

"I didn't say I was going."

Koski didn't seem bothered by that, either. After asking, "Got a pan I can run a little water for the dog in?" he walked off, taking with him his aggravating assumption that his orders would be followed.

McIntire might go to Benton eventually, if he happened to feel up to it; the card playing factor sounded promising. But right now he had other plans.

There was something about Hofer—or Hofer as reported—that McIntire didn't quite believe. Reuben had been raised in a strict religious farming community; left as a young man; got involved with a Catholic girl to the point of marriage and pregnancy—probably not in that order; turned into a hell-raiser for a cause he believed in; spent time incarcerated; got out and went back to his roots. That all sounded perfectly reasonable, even predictable. But the man who ruled his family with that proverbial iron fist, and presented that accusing face to the world, was impossible to reconcile with the one who spent his Sunday evenings boozing it up and playing cards, maybe in the back room of Wanda's Cut 'n Curl. Although looking into those icicle eyes over a poker hand might well have inspired retreat in the most confident of opponents.

Reuben Hofer had been killed by someone who hated his guts. McIntire could see it no other way. That sort of loathing didn't come about overnight. It didn't come about in two months. The person who'd sent a shotgun slug into Hofer's head must have known him for a long time, and that narrowed things down a whole hell of a lot. One person had already admitted to hating the son-of-a-bitch. It was a horrifying thought, but wouldn't be the first case of patricide the world had seen.

McIntire let the coffee stay cold for once and went outdoors. The suffocating heat was gone, and the sky was scattered with puffy clouds that really did look like the stereotypical flocks of sheep. They were mirrored in a drift of white along the garden fence; the rain had tempted Leonie's roses from their buds at last. He'd send her a picture. Maybe it would make her homesick. But this wasn't her home, and homesickness was the reason she'd left. Suddenly he missed her terribly.

◇◇◇

When he pulled into the Black Creek School drive, he could see that the front door, behind the screen, was open, signaling that the house was not empty. As he left the car, Mia Thorsen stepped out onto the concrete porch. She walked toward him, chary as the child she'd become so enamored of.

"John, what brings you back? It's not Mary Frances—?"

"No. Just making sure everything is okay. I didn't figure you to still be here."

"We stayed to clean up the worst of the mess." She brushed at the front of her blouse. "Or transfer most of it to me."

"Would that all our messes were so easily handled."

McIntire felt that it was positively profound, but Mia only gasped, "Easy? Put your muscles where your mouth is. I'm sure we can scare up a bucket and a spare mop."

"Maybe later. How're the kids doing?"

"As well as can be expected, as they say. They still seem to not know what's hit them, which may not be such a bad thing. I expect Mary Frances will be home tomorrow or Sunday."

"What about the older boys? Any idea when they'll get back?"

She shook her head, and McIntire said, "I'd like to talk to the girl."

"She's scared stiff of you."

"I know." McIntire admitted. "I can't think why."

"Maybe she's leery of all men, thinks you're all like her father, possibly. Or maybe it's just your standoffish attitude."

"I suppose I could make an ass of myself buttering her up like Pete Koski. She's not scared of him."

"That's for sure! I think she has quite the crush on our handsome sheriff."

"Kind of old for her, ain't he?"

"When everybody's too old for you, it's beside the point. If you can behave yourself, I'll get her to come outside."

That was a good idea. He might look smaller sitting on the steps, less intimidating.

Obviously he didn't. The girl sidled out the door and stood rigid, clutching the handle, poised to flee. The dog was not in evidence. Mia lingered just inside the door.

"Hello, Claire," McIntire began. "How's the cleaning going?" What a start. He was just plain boring, that was it. No wonder she preferred Koski.

"Fine."

"Mrs. Thorsen says your mother might be home tomorrow." Claire nodded.

Her hair was braided. He could try saying something about how pretty it was. But there was no getting around that he wasn't Pete Koski, and it didn't look all that pretty. One pigtail was about twice the size of the other. He settled for, "What about your brothers? Will they be home tomorrow, too?"

"I don't know. Could be."

"That burglar probably thought nobody was home. He wouldn't have broken in if your brothers or your mother were here."

She stared and rubbed at her breast bone under her dress. There should be some tricky way of extracting information from a kid, but, in addition to flattery, McIntire also wasn't good with either subterfuge or kids. "Claire, if it happened again—" great, throw a good scare into her! He plunged ahead. "In an emergency, would your brothers know how to use a gun?" A sharp intake of breath came from the other side of the screen.

The thin cheeks reddened. "Our father wouldn't let us have a gun."

McIntire could think of no way to follow that without a further reminder that her father had just been killed by a gun. When he stood up, she shrank back against the door. Was he really that terrifying?

"Thank you for your time," He said and started to make his escape. Not quick enough. Mia caught him before he'd reached the bottom of the steps. She pulled him to the side.

"What the devil was that all about?" Mia could put a lot of shout into a whisper.

"They might need some protection, and maybe some food this winter. I was just wondering if either of those boys knew anything about handling a rifle."

"Baloney!" That was definitely no whisper. She lowered her voice again. "Are you actually thinking that one of those boys killed his own father?"

"We have to look at every possibility, and that is possible. They hated him. At least one of them did."

"You hated your father. Would you ever for a minute have considered shooting him?"

It was an intriguing question. McIntire hadn't thought about it before. He pushed back his hat to scratch his forehead. "I suppose I wouldn't have gone so far as to plot it, but there were definitely times that if I'd had a shotgun in my hands, who knows what I might have done?"

"Well, those boys didn't have a shotgun. And even if they had…. It's simply not possible!"

"I hope you're right," he said, "but if you're not, those younger kids are going to need some looking after." When McIntire saw the hunger in her eyes, he'd have given anything to take the words back.

He walked past the barnyard and up toward the field where the boys had been tending their spuds. It was a good sized patch, six or seven acres. Hofer must have intended to sell most of the crop. It was a lot for two boys to take care of by hand, but so far it looked good. The hilling was complete, every plant neatly banked with soil, and not a weed in sight.

A woven wire fence topped with a double strand of barbed wire separated the field from pasture on two sides. McIntire walked along the fence line until it abruptly ended in a weedy strip a couple of yards wide that lay between the potatoes and a field planted in oats, hardly larger than the potato patch. On the far side of it, he could make out another stretch of pasture, beyond that, he knew, lay the hayfield where Reuben Hofer died.

McIntire slowed his steps and studied the ground until he found what he was looking for. The hazy blue carpet of oats was bisected across its width by a straight line of clearly trampled stems. It might have been done by a deer. McIntire bent and peered under the stems. The soil was soft and moist from the night's rain. It had rained hard, but not hard enough to obscure the deep imprints of a deer's narrow hooves, had they been there. The tennis shoe covered toes of an adolescent boy in a hurry might not have made remaining impact.

McIntire skirted the field to the point where the path emerged on the other side. From here, a quick jog through the adjoining pasture would bring him straight to the north end of the hayfield. In little more than five minutes one of those boys could have dropped his hoe, picked up a shotgun, and had it trained on the back of his father's neck.

It was a disgusting thought, but barring any new information, the two were the most likely suspects. They probably hardly knew their father. They couldn't have been much more than six or seven years old when he was drafted; they hadn't grown up with him. In their early years he must have been home only long enough to conceive a couple of siblings, before he was off again to be locked up somewhere, including a federal prison. When he finally turned up for good, he treated them like indentured servants. They had every reason to despise him, to not even think of him as a father.

But still, the sort of kid who could blow someone's head off—let alone his own father's—and then calmly go back to hilling spuds, McIntire wouldn't want to have a run-in with.

But Sam and Jake Hofer hadn't been responsible for the shenanigans of the previous night. Koski was right. In all probability, that been the work of one of Reuben's old buddies. Maybe he would take that trip to Benton.

Chapter Twenty-three

She'd managed to act half way normal when the sheriff was there. Even when he asked her if Pa had a shotgun, she didn't look away when she said that Pa didn't believe in guns. Now that skinny guy comes snooping around, and she was shivering so hard that her teeth were chattering, and she couldn't stop. Like it was the middle of winter instead of a warm summer afternoon. It was those glasses. The sun glinted off them and you couldn't see his eyes inside. He looked like some kind of giant beetle; it gave her the creeps. Whether her brothers knew how to shoot a gun was none of his business. She should have told him off. She should have said right to his face, *None of your damn business!*

Mrs. Thorsen was on her knees scrubbing the syrup off the kitchen floor. Claire could have gone in and told her that it would work better to use hotter water, but she didn't want her to notice the shaking.

She folded a sheet and stuffed it in the bottom drawer. The drawer where the gun used to be.

Ma had said the same thing when the sheriff asked her. Pa was a pacifist and wouldn't allow guns. And now bug-eyes was nagging about it, too. What would Joey say if they asked him? He wouldn't know to lie, and if she told him to, he'd want to know why, and Claire wasn't sure why, herself. She didn't want to think about the reason Ma didn't just tell the sheriff that they had a gun. It was gone now anyway, stolen by the burglar, so it didn't matter. It would matter plenty if they caught the person who stole it, and he confessed, and the sheriff found out that they all lied. Claire didn't want the person who made her sit in the barn all night to get away with it, but she wasn't sure she wanted him to get caught either. Unless it was the same person that killed Pa. He might be wanting to kill them all, and now he'd have two guns to do it with.

Joey didn't ever look in the chest of drawers, and he probably didn't even know that the gun used to be there.

Mrs. Thorsen came to the doorway. "I'm going out for more water. By the time I get this syrup off the floor, the well will be dry!"

"Okay." Claire scrunched down to look under the davenport and stayed that way until she heard the door shut.

She stood up and said low, "Joey?" He was wandering around, picking up marbles from the Chinese checkers game.

"What?"

"Remember when we used to have Grandpa's gun?"

His eyes opened wide. Maybe she shouldn't have mentioned guns after what happened to Pa, but it was too late now. "It's too bad Ma didn't bring it along when we moved here. If we had it, we could go hunting."

He kept staring at her like she was nuts.

"I could shoot a deer," Claire told him.

"You couldn't hit a deer in a million years."

"I could practice. You never know what you can do until you try. I bet I'd be a darned good shot. It doesn't matter now, anyway. Ma left the gun at Grandpa's house."

"Ya," Joey said. "That's too bad."

"What's too bad?

Claire jumped. She hadn't heard Mrs. Thorsen come back. "Some of the marbles are missing." She spoke up quick before Joey could answer. He looked at her funny, but he didn't say anything.

"They always are. It's one of life's rules. Checkers, marbles, and mittens. They disappear." She straightened the shade on the table lamp.

"Our father made that." Claire had forgotten about the lamp when Mrs. Thorsen said her father made things. "He carved it from wood." It was painted plain black with some designs, blue and red and gold, and Pa had done a good job of making it perfectly round. The shade slipped sideways again. It wasn't that the burglar had broken it. It was always that way.

Mrs. Thorsen picked it up in both her hands and bounced it up and down, like she might be planning to shoot a basket. "Don't you think we're about done here? I'm ready for some afternoon coffee."

Chapter Twenty-four

McIntire had never entered a beauty parlor. He wasn't sure he could do it. He stretched across the seat, pretending to be engrossed in retrieving something from the glove compartment, and strained to see through the front window of Wanda's Cut 'n Curl. It was no use. The Venetian blinds were closed just enough to keep out the late afternoon sun and prying male eyes. The only thing visible beyond their slats was a feline shape on the window sill.

He exited the car and strolled nonchalantly past the brightly painted door. The sign said that Wanda closed things down at five thirty. He dawdled, staring into the window of the drugstore next door, and made a lengthy show of checking his watch. It was now five-twenty five. Wanda might live on the premises, in which case maybe McIntire could find another entrance and avoid the shop entirely. But if she didn't, she might leave by the back way while he was snooping around out in front, or vice versa, and he'd have wasted a trip.

He strode resolutely back, resisted the urge to cross himself, and opened the door. The bell above jangled like the voice of doom. McIntire had never seen a place that looked so pink and smelled so…acid green. An odor of ammonia burned his nose. All eyes—all seven of them—turned his way. The apparent Wanda froze in the act of applying a whisk broom to the back of a closely-cropped neck. The neck's owner, a youngish woman with an overbite, stared at McIntire's reflection in the mirror, while a rigidly coifed blonde near the window gaped at him above the pages of the *Saturday Evening Post*. His entry could have inspired the perfect Norman Rockwell cover for that magazine—*The Invasion*. The tortoise-shell cat recovered first and settled back onto its haunches, closing its single eye.

"May I help you?" Wanda Greely was, no question about it, stacked.

"I was hoping to have a word," McIntire said, and added, "once you've finished for the day."

"I'm done now." She lifted the cape off her client's shoulders and shook it over the floor with a flourish that jiggled anything remotely jiggleable.

The ladies took their time settling up their bill and arranging for their next beautification, sneaking occasional peeks at McIntire from under blackened lashes. At last the doorbell pealed raucous relief as they walked out onto the street.

Wanda leaned on her broom handle, her hip protruded in an attractive curve, and looked at him expectantly.

"John McIntire. I'm here from the sheriff's department. I understand that you were acquainted with Reuben Hofer."

"I thought I was also acquainted with Sheriff Koski's deputies."

"I'm on special assignment."

"Is that so? Special assignment? For little ol' me?"

"That's right."

"Well," Wanda shifted her weight, and the other hip took over, "Special Deputy, what's on your mind? My husband will be here to pick me up soon."

For no good reason, McIntire hadn't expected Wanda to come equipped with a husband. It could complicate things if her dealings with Hofer hadn't been restricted to poker hands.

"How did you meet Reuben?"

"I don't remember. Through friends, I suppose." An auburn wave fell across her face as she began sweeping up the piles of hair clippings. What would it be like to mess around with other people's dead hair for a living? Just wiping his own out of the sink, where more and more of it was ending up these days, turned McIntire's stomach.

"Which friends?"

She straightened up and pushed the hair from before her eyes. "What do you mean?"

"We're trying to locate people who knew Reuben Hofer when he was in the CPS camp. So if you can tell me who introduced you...."

"I just said, probably through friends. I don't remember the details. I doubt we were 'introduced,' as you put it. We most likely just ran into each other somewhere."

"Word is that he played cards with some of your friends."

"Well, that's it then, I imagine that's where we ran into each other."

"And that 'where' was right here."

"Some of the guys liked to get together, and I let them use the room...." A crimson tipped finger pointed to the ceiling. "I didn't join them." She flicked the hair back again and effected an innocent stare. "I'd have lost my shirt."

Subtlety wasn't one of the lady's failings, but then subtlety was generally lost on McIntire. He hoped his glasses didn't start steaming over. "Can you tell me who some of those men were?"

"No. I don't remember."

It was a blatant lie, but names weren't something McIntire could force out of her. He sighed, trying to sound like the embodiment of reason and kindly forbearance, "Mrs. Greely, someone hated Reuben Hofer enough to murder him. Very possibly it was someone who knew him during the war. We need to know who he was involved with back then."

"He wasn't *involved* with me."

"You were close enough friends that you paid a call on his widow."

She went back to sweeping and hiding behind the hair. "I had something I wanted to give her. Something that belonged to her husband."

"What was it?"

"None of your business. I drove all the way out there to have my casserole grabbed out of my hands and the door slammed in my face. Far as I'm concerned, she can forget it!"

It did sound sort of rude. McIntire said, "Her husband was murdered, and she's not in good health. She might not have been feeling up to having company."

"I wasn't expecting to be company, but I didn't expect to be sent packing by some scrawny.... Well, I won't be troubling myself to go there again. I can get another baking dish!"

The angry words were softened by the view of Wanda's well-rounded backside as she bent to sweep the hair into a dustpan.

"What kind of person was Reuben Hofer? When you knew him?"

The wad of hair plopped into the waste basket. How much did she collect in a given year? It ought to be good for something. Stuffing pillows? No, that would be disgusting.

Wanda rested her chin on the tip of the broom handle. "Not a bad guy. Good looking. He didn't have the beard then. He was the sort that didn't waste time. He stuck to his principles and got things done. And the sort that couldn't hold his drink." McIntire hadn't been conscious of the vampirish look of her flame-red lips until a smile playing around them wiped it away. "He was a heck of a lot more fun when he'd had a few, though," she went on. "Get some drink into him, and he actually had a sense of humor. Well, maybe he always did, but just kept it under wraps when he was sober." The smile grew into a full-fledged grin. "Walking around with that ball and chain *was* funny. I suppose you heard about that?"

McIntire nodded. "Didn't he ever take it off?"

She shook her head. "It was welded. He'd have had to use a blowtorch. Or a hacksaw."

It was time to get to his real reason for coming. At the risk of losing the new, friendlier, Wanda, McIntire began, "Do you always close at five?"

"No. I keep working as long as there's somebody here, and I take appointments until eight on Fridays. You looking for a permanent wave?"

"I'd like permanent hair, if you can arrange that." They were getting positively jolly. That wasn't going to last. "Where were you last night?"

"Why?"

"Last evening somebody went into the late Mr. Hofer's house and tore it apart. Ransacked it."

"No kidding? And you think it was me? I was peeved about driving all that way to see his wife for nothing but not mad enough to go all the way back!"

"Somebody was pretty damn mad, or looking for something, or both. Where were you around nine o'clock last night?"

She smiled again, but this time the lips stayed the color of blood. "I was home with my husband and my son."

Chapter Twenty-five

The two little imps were filthy, and Mia was none too clean herself. She had never claimed to be a world champion housekeeper, but the state of the Hofers' home, even discounting the previous night's destruction, was utterly wretched. It was easy to see that Mary Frances wouldn't have been crawling around scrubbing out corners, but they'd only been there a couple of months. The grime in that place had to have been building up since at least the Hoover administration.

She was overjoyed to see a trickle of smoke wafting up through the trees. "Nick's got the sauna going," she said. "We can get cleaned up."

The children looked at her, then at each other, but didn't say a word.

"Have you had a sauna?"

Claire's eyebrows drew together. "Probably. I can't exactly remember right now."

"A small room, with a stove. It makes you sweat to get clean."

"Oh, sure. I forgot."

Organizing the sauna proved to be an unexpectedly complicated undertaking. Joey was a boy, he pointed out, and was too big to go with Mia and Claire. That meant he had to either wait for Nick, which would be hours, or go by himself. Mia decided to table that decision until she and Claire were finished. They left Joey picking clover for the rabbits and set off down the path.

Halfway along, Claire slowed and, without a word, circled the great fan of tangled roots, all that remained of the giant white pine that had stood for so many years.

"It fell down last winter," Mia told her, "in an ice storm." She waved to the jagged stump of its twin. "We had two of them. This one hit that one, and, kaboom! It sounded like an atom bomb."

"Did it scare you?"

"It was in the middle of the night, in a terrible lightning storm, and it scared the liver out of me! But it makes a fantastic sculpture, don't you think?"

Claire nodded.

"My mother called roots like that a witches cradle." A term that was even more apt, considering that those roots had cradled two generations of stillborn infants. Claire looked up quickly, but she didn't respond, and Mia directed her back down the path.

The girl stalled again when the reached the sauna. "It's a cute little cabin."

"It's been here since before I was born," Mia told her. "I think it's older than the house, even. It was built by a man named Mr. Touminen. I don't remember his first name. He was a Finlander. Finlanders do like their saunas. They build a sauna first and live in it while they build their house."

"It must have been a little crowded." Did the child have a sense of humor after all?

"Finlanders are a close-knit bunch," Mia told her, and was relieved to hear a laugh.

They stepped around the ladder leaning against the faded log wall.

"Nick's at war with the starlings," Mia explained. "They're given to building nests in the chimney. After they plugged it up and smoked Nick out a few times, he got smart and decided to leave the ladder up, so he can check it every couple of days."

"We got smoked out once. The stovepipe fell right out of the wall. Sam had to fix it, and the smoke made him throw up."

"Smoke can make you sick in a hurry." It could kill you in a hurry, too. Only the past winter, an old couple from Marquette had died of smoke inhalation. But maybe death wasn't a good topic of conversation right now.

It didn't take long to figure out that the child was not about to take her clothes off in front of anyone, and would die of shame if Mia did. Claire solved the problem by wrapping a towel snugly under her arms and clutching it to her thin chest, an option not open to Mia; the towel wide enough to cover her with any degree of modesty did not exist, and she didn't have a bedsheet handy. She finally opted for leaving on her underwear, provoking a beet red flush of the child's face, but prompting her to abandon her towel and enter the steam room in grayed and saggy underpants that made Mia want to cry. An amulet of some sort dangled from a frayed shoestring tied around her neck .

"You'll need to take off your necklace," Mia told her. "It'll get hot enough to burn your skin."

Claire pulled it over her hair and laid it on the bench beside her. "It's my good luck charm." She hesitated, then added, "My father gave it to me." The center of her chest was scraped raw. Obviously she'd only recently begun to wear it. A tribute to her dead father.

Mia touched her own momento mori, hung in a soft pouch between her breasts. "I'll make you a bag, like this. Then it won't scratch, or get hot in the sauna."

"I know how to sew." She gasped at the blast of steam when Mia threw a dipper of water onto the rocks. "I just haven't had time."

Did the kid ever admit to being only eleven? "Do you have a machine?" Mia asked.

"Ya." She wiped at the rivulets of dirt running down her arms. "But mostly I sew by hand."

Mia didn't know what to make of this girl. Hardly a child at all in some ways, but barely more than an infant in others. Capable—she had no doubt Claire was proficient at sewing—but desperately in need of the most basic care. Incredibly shy on the one hand, and a bossy little know-it-all on the other.

How had she felt about her father? Was her curious behavior because of her recent bereavement, or had she always been that way? She didn't act as if she was sad, exactly.

"Do you know who killed your father?" It slipped out before Mia knew what she was saying.

Claire didn't even look surprised, apparently accepting that such wisdom was expected of her. "At first I thought it might be that skinny man, the one that came over today. He was in the field. But now I think, probably not."

"John McIntire?" Mia stopped herself from laughing.

"I don't know his name. I saw him walking around the field when I went to bring Pa his dinner that day."

Where do kids get their ideas? "He was there because Father Doucet went to get him after he found your father. Mr. McIntire is the constable. Sort of like a sheriff."

"Oh."

"Do you think he's scary?"

"I'm not scared of him. I just don't like him very much." She rubbed at her knee. "Do you like him?"

It was an interesting question. Mia didn't ordinarily think of her feelings for John in quite those terms. "Most of the time," she said. "Most of the time I like him just fine. We lived together when we were small. He was like my twin brother. There was three of us kids, all the same age, so maybe it was more like triplets."

"I thought you lived here when you were a kid, because you walked through the woods to go to school."

"I did. We all did. The three of us slept in the room where you were supposed to be sleeping last night. There were five families living in my house then. This was a big farm, and everybody worked together."

"Like Prairie Oak?"

"What's that?"

"Where my Aunt Jane lives. Where my father lived when he was a kid."

"Oh. Yes, if Prairie Oak is what I think it is, then this farm was sort of like that, but not exactly the same. I think where your father's family lives, everybody is… alike, the same nationality and the same religion. All the people in the Association—it was called the Gitchee Gummee Association—were from different countries. They didn't even speak the same language, and it wasn't a group based on religion like I think Prairie Oak must be."

"It is. Sister is forever going on about God, way more than Father Doucet does."

"Well, the Gitche Gummee Association didn't have that to hold people together. So it didn't work out for very long. When I was about four, I guess it was, everybody moved out except me and my mother and father. But John McIntire's parents only moved a short distance away, so we stayed friends."

"Was he your childhood sweetheart?" She must be loosening up.

"I suppose you could say that," Mia admitted. "We were close friends until he until he went into the army. I was very sad to see him go, and he stayed away for a long time. I never saw him again until a couple of years ago." Why was she telling all this to a child? It was years since she'd thought about the old Association, and certainly she'd never before spoken aloud of her past with John McIntire.

"What about the other triplet? Was she always your friend, too?"

"He. It was another boy. His name was Wylie. We all three stayed friends for along time, but when we got older, in high school, Wylie more or less went his own way. He was good looking and popular, and John and I weren't." She amazed herself again by going on, "He got hurt last year. He…fell, and he's paralyzed. He can't walk." She'd said enough and was relieved that Claire asked no more questions.

Chapter Twenty-six

Maybe if McIntire quit now, Koski would get the lead out and do his job himself, or send out one of those intrepid deputies Wanda had alluded to. But McIntire had come all this way, and even knocking on doors, he could probably cover the entire town before dark. He could certainly cover the one place he'd potentially get the most information, the single watering-hole, and still be home for supper.

The man behind the bar of Ole's Timber Inn looked up with a crooked-toothed grin that hadn't changed in thirty-five years. "Johnny Mac, what the hell!"

"Fergie, what the hell."

The last time McIntire had seen Fergus Olson he'd been wearing a cap and gown. He'd also had a bottle in his hand, as he did now. The man plunked two glasses on the bar and dumped a splash into each. "Have one on me. Long time no see. Where the hell you been all this time?"

"Here and there. I've been back in St. Adele for the past year and a half."

"No shit? Well, here's to ya."

McIntire was glad he'd come on business. Making small talk with Fergus Olson once the guy had run through his, admittedly comprehensive, stock of ready-made phrases, had been hard enough back when they'd shared a table in the high school science lab. He couldn't imagine what they'd find to chat about now. Of course murder was a great little ice-breaker.

"I guess you heard about Reuben Hofer?"

"Who hasn't? Poor bugger. If it had happened seven or eight years ago, it wouldn't have been much of a shock, but now? What do you suppose made him move here, to the scene of his crimes?"

"You knew him back then, I take it?"

"Oh, sure. He was in most every week, along with the rest of that chicken-shit bunch."

"Big bunch, was it?"

"Not by the time I was through with them. Somebody that made trouble, I booted their ass out the door before they knew what hit 'em, and they didn't get back. Reuben Hofer wasn't so rowdy as some."

"Can you remember anybody special he used to hang around with? Anybody who's still around?"

"Somebody that might have killed him, you mean?" He smiled conspiratorially and tossed back his drink. "Why're you asking about Reuben? I ain't saying it's none of your business, but, is it?"

"Oh, you bet it is," McIntire sipped at his own whisky. "I'm sent direct from Sheriff Peter Koski, himself."

"Well, it ain't like he'd ever bother to drag his own butt out here, unless it's getting close to election time. Maybe we need our own murder." He indulged in a spell of finger-drumming concentration before shaking his head. "I can't think of anybody Hofer was particularly chummy with. Although," he raised a finger, "there were a few rumors about him and a certain beauty operator whose name I won't mention."

"Any truth to the rumors, you think?"

"I definitely think. She lived over her shop then. Right on the street. You could hardly keep anything like that a secret."

Weren't bartenders supposed to maintain confidentiality, like priests and attorneys? Maybe that only applied to what they were told by inebriated customers. "What about Bruno Nickerson? You ever see him, then or now?"

"Oh, sure. Then *and* now. He stops in damn near every night. He used to be a guard at the camp, so I guess he'd have known Reuben back in those good old days, too. What about him?"

"Was he here last night?"

"Last night? Why last night?"

"Koski was asking. He wants to talk to him, since he knew Reuben, I guess. He must be trying to track him down."

It was the only pretense McIntire could come up with on such short notice. He couldn't have done much worse. Olson looked mystified. "If the sheriff wants to talk to Bruno Nickerson, he knows where to find him."

"He does?"

"Bruno works for Sid, at the hardware store. Strange that the sheriff would have trouble getting hold of him."

Sid, Sheriff Peter Koski's father. "Hmph," McIntire agreed. "That is strange. I'll have to ask Pete about it, he must be getting senile. *Was* Bruno here last night?"

McIntire must be a better liar than he thought. Olson shook his head at Koski's incompetence, and said, "No he wasn't, now you mention it. His wife called looking for him. Said if he came in, to let him know his brother had showed up unexpected."

"What time was that?"

"Hold on." Fergus handed bottled beer to a pair of youthful pool players. "Time? I can't say for sure, because I only heard later from *my* wife. She takes over Thursday nights when I bowl. I didn't get back here until about eleven, and Diane said that Belinda called and said, if Bruno turned up, to let him know that his brother was in town. I guess that would have probably been around eight-thirty or nine. People don't hang around late on a week night, especially in summer. Why you asking about Bruno?"

"We're asking about everybody that knew Reuben Hofer." And, despite McIntire's assurances to Pete Koski, that list wasn't getting much longer. Fergus made four. Should McIntire check with his bowling buddies? "Do you know if anybody had it in for Reuben? The COs couldn't have been too popular around town."

"They couldn't have been a hell of a lot less popular. Like I said, I wouldn't have been surprised to see one of them end up on the wrong end of a gun in 1943. Now? I can't think there'd be much point, but some people don't forgive *or* forget."

"Anybody in particular?"

"Naaa." He flashed the contorted teeth again. "Unless Wa—that beauty operator I won't mention—is one of those women that hell ain't got no fury like."

Chapter Twenty-seven

They were so thin. And, once again, so quiet. Mia cut two more slices of chocolate cake and refilled their plates. "Would you like a glass of milk?" She hadn't thought of it before. She never drank milk herself, but she supposed kids would. Joey nodded, but Claire just said "no" and picked up the cake in her hand. Then she said, "The coffee smells good."

Did that mean she wanted a cup? Why didn't she just ask?

"Would you like some?"

She nodded, and Mia brought out another cup. "Cream?"

Another nod. The child diluted the coffee to the color of sand, and took a sip.

Mia shook the bottle and poured Joey's milk. "The frosting got sort of hard."

"If you put a teaspoon of syrup in, it's better." They were the first real words the girl had spoken since they sat down.

"Is that what your mother does?"

She searched Mia's face, apparently baffled by the question, before responding, "I know how to make cake...and frosting."

Mia's cake had come compliments of Betty Crocker. She wracked her brain for a topic that wouldn't further demonstrate her inadequacies, and was saved by Joey, who swiped the back of his hand across his upper lip and stated, "I think I'll go outside." The screen door slammed behind him before the words were out of his mouth.

"There's a young man in a hurry," Mia said.

"He likes to play outside."

"What about you?"

Once again her dark-circled gaze showed only bewilderment. Mia elaborated, "Do you like to play outside, too?"

"I'm too big to play." She seemed genuinely incredulous that Mia should mistake her for a mere child. "I like to *be* outside."

"I do too. Let's take this out."

They picked up the plates and transferred themselves to the porch. Claire perched on the edge of the wicker chair, barely reaching the table.

Mia went back to searching for a safe topic of conversation. "I know you're a big help to your mother."

She could have done better; Claire only took another bite of her cake.

"She'll need even more help now."

That brought a nod.

"Maybe your aunt will come back to stay for a while."

"Probably she will." She picked a lump of the fudge-like frosting from her plate and popped it into her mouth.

"You don't sound particularly happy about that."

"She used to come sometimes, when we lived in Iowa."

"Wasn't that good?"

"She was always after us to talk German, even though we don't know how."

Reuben had spoken with a pronounced accent that made Mia think of her father. "Doesn't your aunt speak English?"

"Sure. She just thinks we should learn to talk German, that's all." She sat back and folded her arms across her chest. "And besides, she's bossy as all get out."

"Oh?"

"She acts like she has to do every bit of the work herself, and she's all disgusted about it, but she can't bear to let anybody else do anything if they did want to."

"A martyr?"

"What?" Was the child finally admitting to not knowing everything?

"A martyr," Mia said. "Somebody who does things they don't really want to do just so they can make a big deal of sacrificing themselves for the good of others, even if the others didn't want their sacrifices in the first place."

"Ya, that's Sister. One of her best martyr tricks is putting stuff up high where I can't reach it. Then she sighs and rolls her eyes when she has to get it down herself."

"If she takes over most of the housework, won't that make up for the bossiness? Why not just go read a book and leave her to do it? Take a walk? Play in the sand with Joey?"

Although it was sometimes difficult to determine if Joey considered his activities play or work. Whichever, he was thoroughly engrossed in it now, turning a handful of spruce twigs into a three-inch high grove in Mia's driveway.

"I just might," Claire asserted. She gave a grown-up snort. "She's forever telling me how to do things."

"Things you already know how to do?"

"Ya." It was accompanied by an emphatic nod.

"I know how aggravating *that* can get," Mia agreed. "Since Nick got sick and had to quit going to work, he spends half his time telling me how to do things I've been doing just dandy fine for thirty years."

"Why don't you tell him to do it himself then?"

Now that was a good question. "Is that what you tell your aunt?"

"No. I just act like I don't hear her."

"Me too."

"But someday I'm going to tell her to mind her own beeswax."

"Me too."

"Maybe I'll learn how to tell her in German."

"Good idea!" Mia's words were drowned in the honking of the geese and the roar of a rapidly approaching car. They looked at each other. "Father Doucet," Claire said. Mia nodded. She looked out to see Joey scrambling from his miniature landscape.

"Is this Thursday?" Claire asked. "Father comes to teach Joey his catechism on Thursday." She walked to the rail. "He's not wearing his priest outfit."

Indeed, outside of the Roman collar, nothing about Adrien Doucet said "man of the cloth."

"It's Friday," Mia said. "Maybe it's his day off."

Claire continued to stare. "He looks…different."

He certainly did, less like a priest than a down-home leprechaun, slight and brown-skinned in bluejeans and a faded work shirt. Even Joey approached his favorite person cautiously.

He waved to Joey and opened the car's back door. At the sight of the violin case in his hand, the boy's face lit up like a sunrise. The promised fiddle lessons. Perfect timing for it.

Mia remembered the sink full of unwashed dishes and hurried down the steps to head the priest off.

"Good afternoon, ladies." He spoke, as usual, in a muted and tranquil manner, suitably clerical. "Have you caught up on your sleep?"

"Almost." Claire answered for both of them.

"So have I," Joey chimed in. The little tyke should have been caught up for the next month.

"That's good. I've been to see your mother. She's feeling much better and said to tell you she'll be home tomorrow."

Claire smiled and turned her attention to Spike, straining at the end of his rope to make after the squawking geese.

"It's good of you to come," Mia said, "but if you're looking for the hoe-down it was last week."

The priest smiled with the same perplexed expression Mia had seen on Claire's face a few minutes before. "What's that?"

"Just a joke, Father."

"Oh?"

How thick was this guy? She floundered, "You look kind of like you could be headed for the Grand Old Opry."

The light apparently dawned. "Oh! I guess maybe I do. I thought I'd go over to milk that cow after I leave here. But first—" He waved the instrument case—"do you have a quiet spot we could use?"

"Most all our spots are quiet, you can take your pick." Mia began to feel that she was needling the priest and took pity. "The living room is fine." She touched the child's shoulder. "Joey, you'd better go wash up before you handle Father's violin."

He scampered off, and Mia herded the priest along the porch to the front door, out of the way of her unsightly kitchen. "You've been to see Mary Frances? What sort of shape is she in?"

A twinkle danced in Doucet's eyes, but he answered gravely, "No better than before, but no worse right now, thank God."

If she wasn't better why was she coming home? "Is she expected to get worse?" Mia asked.

"She's not going to recover." The reply was blunt and seemed somewhat indiscreet, especially coming from a clergyman.

Claire's footsteps and those of her dog sounded on the wooden floor. Mia drew the priest inside and away from the open door. "What is it that's wrong with her, exactly?"

"Myxedema. An underactive thyroid. It went on for years and got way out of hand before she had any treatment. She takes medication now, but her heart is damaged far beyond repair, and with her weight, it only gets worse."

"Will Reuben's sister take the children?"

"And raise them in that...*Deutsch* penal colony? I hope that won't happen. The last thing this world needs is three more Reuben Hofers." There was a chill in the strong words, expressed, as they were, in gentle monk-like tones.

"They're going to need someone to take care of them," Mia said. "Especially these little ones."

"Yes, they will."

"I've got a big house."

"You've got a very sick husband."

It was true. Nick didn't take so much of her time now, but he would. And he wasn't going to recover any more than Mary Frances Hofer was. Eventually he would need her twenty-four hours a day. But these two babies needed her now. Mia looked down into the priest's curious brown eyes. "Please let Mrs. Hofer know that I'll help any way I can."

Chapter Twenty-eight

Three local people had admitted to knowing Reuben Hofer when he was a prisoner—Nickerson, Olson, and Wanda Greely. Two of those three had so far not accounted for their whereabouts when Hofer's house was being ransacked. You could possibly make that all three; Wanda Greely's claim to having been with her family was only worth how much her husband was unwilling to lie for her. It wouldn't be a bad idea to find out how long Wanda's mister had been around. He might have known Hofer, too. There was no reason, so far, to suspect any of the old acquaintances of skulduggery, and McIntire was prepared to reject Fergie Olson as even the most remote of suspects.

Before taking himself back to his own empty house, McIntire decided to swing by the Hofers'. He'd sleep better knowing that things were as they should be.

The cow stood near the barn, a deeper shadow in the dusk. When McIntire approached, she pushed her nose between the bars of the gate and licked at his sleeve. Her udder hung limp. Someone had done the milking, and, McIntire saw, latched the hen house door.

It was all peaceful enough, but he might as well check the house, just to be sure, and turn off a light that had been left burning in the kitchen, attracting a cloud of insects to the windows.

The cloakroom was uncluttered and smelled only faintly of old shoes and cellar.

The inner door was unlocked and had shrunk back to its pre-tropical dimensions, opening without a whimper.

Mia and the kids had managed to do a fine job without his help. The kitchen was swept and scrubbed to an unrecognizable level of spickness-and-spanness. He walked through to the living room.

The single day of dry air had also gotten to the maple floorboards, and the ominous creaks drawn forth by his footsteps transported McIntire ever deeper into a segment of his past he did not look back on with misty-eyed nostalgia. His memories of time here were almost universally dismal, capped by the time, when he was about ten years old, that he'd been forced to spend the night, trapped at school by a blizzard. Despite the presence of twenty or thirty other pupils, some of whom appeared to be enjoying the experience immensely, he'd been petrified. While the whispers and giggles around him died away, he lay on the floor with his knees pulled up under his coat, shivering at the scream of the wind through the bell tower, and watching grotesquely elongated shadows cast by the oil lamp dance across the mournful face of Abraham Lincoln, an image that still figured in his nightmares.

During his visits of the past twenty-four hours, he'd been too distracted to pay much attention to his surroundings, and he now looked around with curiosity. The space had been considerably chopped up, so that the room was less than half the size of the original classroom. But Honest Abe was still there, spooky and sad-faced as ever, flanked by George Washington and…. What the hell was that? No dead president, but some sort of animal pelt. McIntire drew closer. A badger. Did they have badgers where the Hofers hailed from? Iowa or where ever it was?

A partition wall at the back separated off a small bedroom and the set of steps ascending to the two rooms under the eaves. McIntire didn't go up. Everything seemed to be in order, and he was beginning to feel uncomfortable about committing this invasion, even with the best of intentions.

He wasn't sure the remodeling would serve to put his goblins to rest. Even with the braided rug, and the lace curtains softening the tall windows, there was still more of bleak institution than family home about the place. He straightened the shade on a globe-shaped table lamp, flicked out the light, and hurried back through the kitchen.

That's when he saw it. Dead center on the jolly oilcloth covering the table, obscuring a robin feeding her young. A stone—smooth, shiny, doughnut shaped, sharply excised lines radiating from the hole in its center—lay glinting in the light, held delicately in the skeletal remains of a human hand.

Chapter Twenty-nine

It was dark. Pitch black, absolute dark. Claire couldn't even see where the window was. It was like she was wearing a blindfold. She could hardly tell if her eyes were open or shut.

Mrs. Thorsen had said it was bedtime and came upstairs with her. She talked while Claire got into bed, about what a long day it had been and Ma coming home tomorrow. Then she turned out the light and went downstairs. Just like that.

Claire stayed curled up stiff and quiet with the sheet pulled around her head like a hood and only her nose out poking so she could breathe.

She hated being scared. Some kids just snuggled down under the covers and went to sleep until morning. Joey did. But Claire was always still awake when Joey fell asleep. He didn't need to worry. Claire wouldn't be scared either, if she knew someone else was nearby, awake. It wasn't fair that she always had to be the last one to go to sleep.

Joey might be scared tonight, though; he'd never gone to sleep in a room by himself.

If only she could turn on the light. Even if she dared get up, she probably couldn't reach the string without a chair. Anyway she wouldn't want to reach for the string in the dark. Last year, at Angie Greenbush's Halloween party, Angie's cousin told a story about some kids that played a joke on a girl and tied an arm from a dead person to her light string. The girl went into her room and the other kids stayed outside the door to hear her scream when she grabbed the dead hand, but they waited and waited and didn't hear a thing. When they finally opened the door, the girl had gone crazy and was sitting on the floor, chewing on the arm.

Claire began to count in her head to push the memory of that story out of her brain.

At home she had a long piece of rag tied to the light string and then to the bedpost, so she could turn off the light after she got into bed. But she didn't. She never turned off the light until she could see the sky starting to turn pink. She stayed awake and she read. Even if she had to read *The Eagle's Mate* so many times that she knew it by heart. Even if she had to read the *Farm Journal*. She should have brought some of her books with her.

She heard a creak like somebody was coming up the stairs. Maybe Mrs. Thorsen really was a witch, or a murderer. She had a witch's cradle in her yard, and the biggest knife Claire had ever seen that she cut the bread with. She told Claire to be careful using it because Nick had started sharpening the knives every day. Maybe she tricked them into coming here to kill them.

Claire knew it wasn't true. When morning came, everything would be normal, and she'd wonder how she could have been so silly.

Being scared was a punishment for her sins. She knew that, too. Tomorrow she would be good. She wouldn't think any bad things, and she wouldn't tell any lies, like about Pa and the gun or about the burglar's car. But it wasn't fair. Jake and Sam committed lots of sins. They swore and they sneaked to the store and bought cigarettes, but they weren't scared of anything, and they snored like crazy all night long.

This was an old house. Mrs. Thorsen used to sleep in this room when she was a little girl, and she was old now. Sometimes old houses were haunted. Mrs. Thorsen's mother and father must have lived here, and they were both dead. Maybe their ghosts were here now. What if her mother's ghost knew Claire was in her daughter's bed and didn't like it? What if Pa's ghost followed her here?

Claire had dreamed about her father, that he was alive again. In the dream he was mad because she left the milk in the pail and let it go sour, and he wanted to take her lucky charm back. She tried to run, but her legs were too heavy.

A square of light flashed on the wall and moved around the room. It looked eerie, but it was only a car driving into the yard. The light disappeared and a door slammed, and Spike started barking.

The door at the bottom of the stairs opened, and Claire heard Nick say, "Get up there. One more yip and you're crow food!" In two seconds, Spike came bounding onto the bed, and Claire hugged him tight.

More doors opened and shut, and another man was talking. It was the google-eyed one. John McIntire. Mrs. Thorsen could like him if she wanted to, but that didn't change Claire's mind. He was mean to Spike, and she didn't like him hanging around Jake and Sam and asking her if they had a gun, and if Jake and Sam knew how to shoot. When she thought about that, it made Claire feel sick. Now he was coming to Mrs. Thorsen's in the night.

Jake and Sam weren't nice. They were mean, but they were her brothers. John McIntire was her enemy.

Chapter Thirty

McIntire had hated leaving the house unguarded. Someone had been there, and that someone could be back. But he didn't have much choice. He couldn't take the evidence with him, and he couldn't lock the door. His best course of action would have been to leave his car to make it look like the house wasn't empty, and take the path to Thorsens' that Mia had been traversing so frequently of late. But he hadn't used that path in better than forty years, had no idea where to find it, and his flashlight batteries were dead. He'd finally decided to compromise by turning on a few more lights and moving Hofer's Oldsmobile from under the trees to a more prominent position. It might fool anybody who didn't know better.

He'd stood in the Thorsens' doorway only long enough to ask Nick to track down somebody from the sheriff's office, and to determine that Mia and her charges had left no bones or fancy stones on the table when they finished their cleaning.

"You might ask Father Doucet," Mia told him. "He went over to do the milking."

"Maybe you could call him?" McIntire asked. "Just say we'd like to talk to him. You don't have to tell him what it's about on the phone."

"Really, John, I'm not a complete idiot!"

McIntire left without taking time to placate Mia's injured ego. Life would have been much simpler if the Hofers had put in a telephone.

The entire trip couldn't have taken more than fifteen minutes, twenty at the most, but as he rounded the corner toward the old school, he swore to himself. A hulking shape showed through the trees directly behind Hofer's car. When he approached, his headlights illuminated Periodic-Deputy Sheriff Adam Wall's pickup truck.

Wall stood waiting at the foot of the steps. "She back?"

"No," McIntire told him. "How'd you get here so fast?"

"Fast? In my old beast? I was just driving by to check on things. What's going on?"

"Step inside. You just might be the man who can tell me."

Wall stared at the grotesque centerpiece for some time before turning to McIntire. "Why? You figure I've had experience with this sort of stuff? Sneaking through the bushes in my loincloth, tracking down deer? Maybe chipping out a spear point or two in my spare time?"

The reply was cold, as it might have every right to be, if McIntire didn't know for a fact that Adam Wall *had* attempted once or twice, with pitiful results, to reproduce the weapons of his ancestors. He waited.

Wall gave in. "It could be a weight for a net."

"Fish net, you mean?"

"Ya."

"Would it have been used by Indians around here?"

"Indians and plenty of other people around here." The hand glistened in his flashlight beam. "Where did this come from? Why would these people have it on their kitchen table?"

McIntire shook his head. It must have taken some trouble, shining up the bones, wiring them together, arranging them in a properly grotesque position. "Someone had to have come in early this evening or late this afternoon. What kind of person would leave such an object for a sickly widow and her children?"

"Someone who wanted to scare them?"

"It scares me." Not the least because of its spooky resemblance to Reuben Hofer's slender hand in death, extended in an offering of his own blood.

"Are you sure it's not something that was here in the house? This was a school once, maybe there was a skeleton for the science classes?"

"There wasn't. At least not when I went to school here, and it closed not long after. Everything worth having would have been moved to the new school."

The two men went silent as vehicles approached from opposite directions—Pete Koski's lumbering Power Wagon and another McIntire was rapidly learning to recognize, Father Adrien Doucet.

Apparently Wall did, too. "What's he doing out here?"

McIntire hadn't expected Mia's phone call to bring the priest running. He said, "Beats me. It's a little late for bird watching."

"What's that?"

"Guibard says the father is a bird watcher."

Adam Wall threw back his head and laughed like a lunatic. "Bird watcher? He's a bird stalker!"

"What does that mean?"

"He ain't admiring their plumage. He *eats* them. Tweety birds, robins, blue jays, hummingbird tongues, for all I know."

Wall didn't sound like he was kidding. McIntire had heard of such in Europe, but…. "He *eats* them? You mean…? How?"

"Roasted, maybe with a dash of wine, wrapped in bacon, possibly, on a nice bed of rice."

"I mean how does he catch them? Nets?"

"Bite your tongue! He shoots them with a twenty-two. He can pick the eye out of a sparrow at a hundred yards." Now he did sound like he was kidding.

"Are you sure this isn't all just talk?" McIntire asked. "Have you seen it for yourself?"

"Seen it? I've tasted it. Not bad either. Not something I'd go to all that trouble for myself, but not bad."

Adam Wall's parents were regular church goers, and Adam would be likely to know more about Doucet than McIntire did. Maybe the man had other unseemly habits.

"Has he been here long?" McIntire asked. "He seems fairly young."

"He's older than he looks, I think. He was here before I left for the army, and he was here when I got back. After that he was away on sabbatical—odd thing to say, 'sabbatical' sounds like something priests should be on permanently." He glanced toward the door as the roaring of engines drew closer. "Anyway, he went home for a while after the war, back to France for a year."

"Back to France? Does he have family there? I had the idea he was from down south somewhere. His bragging it up was one of the reasons my mother decided to head for warmer pastures."

"He grew up in Louisiana, but his mother was from France, and I think he might have been born there. In a small village, Oradour-sur-Glane. He still *had* family there."

"All killed?"

"I would imagine so."

Brakes and gears shrieked like a covey of banshees, and a minute later the Mutt and Jeff pair of sheriff and priest trotted up the steps.

Koski circled the table, peering at the object from all directions, while Doucet hung back, staring as if he half expected the hand to hurtle through the air and grab him by the throat.

McIntire asked, "Was it here when you came to milk the cow?"

"No." Doucet spoke distractedly, his gaze still trained on the bones, then gave a shake of his head and came back to life. "That is to say, it might have been, but I wouldn't have seen it. I only came inside to put the milk in the cellar. I didn't go into the kitchen."

"What time did you get here?"

"I can't say, exactly. Seven-thirty, quarter to eight, something like that. I was here about forty-five minutes. I know, it's only one cow, but I'm a little rusty. " His gaze went back to the hand, and he took a step closer. "What do you suppose is going on here? I can see that someone might have had a grudge against Reuben. Someone who knew him from the CO camp. But he's dead now. Why keep after his widow?"

"Did you know all along that Hofer spent time here?" Koski, leaning with his hands on the table, didn't look up. "You didn't say anything?"

The Adam's apple bobbed above the white collar. "I didn't think to mention it. I suppose I thought it was up to Mary Frances to tell you. She didn't like people knowing."

"But she told you."

"I'm a priest."

Koski straightened up, eyes narrowed as if he might like to see proof of that, but then he smiled tolerantly and nodded in understanding. Obviously he still intended an attempt at availing himself of those priestly confidentialities. He turned his attention to McIntire. "What time did *you* get here?"

"Quarter past nine, maybe. I'm just guessing. It could have been later. It was getting dark when I got here, and completely dark by the time I left."

"The bones look pretty old," Koski observed. "Whatcha think?"

He addressed the question to Adam Wall, whose face froze as it had with McIntire's earlier implication of possible genetically bestowed expertise. "Believe it or—"

"That thing," McIntire hastily indicated the carved stone, "is almost certainly pretty old." A spark kindled in a far corner of his brain.

Koski tucked his shirt-tail in more snugly and hitched up his belt. "I'll get the camera and the fingerprint stuff," he addressed Adam Wall, oblivious to the set of the deputy's jaw. "In the meantime, you might as well have a look around."

McIntire followed the sheriff down the steps. He felt mildly guilty over his attempt to get out of earshot of Doucet, but nudged Koski off a few yards and asked, "Remember our pseudo-prospector friend from last summer, Professor Gregory Carlson?"

"How could I forget?"

"He's the expert on this sort of thing," McIntire reminded him. "We could send him a picture."

"No need for that. He's back. All settled into his old camp. Can't stay away from us. "

He'd stayed away from McIntire, hadn't looked him up, let him know he was back in the neighborhood, and McIntire felt an embarrassing unmasculine discomfort at the slight. He wasn't particularly surprised that Carlson had returned; the guy had been positively enraptured with whatever it was he was snooping around for.

The narrow silhouette of Father Adrien appeared behind the screen. Koski slapped a mosquito on his neck. "I still think there's something funny about that guy. He looks like a Goddamn cat burglar."

"Worse," McIntire told him, "he's a bird watcher."

The drive home was no where near long enough to sort through the Hofer family saga's latest episode. If Reuben Hofer had gotten hold of some sort of Indian artifact, he might have passed it on to someone he knew for safekeeping while he was in prison, and they could have wanted to give it back. Was that what Nickerson and Wanda were getting at? Then why not just turn it over to Mary Frances? Why give it back at all at this point? And why leave it perched on the kitchen table, offered up in such a macabre way, in a slightly used hand? Did this have anything at all to do with Hofer's murder, or was it just that his death let his old friends know he was still around?

The mailbox held another letter from Leonie, and the light bill—a bill that might be bigger than necessary; lights were glaring from the kitchen and bathroom windows. He'd have to be more careful to turn things off.

Kelpie waited at the door, thumping her tail without a hint of accusation, which only increased McIntire's feelings of guilt. She should have been let outdoors hours ago. He carried her down the steps to set her in the grass, and watched her toddle off into the dark. Her backbone was getting sharper by the day.

How old was she now? Sixteen? He had no idea. It would be sad if she didn't last until Leonie got back.

He sat on the steps to read the letter by the porch light. Leonie had spent the past few days visiting Stevie and her husband, and the adored grandson, Charles. Charles must be growing up; he'd been "Chuckie" until now. Stevie had been out of sorts, and Leonie wasn't sure that she and Angus were getting along all that well. She missed him and wished he had come along with her.

McIntire didn't recall being invited. Not that he would have gone if he had been; he had scant interest in passing the time with out of sorts step-daughters.

Porch lights and summer nights were a bad combination. He hadn't finished reading the first page before the mosquitoes drove him indoors.

How had he managed living alone all those years? He'd seldom cooked his own meals, that was true, and he'd lived most of that time in a city of eight million people and gone out to work every day. And gone home alone every night. When he thought back on it, it made him sad. So much of his life had been wasted.

He cracked three eggs into the pan and shoved them aside to make room for the dry heel of the last loaf of bread.

It still nagged at him, the idea that it should be simple to discover who had killed Reuben Hofer. There were such a limited number of possibilities. Bruno Nickerson would probably not have come waltzing over to see the widow the next day if he'd done it, and certainly Wanda Greely wouldn't have. Sure, there were others, but presumably the sheriff had done a thorough job of checking around the neighborhood, and hadn't turned up anybody with either the weapon or a motive.

Try as he might, McIntire couldn't ignore it. There were two formerly independent young men who'd had every reason to resent, and despise, and fear, the virtual stranger who'd invaded their territory and rendered them slaves.

The girl had squirmed like an eel when he asked if her brothers knew how to shoot a gun. She'd been slippery as an eel, too, only staring off into space and singing the same old tune; her father didn't allow guns. It might be worth asking the youngest one. He probably wouldn't have the wit to lie about it. McIntire could have taken the opportunity to search the house again when he had it, but it would have been a waste of time. If they had owned a gun and were lying about it, it followed that they had a damn good reason for lying, and the gun would now be long gone. If they hadn't got rid of it, Koski and his deputies would most likely have found it in the aftermath of the ransacking. The minute Reuben Hofer turned up dead, the entire area, including his home, should have been closed down and every nook and cranny searched. No point in fretting about that now.

McIntire swallowed the last of his supper and got up to answer the clatter of claws on the steps and the scratch at the door. Kelpie's tail thumped as she sniffed at his ankles.

"Yes, I'm afraid I've been seeing another dog," McIntire admitted. "He means nothing to me, I assure you." He straightened the rug by the stove so she might have the pleasure of rumpling it to her satisfaction. "Time to turn in, tomorrow is another day." He looked at the clock. "I stand corrected. Tomorrow is today."

Chapter Thirty-one

Ma was already home when they got there. She was sitting by the table, reading a magazine and listening to the radio, same as always, but she seemed different. It had something to do with her having been someplace without them. She knew about things they hadn't seen. Claire couldn't put her finger on it, but it seemed like Ma'd been gone a month instead of only two nights. She seemed more her old self when she folded the magazine down the middle and flipped it over. "You've been cleaning, I see. It looks good."

Claire put the box that had her and Joey's clothes in it on the floor. "It should look this way all the time."

"Maybe not quite *all* the time. We'd be picking up constantly."

"Other people manage."

She didn't answer that, and Claire felt kind of ashamed. Ma was just home from the hospital, and she was sick, and here Claire was, already nagging at her about the mess. Sometimes Claire couldn't help it. She knew she was being mean, but she just couldn't stop.

Joey came in with Mia Thorsen. He stood by Ma and leaned against her knee.

Mia Thorsen put the sack she was carrying on the table. "It's just some bread and macaroni salad. You won't have to bother with cooking dinner. How are you feeling?"

"Thank you, that's very kind of you. I'm feeling much better."
Ma was using her company voice again. "And thank you so much
for looking after Claire and Joey."

"It was a pleasure having them," Mia Thorsen said.

The nice words made tears burn in Claire's eyes, and she felt
stupid. She kept her back to them all and took the pail out to
the pump to get water for coffee.

Mia Thorsen let Claire make the coffee without butting in.
Maybe she remembered what Claire said about Sister being
bossy. Or maybe she just didn't think that making herself at
home in somebody else's kitchen was polite. But she got a knife
from the drawer without asking. She cut some of the bread and
put it in the toaster.

It was a new toaster; Ma got it with green stamps. Claire
wondered if Mrs. Thorsen would know how to use it. The
toast didn't pop up by itself when it was done like it did with
the Thorsens' toaster. You had to open it up and turn the bread
around. It worked better than using a pan in the oven, but you
could only do two slices at a time, so it was slow. Store-bought
bread was better for toast.

Ma laughed when she heard about Father Doucet milking
Opal. "Last run-in he had with Opal, she threw quite a scare
into him."

"Is that right?" Mrs. Thorsen started spreading butter on the
toast. "He looked like an old hand—an 'old cow hand from the
Rio Grande'—when he came over yesterday."

"Oh," Ma said, "It wasn't much of anything. She just mooed
in his face and gave him a start." Then she looked at Claire. "I
thought you'd be able to do the milking."

She'd been itching to tell about it, but now she wasn't sure how.
"I couldn't. I mean, I *was* milking, but than a burglar came."

"A burglar?" Ma looked at Mrs. Thorsen.

"Claire," Mrs. Thorsen said, "maybe you'd better check to see
if anybody milked your cow this morning, and," she looked at
Joey, "you can collect the eggs. Do you know how to do that?"

She wanted to get rid of them, which was nothing new, but this time Claire couldn't figure out why. After all, she knew all about the burglar; she was the one who'd been here when he came, for Pete's sake. She felt like she might start bawling again. She went to the cellar to skim some cream off last night's milk. The can was full, so Father Doucet, or somebody, must have milked Opal that morning.

When she came back up, Joey had already gone out to pick the eggs. Then he'd head for his regular spot with his regular stupid rocks and scraps of wood. Mrs. Thorsen would get to tell all about the burglar, and she hadn't even been there.

Claire went outside too, but then circled around to go in the back door up to her bedroom. The boy's room was still a mess, because Claire didn't have time to straighten it up herself, and she was way too ashamed to let Mrs. Thorsen upstairs. Jake and Sam would probably like seeing what the burglar did, anyway, so they could brag about it.

Some of the pages had been ripped right out of *The Eagle's Mate*. She laid the book on the bed and set to work putting them back in the right place. The one with the picture of Anemone standing by a big fireplace was first. Anemone had messy hair and eyes that were put in with "the dirty finger of beauty." Claire's hair got snarled, too, and her eyes had purple bags under them, but it didn't look beautiful.

She couldn't stop thinking about if the sheriff had caught the burglar yet. When he did, he was going to find out about the gun, and know they all lied. But maybe the burglar was a killer, too, and it would be better to catch him. Claire was starting to wish she hadn't panicked and lied about the car. When she said it was black or dark blue, she was thinking that it was really red. Now she couldn't remember for sure what color it was. That was the problem with lying. Sometimes you forgot what the truth was and started to believe your own self.

Ma hadn't told the whole story about Father Doucet and the cow, either, but Claire knew why. When they first bought Opal, Father went to have a look at her, and she walked right up to him and let out a long sad moo, right in his face. Father jumped like a scared rabbit. Then he laughed and said when he was a little boy, his grandmother was very superstitious. She believed in all kinds of signs that told the future, and she called them 'advertisements.' She said a cow mooing at you was an advertisement that somebody in your family was going to die. That's why Ma stopped telling the story. Of course it wasn't somebody in Father Doucet's family that died, but it still gave you the creeps to think about it.

Father Doucet said he wasn't worried, because everybody in his family was already dead, except for his Great Uncle Sal, who was ninety-seven years old, and he didn't need a cow to tell him Sal couldn't last much longer.

Chapter Thirty-two

McIntire was beginning to feel like a vampire, prowling by night, falling asleep at sunup. At least today he was up before ten—by about four minutes. Leonie, who, like Beau Brummel, preferred her mornings well-aired, would be proud.

The cool front that had brought the rain stuck around, and he was grateful for it. It made sleeping in one's clothing a tad more comfortable.

It also made thinking marginally less painful. McIntire couldn't get past the idea that finding the murderer shouldn't be so difficult: A shot to the head from the edge of a field by a killer who had access to that field and knew Hofer would be there. Of course strangely carved stones and long-dead hands complicated things. Where in hell would somebody have dug up the artifact and the hand that held it.

Maybe Greg Carlson could tell him that. He'd do Koski a favor and fetch the professor himself. Even if the guy hadn't had the decency to stop in to say hello.

He'd have to call Koski to let him know that he was going, which meant he'd want to keep that call confidential, which gave him an excuse to beg Mark Guibard for the use of his private line, and, to complete the ingenious thought, get the chance to glean whatever information he could from the doctor.

He remembered to pump some fresh water for the horses before he left, and to leave Kelpie outdoors.

◇◇◇

Marian Koski oozed such sympathy over Leonie's defection that McIntire wondered if she might have heard something he hadn't. McIntire gave his message and assured her that, the next time he went to town, he'd drop in for dinner.

He put the phone on its cradle and turned to Mark Guibard who had amassed an arsenal of equipment preparatory to forcing the wrinkles out of a pile of neatly rolled, dazzlingly white, shirts. "Many thanks."

"Don't mention it, except maybe in the process of telling me what the hell that was all about."

McIntire told him.

"In a human hand?"

"Human hand bones. A skeleton hand, all wired together and bent so it could hold the…whatever it is."

"That sort of adds a new dimension to things."

It did, McIntire agreed, "But I can't figure how it might be connected to the murder."

Guibard frowned, touched his forefinger daintily to his tongue, and tapped the bottom of his iron. It apparently wasn't to his liking; he sighed and turned the dial before commenting, "It would seem damned odd if it wasn't."

That was hard to argue with, too. "Could somebody be after the whole family? It seems like the only point in leaving the bones could be to scare them, but why?"

"Could be it's some lunatic," Guibard said, "except that we're thoroughly familiar with all our village idiots. If we had one given to leaving body parts around, we'd know it. There's nobody new except the Hofers. Anyway, it's a good thing you found it before Mrs. Hofer or one of the kids did."

"Yes," McIntire said. "It would have been some great welcome. Speaking of which, will she be getting out today?"

"I took her home this morning."

That put the kibosh on any chance McIntire'd have to extract information from the little boy. He could try the doctor, although he was only marginally less close mouthed than Father Adrien was likely to be. "Mark," he ventured, "according to his sister, Reuben Hofer was a 'harsh man.' Do you by any chance know how harsh?"

"Did he beat his wife, do you mean?"

"Or his kids."

The doctor unrolled a dampened shirt and applied the iron to its stiffly starched collar with surgical precision. "I didn't see Reuben often. Whenever I was at the house, he was mostly outdoors working somewhere, and I only talked to him more than just to say hello once or twice. I couldn't help but get the idea that he was almost intimidated by his wife. Maybe that's why he stayed out of the house." He leaned on the iron with both hands. "But the kids? I've no idea. He sure managed to keep them in line one way or the other. He kept the whole bunch on a rigid schedule every minute of the day, and night, too. He looked like the type to subscribe to the spare the rod and spoil the kid philosophy, but maybe that's just my bias showing. Even if he did administer a whack or two, I wouldn't call it a motive for patricide, if that's what you've got on your mind. If it was, half the men in the county'd get bullets to the head."

"But it could be a motive for husbandicide. Mary Frances wouldn't want to die and leave her children at his mercy."

"Mary Frances did not tippy-toe out to that field and blast her husband into the next world. I can guarantee you that!"

"She doesn't seem to be sorry he's in that next world."

"I imagine she's ecstatic. Why the hell shouldn't she be? He only hung around long enough to get her pregnant and turn their home into a boot camp. She wasn't afraid of him, and she didn't hate him, but she was realistic enough to know that those kids would have a miserable existence without her around to protect them."

Which sounded like a half-decent motive for murder to McIntire, and when there's a homicide, the first place to look was at those who had the most reason to want the victim out of the way. As a general rule that was right at home. But Guibard was right; Mrs. Hofer hadn't done the shooting herself, and probably wouldn't know where to hire an assassin or have the money to pay one.

There could be others with good reason to have wanted Hofer dead.

He thanked the doctor again, even though he'd not learned much more than the secret to his relentlessly crisp appearance.

Chapter Thirty-three

"Burglar?" Mary Frances wheezed out the word again.

"Didn't the sheriff tell you?"

"I haven't seen him."

It shouldn't be up to Mia to tell the story. But it wasn't Mia's responsibility to keep it from her either. If Koski wanted to be the first to let her know, he could have done it by now.

"It's all right," she began. "Nothing was stolen, but someone came into your house Thursday night." She hesitated before admitting her own negligence. "Claire had come back to milk the cow. She was in the barn when they came, and she ended up hiding in the hay mow all night."

Mary Frances Hofer's face reflected a horror that Mia was rapidly beginning to feel. What kind of idiot was she to tell a woman with a badly failing heart that her daughter had spent a night of terror hiding from intruders? Chatting about it over coffee, like it was the latest gossip. What would she do if Mrs. Hofer fainted or even had a heart attack? If she ended up on the floor, Mia would never get her up. She scrambled for water, saw no glass, and held the dipper to her hostess' lips.

"I'm all right." Mrs. Hofer closed her eyes and let out a puff of air. She grasped the dipper in both hands and took a small sip. "Thank you." She handed it back.

"I'm so sorry. I shouldn't have said—"

"Of course you should have." She waved her incongruously dainty hand. "I hardly think you should keep it from me! Who was it?"

Mia shrugged and shook her head. The rest of the story didn't take long to tell. Whatever had happened last night, involving bones and stones and Pete Koski, she didn't know the details of, and didn't mention.

"Ransacked? But why?" Her agitation gone, Mrs. Hofer seemed unconcerned about what trauma her daughter might have suffered.

"Who knows? Is there something they could have wanted to steal? Something specific that they expected to be hidden, maybe?" It sounded ridiculous when Mia said it aloud. Mrs. Hofer apparently thought so, too.

"Now what do you think?" she asked. "We have nothing worth stealing. What reason could anybody possible have for ransacking this house?"

"Maybe some acquaintance of your late husband?"

"You mean that woman that was here? I hardly think—"

Mia also hardly thought the mess could have been the work of Wanda Greely. "There could be others," she said. "For sure your husband would have met a fair number people during his time here. Did he ever mention anybody? Maybe somebody he'd gotten into some sort of tiff with?"

"My husband never mentioned a soul. During most of our marriage, I barely saw him. He was home long enough to give me four children, and that's about it." She glowered, daring Mia to contradict her. "They were gifts I'll always be grateful for." The scowl might have been meant for her husband; she went on, "He left us to fend for ourselves. He had a choice. He could have gone into the service as a non-combatant—a medic or something. He'd have been paid, and the boys and I would have gotten an allotment. We'd have been taken care of. There was no support for families of conscientious objectors. Reuben was paid five dollars a month, and he was expected to pay thirty-five for his keep." She repeated, "He could have gone into the service."

"And your other two children might not have been born," Mia reminded her.

"No, probably not. But he had no right to have those children, desert them, and then come back expecting them to work night and day for him." Her resentment brought some substance to her thin voice. "He hated that we managed to get along without him, but he was never bothered enough to stay and take care of us."

"How *did* you get along? Alone, with four children to feed and clothe?"

"Oh well, I wasn't completely alone. We lived with my father. In the last few years before he died. That mostly just gave me another person to care for, but we always had a roof over our heads."

Mia and Nick had lived with Mia's father, too. Her father had died suddenly, giving her no chance to nurse him, or even say goodbye. Well, she'd have her chance with Nick.

Like her children, once Mary Frances got started, she didn't stop. "Reuben was starting his second year of college when we met. He had to quit when we got married, of course. He wasn't doing well, anyway. He was smart, but he'd never been to a real school, his English wasn't so good, and there was too much he simply didn't know."

"It must have taken some courage for your husband to try at all."

"If there was one thing Reuben didn't lack, it was courage. It was a shame that he had to quit school, and of course that was partly my fault, but he never blamed me." She took a long drink of the water. "My father was getting older and needed help running the farm, so Reuben moved in. There were no jobs then, anyway. We didn't have any money, but, like I said, we had a roof over our heads, and we had enough to eat, which was more than a lot of people could say. Reuben wasn't so happy about living off my father, even if he did do all the work, and it was really more that my father lived off him. You'd think it wouldn't have bothered him. He was used to the generations together."

"Maybe it was too much like home," Mia offered.

"Maybe," Mary Frances agreed. "Anyway, as soon as he could, he went off and got a job at a meat packing plant in Des Moines. Then he was drafted, and the rest I imagine you know."

Mia nodded. "That was that. We never knew what was around the next corner, so I stayed on my father's farm. He was good with the boys. They had to work hard, but no more than the usual for farm kids. We managed. "Reuben came when he could, I guess. During the war, that wasn't very often. He wasn't ever home long enough to…fit in, you know? And he was like a stranger to the kids, in Des Moines most of the time when Jake and Sam were small. Claire was barely a year old when Reuben was drafted, and after that he was hardly home at all."

Mia wasn't sure if she should bring it up, but Mary Frances seemed in the mood to talk. "When did your health start to…?"

She smiled, "Deteriorate? I hadn't felt very well for a long time, not for years, really, but I started getting worse after the boys were born. My father was providing us with a home, and I didn't like to ask him for money for the doctor, and mostly I just felt tired. Then I began putting on weight like nobody's business. I had always been on the plump side, but nothing like now. No matter how little I ate, I just seemed to keep gaining, and I was too exhausted to do anything to work it off. The heavier I got, the more tired I got. Just staying awake was a chore."

"How awful, and to have so many people depending on you." Mary Frances would have been a young woman then. She was still a young woman, at least ten years younger than Mia.

"Then my hair started to fall out, and I noticed I was losing my hearing, so I knew something was definitely wrong. I went to the doctor. He told me it was just nerves, I should lose some weight, and I'd be fine, when my husband got home."

"Naturally." Mia wondered how may women ended up dying of their "nerves."

"Not long after that, Reuben got out of prison, and he came back for good."

Or for bad. Mia poured more coffee.

"My father had died a few months before. Dad owned the farm with his two brothers, and they insisted on selling, so we were out. We'd have never been able to stay there, regardless. Not with people feeling the way they did about Reuben, that he was a coward and a traitor. He had some money saved up, enough to buy this place outright, and here we are."

"Do you plan to stay here, then?"

"We have nowhere better to go, and no reason not to stay for the time being. We haven't gotten acquainted yet, but these last few days people have been kind. Father Doucet has been a great help and a comfort. I'm not able to get to mass, or to take the kids. He's been seeing to Joey's religious education." Her chins jiggled when she laughed. "Even milking the cow. My boys can handle things as long as I'm around to sign papers and that sort of thing until they're of age. That won't be much longer. Jake turned seventeen in April. And," she cleared her throat before going on, "if I'm not here, there's always Jane."

"Your sister-in-law?"

"She'll see that they're taken care of, when I'm gone."

"Surely it won't come to that."

"Almost certainly it will come to that."

Mia wasn't sure what to say.

Mary Frances stuffed the crust of the toast into her mouth and swallowed. "It may sound harsh, but my mind is much more at rest now, knowing that I won't be leaving my children with their father."

Once again Mia was left floundering for a response. Was the woman telling her that she was glad the old boy was dead? Her hesitancy gave her hostess the chance to really set her back on her heels. "There have been times," Mary Frances sounded absolutely serious, "when I'd have seen to it myself if I'd had the means—and the courage. I don't know what would be the greater sin, breaking the sixth commandment, or abandoning my babies to slavery."

The bloated features showed such utter sadness, that Mia forgot her own discomfort. "I'm so sorry. But surely—"

"I talked about it with Father Doucet. If it weren't for the manner in which my husband died, I'm sure he'd be agonizing right now over whether to turn me in to the sheriff." A genuine laugh bubbled out. "I told him I was tempted to accidentally roll onto Reuben in the night! He wasn't terribly shocked, almost sympathetic, but then I suppose there's not much a priest hasn't heard."

No, but there probably weren't many who'd heard that one. It might have worked, too.

"He promised to keep an eye on the children if I wasn't around to do it. But he wouldn't have been able to do anything. A man's home is his castle."

"You're probably right about that," Mia said. "People don't like to interfere."

"I asked him, don't you think it's odd that God commands us to honor our mother and father, but doesn't make so much as a peep about how we should treat our children?"

Mia hadn't thought of it before. It was a good point.

"If I could get anybody to believe I'd done it, I'd confess right now and put an end to the fol-de-rol."

Fol-de-rol? Investigating her husband's murder? "But you must want to know who's responsible. Apart from the rest of it, if it's the same person who rifled your house last night, your family might still be in danger."

"I can't believe that!" She did sound incredulous. "We don't know anyone here, and we've done nothing that could possibly have got anybody mad at us. My husband, maybe—I don't have any idea what he might have gotten up to here, years ago—but me and my children? There isn't a person in this state that could possibly have anything against us."

"Somebody made an awful mess of your home. Somebody vicious enough to break a little dog's leg."

"There's no telling what people might do." It was a matter of fact statement you could hardly argue with.

Mia hadn't intended to be so nosy, but Mary Frances didn't seem to object to frankness. She took a fortifying sip of coffee and asked, "Have you made legal provisions for your children?"

"As I said, Jane will see that they're all right. Their—Jane's and Reuben's—mother is still living. She's the children's next of kin. They have a rule at the colony that children born to outsiders aren't allowed, but they'll make an exception after I'm gone. Custody of the children will be given to their grandmother even without a legal agreement, if there's nobody to object, and there won't be. So they'll be with Jane at the colony. It's not the best thing, but at least they'll be taken care of."

"In the community that produced your husband?"

"And his sister. No, Prairie Oak didn't make Reuben into the monster he was. It was leaving the place that started all the trouble."

"Monster?" Mia couldn't let it pass. She'd said it in such a matter of fact way. No qualification and no animosity.

Mrs. Hofer's mouth worked for a time before any sound came out. "He allowed my children, our children, no peace. He controlled every minute of their lives."

She coughed. Mia located a real glass, poured more water, and waited for her to sip and continue.

"None of it made sense. He'd wanted that education himself, but he forced Sam and Jake to leave school, and Claire had to sneak to read and do her homework, mostly when she should have been asleep. He'd hated the lack of freedom when he was growing up, but he gave his own children far less. They had not one minute to themselves or a single thing to say about their own lives.

"Things hadn't been all that rosy with my father, but the kids were doing okay, growing up to be responsible people, happy people, good people. Six months after Reuben returned they were frightened, nervous, angry, hardly kids at all. They'd learned to lie and sneak and…hate." She repeated, "He allowed my children no peace. It was monstrous."

It sounded ugly and, as his wife indicated, bizarrely at odds with Hofer's supposed beliefs. "How did it come about?"Mia asked. "His leaving the colony?"

"Like I said, when he was young, he hated the life there. He convinced them that it would be good for one of them to have a college education. I don't know where he got the idea. Since the GI bill, everybody and their brother is in school, but in 1931? How he even knew colleges existed is beyond me. Anyway, he managed to convince them that the outside world was changing, and they needed to be ready for it, so off he went to Drake University." Her grin showed a missing molar. "He even got the colony to pay for it."

The ceiling creaked overhead, and she lowered her already weak voice. "Then he married me, and they kicked him out for good. Even his parents would have nothing to do with him, or our children. Only Jane, who should have been the one to go to college, kept in touch. From the minute he knew he couldn't go back, ever, the colony started looking better and better. When he got drafted, he plunged head first into pacifism. By the time he got out of prison, you'd think he'd never left South Dakota.

"He tried to go back to leading the kind of life he grew up with. He couldn't see that it just wasn't possible. Prairie Oak colony was a big group, a hundred or more, and they lived well. They had thousands of acres of the best farmland and all the modern machinery. Yes, everybody had their jobs to do, even the smallest children, but there were dozens of them, and they did it together. Work was a social thing, if you see what I mean. It's not the same as sending a seven year old boy out alone before sun-up in the middle of January to pump water. Thirty gallons before he was allowed breakfast, whether we needed it or not. Reuben forgot all about the reasons he left Prairie Oak. He was obsessed with recreating it here. But what he created was closer to the prison he despised than the home he idealized. And when the one of the kids couldn't do something he expected of them, he took it as a personal attack. Like they were doing it on purpose, just to aggravate him. It was especially hard for Jake. He was old enough to remember when he was small and crazy about his father…and when his father was crazy about him."

It was so terribly sad. "Do you think it was the time spent in prison? The war? I know Reuben didn't fight in the usual way, but—"

"No. My husband was like a horse with blinkers, he couldn't see anything except exactly what he wanted." The chins bounced again. "At one time that was me, and if it meant being ostracized by his family, so be it. If having a self-supporting farm meant turning his children into indentured servants who hated him, he was more than willing to pay that price, too. But it wasn't Prairie Oak that made Reuben the way he was. I think he was probably born...ruthless, in a way, and leaving the place that...protected him, put limits on what he could do." She shook her head. "He just wasn't prepared to handle it."

Maybe it was the colony then, or heredity. From what Claire had told her, Jane Hofer had her own ruthless streak. Mia asked, "Does your sister-in-law have children of her own?"

Mary Frances shook her head. "She was married years ago. Her husband disappeared less than a month after the wedding. Fell off a footbridge trying to drive home some cows in a flood. He was drowned, of course, but they never found his body, so Jane had a good excuse not to marry again no matter how much they hounded her. Well, who can blame her? She's the only one of those women that has any time to herself at all, or anything to say about her own life. The rest of them never leave the farm. They barely speak English. Get married, have children, that's it."

It didn't sound different from Mary Frances' own life.

"Jane is smart as a whip and not afraid of anybody. She'll take care of things. Prairie Oak will take my kids back now, and be overjoyed to have a couple more farm hands and another kitchen maid for a few years."

"Is that the best thing for Claire—or Joey?" Would those few years stretch into life?

"It's the best I can do. It will keep the children together, at least until they're grown up."

Mia refilled the glass and placed it within Mary Frances' reach before she left. "If you should need anything, just send one of the children for me. They know the way, and I'm always at home."

Joey was in his place under the kitchen window, repairing the damage a night's downpour had done to his stick fences and miniature canals. His face showed such intensity, it was hard to believe he was getting any joy from his play.

Chapter Thirty-four

The last time McIntire visited Greg Carlson in his rustic lair had been the previous October—crisp air, foliage brilliant or lying on the ground, and, more to the point, no bugs. He smashed one of the advance guard on his ear, and rolled up the window.

The road—nothing more than a track for logging equipment, was rutted and still soft from the rain. McIntire gripped the wheel and strove to keep a constant pressure on the gas pedal. Lost momentum could mean a long walk back for a tow truck.

He pulled in behind Carlson's panel truck and winced as the Studebaker's bottom scraped sand. Maybe it was a good sign; at least it wasn't mud. He sat for a time, not thinking, absorbing the green-dappled light and the cool moist air, the only sound the almost imperceptible rustle of leaves. Hypnotic, as long as he stayed in the car.

Entering that jungle was going to take some serious getting ready for. He stuffed his trouser cuffs into his socks and reached for the long sleeved shirt he'd, for once, had the presence of mind to bring along. Turning up the collar still left an enticing expanse of neck at the mercy of the winged vampires. He draped his crumpled handkerchief over the back of his head and snugged his hat down onto it. It was good enough for Lawrence of Arabia, but he'd only had to worry about sunburn.

He gave a blast on the car horn as a warning to Carlson to get decent or hide out, took a deep breath, and launched himself into the breach.

The small brook was now rendered a substantial stream. McIntire congratulated himself on leaping across with only one resulting wet foot, and headed up the slope with long strides, eager to leave the hum of insects behind. It was about a quarter-mile walk to Carlson's camp. Despite the discomfort, McIntire was glad he'd volunteered to make this trip himself. Getting away from what passed for civilization in St. Adele would do him good. He must be in withdrawal from the surges of adrenaline brought on by battling the past winter's snow. Maybe mowing the lawn, which was fast reaching hay-height, would have done the trick.

He hoped he wasn't facing the challenge for nothing, that he'd get there early enough that Carlson would still be hanging around his shack. Why the guy was there at all was a mystery. McIntire was under the impression that most of the places he was snooping into were some distance away. Like, for instance, the Shawanok Club grounds. He could have stayed more comfortably in Thunder Bay. More conspicuously, though, which might well have been the deciding factor. Or possibly Carlson liked a challenge, too.

The man had been indulging in some non-archeological work; the clearing around the cabin was—clear. Brush cut away, ferns and weeds trimmed or trampled, low branches lopped off trees. Light shone into places that hadn't seen the sun in a thousand years, and onto a chair fashioned from split willow. A couple of shirts hung from a line strung between beeches.

Even the cabin looked more civilized. The low roof had its sag pushed up and was covered in corrugated metal. A tidy railing of peeled cedar surrounded the porch leading to the shiny new screen door.

The inner door was open, and the aroma of bacon and coffee vied with that of balsam trees and birch firewood.

Carlson came from behind the cabin—to where he had retreated until he saw whose visit the car horn heralded? At least the man hadn't been intentionally avoiding him. He'd put on weight. Of course when McIntire last saw him it was at the tail end of four or five months in the bush. It was early days of deprivation now. The clearing didn't smell deprived.

The hand Carlson extended in greeting was roughened. "Howdy. My first real guest of the summer, and just in time for a late breakfast."

McIntire accepted with thanks. It just might be his first real *meal* of the summer.

The interior of the cabin was as spruced up as the outside, right down to a pot of chives on the window ledge. First Guibard with his ironing and now...it was a conspiracy, no two ways about it. Leonie had paid them off.

"What the hell's going on?" McIntire demanded.

"With what?" Carlson pulled a pan of biscuits from the wood-fired oven. His face, normally ruddy, hot-looking, glowed like neon.

"What's with all the domesticity? No dirty socks, no month old bacon grease. You hiding a wife or something?"

"I've only been here a couple weeks. It takes time to get the place lived in."

"Sounds like a damn feeble excuse to me."

"I can take my shirt off and spit a wad of snoose into the corner if it will make you feel more at home."

"No thanks. It might be too much like home. My wife's been away. Maybe you could give me some lessons...or move in?"

"Is that what brings you here?"

"Can't a guy just pay a friendly visit?"

"Is *that* what brings you here?"

"No." McIntire admitted and explained his errand.

The turquoise eyes lit up. "You got the stuff on you?"

Carlson was only mildly disappointed at the request to come back to town. His eagerness to get on the way was downright uncivil. He stuffed down his breakfast, shoved back his chair, and began pacing the room, while McIntire savored every tidbit. The man was a genius. The bacon was lean and crisp. The coffee robust. Compared to his biscuits, Leonie's scones had all the flavor of wall-paper paste.

After a third cup of coffee and a fourth biscuit, McIntire stood and brushed the last crumbs from his knees. Maybe he *could* get Carlson to give him a baking lesson. As long as he forgot everything he learned when Leonie got back.

Pete Koski removed the cigarette from between his lips and dropped the stone into the archeologist's eagerly sweating palm. "Wall thought it might be a weight for a fish net."

"Good guess." Carlson's verdict didn't take long. "But, no, it's an earspool. A body ornament. It fit in a hole in the earlobe." He held it up to his own ear. "It took a bit of stretching."

"Very becoming. How old would you say it is?"

"Pre-Columbian. Early Woodland period. Five hundred BC or so, at the oldest."

"Twenty-five hundred years." The sheriff released a stream of smoke through his teeth. "So it'd be worth a little money then?"

"Some. Not a king's ransom. Maybe a few bucks. It depends."

"On what?"

"Like anything else, who wants it and how much they're willing to pay. If it can be dated, established where it came from   " He carried the artifact to the window, turning it in the light.

Koski followed at his elbow, oblivious to the scientist's glower at the smoldering Camel. "Could it have come from anywhere around here?"

"That's what I'd like to know. Where was it found?"

"We found it in a kitchen," McIntire said, "held in a disembodied hand."

"Damn, you jackpine savages lead exciting lives."

Koski left McIntire to fill in the details of their exciting lives while he went to fetch the bones.

Carlson squinted and leaned in. "Okay if I take a closer look?"

At the sheriff's nod, he placed the hand on his own palm. "I can't tell you where these came from, but I can tell you this much, they aren't all that old. Not more than a couple years, at most. You'd better get looking for the rest of this guy."

"Shit." Koski stubbed out his cigarette.

"Not me," McIntire said. "I ain't looking for anymore bodies, and if one surfaces, I'll be burying it again—a whole lot deeper. I've had all I can take of dead people. Any more turn up, they can damn well just stay dead."

"That's up to you. Mind if I take some pictures? Of the earspool, I mean. I got no interest in the latest victim of your Yooper carnage."

Carlson went for his camera.

"Shit," Koski said again. "We can't just go out and dig up the whole damn countryside, looking for a body without a hand. Maybe we could put an announcement in the paper. Make it a contest." He shook the hand like a rattle. "On second thought, maybe not. We'd probably end up with a half dozen."

"No, we can't dig up everything, but," McIntire remembered, "we can dig where Reuben Hofer dug."

"His spud field?"

"Pete," McIntire prepared to lay out his reasoning, "according to Gary Cooper, when Reuben was at the camp, he was always making some sort of trouble."

"Ya, so I heard. He wasn't the only one."

"The common punishment was being put to work filling in a swampy spot behind the buildings."

"Oh?"

"They had to dig sand from a few hundred yards away and carry it over in a wheelbarrow."

"That could be punishment."

"Some of the guys mended their ways, most flatly refused. But Hofer was stubborn, he never learned his lesson, always ended up with that wheelbarrow. Of course he never accomplished much. Just seemed to spend the whole day fiddling around."

"Are you going to get to the point?"

It was gratifying to see Koski on the begging end for a change. McIntire explained with exaggerated patience, "They got the sand from a big dune, sort of a small hill. That's where Hofer worked all day. Mostly by himself."

"A dune? Or maybe a mound? Like the ones over on Sand Point, you think?"

"Could be."

"What's that?" Greg Carlson walked through the door, laden with an amount of photographic equipment that seemed far out of proportion to his unassuming subject.

McIntire ignored the interruption. "So, we could dig up the spot where Reuben Hofer dug."

"I guess it'd be worth taking a look."

"Hold your horses! If you're saying that's where this," Carlson waved the stone, "came from, you can't just go barging in with a shovel—"

"But if the hand died more recently...." McIntire shook his head. It had been six or seven years since Hofer and his compatriots were put to work on that dune.

"Carlson ain't infallible."

"Who says so?" Indignation was underscored by the sudden glare of a flashbulb. "I could be off by a few years. I didn't look at them that close. Things stay pretty well preserved around here."

"That's true," McIntire said. "Look at our J.P."

"Shit." The sheriff's favorite word, evoked by the mention of his least favorite person, was accompanied by another flash.

Blue spots danced in McIntire's field of vision. "It wouldn't hurt to find out if any of the COs went missing."

"You know damn well they didn't. There'd have been hell to pay."

"Somebody from outside the camp, then." There had to be some reason that hand ended up in Mary Frances Hofer's kitchen.

"Reuben buried a body in an old Indian mound? Sneaked it in when the guards got their backs turned?" Koski rolled his eyes and lit another Camel.

McIntire turned to the window. The wind had churned up white-capped waves on the bay. A young couple strolled along the shore, the girl's long pony tail lifted above her head in a sooty plume. "Maybe Hofer *found* the body," he said, "one put there a few years before, when it was a CCC camp."

"The hand is supposed to be recently deceased, remember. Anyway, If Hofer found a skeleton, why'd he keep it quiet? Seems to me a body turning up in the camp would have had those Conchies dancing in the streets."

The glare of sun on water was as blinding as the camera flash. McIntire walked to the table. "Unless He had a good reason for keeping things to himself. He spent time digging. A lot of time. Alone. Days poking around, scooping up a teaspoonful at a time. If he dug something up, something like this"—He picked up the earspool, eliciting another protest from the shutterbug—"and maybe more stuff like it, he might not want news of his good fortune to get around. If this was part of his find, he managed to smuggle it out without it being noticed."

"Or with somebody looking the other way, possibly for a small consideration," Koski said, and added, "I think we need a conference with Bruno Nickerson." He scratched his head, "That could get touchy."

"Touchy for you. Won't bother me in the least."

"Go ahead then."

"It's your job," McIntire told him. "But I'll tag along. I like to see you squirm. Anyway I need to check out the power mowers."

"We'll have to go separate then." The sheriff plucked the earspool from under Carlson's exasperated nose, wrapped it in a scrap of paper, and pocketed it. "I ain't hanging around while you window shop."

Bruno Nickerson gave a quick glance up at their entrance and went back to aiding an elderly lady in her search for the perfect picture hanger with more eagerness than he might ordinarily have shown. Koski stalked off to the back room to pave the way with his father.

The lawn mowers sat in a gleaming column by the front window. They didn't come cheap. Maybe McIntire could just get Sulo Touminen to sharpen the blades on his push mower.

The senior Koski came through, nodded unsmiling to McIntire, and took his employee's place behind the counter. With McIntire at his heels, Nickerson headed for the office, a cavern of stacked papers and a markedly oily bouquet.

"Grab a chair." The sheriff had already grabbed the substantial oak chair behind the gray steel desk, leaving the other two to grab one of the metal folding variety leaning against the wall.

Nickerson turned his around and straddled the seat, arms folded across the back in a caricature of relaxation, belied by a feverish blinking. "What's up?"

Koski leaned back and crossed his ankles, swivelling the chair enough to effect his own fraudulent display of nonchalance. "Just double checking a few things. Talking to people that used to know Reuben Hofer. Making sure we didn't miss anything."

"So what do you want to know?"

"You haven't seen Reuben since when? Nineteen-forty-three?"

"Forty-five. I already told that to...." He inclined his head toward McIntire.

"Well, you know how it is, I like to make sure of things. Check for myself." Koski gave a conspiratorial lift of his eyebrows. How could he be expected to entrust such things to a moronic township constable?

"Well, I said it before, and nothing's changed."

The sheriff nodded and picked up a pencil, running it between his fingers, tapping its eraser on the desk. "I stopped in Thursday after supper, but you weren't here."

"I only work until five."

"That's good. Good to be home with the wife and kiddies."

Nickerson shifted on the chair. The casual pose was possibly not so comfortable as he hoped it looked. "I guess. Sometimes I drop in at Ole's for a game of cribbage."

"But not on Thursday."

"Maybe not." He squinted and rubbed at his chin. "No, nope, I don't remember."

"It was the day your brother showed up. Your wife was looking for you, too."

"That's right!" Nickerson slapped his thigh. "Can you believe it? Haven't seen the guy in about eight years, and he turns up—unannounced. Just passing through, he says. Can you believe it?"

"Belinda didn't seem to know where you were either. She sort of expected you to be at the pool hall."

He winked. "Wives don't need to know everything."

"I do." Duty had apparently trumped filial sensibilities.

"Do what?"

"Need to know where you were Thursday night." He dropped both the pencil and the amiable pretense.

"Okay. You caught me," Nickerson admitted with a perfect self-effacing grin. "To tell the truth, I was hiding out."

"From your brother."

"You got it." He shook his head. "Never could stand the guy. I saw his car heading my way when I was driving to Ole's, and I just kept right on going."

"After eight years, you know what he drives?" McIntire butted in.

"It's a Jaguar. He sent pictures." He shook his head again. "Snapshots. Of his *car*. Can you believe it?"

McIntire was having a hard time believing much of anything these days.

"So where were you? When you were hiding out?"

He looked for a moment like responding to McIntire's questions was beneath him, but then shrugged. "I just drove around. Here and there. Mostly there."

"Where?"

"Far as I could get from Wally."

Koski reached into his pocket and pulled out his paper wrapped stone. He placed it on the desk and slowly unfolded the paper. Nickerson showed no particular reaction that McIntire could detect. No unease, but also no overt curiosity to accompany his, "Whatcha got there?"

"You have any idea?"

"Not the foggiest. Should I?"

Koski left it on the desk. "You know anybody that only got one hand?"

That did get a small spate of blinking. "I don't think....Well, ya, there was Wylie Petworth, the poor shit. We used to have to special order for him."

McIntire hadn't even thought about Wylie in connection with the hand. It wasn't his, of course; Wylie's arm had been removed in a hospital in Houghton almost forty years past. But it was only a year now—almost exactly—since he'd last seen Wylie, and it was odd that he hadn't come to mind. Of course, McIntire generally put a fair amount of effort into keeping thoughts of his old friend from coming to mind.

The door popped open and Sid Koski stuck his head in. "You done in here yet? We got customers to take care of sometime before the year's out."

"We're done." The sheriff nodded to Nickerson. "Sorry to take your time."

Nickerson smiled his guilty little-boy grin. "S'all right. I never complain about getting a break."

He closed the door behind him when he left, and Koski leaned back again, swivelling the chair, this time in a more convincing attitude. "That sonofabitch is lying through his teeth."

"That sonofabitch had me fooled."

Pete tossed the earspool in his hand. "He's seen it before."

"What makes you so sure?"

"Everybody I've shown it to has had the same idea of what it could be."

Even head-in-the-clouds McIntire would have figured that it was some kind of weight. Only Bruno Nickerson claimed to be totally befuddled.

"Sitting there with that shit-eating grin! That guy's seen fish nets all his life. If he didn't think it was a weight, it's because he knows Goddamned well what it is."

◇◇◇

When he turned into the driveway, McIntire saw that the big maroon priest-mobile had usurped his parking spot in the shade. The good father himself sat on the steps, wreathed in delicate wisps of smoke. How did he manage to do that? Koski always resembled a puffing stream engine. It was Doucet's second visit in little more than a week. He didn't look as though someone had died this time.

He'd also usurped McIntire's dog. Kelpie, draped across his narrow thighs, barely looked in McIntire's direction. So much for man's best friend.

"Anything new?" he asked.

McIntire supposed Doucet referred to news on the murder front. Weren't priests supposed to be above snooping into the sordid side of life? Maybe not. In a way, it was their bread and butter. He supposed that in Doucet's case the interest transcended common gossip. "Nothing you don't already know," he told him. "Matter of fact, you probably know more than any of us."

"How do you figure that?"

"You're a priest. People confide in you. Confess to you even." McIntire couldn't believe he had said it. Pete Koski would be so proud.

"They confess to God." His smile was bemused, not to say condescending. "Nobody's mentioned homicide in my confessional."

"I wasn't thinking…I only mean that Mary Frances Hofer trusts you. So do her children. You probably know more about that family than anyone."

"I don't know who killed her husband."

"Do you have a guess?"

"No." It was unequivocal, and, cynical as he was, McIntire didn't suppose that priests indulged in outright lies. He commented, "There are those who think his family is better off without him."

"No doubt there are. I'm not one of them."

That was a shocker. Father Doucet had seemed almost smug in his *the Lord will provide* attitude on the day Reuben died, assuring him that the widow would be just dandy fine.

The priest flicked his cigarette into the grass. "A few more years with Reuben might be far better than a lifetime with his sister and her clan."

"So you think she'll take them?"

"She'll try, and who's to stop her? If the kids are under age when their mother passes on, they'll have no choice in the matter, and once she gets her hands on them, they'll never get out."

"Reuben did."

"And look how he ended up!" The words were sharp enough to induce Kelpie to momentarily open both eyes; next thing to a shout. "Reuben Hofer was helpless as a newborn lamb when it came to real life. He wasn't ten minutes out of *Stalag* Prairie Oak before he got Mary Frances pregnant and ended up booted out, shunned, by that whole God-fearing bunch."

"His sister seems capable, and she seems to have the best interests of the children at heart."

"Jane Hofer seems to be the soul of kindness and self-sacrifice. In reality she's every bit the despot her brother was. It's her own interests she has in mind, and she wants those children."

The battle lines were being drawn. Mia, Jane, and Adrien Doucet. A three way tug of war for the Hofer youngsters—bodies and souls.

"What did you find out about the…the things that were on the table?" Doucet changed the subject.

"Nothing that would tell us who might have put them there. As we assumed, the stone was an Indian artifact, a couple of thousand years old."

"Nothing about the…?"

"Not so far, only that it doesn't seem to be that old."

The hairs on the priest's forearms stood noticeably erect. He seemed overly squeamish for a man who'd probably seen much of life—and death. Maybe too much; his roots were in France, in Oradour-sur-Glane, a village whose inhabitants had died at the hands soldiers of the Waffen-SS.

"Adam Wall mentioned about your family, I'm sorry." McIntire sat on the steps, just as the priest stood up, like one of those toys where you push down a peg and another pops up somewhere else.

"Thank you." Doucet pulled out his cigarette pack and turned to go. "There aren't many left of us now, and, given the circumstances, when I'm gone, that will be the end of my family."

That was true of McIntire, too, but he wasn't so despondent about it as Doucet appeared to be. Of course the McIntires hadn't been massacred by German soldiers.

Chapter Thirty-five

Sister brought them some clothes. She said that Sam and Jake had got new clothes for the funeral, so it was only fair for Claire and Joey to have some, too. Sister could be nice sometimes.

There were pants and shirts for Joey, but Sister didn't believe in girls wearing pants, so she brought Claire material for making dresses and blouses, lavender plaid and plain blue. Maybe when Sister went back home Claire would try to make some shorts. She wouldn't mind a cute dress, though. If she got to pick out the pattern herself it would be okay. If Sister picked, it would be another story.

She also got some underpants and anklets, and Sister said they would go to Chandler and buy shoes for when school started. "We don't want to do it right away," she said. "It would be too bad if you outgrew them before you got a chance to wear them!" Did that mean she was planning on staying until school started?

Joey held his new jeans in his arms like they were a baby. "I need shoes for when I have my first communion." Joey was excited about his first communion. He had the white suit from Montgomery Wards. Ma didn't tell Pa about ordering it, but he saw it when it came in the mail and was hopping mad. He carried on for hours about what a waste of money it was, but Ma put her foot down and wouldn't send it back.

Sister patted Joey's head, but she didn't say anything. She wasn't Catholic, and she probably didn't know about communion.

"We'll just make sure they're big enough to let you grow a size," Ma said. She laughed in her throat. "Maybe that's what I should have done."

Sometimes Ma's feet swelled up, more than just from being fat. So if she wanted to wear shoes, she couldn't get them on, even with Claire's help. She couldn't ever reach to put her shoes on by herself.

All the time they were talking, Sister was snooping around like she lost something. Peeking into corners, opening up cupboards and shutting them again without taking anything out. Looking for dirt. Well, let her look. She'd be so disappointed!

Sister was bossy and a martyr, but it felt better now that she was there. Safer. Even Sam and Jake weren't such smart alecs when she was around. But then she hardly ever went outside, so they didn't have to put up with her sticking her nose in their business.

The ketchup was almost gone. Claire poured a few drops of water in the bottle and shook it up. She hated watery ketchup, but the boys would eat darn near anything. Then she went to the cellar for the pan of cottage cheese, and they all sat down. They had a big bowl of summer squash, which Claire also hated, and the last of Mia Thorsen's bread. Claire didn't like to admit it, but Mrs. Thorsen's bread was the best she ever tasted. Maybe sometime she would get the chance to watch how she did it.

Claire put a scoop of cottage cheese on her plate and squished it flat with her fork, like it was potatoes. She sprinkled it with salt and a lot of pepper.

Sister took a bite of her squash. Then she put some salt on it, and added another shake to the squash in the bowl. "Is there any news?" she asked.

Claire just kept eating while Ma told about the burglar and all the rest of it. The boys' mouths practically hung open. Jake said, "You hid in the haymow? All night?"

"I had to," Claire said. "If the burglar found me, he probably would have killed me."

"Did he steal anything?"

"No." She did it again. Lied. "He didn't take anything. He just wrecked the place, and kicked Spike and hurt his leg and locked him in the closet."

"Good lord!" Maybe Mia Thorsen hadn't told Ma about Spike's leg.

Sister made a "tsk" sound, and Jake said, "Now, now, Mater, you shouldn't be taking the Lord's name in vain."

Ma said. "How do you know I didn't mean Lord Henry Brinthrope?"

They didn't have radios at Prairie Oak, so Sister didn't get the joke.

Sam talked with bread in his mouth. "I wish I'd been here."

"Why?" It was okay now that it was over, but it wasn't a night Claire'd want to have again.

He stuck out his chin. "I'd have taken care of them."

Jake choked and milk came out his nose. "You and whose army?"

They were jealous was all.

Jake stood up and gave Sam a poke. "Come on, Superman. We have to go cut the hay."

They didn't make it to the door before there was a knock on it, and they all went still. Sister tip-toed to the window and peeked out. She shook her head; no car. The knock came again, and then the door into the porch opened. "Anybody home?" It was the sheriff.

Sister opened the door and said, "Good afternoon, Mr. Koski. Please come in. We didn't hear you drive up."

He had to duck to make it through the door. "I walked. Left my car in the field." He gave his head a twitch toward the place where Pa was killed, like he didn't want to say *which* field out loud.

Ma said hello, and wasn't it a nice day, not so hot as before, thank the Lord for small favors. Then she started picking up the dishes that she could reach, stacking the plates in front of her. Sister went on, "Please sit down. The children were just on their way out."

"I'd like them to stay for a minute. I've got something I want you all to see." Sheriff Koski shoved Jake and Sam's plates out of his way, and Sister grabbed them up. Then he took a package of folded-up paper from his pocket. "Have any of you ever seen this before?" He put the package on the table and opened it.

Claire felt her heart jump. "That's mine!" She snatched up the wheel. Her special magic charm with the hole in it. What was he doing with it?

Things were very quiet for a minute, then Ma coughed and leaned toward her. "Come here. Let me see."

Claire walked around the table and opened her hand.

"Are you sure it's yours? Where did you get it?"

The wheel lay in her hand. Something was wrong; she could feel her own charm rubbing against her chest. "No," Claire had to say. "It's not mine." It was different. Almost the same but not quite. This rock was a different color and it had some lines cut in it. "I made a mistake. I used to have a rock like this, but it wasn't this one."

"You used to? Where is it now?"

"I don't know." Her heart thumped against the lucky wheel, and her face felt hot. "I haven't seen it for a while. I guess it's lost."

"Where did you get the one you had?" The sheriff looked hard at her.

Clare tried to stare back. "I found it. Back in Iowa. It wasn't exactly all that much like this one, now that I see it up close."

Sheriff Koski took the rock from her and put it back on the table. "Have any of you seen anything like this? Any idea of what it might be?"

Sam spoke up. "It's a weight of some sort, like on the fly nets Grandpa used to have for his horses."

"Have you seen one before?"

"No," Sam told him. "No, I guess not."

No one else said a thing, and the sheriff asked, "Do you know anybody who collects Indian things? Did Mr. Hofer have anything like this?"

"Is that what this is?" Ma poked at the stone. "An Indian thing?"

"Ya. From a couple of thousand years ago."

Did that mean that Claire's charm was an old Indian thing, too? Two thousand years old? That was why Pa said to not lose it. Maybe she *was* kidnapped from a tribe. She scrunched her shoulders in case they saw the lump under her blouse. "It could be it belongs to Mia Thorsen," she said. She knew it didn't, but it might make them forget about her. And about Pa.

"Why?"

"Mia Thorsen is an Indian, you know."

The sheriff looked like he thought she was lying again. "I don't think this is hers," he said. "And it doesn't belong to any of you?" He looked at Sam and Jake.

They shook their heads.

"Okay, you can all run along then. I want to talk to your mother."

For once Claire was happy to run along.

Chapter Thirty-six

"The kid pounced on it like Christmas candy. Sure as hell, she'd seen it before." Koski slapped the car roof. "Then she got all foxy. Said she 'use to' have one like it but it must have got lost."

"Why would she lie about it?"

"Who the hell knows what goes on in a kid's mind? My guess is she knew it was something her old man had, or something her old man had swiped."

"If he'd stolen it, would she know it?"

"Kids know plenty you'd never suspect. Especially girls." Koski, with his three daughters, was no doubt in a far better position than McIntire to make that judgement.

"But Reuben Hofer didn't leave that stone on the table."

"No, I don't suppose he did. The hand's been dead too long to be his. But it belonged to somebody who's either dead or walking around short a limb. That's a little more serious than a stolen rock. Or even a stolen earring."

"But, like you said, we can't just dig up the countryside looking for a one-handed corpse."

"No we can't, and it ain't turning out to be all that easy to dig at the CO camp. It's federal property. We need a warrant, and Carlson is making a god-awful fuss about not messing things up. A one-handed living person might be easier to find."

"It would be crazy to think the hand belongs to somebody who just misplaced it."

"This whole damn thing is crazy. I sent it off to the state police. No point in doing anything much until we get it checked out by an expert. If they can say approximately how old it is once and for all, we can put out the word for any people missing around that time. I don't know what else we can do now."

There didn't seem to be anything else. He was right; if the bones postdated Reuben's time at the CO camp, as Carlson seemed to think, there was no point in looking for the rest of the body there.

McIntire said, "If Reuben was walking off with some valuable artifacts, he'd have had to find some way to smuggle them out of the camp—and somewhere to smuggle them *to*. I can't think he'd have turned it all over to Bruno. He could have passed the stuff on to somebody in town, somebody he trusted more, as in Wanda Greely. Wanda and Bruno might been more than just casual acquaintances, or card playing buddies. And one more thing, he added. "Wanda Greely lied when she said she hadn't seen Reuben Hofer since he left here in forty-five."

"Ya?"

"She mentioned that back in those days he didn't have the beard, so she apparently knew he'd grown one lately."

"Was his picture in the paper? That might have shown him with the whiskers."

McIntire hadn't thought of that. But, "No. I didn't see a picture, and photographs might be another of those things Hofer didn't believe in. Their wedding photo was of Mary Frances alone."

"Wanda might have heard about it."

Koski had a point. Hofer's whiskers were unusual enough to provoke comment. "Well, you kind of had to be there. The way she said, 'He was good looking. He didn't have the beard then,' gave me the distinct impression she'd seen him with that beard."

"Well, we'd better get back at her. Check out her alibi with her husband, for all the good that'll do."

"There's a kid. He might not lie."

"Surely you jest."

McIntire hoped it wasn't Leonie's absence that led to his ready agreement to once again pay a visit to Wanda Greely.

Chapter Thirty-seven

Sister came into the kitchen and turned off the radio right in the middle of Queen for a Day. At first Ma didn't say anything. Then it was like she remembered that Pa wasn't there, and they could do what they wanted.

"Jane, this isn't the colony." She made a 'tut' with her lips, but she didn't turn the radio back on or tell Sister off.

Sister didn't pay any attention. She talked softly, like that was the only polite way to talk, and you couldn't do it with the radio on. It made it sound like she was saying nice things, even if the words weren't nice. "Are you sure Joseph should be spending so much time with that man?"

"What man? Father Doucet?" Ma sounded like she couldn't believe her ears. "He comes to see to Joey's religious instruction. I think it's very thoughtful, since I can't take him to the catechism classes."

"They are not studying religion now." She grabbed the kettle of water out of Claire's hands without asking.

Father was outside with Joey, watching Sam put posts in for a new fence by the barn.

Sister dumped the water in the dishpan. She turned away quick when the cloud of steam hit her face and said, "He might not be the best influence on a young boy."

"A priest? A bad influence?"

"He smokes, and he probably drinks." She looked at Claire and spoke even softer. "Who knows what else those people might do. It's all secret." Ma didn't answer that, and Sister said, "Not to mention that he keeps Joseph from his chores."

"He's eight years old!" Ma just shook her head. "Like I said, this isn't the Colony." She switched the radio back on.

Sister had to talk louder. "No, it is not, and I think it is time I went back."

She'd just got there. Claire had been thinking she was going to stay for a long time.

Ma said, "Oh, my goodness!" like she didn't want her to go, but then right away she added, "If you think it's best. When were you planning on leaving?"

"In a day or two." It sounded like Sister's mind was made up already, or else Ma not asking her to stay made it up then and there. "And I will take Claire and Joseph with me. With all that's happening now, this is no place for them."

Claire almost dropped the bowl she was carrying. Sister sounded like she'd made up her mind about that, too.

"I couldn't get along without Claire, you know that."

"Just Joseph then. For the time being, anyway."

Ma didn't say anything for awhile. She just stared out the window to where Joey was standing with Father Doucet. Now they were looking at the swallow nests on the barn. "I don't think that would be a good idea."

It was funny. When Sister talked, she sounded all gentle, but her words were like there'd be no arguing with her. Ma said, "I don't think," like she wasn't quite sure, but you could tell by the sound of her voice that she meant, "nothing doing!"

Sister didn't seem to know that. She scrubbed at the scalloped potatoes burned onto the sides of the roaster until Claire thought she'd go right through. "Joseph will be much better off away from here. At least until this business about Reuben is over."

Ma just tapped her fingers on the table for a while. Then she said, "Claire, go out and ask Father to come inside. You can stay out and keep Joey company."

"What kind of advice do you expect to get from him? He is not going to give up one of his merry band."

"I'm not looking for advice. I just told you. My children are staying with me. All of them."

Sister dumped the dishwater down the sink with a whoosh. It probably flooded out Joey's farm. She dried her hands on her apron. "I'll go fetch the pied piper. I need Joseph now, anyway." She stomped out the door without waiting.

Claire stood next to Ma, and they watched out the window.

"Maybe we'll have a fist fight on our hands," Ma said.

"I'm betting on Sister."

"She's got the power, I'll grant you that, but Father's light on his feet."

They couldn't hear what the two were saying, but it was enough to make Sister send Joey off to the hen house, and Sam stop his hammering to listen. He was around the corner of the barn, so Ma and Claire could see him, but Sister didn't know he was there.

They talked for a few minutes. Mostly Sister talked, with her hands folded in front of her, and Father listened. Then Sam must have made some noise, because Sister looked in his direction, and walked farther away. She talked a little more, lifting her clasped hands to her chest like she was praying. Then she went after Joey, and Father Doucet headed for the house, looking sort of pale.

"Seems like I owe you," Ma straightened her dress. "She certainly seems to have got the better of him."

Claire zipped outside to where Sam was nailing the top wire to the fence posts. He was nicer when Jake wasn't around. He might tell. Claire asked, "What were they talking about?"

"Never you mind."

"Ma wants to know."

"Liar." He gave a whack with the hammer.

"She wants to take Joey away with her, was that it?"

"She wants to take you, too, Smarty Pants." Sam looked at the sun and sneezed three times. Claire wished she could do that.

"Ma already said no. Tell me what she said, or, next time I sweep up, I'll accidentally find your cigarettes."

That did the trick. Claire was proud of herself. She didn't have any idea where the boys hid cigarettes.

"She said Ma was too blind to see what needed to be done, but that Father Doucet had…influence. Ma'd do what he said, and if he let religion get in the way of children being protected, she didn't think much of his precious church. And then," he squinted at the sun and gave another loud sneeze, "she said she knew he'd see reason, and she'd let him know how to get in touch when that time came."

"She's going home in a couple of days." Claire was glad to be able to tell something Sam didn't know. "I'll get her to make some cinnamon rolls before she goes."

"Sister ain't gonna take orders from you."

"All I have to do is get out the yeast. She'll come nosing along and take over."

Chapter Thirty-eight

Wanda Greely's home was damn near as pink as her shop, and that was only on the outside. She stood in the doorway in a sunset-colored blouse blinking her astonishment, or perhaps it was meant to be a seductive batting of eyelashes.

"Not to be rude, but what do you want now?" It was definitely run of the mill blinking. "Sheriff sent you on another little errand, has he?"

She opened the door just wide enough for McIntire to get through without quite brushing against the parts of her body that thrust out the farthest. McIntire decided to take that as a welcome.

The door opened directly into the living room. McIntire was getting so habituated to the rosy hues surrounding Mrs. Greely, that he hardly noticed more than the puce-colored scrollwork that trimmed the case filled with fishing rods and hunting rifles. That was a novel touch.

"Is your husband at home?" he asked.

"They've gone fishing. You're safe."

"I was hoping to have a word with him, too."

"Corroborate my alibi, as they say? Why bother? We've had plenty of time to cook up a story between us." She stood with her arms folded, not exactly tapping her foot, but her toe was twitching.

"A story for Thursday, maybe not for Friday."

"I need one for Friday now, too, do I? You have a remarkably short memory. On Friday, I was trying to chase you out of my shop."

That was true. For a short part of Friday anyway.

McIntire took the earspool from his pocket. "Have you seen this before?"

"No. Not to remember. What is it?"

"Don't you know?"

She held it between her thumb and forefinger and put it to her eye, peering at him through the hole. "I spy." She dropped it back in his hand. "It could be a curtain weight, but it's sort of thick and lumpy."

"A curtain weight?"

She walked to the window, toes protruding from her fluffy mules that sank into pale coral carpet, then bent, in a way that tightened her clothing across all the rounder areas, to lift one of the magenta colored draperies. "It's sewn into the hem. To keep them hanging straight." She smoothed the curtain over her hand, exposing a circular shape in the cloth. Then she let it drop with a thump.

"Do you know anybody with only one hand?" McIntire asked.

"I don't think so." It was accompanied by no blinking or batting. "I met a woman the other day with only four fingers, though. She was at the Hofers'. Maybe you should go after her."

A slam sounded at the back of the house. "Mom!" Quick footsteps sounded and a door at the end of the room swung open bringing a rush of cool air and a stocky white-haired boy holding a stringer with a pair fat walleyes. "Two! I landed them myself!"

His excited babble was joined by a voice deeper and filled with laughter. "Bring them back to the sink." The door opened wider. "Hello! I didn't know we had company. Let me just wash this fish off my hands." The two of them disappeared, leaving the door swinging.

None of Reuben Hofer's son's had inherited his hungry-hawk eyes. None except this one.

Wanda Greely's hand, and her eyes, extended toward McIntire in a gesture of defeat and pleading.

She waved him into a chair, seated herself on the sofa and took a cigarette from a box on the coffee table. By the time her husband was back, all soapy-clean, she was herself again. "This is John McIntire, Darling. He's been sent direct from the county sheriff, investigating Reuben Hofer's death."

From all appearances, Chet Greely was older than Wanda by a few years, but not by enough to be some doddering sugar-daddy who'd be likely to have had the wool pulled over his eyes. He sat next to her, his body turned slightly away to face McIntire. "That was an awful business. Four kids."

"Did you know Mr. Hofer?" McIntire had to start somewhere.

"Not really. Wanda mentioned him a time or two. But I don't recall that I ever met him. I was away most of the time then, working at the shipyards in Superior. 'Course Wanda had them flocking around, soon as they heard her old man was out of town." It was a simple statement of fact, delivered with neither jocularity nor rancor and with a squeeze around his wife's shoulders. He said again, "Terrible thing for that family. Four kids."

Mr. Greely seemed genuinely concerned, relaxed, and amiable. A different animal from Wanda.

"There was some disturbance at the Hofers' home on Thursday evening, and again on Friday. We're asking everybody who knew them to tell us what they were doing on those two occasions."

"Disturbance? And you're asking Wanda?"

"And you. If you don't mind."

"Far as I remember, we were here, together, like always." He didn't turn to see his wife's affirming nod.

"With your son?"

Wanda spoke with cold formality. "Would you like me to call him?"

"That won't be necessary, Mrs. Greely." McIntire addressed her husband. "You say you never met Reuben Hofer?"

"No…. No, I never laid eyes on the man." His demeanor remained bemused and affable, but when McIntire stood, he could see that Greely's hand, behind his wife's back, was clenched into a fist.

The earspool hadn't been found dangling off Mia Thorsen's absent finger, but she might be worth consulting. She'd spent that afternoon cleaning the Hofers' house and had done a damn thorough job of it. If Reuben had a stash of artifacts, she might have seen something.

McIntire found her on her knees, pulling weeds from around some beets, a reminder that he hadn't touched Leonie's vegetable garden since she left.

Mia's garden had always been the source of undisguised amusement, bordering on ridicule, in the neighborhood, but she seemed to be putting a little—or possibly a lot—more effort into it this summer. Her husband's lack of employment might have something to do with that, both from its impact on her grocery bill and…"Hiding out?" McIntire asked.

She straightened up, rubbing both knees. "I used to read at this time of day, have a piece of cake, a cup of coffee, maybe a wee nap. Now, with Nick home all day…."

"He disapproves?"

"Naps and cake are only worthwhile when you take them on the sly."

Maybe that was why existence without Leonie had lost so much of its punch. Had Mia discovered the secret of life? Guilty pleasures?

"How's Nick doing?"

"Not so bad. It's easier now, with the weather good. I'm not looking forward to winter."

Here was another situation in which McIntire was lost without Leonie. She had ways of finding things out without seeming snoopy. The best McIntire could do was, "Is he getting any sort of treatment? Medication?"

Mia shook her head. "He won't hear of it. He doesn't even drink anymore, not even though Guibard said it might do him some good, in moderation." That brought a smile. "Nick never was one for moderation."

She wiped her hands on her baggy, too short, trousers. "I was hoping that you'd come to tell me what went on at Hofers' house that sent you scurrying over here the other night."

"I came to show you." McIntire dug into his pocket. "I thought maybe you might have seen something like it when you were cleaning."

Mia took it from his hand and held it up to the sun. "I have. Not when we were cleaning, and not exactly the same. Fancier. The carving was different, and it looked like it had some copper on it at one time."

"You saw it in their house?"

"No." She twirled the stone on the tip of one of her remaining fingers. "It was on a string around Claire Hofer's neck. She said her father gave it to her."

"You didn't see this one anywhere?"

She shook her head. "You're not going to take it from her, are you? The poor little waif has practically nothing, and she was so proud of it. I stupidly told her that Papa made the furniture in the bedroom for me when I was a kid."

"It might have been stolen."

"From where?" A trickle of blood, dark and crusted, ran below her ear, the attack of a late season black-fly.

"Reuben might have dug it up when he was in the CPS camp."

"Dug it up? That's not stealing."

"It is if it's on federal land." According to Carlson, digging on federal land was illegal, but maybe he had ulterior motives.

"Stealing from the government doesn't count. It's almost anti-American not to."

"It could also be the item whoever ransacked the house was looking for." And so might not be the safest thing for a small girl to have hanging around her neck.

"Is it valuable?"

"Greg Carlson said not terribly. But if Hofer had an entire collection of the stuff, all together it could be worth a tidy sum."

"They're dirt poor. If Papa Hofer had a pile of gold doubloons and pieces of eight, wouldn't he have sold them long ago?"

"I suppose he would have. That's probably why the burglar doesn't seem to have found what he was looking for."

"You didn't answer my question. Are you going to take it from her?"

"That's hardly up to me."

"Is it important? You've got this one." She handed it back. "And you know that she's got the other one. Why would you need to actually have it in your hot little hand? If Reuben Hofer stole it, I doubt he told his daughter that when he gave it to her. It's hers. What do you need it for?"

Mia could make the most ridiculous thing sound so perfectly reasonable. "It's evidence," McIntire floundered. "Evidence in a murder case. Maybe two murder cases."

"Two?"

He told her about the hand. "Well, just bones. A skeleton hand."

"Wylie didn't save his, did he? Pass it on?" She'd thought of it right away. Mia had always had a penchant for the macabre, but given her role in Wylie Petworth's present circumstances, he was amazed that she spoke of it so lightly.

"Don't be morbid. Anyway Carlson says the bones aren't more than a couple of years old."

Her smile disappeared like a light switched out.

"A couple of years since they were alive, I mean." McIntire explained.

"Are you going over to Hofers' now?"

"No. I'll leave that to Koski."

"But you'll tell him."

"Of course, I'll tell him."

"I suppose you have to. And he'll figure he's got to confiscate it and tell Claire that the only thing her father ever gave her was something he stole. He was a thief as well as a…pacifist."

It did sound callous. "I'm sorry, Mia. She might be able to keep it. But," he added, "she shouldn't be wearing the thing, in case the wrong person sees it."

Mia picked at the green stains around her fingernails. "Let me tell her?"

"Well…."

"Please. I'll try to explain so she can understand. She's afraid of you, and she might change her mind about Pete Koski, too, once he starts trying to take away her keepsakes. And it will make me seem less of a snitch."

"I guess it'd be okay." She might be right after all. It probably didn't matter very much anyway, unless, of course, Claire did know where her father got the artifact.

"It might make things slightly better. None of this is okay."

No, not for the Hofer family or for Mia herself. "How are *you* doing?" McIntire asked.

"Me? Just fine. I've got an indoor toilet and Nick helping out with every little thing. What more could I want?"

"You're trying to say that like it's true."

"It should be true."

"What? You should be happy to have Nick home, underfoot all the time, invading your territory?" It wasn't quite like Reuben Hofer's return to the bosom of his family, but there were parallels.

"I didn't used to think I *had* a territory. When Nick first started getting sick, I agonized over what a fool I'd been for letting myself get so completely dependent on him. I figured that without his income and his driving, I'd be helpless, and we'd both wither away and die. Now I realize that I ran things around here exactly the way I wanted them, and I worked hard at it. I liked it that way. I know he's had to give up just about everything that was important to him, and it's only going to get worse, but his incessant interfering is driving me crazy!"

"That's not hard to understand—and to sympathize with. Anybody would feel the same." McIntire wondered if Leonie felt that way. She'd been single almost as many years as he had. Did he interfere with her running things the way she wanted them. He didn't think so, but she might see it different. Was just his being there, in her way twenty-four hours a day, enough to get on her nerves?

"I need something else," she stated. "I need some new territory."

"What about…?" McIntire inclined his head toward the workshop.

"No. That's just something to keep busy. An excuse to kill time. It always has been. I need to do something with my life, with whatever years I have left. Something more important than hope chests and clock cases. I need to do something that makes a difference to people."

To two small people in particular. She'd been hovering—scrubbing, combing hair, pushing food like she was fattening them for the county fair. She wanted more, and he sympathized with that, too. He also knew that it wouldn't happen, and she would be hurt once again. Mia's life had been a string of pain, and McIntire had been responsible for some of the worst. That indoor toilet might just be its high point.

"You're thinking that soon I'll have my hands too full for anything else."

He hadn't been, but it was undoubtedly true.

"I'm not going to let Nick's illness take over both our lives."

"Do you think you can stop it?"

"No, of course not." The smile was bleak. "I'm not a complete idiot."

Mia handled her adversities well. McIntire wasn't sure how she'd deal with good fortune, if it ever came her way. Would she recognize it if she saw it?

"Well, if you can direct me to him, I'll get Nick out of your hair for a while right now."

"He's inside, working on the radio."

"What's wrong with it?"

"There wasn't a darn thing wrong with it, until Nick decided it needed fixing. Now I imagine it's a lost cause."

Nick was at the table in the seldom-used dining room, his nose about six inches from a line-up of tubes and screws. His hand shook as he attempted to poke a wire through something in the guts of the radio. "I think the damn thing's shot."

The damn thing was almost certainly shot. "Good excuse to get a new one." McIntire took a chair. "I'd help you out if I could."

Nick put his hands in his lap. "What's new?"

"Not a hell of a lot, unfortunately. Maybe *you* can help me out."

"Long as your radio don't need fixing."

"Who's lived in the old schoolhouse before Hofers? I know he bought it from Maki, but I don't suppose he and Grace ever lived there."

McIntire leaned forward to catch Nick's words as they bubbled out, soft, rapid, monotone.

"Matter of fact, they did, for a while. Mike bought the school and the land it stood on when he wasn't much more than a kid. It was only a couple of acres, but it was joined up to his old man's farm. He built that midget barn, and the hen house, too, I suppose. When he got married, him and Grace lived there for a few years until Sumo died, then they moved back to the old place with Mike's Ma and rented the school out."

"To who? Whom?"

Nick ran his fingers through his enviably thick hair. "There was a young couple with a baby. Some kinda Bohunk name, I forget. He worked for the REA when they put the highline in. They pulled out when it was done. It was for a couple years, and then Hector Monson moved in."

"The old trapper?"

"Trapping, ya. And trying to learn taxidermy. He was taking a correspondence course. But he wasn't old. I don't think he was forty yet."

"I thought he died?"

"Electrocuted. Looked like he was trying to stick a mousetrap in the attic wall and touched the wrong wires. Threw a scare into Mike. He figured if Hector'd had any relatives, he'd have got the shit sued out of him. So he decided to retire from the landlord business. Got the wiring fixed and sold the place, along with about twenty acres."

"That's all Hofer had? Twenty?"

"He was farming the rest on shares. Mike's had to cut back. He ain't been the same since he took that nose-dive off the roof, and with Ross in Korea...."

So that's where the badger had come from. "You say Monson didn't have any relatives?"

"None they could locate."

"So his personal stuff, was it just left in the house?" His personal shotguns, for instance?

"Some of it. He owed money here and there. His car, traps, anything worth selling, the county auctioned."

"That would include guns, I take it?"

"I see what you're getting at. It would include guns. But Koski knows that. It was only a couple of years ago. He'd have handled the auction."

Chapter Thirty-nine

"What did Wicked Wanda have to say?" If Koski had made the trip all the way to McIntire's house just to find that out, he was going to be disappointed.

"She said it looked like a curtain weight."

"I rest my case. Nickerson's full of shit. Did she mention how she knew Hofer died with a beard on?"

"I didn't bother to ask." Truth be known, he hadn't thought to ask, but Koski was right, anyway. She'd just say she'd learned about it through beauty shop gossip. "What about you?" McIntire asked. "Heard anything about the hand yet?"

"Not a peep. And they're taking their damn sweet time with it. Last I heard they sent it off to the university."

Carlson had seemed to think that dating the bones wouldn't be much of a trick, and what more could they do? Bring in a clairvoyant to conjure up their owner? McIntire said, "I can see Bruno and Wanda in cahoots with Hofer on making off with some valuable souvenirs, but I can't see them chopping somebody's hand off."

"Or shooting their partner in the head?"

"Especially if he's the only one knows where the loot is stashed."

"They're just ain't anybody else." Koski said. He plucked a soiled dishtowel off a chair and sat down.

"There are two young men who hated his guts."

"Shit."

"For Christ's sake, Pete, get your head out of the sand! They had motive, they had opportunity, and they might damn well have had the means. There was a trail straight through that oat field. They were less than a half mile from where Papa ended up dead, but they still claimed not to have heard a shot." That was curious. Even if they'd done it, they'd have no reason to lie about hearing the gunshot. Better to lie about *when* they heard, if that would give them an alibi. Of course Sam had made that vague statement about a car backfiring.

"They killed him just because he made them work hard? With him gone, they'd have twice as much work piled on them. What good would it do?"

"They'd have done it because they hated him, not because they're a pair of do-gooders. They're kids. They're dumb."

"What about the weapon?"

"We don't know they didn't have a gun."

"They all tell the same story, even the girl."

"Right," McIntire said. "They sure do, same old song and dance. 'Pa was a pacifist. Pa didn't believe in guns.' None of them have come right out and said they don't have one." There was still a member of the family they hadn't asked. "What about the little guy?"

"What about him?"

"Nobody's talked to him," McIntire pointed out. "He might be too young to lie."

"I ain't sure they're ever too young. But unless he tells us where it is now, what good would it do? We can't haul him into court to testify against the rest of the family."

"We could get a warrant, search the place."

"I went through the place with the girl, remember. There is no gun in that house, unless it's damn well hid."

"There wouldn't be, would there? They wouldn't keep it around." They should have had that warrant in their hands the day Reuben Hofer died. McIntire knew that, and Koski surely did, too. But they wouldn't have found anything then, either.

"If those boys shot their father, they'd have got rid of the gun. The question is how and where."

"They were digging in a potato patch at the time." Koski raised his eyebrows.

"Nothing doing! We can't plow up their potatoes, or their oats, or anything else."

"Gopher Hansen's got a metal detector. War surplus."

It sounded like a good idea to McIntire. If the kids had planted a shotgun along with the potatoes, they'd find it without doing too much damage. There was another aspect to things, and he couldn't very well ignore it. "Pete, when Wanda Greely ran those card games which may or may not have been just gossip, was Mr. Greely involved?"

"She might not have been married then."

"Okay, did the future Mr. Greely take part in the socializing?"

"Beats me. Why?"

"Have you seen Little Greely Junior?"

"Their kid? Not to notice. Should I?"

"You don't need to bother. You just have to take a gander at Little Hofer Junior."

"What are you trying to say? Is this your evil mind at work again?"

"It doesn't take a mind anywhere near as evil as mine to figure out that Hofer was playing more than five card stud with Wanda."

"Why the hell didn't you tell me this before? Finally! Somebody with a motive!"

"What motive?"

Koski stared. "Hofer was fiddling with Greely's wife and you ask me what motive?"

"I thought you said she wasn't married then."

"I said *maybe* she wasn't. But maybe she was, and I intend to find out. Even if she was single, she sure as hell must have been married by the time the little tyke was born. Greely probably didn't even know the kid wasn't his." His brows drew together in a cartoon-like parody of shrewdness. "Until maybe he ran into Reuben Hofer and his boys in town."

"In that case wouldn't he have more of a quibble with the little woman?"

Koski turned to the door. "Maybe she'll be next."

Chapter Forty

Claire Hofer was stretched on her toes, hanging out washing, and Mia was cheered to be greeted with a spontaneous smile, the first she'd seen the child direct at anybody save the charming Pete Koski. She might as well enjoy it. Once she'd commandeered the earspool she wasn't likely to be so welcomed.

"Can I give you a hand?" Mia asked.

She shook her head. "My aunt is here." That explained the boxy plaid dress with the hemline six inches too low for a young girl.

"I'll just go in and say hello." Mia wasn't particularly eager to spend the time of day with Jane Hofer, but curiosity overcame her hesitancy.

The sound of her approach was masked by the thumping washing machine, and Mia had the advantage of getting a good look at the aunt before she knocked. The woman had stayed in the background at Reuben's wake, and Mia hadn't met her, or even seen her, except from the back. Miss Hofer was not the plain, old maid type Mia had anticipated, maybe even hoped. Despite a body that might be called 'sturdy,' Jane was neither plain nor particularly old. She stood with sleeves rolled past her elbows, feeding towels into the rotating wringer, singing in a clear, strong alto, words Mia couldn't work out over the noise of the machine. Her pale hair was pulled back and covered with a kerchief in a way that would have been dowdy on someone without the peaches and cream complexion and with a less dreamy smile on her face.

The cerebral expression was wiped away by Mia's rap at the door. She looked up with as much annoyance as if Mia had been peeping through her bedroom window.

"Good morning," she said and switched off the washer. Mia might not have known the smile was a false one if she hadn't just seen the real thing. "You must be Mrs. Thorsen."

Mia nodded and ducked under the doorjamb, not wondering how she'd guessed. She gave the commonplace "just stopped by" introduction. "How are you all doing?"

"Very well, thank you."

Mia couldn't believe that any of them were doing very well, outside of Jane Hofer herself, perhaps. "They're lucky to have you," she said, and couldn't help adding, "Will you be staying long?"

"As long as is necessary."

Which could mean anything from five minutes to five years, "That's good. I'll just go in and say hello to Mary Frances."

Jane smiled and bowed her head in acquiescence and dismissal. As Mia entered the kitchen, the rhythm of the washer began anew.

The shock at first seeing her never wore off. Did the woman ever move? More than that, *how* did the she ever move any distance? Had her husband helped her in and out of bed? Without him would she have to call upon her sons to do it?

Mrs. Hofer sat wrapped in a bedsheet-sized apron, pallid and damp looking like a colossal infant fresh from the bath.

Her smile, like her daughter's, was welcoming to the point that Mia pulled out a chair and sat, without waiting for an invitation. In response to her "How are you?" Mary Frances spread her ludicrously tiny hands. "Getting back to normal, slow but sure." Her nervous chuckle fluttered out. "Well, I don't suppose life will ever be completely normal again."

"No," Mia agreed. "I don't suppose it will, not for you anyway. Your children seem to be coping."

"Yes, thank the Lord."

There was not much more to say about that, and Mia had come on a mission. "Speaking of which, I was hoping you could spare Claire for an hour or two. I promised to help her make something in my studio—my workshop. A toy for Joey."

Mary Frances' smile was a delight to see. "That's very kind of you. Claire mentioned that you did woodworking. She could certainly use some fun for a change."

"I think today might not be a good time." The omnipresent spirit-dampener that was Jane Hofer spoke from beyond the open door.

Mrs. Hofer's lips thinned more than Mia would have supposed possible. "What's the problem?"

"We're planning a sewing lesson for this afternoon." Jane strode in, oxfords clippity-clopping on the wood floor. "And I've sent her to find some lamb's quarter." She swept through to the living room, as though the final word had been spoken. Apparently it had; as her sister-in-law's steps faded up the stairs, Mrs. Hofer rolled her eyes, but sighed, "Maybe some other time."

"Most any day will be fine." Mia's irritation was tempered with relief at the reprieve for telling Claire where her charm had come from.

Mary Frances spoke softly. "All of a sudden she's got all-fired up to leave, and she's going tomorrow. I guess it won't hurt to humor her for one more day."

So that was how long her presence would be necessary. Odd that she'd been so circumspect about her plans when Mia asked. She should tell Mary Frances about Claire having the earspool and its possibly being stolen. It didn't seem right to keep it from her, but once again it didn't seem like her responsibility. Footsteps sounded on the stairs again. She'd leave it for now.

Sister Jane didn't return to the kitchen, and Mia left the house without bidding her goodbye.

Joey was engrossed in his lilliputian agricultural pursuits, directing a silver and grey tractor, pulling a wagon loaded with stones, along his miniature roads. So that was that. When she did get her hands on Claire, they'd have to come up with a different sort of toy. Maybe she'd go all out and build a barn, with real windows and a cupola, paint it red with…. She knelt by his side. "I see you have a new tractor."

"Sister brought it from the funeral."

"Your farm is growing. Before you know it, you'll need two tractors, and maybe a few hired hands."

"It's like Grandpa's. Where we used to live." Any wistfulness was counteracted by the enthusiastic spark in his eyes.

"Did your Grandpa have a tractor like this?"

"No. His was red, all red."

"I like this one."

"Me too. Look out, here it comes! *Kabloomp!*" He dumped the load of stones. "It's a Ford."

"It would have been nice for her to go." Their conversation was interrupted by Mary Frances Hofer, clear as if she was hunkered down in the dirt next to them.

"Sewing will be of much greater good to her than playing around in a woodshop." The words came through the drainpipe in the wall, a direct line to the kitchen.

"I'm still alive, Jane, and they're still my children." Mrs. Hofer might have been shouting through a megaphone.

The boy began piling peeled twigs into his empty wagon, fuzzy white head bent close to the ground.

"Jocy—" Mia intended a reprimand, an injunction against eavesdropping on one's elders, but stopped short at the tear that splashed onto the tractor's thumb-sized seat. She stood and held out her hand. "Come with me," she commanded. "I'm going to show you how to make a willow whistle."

He scrambled up. Mia hoped she remembered how to make the whistle.

Chapter Forty-one

"Just stand normal, don't suck in your breath." Sister's hands were like ice, as she measured Claire around the waist and chest. "You haven't grown hardly at all since last summer." She made it sound like that was Claire's own fault.

When she was done, she moved Ma's magazines off the table and laid out the plaid material. She didn't have a pattern; it would just be a plain dress like her old ones, or maybe a jumper.

Claire left her doing the cutting and went to the living room to wind two bobbins and thread the machine. She took a piece of brown flannel from Ma's box of scraps and made a little bag like Mia Thorsen's. It was kind of puckery when she turned it the right way out, and she couldn't get it under the needle to hem up the top. She'd have to do that part by hand.

Sister came and started setting up the ironing board. "Are you making something?"

"A pillow case," Claire told her. "A doll pillow case."

"I didn't know you played with dolls."

"I don't. It's just practice sewing."

Sister hung over Claire's shoulder for a while, which made Claire feel like screaming, then she held out her hand. "Let me see."

Claire wanted to tell her to mind her own business, but she handed it over. Sister turned it inside out again. She took the scissors and snipped at the corners. When she turned it back the right way, the puckers were gone. "There. If you iron it now, it will stay flat."

Claire smoothed it with her fingers.

"Isn't that better?" Sister didn't mean it like most people did, saying it just to have something to say. She wanted an answer.

"Yes, it's better," Claire stood up. "I was just waiting for you to get done with the scissors."

"I see." She said it with a sigh, like Claire was an idiot. "Do you want to use the machine now? To hem the edge?"

"No, I'm going to do it by hand." Claire stood up. "Later." She went out to the kitchen and gave Ma back her magazines and poured her a cup of coffee.

Ma put down the magazine. "Is the bread sponge ready?"

Claire peeked under the dish towel. It looked ready to her. She put the pan on the table and got some flour from the sack in the bin.

Ma dipped flour and sifted it onto the sponge. It wasn't easy for her to reach. "Is that a car?" She started brushing the flour off her arms and the front of her apron.

Claire looked out. It was Mike Maki, the man Pa bought their house from. He had a bad limp.

If they hadn't seen him coming, they'd have never known he was there, his tap sounded like it was a chipmunk at the door. Claire grabbed up the sifter so he wouldn't see the mouse turds left in the bottom, and Ma called to him to come in. He opened the door but just stood leaning against the frame. His hair was stuck to his head in a circle when he took his cap off. He said if the boys finished cutting and raking up the hay, he'd come and bale it for them. Some of what had already been cut might be shot from being on the ground so long, but they'd do what they could. Then he said how awful it was about Pa not being here to do it himself.

Usually Claire hung around to listen when they had company, if she could get away with it, but today she didn't want to hear any more.

She had to go through the living room to get outside, because of Mike Maki blocking the kitchen door. Sister was fiddling around with the iron, holding off on her sewing so she could hear what was going on.

Claire threw the turds out of the sifter and sat on the steps for awhile trying to decide what to do. Spike put his paws and his head on her knee. He was almost too big now to get on her lap, and probably his leg still hurt. She felt around his ears and on his stomach for woodticks. He only had two, and one was still flat and brown. She pulled them off and threw them across the yard. The boys always killed them, by burning them with a match or popping them with their fingernails. Claire didn't mind touching woodticks, but killing them was way too ishy.

She could hear the tractor, far off, like on the day Pa died. Jake was already finishing raking the hay. She wondered if he was scared, looking behind him every so often. What if Jake was murdered, too?

She hopped up. "Come on, Boy. Let's go for a walk."

When she got down the driveway on onto the road, Joey was right behind her. "Where you going?"

"Berry picking." It was the first thing that came into her head.

"You don't have anything to put them in."

"I'm just scouting, for later on."

"That's stupid."

Making things up sometimes meant you had to act like what you said was true. "Oh, okay. Go get something."

"Why should I have to do it?"

"Because if I go back in, Sister's gonna put me to work."

"I'll be back in two shakes!" Joey went barreling off to the house. He wasn't back in two shakes, not even ten shakes, but when he came, he had an empty coffee can.

"That took long enough."

"Sister put *me* to work, putting away the dishes. It's your job, but I did it for you."

"Don't be such a martyr," Claire told him.

They walked slow. The warm sand felt good on the bottom of Claire's feet. Joey picked up a rock and chucked it at a crow sitting on the electricity wire. If the crow had stayed put, he probably would have hit it. Claire wondered if boys really were just naturally better at things like that than girls, like they always said. Joey was younger than her, but he could already throw better.

A car was coming, and she picked Spike up so he wouldn't get run over. It was Mike Maki going home. They waved, and he waved back, but he didn't smile or anything.

"He looks like a grouch," Claire said.

"He's grouchy about Korea."

"How do you know?"

"His boy is there. In the war."

Joey was a little kid, so people hardly noticed he was around, and they weren't careful about what they said. Even if they realized he was there, they figured he didn't understand anyway.

All of a sudden he stopped, right in the middle of the road.

"What's the matter?"

"Nothing." He started walking again, but even slower. "I don't think there are any berries around here."

The tractor sound was getting louder. When they went around the bend, they could see it, bumping along with Jake on top, raking up the hay, not looking behind him. When he spotted them he stopped the tractor and got off. He came close enough so they could hear him holler, "You'd better get back home!"

"Why should we?"

"Because I say so! Beat it!"

Joey took off like a scared rabbit, back the way they came, not running, but walking about as fast as he could. Claire wasn't about to give Jake the satisfaction. She yelled, "I'll go home when I'm darned good and ready!"

Jake got back on the rumbling tractor.

He was headed toward the road, and if she kept walking they'd come right together, so she'd have to decide how brave she was before that happened.

Then she saw the big hole. It must be the place where Pa's tractor went into the ditch because he was dead. It was what she saw from her tree, the tractor hitting the fence before it ended up in the ditch. When she saw it, Pa was dead, but she didn't know it. It was right then that Ma yelled for her to make Pa's dinner and take it out to him. If Father Doucet hadn't come along first, it would have been her that found Pa when he died.

The brush was all knocked down, and even a couple of spindly trees were bent over with the bark scraped off. Two deep ruts showed where the back wheels of the tractor sank in. The rest was black mud and water. This was the place where Pa died, and Jake was out here, all alone, on the very same tractor. He was braver than she was, any day.

Maybe he didn't care. He might be glad Pa wasn't around any more. Pa usually liked Jake better than the rest of them, and was friendlier to him, but not the day he died. Not after the fight they had the night before. Pa told Jake to go get a can of gas for the tractor, and Jake fell asleep driving the car and got stuck in some sand. He got out, but by that time the store was closed, so he couldn't buy any gas. Pa was mad, and he hit Jake and made him cry. It was scary, seeing Pa hit him, and seeing somebody that was as big as Jake crying was even scarier.

She stopped in the road. Jake was turning around, heading back the other way, like he didn't even remember that she was there.

Chapter Forty-two

Well, my dear, I'm going to have to leave you for a short while. An eager-looking female is sashaying across the yard, headed straight for my front door.

McIntire laid down his pen, slid his feet back into his shoes—his bare toes were probably not nearly so fetching as hers—and got up to greet Wanda Greely. He'd wondered how long it would be.

She said hello with a brilliant fuschia smile. "I guess it's my turn now. Could I have a few minutes of your time?"

"Turn about is fair…whatever it is they say. Come in out of the sun and have a seat." A couple of courtesies she hadn't so graciously extended to him. He added a third, "May I get you something to drink?"

"What are you offering?"

"Gin?" May as well take the opportunity to render her tongue as loose as her hips. "For all I know, my wife may even have left the makings of the pink variety."

She followed him to the sideboard and then into the kitchen, peering around his elbow while he placed his armload of bottles on the counter.

McIntire studied the labels, "Ice or not is about the extent of my bartending abilities."

"Don't apologize."

"Apologize? I'm bragging. Far as I'm concerned, it's a mark of purity."

She sidled him aside, "You'd better let unpure me do it then."

When they were seated in the living room—Wanda, indeed, holding a glass of sparkling rose-colored liquid—McIntire asked, "What can I do for you?"

"You can leave my husband alone."

Had Koski gotten to Greely already? "I haven't bothered your husband."

"You will. You or that now-you-see-him-now-you-don't sheriff, once you've told him.... Chet will be a suspect, won't he?"

"He has a motive."

"Motive, my foot! He hasn't got a motive. It could only, just barely possibly, be a motive if he knew, which he does not."

McIntire could still see Greely's ship-builder fist, inches from his wife's russet locks. "How can you be so sure of that?"

"Do you think I wouldn't be able to tell? He doesn't have any idea that Kevin is not his natural son. I didn't know it myself, not to be absolutely sure, until I saw Reuben's little boy. If Chet found out, it would kill him. It would absolutely destroy his life and my son's life, too."

It surely would. Why was it that any time something bad happened it seemed to mushroom, spreading tragedy like a contagious disease? How many innocent bystanders had to be knocked out of the way before you got to the guilty party? "If your husband has an alibi for the time Reuben was shot—somebody besides you to vouch for him—he's in the clear. He won't have to know why we asked."

"He doesn't have any alibi. He's been taking his two week's vacation, and so far he's spent ninety-nine percent of that time fishing."

"Alone?"

She nodded. "Except when he brings Kevin along."

"On the ninth, the day Reuben Hofer was killed?"

"All by his lonesome. He was away all day. I drove Kevin to sleep over at Chet's mother's."

"You're sure of the date?"

"Positive. That's why I was able to go to see Mrs. Hofer the next day without bringing Kevin along. And a darned good thing! Can you imagine if I'd turned up with…?" She took another swallow.

"So you didn't stay there with him? At the grandmother's?"

"No. I mean, that's right, I didn't. I just dropped him off."

"Presumably you were working, so you have an alibi?"

"For what time, exactly?"

"Exactly, I can't say, but can you account for your time around noon?"

"Nope. After I dropped Kevin, I had the whole day to myself, and I made the most of it. I did my nails and a little sunbathing,"—Now she *was* batting those eyelashes—"you know, that sort of stuff."

It would be too bad if the sins of the wife were visited on the husband and son, but McIntire didn't see how it could be otherwise. "So why are you here? Not that I don't appreciate the company, but what do you think I can do about this?"

"You can have some compassion!"

"I feel all the compassion in the world, something that didn't trouble you when your husband was off building boats."

"What would you know about it?"

Maybe more than she imagined, but McIntire wouldn't get into that.

She glanced down, running a richly enameled fingernail slowly around the rim of the glass. "I could give you some information."

"I'm sure you could."

"And I will."

"For a consideration?"

"For some basic human compassion, I'm sure we could come to an agreement." The downcast eyes perked up, and the shy maiden disappeared. She put her glass, and her cards, on the table. "Your wife's away, I hear."

He'd have to rewrite that tongue-in-cheek letter. "Been checking up on me?"

"It must be lonely."

"I'm used to it." McIntire said. Was she truly implying—?

"Not much fun, though." She was.

Either the woman was truly desperate, or McIntire was far sexier than he'd given himself credit for. "Mrs. Greely, I can't take advantage of you under false pretenses. It's too late for me to indulge in compassion."

The vamp, too, evaporated in the blink of a black coated eyelash. "You've already gone running off to the sheriff." She made him sound like the busy-body he was.

"This is a murder investigation. You couldn't have thought I'd keep it to myself."

"Koski hasn't come to question Chet so far, or sent his boy-wonder nephew."

He wasn't likely to do that. Too bad, McIntire would pay money to see Cecil Newman's annihilation at the hands of Mrs. Chester Greely. "He's been busy."

"The paper said that Reuben was shot with a twenty gauge shotgun."

"Did it? I don't think I read that." It was a feeble attempt at a bluff and a failure.

Wanda smiled tolerantly. "Yes, it did." She uncrossed her legs and put her hands on her knees. "I've got Chet's twenty-gauge in the car. You can have a look at it. He'd have cleaned it last fall, after partridge season. You'll be able to tell that it hasn't been fired since."

"We won't know when it was cleaned. It might have been last night."

"Oh." Her disappointment was the first genuine emotion she'd shown. "Are you sure? There might be dust in the barrel or something."

"I guess there could be, and sometimes you can tell if a bullet came from a specific gun."

This time the bluff worked. The remnants ice cubes rattled as she reached for the glass. "Really?"

"The inside of the barrel sometimes leaves distinctive markings."

"Good! Then you'll see that this is not the gun that killed Reuben Hofer."

"Mrs. Greely, how can you be that sure? Are you so positive that your husband *didn't* murder your former lover?"

"Don't be an ass."

If she wasn't sure, bringing the gun was a gamble, if only because Greely would notice it missing. But Wanda had a history of gambling, and her husband might well have a whole fleet of shotguns.

"What good will all this do anyway?" McIntire asked. "The kids only live a few miles apart. Sooner or later somebody's going to notice."

"Sooner." She still clutched the glass, which now contained only an inch of straw-colored water. "In about six weeks."

Six weeks. In about six weeks school would start, and two small boys would walk into the second or third grade classroom and see themselves in a mirror.

"Good lord, it was *you!*"

"I want them out of here." Pink never sounded so cold.

"You shot a man in the head, the father of your child, just to keep from—"

"Oh, for God's sake, you *are* an ass. I don't know who killed Reuben. I went to his home to...pay my respects, and when I looked at his son, I saw *my* son looking back." She didn't elaborate, only asked, "I suppose they'll be going back to where they came from now?"

"I believe they intend to stay."

"They can't! They have got to leave!"

"So if anybody had a motive to kill Reuben it was you. "

She sat still for a moment, wheels turning, before responding. "Yes, you're absolutely right. There's no need to go after Chet. It was me with the motive, and I can give you another one, maybe even a better one."

"Go ahead."

"Reuben Hofer stole from me—some things worth a bundle."

"And what was that?"

She looked for a moment like she regretted her impulsiveness, but finally stated, "Fossils. No, not fossils exactly, relics, ancient Indian relics."

"Ancient relics that belonged to you?"

"A share in them belonged to me."

"And another share to Bruno Nickerson?"

"That stool pigeon!"

"Don't worry, your secret is safe with Bruno, so far. But somebody's been dropping hints, and 'ancient relics.'" McIntire lifted his glass. "Let's hear the whole story."

"Well," she hunkered forward, no hesitancy now. "It was like this. When Reuben was at the camp, they got put to work shoveling up sand from a dune to fill in some swamp. The other men just sort of hung around bullshi—passing the time of day, you know. But Reuben kept working. When he was digging he found some things. Funny shaped rocks, stuff like that. The rest of the guys quit, but Reuben kept going. He found a pile of old…implements, I guess you'd say, arrowheads, fish hooks, things we didn't know what they were. Bruno Nickerson was working there, which I guess you know. He started wondering what was going on and caught Reuben at it, so they hatched up a plot."

"A plot that included you?"

"I was supposed to take care of selling it. They didn't want anybody to know where it came from, and we figured nobody would connect me with the camp. It wasn't illegal."

"Selling it might not be. Digging it up was."

"I didn't do any digging," she reminded him, "and neither did Bruno. They'd smuggle the stuff out—It was small enough to fit in their pockets, so that wasn't hard—and they'd bring it to me. We had a shoe box chock full. A big shoe box. It would have been worth a fortune!" Her cheeks blazed almost to the point that their painted circles disappeared. "Then they closed down the camp and sent the whole bunch of them to California."

"And Reuben took off with the loot."

"He sure as hell did. I don't know how. It was a Sunday. They always got Sunday afternoon off. He wasn't supposed to be gone overnight, of course, but the punishment for getting back late was canceling their leave privileges, and, since they were going to be leaving in a few days anyway, it didn't make any difference. So he stayed in town."

"With you."

"Yes. The next afternoon, I went to look in the box, and it was empty. I can't for the life of me figure how he did it. Every single solitary bit was gone. Right down to the last fish hook. He couldn't have taken it all out in his pockets. All I can think is that sometime during the night, while I was asleep, he sneaked it out to somebody, and that somebody had to be Bruno Nickerson!"

"Reuben might have had other friends."

"I guess he might have," she admitted. "Bruno swears up and down he never saw any of it. I've been keeping tabs on him, and he hasn't been spending like a drunken sailor or anything."

"And you swore up and down you didn't know Hofer was back here until he died. What does that do to your motive, both of your motives, for that matter?"

"I just give you two good reasons that I could be a murderer, and you say I can't be, because I would also have to be a liar?"

McIntire had to own up to some respect for the woman's willingness to lay her shapely neck on the block for hearth and home.

"Strictly speaking, I didn't lie about that," she went on. "I told the sheriff that I hadn't seen Reuben, which was true, but I did know he was back. Grace Maki came in for a permanent wave, and she told me about selling the place." She shook the glass. "Are you ever going to offer me a refill?"

"Help yourself. Don't dawdle."

She went off to the kitchen and was back, without dawdling, carrying two glasses; one something fizzy, one whisky, with ice. McIntire could have done that himself.

She kicked off her shoes and dropped to the sofa, legs curled under her. "I wrote him a letter. I told him I knew he'd taken the stuff, and I wanted my share. I said it in a cagey sort of way, so if his wife read it, she wouldn't catch on." The thick lashes fluttered again, "I also put in a picture of Kevin. I didn't say anything in the letter that would, you know, make his wife suspicious if she saw it. I didn't know then that he had a child that was Kevin's double. If she saw that picture...." She looked up. "She must have seen it. That's why she wouldn't talk to me when I went to see her."

That sounded plausible.

"I didn't hear anything back from him, of course. I didn't expect to, but I figured it couldn't hurt to give him a little reminder. I couldn't think why he'd come back here, unless he had it in mind to do a bit more treasure hunting. I wanted him to know that he wasn't going to be fooling anybody this time around." She smoothed the fabric of her ankle length pants, which had absolutely no room to wrinkle. "And now he's dead."

The man who'd fathered her son. Was it sorrow and grief that caused her to look away? Perhaps remorse?

If so, it was short-lived. She looked up and rattled her ice at him. "Somebody took that loot," she said. "And whoever it was damn well still has it!"

"What makes you think so?"

"If they sold it, they would have had to say where they found it, and there'd have been archeologists swarming over Gibb's Bay like ants."

She wasn't so dumb. And if she thought her loot was still around, she was also smart enough to think that there was only one likely place for it to be, and that was in Reuben Hofer's house.

Chapter Forty-three

"I've got something for you and you're going to have to come and get it." McIntire didn't wait for the sheriff to invoke his back, his fatherly duties, his son-ly duties, or his lack of time and deputies. Before Koski showed up to get Chet Greely's shotgun, he intended to take care of an errand of his own.

If Jacob and Samuel Hofer had shot their father, they'd got rid of the weapon. Why? If it belonged to the family, why not just clean it up and put it back where it came from? If the Hofer boys had a twenty gauge, which was now missing, their whole family knew it and was protecting them, or they were all in on the crime together. Nobody in the neighborhood had reported a gun missing, and it would be hard to believe those kids could have gotten hold of one any way other than theft without their parents, or snoopy younger siblings, catching on. They hadn't bought it, not around here. Another possibility was that the trapper, Hector Monson, had left one in the house, and that it had been overlooked in settling up his estate.

It was time to quit pussy-footing around and go straight to one person McIntire might have a chance at cowing into telling the truth. Joseph Hofer.

He was playing catch with his sister, looking so much like a real kid that McIntire hated to break the spell. He didn't need to; Claire spotted him, missed the ball, and headed for the weeds to look for it. A few seconds later, Spike bound up with the ball, but without his mistress.

McIntire wrested the ragged drool-covered orb from the animal and wiped it on his pants leg. He tossed it to the boy, who didn't recover from his dumbstruck stare in time to keep it from rolling through the grass and back into the dog's mouth.

Any further attempts at getting friendly would probably only show him up for the fraud he was. McIntire bent low enough to allow the child to hear him without letting his words carry to anyone who might be on the other side of the open windows. "Joey, the sheriff would like to know, does anyone in your family have a gun?"

It was a simple question, one that shouldn't have required the agony of concentration on the round face.

"Pa doesn't allow guns." Was it a family of parrots? Did Ma line them up every night to practice their lines?

McIntire was halfway erect when Joey went on, barely above a whisper. "We use to have one, but we left it at Grandpa's. It's too bad, 'cause now we can't shoot a deer."

"They *use* to have one. That's what he said. They left it at Grandpa's."

"So maybe they did. Reuben didn't want it. Did he also tell you it was a twenty gauge?"

"No. He's a little kid. But he implied it was something you could kill a deer with."

"If any of the others say it wasn't that kind of gun, are you going to believe them?"

"I ain't gonna believe much of anything that bunch says."

"So where is it, if it ain't back at Grandpa's?"

"The way I figure it, they could only have done two things—buried it, or hidden it somewhere around the house or barn."

"Or thrown it down the well, or drove off in the night and dumped it somewhere, or packed it in a suitcase and taken it back to South Dakota. You got a mighty poor imagination. Why get rid of it anyway?" Koski reflected McIntire's thinking. "It only makes them look guilty as all hell."

"Because they're dumb kids. Although," McIntire said, "maybe not all that dumb. A missing gun might make them *look* guilty, but the actual weapon might prove them to be guilty. Did you check the well, by the way?"

"Yes, as a matter of fact, and, speaking of weapons, can I have the use of your phone a sec?"

The sheriff gave a couple of hefty cranks. "Give me Wanda's...?"

"Cut'n Curl," McIntire supplied.

"Right. Wanda's. You know the place?" She did.

"Hello there, Mrs. Greely. Pete Koski here. I—sure." The sheriff waited, picking at his teeth, while Wanda took care of whatever urgent occupation he'd caught her in.

"Sorry to drag you away from your work. I have something that belongs to your husband. I might need to get some information about it. Will Mr. Greely be home this afternoon?" He held the earpiece away from his head and winked. When the squeaking subsided, he drawled, "Weeellll, I guess that might be okay for the time being. Tomorrow it is, high noon. We'll see you then.

"I think it's time we reunited the Bobbsey Twins." He held the cradle down for a few seconds before releasing it with a pop. "Put me through to Koski's Hardware."

Arranging Bruno Nickerson's lunch hour activity did not take long. "He says Belinda will have the car, maybe you can pick him up?" Koski slapped his hat back on his head and picked up the case containing Chet Greely's shotgun. "All right, let's go tackle that widow."

◇◇◇

"Mrs. Hofer, I don't think you've been entirely honest with us."

Her hands fluttered up and settled back, like a pair of startled blackbirds. "Well, I can't imagine why you say that. I've certainly tried to be."

"I asked if you own a shotgun."

"And I said my husband didn't approve of firearms." The trembling in her chin started in the center and spread, like waves from a pebble dropped in a pool.

"Do you own a gun?"

"No! That is...I think there was an old one of my father's around somewhere. No one ever used it. I'm not sure if it works anymore, or if all the pieces are even there."

"We'd like to see it, if you don't mind."

Mary Frances stared in astonishment at Koski's brusqueness that said it didn't matter a hell of a lot whether she minded or not. Then she called, "Claire!"

The girl came from upstairs, hair arranged to obscure one eye, *ala* Veronica Lake, and a suspicious dab of red on her lips. She'd no doubt seen the sheriff coming.

"Claire," her mother said, "See if you can find Grandpa's old gun for Mr. Koski."

The child didn't move.

"What's the matter?"

She turned and left the room. The sound of drawers being opened and closed came from the other side of the wall. She called out, "It doesn't seem to be here."

"Of course it is. Where else would it be?" So much for her remark about thinking there might have been one "around somewhere."

"I think maybe the burglar took it!"

Koski called for her to come back into the room. She stood in the doorway, ready for flight.

"Up 'til now, you were pretty sure nothing was missing."

"I guess I forgot we had it. We don't ever shoot it." She echoed Mary Frances' words. Not surprising with her bedroom directly above. Her mother hadn't had to call her twice, even with that feeble voice.

The sheriff asked, "What kind of a gun was it, Mrs. Hofer?"

She glanced toward her daughter before she replied, "I'm not sure. I don't know anything about guns."

"Did your father use it for hunting?"

"Sometimes, I think, when I was a child." Her hand flitted up to cover her mouth. "There wasn't much of anything to hunt where we lived."

"One barrel or two?"

"I don't know. One, I think." With each reply, her tone became higher and thinner, a building hysteria.

"When did you last see it?"

She looked again to Claire when she spoke, but answered without hesitation. "The day after my husband died. It was in the chest when we took out sheets to make up a bed for Jane."

"Why didn't you tell us about the gun when we asked?"

"I didn't see any reason to. I didn't even think about it. Maybe I blotted it out of my head. After all, my husband had just been killed by a gun. It wasn't something I liked thinking about. Surely you can understand that. What does it matter? It was just a beat up old gun of my father's. It didn't have anything to do with Reuben."

"Doesn't it seem strange to you that it's not there now?"

"Yes, of course it does. But the house was broken into." Her self-conscious snicker returned. "It might have been about all we had worth stealing."

It was no use. Mrs. Hofer might be lying through her teeth, but as long as they all stuck to the same story, there was no chance of proving them wrong. Although she seemed genuine in her belief that the shotgun was in the chest. If it was true what she said, that the gun was in that chest the day after her husband died, then it had disappeared sometime between then and the morning after the burglary. It might be anywhere between here and South Dakota by now. Once again McIntire realized how short-sighted and irresponsible it had been not to search the house immediately.

"Where is your sister-in-law now?" McIntire asked.

"Gone home. She left early this morning."

"Claire, come over here. Sit down."

She crossed the room, skirting McIntire like he was a boa constrictor, and slid onto the edge of the chair offered by the sheriff, facing him.

"On the day your father died, you took his dinner out to him."

She nodded. "I always did."

"Did you also take dinner to your brothers?"

She squirmed. "That's Joey's job."

"So Joey took the lunch?"

"It's his job."

Once again it wasn't answering the question, but Koski didn't press it. "Your mother said you left here at a quarter past twelve."

"I don't know exactly."

"The news was just getting over. Your father wanted his dinner at twelve-thirty, on the button."

"He was kind of persnickety."

Koski nodded in understanding. "When Mr. McIntire saw you coming, it was getting toward one o'clock."

"It's a long ways. A half mile."

"Which should be a ten or fifteen minute walk for a sprite like you. It took you at least a half hour."

She nibbled on a dirty forefinger, "I think maybe I had to help Joey. It might have been too much for him to carry."

"So you went to the potato field yourself?"

"I might have. Ya, I guess I did."

"When you got to the potato field, were your brothers there?"

Her hand went to the lump under her blouse, and then quickly down. "Sam and Jake, you mean?"

"Yes. Were Samuel and Jacob Hofer in the field?"

"Oh," she met the sheriff's gaze, "I didn't bother to look. I was in such a big hurry that I just put the dinner pail and the thermos in the pickup and took off."

Koski stood up. "Mrs. Hofer, I believe we need to talk a little more with your sons."

Mary Frances spoke through tremulous lips. "I think it might be best if they had an attorney present. They're underage."

"We'll take them into town. You can ride along, and we'll keep them entertained while you round one up."

"I don't think I'm well enough for that."

Koski relented. "It doesn't have to be right this minute. We'll give you a chance to find somebody."

"Do you have any lawyers in Chandler?"

"A few."

"A decent one?"

"All well and duly licenced to practice law in the state of Michigan," Koski told her. "I can't vouch for their decency."

Chapter Forty-four

Bruno Nickerson and Wanda Greely faced each other across the sheriff's pitted table like a pair of banty roosters. Wanda recovered first. "Hello, Bruno, how have you been?"

"Just fine. You?"

Her smile showed a smear of scarlet on a front tooth. "Very well, thanks. Belinda and the kids doing okay?"

Koski butted in on the chance to get the scoop on Belinda and the kids. "Okay, cut the gab, I didn't get you here for a tea party."

"What did you get us here for?" Wanda sat primly, handbag on knees. "I don't imagine us being here together is a case of bungled scheduling?"

"Your old business partner's been shot in the head. This is a murder investigation."

Nickerson gave a huff of disgust. "I might have known you couldn't keep your mouth shut."

"Mouth shut about what?" Wanda demanded. "We didn't do anything illegal. At least *I* didn't."

"Theft ain't legal last I heard. That stuff belonged to Reuben and me."

"And one of you still has it."

"If I had it, I sure as hell wouldn't be peddling nuts and bolts now!" Bruno glanced at Koski. "Sorry."

"No," she responded, "you'd have drunk it all up, and your kids would be sleeping in a tent!"

"Well, the three of you had it," Koski interjected, "and as far as we know, it's not been sold. So one of you has still got it."

"It ain't me!" The two spoke in unison.

McIntire said, "Mrs. Greely has indicated that it disappeared from her home after a visit from Mr. Hofer."

"So it seems reasonable to assume that Reuben walked off with it." Koski stated.

"He couldn't have!" Wanda slapped the purse on her thighs. "When he left, he didn't have a thing on him."

Nickerson snickered. "That must have caused some talk around the neighborhood."

"Oh, shut up. I gave him a ride back to the camp. He was in my car, and he wasn't carrying anything. We'd looked at the stuff before we went to…earlier in the evening,"she corrected. "We each chose one thing for ourselves. Sort of for a keepsake." She reached to pat Bruno's hand. "You could have done it, too, if you hadn't waltzed off with the whole she-bang!"

"The last time I saw that stuff, you had it, and you're the one with the fancy pink—"

Koski quashed the tiff with a wave of his hand, and Wanda went on, "That was the thing I saw Reuben take when he left. But the next day it was all gone. The only way it could have disappeared is if he got up in the night and handed it off to somebody."

"It sure as hell wasn't me!"

"Could somebody have broken in?" McIntire asked. "Taken it in the night?"

"It was under my bed." Which she and Reuben were in, presumably not so deep in slumber that they wouldn't notice an intruder.

"What about while you were off driving Reuben back 'home'?"

"I never thought of that. I don't lock the door," she admitted. "Of course it would have to be somebody who knew the relics were there. In other words—" She waved across the table.

Koski jumped in quick, heading off another round of squabbling, which McIntire might have enjoyed. "If either of you have it, I imagine it isn't something you'd keep from your spouses. I don't suppose you have any objections to my talking to them?"

"Go ahead. I got no secrets from Belinda." The wife who a few days ago didn't need to know everything.

Mrs. Greely was not so sanguine.

"You got no right to drag my husband into your sordid little piddling investigation."

"Homicide is sordid, no doubt about it, but I wouldn't call investigation of it little or piddling."

"Is that what we're talking about? Homicide?"

"What else?"

"I didn't kill Reuben because I thought he'd swiped a few trinkets."

"What did you kill him for?"

"You're as big an ass as what's-his-name here!" And to think a mere forty-eight hours before, she'd been itching to repay what's-his-name's compassion.

"All right, " Koski said. "Forget about murder for the time being. Try to follow me here. Somebody ransacked Reuben Hofer's house, obviously looking for something. Something we figure they didn't find. You," he aimed a forefinger at each of them, "have lost something. Something you think Reuben might have taken. Ergo…."

His encouraging nod was met with twin blank stares.

"All right, back to murder. A murderer has to have a motive, of course. Revenge is one of the all-time favorites, but revenge over a few missing trinkets, as you say, Mrs. Greely, is weak, especially if the victim may still be able to produce said trinkets, unless, of course, he was dead."

"I'm glad you are at least able to figure that much out."

"'Course there's other motives. Maybe just wanting to get rid of somebody inconvenient. Somebody that could do a good job of messing up your life. Or plain old anger. Rage at something that isn't the way you thought it might be. Fury at betrayal, that sort of thing."

Bruno sat dazed. Wanda turned clownlike, skin pale with pink circular cheeks and crimson lips.

Koski heaved a despondent sigh. "I guess maybe we have no choice but to contact those spouses."

"You can't!" The screech could have shattered glass.

"I'd have to have a damn good reason not to."

"All right then, how's this? I did it."

Bruno's jaw dropped. "You shot Reuben Hofer?"

"Oh for cripe's sake!" Wanda Greely faced Koski and put her hands on the table, ready for the cuffs.

"I searched his house. I know he took the stuff. He got me into…he took advantage of me, and, when my back was turned he made off with the stuff. He couldn't have lugged it all the way to California, so he must have taken it to his wife, and she's still got it somewhere.

"I didn't plan to look for it myself. I thought I could make his wife see that Reuben and I had an agreement, and she should honor it."

Nickerson sat dazed, not even objecting to being left out of the "agreement."

"But the house was empty, so I just thought to have a quick snoop around. I know it was wrong, but it had to be there! Anyway, one thing led to another, and…"

"So you searched all through the house?"

"And made a big mess, I'm afraid. I'm sorry. I'll try to make it up to them, somehow."

They could definitely use the services of a hairdresser. McIntire asked, "You did this by yourself?"

"Of course."

"You searched the house—and the barn."

"That's right."

"The little girl was in the barn when you got there. She hid under the hay in the loft. All night."

"Oh, God." After a quick glance in Nickerson's direction, she dropped her forehead to her hands.

"She heard someone come into the barn and up the ladder to the loft. I guess that was you," Koski said.

She nodded, head down, fingers buried in her hair.

Koski bent down to peer at her four inch heels and pencil wide skirt. "You'd gotten all dolled up in your bib overalls and shit-kickers, I take it?"

She raised her head and said with an anemic smile, "Not exactly, but close."

"To pay a visit to a bereaved woman, asking that she honor her late husband's business agreements?"

Mrs. Greely sank back into her chair. "Sorry, Bruno."

"You moron!"

She studied her ruby enameled claws for a moment, then seemed to come to a decision. "Send him out of here."

Koski nodded to Nickerson. "Take a walk. Don't go too far."

The door closing on Nickerson's back was Wanda's signal to turn all business. "I figure his wife killed him, and it's my fault," she said with no preamble. "Like I told"—She gave a twitch of her head toward McIntire—"I sent a letter to Reuben with a picture of my son." At McIntire's cough she added, "Our son. Reuben's and mine. I shouldn't have done it, but I didn't know then that *my* son looked so much like *his* son. I didn't think Kevin looked much like the Reuben I remember. Maybe some around the eyes. I went to see Mrs. Hofer more out of curiosity than anything else. I didn't so much want the money, as just to know once and for all what happened, and that it wasn't that bastard Bruno! Pardon my French.

"After I saw the boy, I knew she had to have done it. She'd have known the second she saw that picture. They could be twins...damn!" She slapped her hands to her cheeks.

"What?"

"I was right! If our two boys are about the same age, and they *must* be, that means that Reuben was back with his wife close to the time he was...with me. Right before he was sent off to California. He *did* leave the stuff with her!"

They weren't the same age. Joey Hofer had to be a year or so older, maybe more, for all the difference that made.

Koski waved his hand, "Get back to the story."

"What else is there? You were talking about motive. Mrs. Hofer must have seen the snapshot, and known right off what Reuben had been up to, so she killed him."

The sheriff took time to light a Camel before saying, "Mrs. Greely, Mary Frances Hofer weighs in at around three-hundred-fifty pounds. She can barely get off her chair. I ain't sure she *can* get off her chair. She didn't sneak out to the hayfield, shoot her husband, and sprint back to the kitchen in time to be shelling peas when the law showed up."

"Three-fifty?"

"At least."

"Cripes." The penciled on brows drew together. "So she didn't shoot Reuben then?"

"No. That we can be sure of."

Her head dropped again, this time onto her folded arms. Only the regular twitching of her back and shoulders indicated that she hadn't been overcome with the urge to take a nap.

The two men regarded each other through the haze of smoke, and waited. A long time. McIntire contemplated the dark roots of Mrs. Greely's copper penny hair. Koski reached toward her shoulder but pulled back. The spasms went on, counterpoint to lapping of the waves outside the window.

When she lifted her head at last, her face was blotched with red, smeared with pink, and streaked with black.

Koski handed her a lighted cigarette and McIntire contributed his folded handkerchief. The last of the three dozen Leonie had insisted on leaving clean and pressed.

"It wasn't Chet. I know it wasn't." McIntire flinched as she blew her nose. "I thought she'd killed him. I was sure of it. Otherwise, I'd never have bothered her again, a new widow. But I wanted to know what had happened to those artifacts. I talked Bruno into going to see her. We didn't drive together, of course. It wasn't Bruno's fault. He's not too smart. I just wanted to know what happened and—"

"Bullshit!"

"What?"

"You wanted her gone," McIntire said. "You might have visited the first time for the reasons that you say, and once you saw Joey Hofer, you might have thought Mary Frances had killed her husband, but most of all you wanted her to pack up and leave."

"Okay, I admit it. I hoped with Reuben dead, they'd move away. Why wouldn't I?" She sucked at the cigarette. "I knew that they'd taken Mrs. Hofer to the hospital, and that there was nobody home. You hear everything in a beauty parlor."

"So you decided to try your hand at burglary."

"I talked Bruno into going. I said that maybe she didn't know about our agreement with Reuben, and we could at least talk to her about it. I didn't tell him she wouldn't be home. Then I convinced him to search the house. I waited in my car, out on the road. If anybody came along, I was going to honk the horn, so he could come outside, and we'd act like we just got there. He was gone for ages. Finally I saw him come out the back door and head off to the barn, so I got out to check. He'd gone crazy! The place was a disaster. I high-tailed it back to my car and got the hell out of there."

McIntire dwelled only for a second on the tantalizing image of Wanda's high tailing. So far what she said may have been true. Had Bruno been getting posthumous revenge for the destruction he'd had to deal with compliments of the "Tobacco Road Gang?" But there was more. "So why'd you go back?" he asked.

"I didn't go back. I went straight home."

McIntire gazed at the gun case in the corner.

"All right!" It was venomous, but she inhaled, and continued measured and civilized. "The next day, after I finished work, I went back. I felt terrible about all the mess, even though I hadn't actually done it myself, of course. Bruno wouldn't have gone to the house without me. It was my idea that got him there. So I went back and brought the relic that I kept." She nodded to McIntire. "The stone with the hole in it. There were two of them, and Reuben and I each took one. I thought giving mine to his wife might be a sort of peace offering. Of course I know it couldn't make up for—"

"Bullshit!"

"I second that bullshit," Koski said. "It wasn't just the earspool there. That's what it is by the way—antique jewelry."

"No kidding?"

"So here's the million dollar question, Mrs. Greely. Who's hand was it?"

"Hand?" The laughter looked ludicrous on the tear-ravaged face, and went on almost as long as the crying jag had. "Some detectives! Hand? Did you really think? That must be...." McIntire's already black-smeared handkerchief suffered further indignities. "It wasn't human!"

Koski stared. "Martian?"

"*Bear*. It's a bear paw. Chet made it for Kevin last Halloween. It was on a stick so he could pull a string and it would—" She opened and closed her hand.

"A bear paw?"

"I thought it might fool an Iowa farm girl."

"The Iowa farm girl never saw it."

"I'm glad of that." She dabbed at her nose. "Three hundred-fifty pounds?"

"Maybe three-seventy-five."

"Cripes." She pulled a compact from her handbag, opened its gold cover, took a quick peek, grimaced, and snapped it shut. "Are you going to question my husband? About the murder?"

"I don't think we need to do that. You should keep better tabs on your old man. While Reuben Hofer was getting shot, Chet was cooling himself off at the Moosehorn bar in Thunder Bay."

"You bastard."

Koski accepted her tribute with a bow of his head. "We'll hang on to the gun for a while, though. Just in case. Which reminds me. When you paid your kindly visit to the widow, did you see a gun in her house?"

"I told you, I only took one look in the door and skedaddled. You'll have to ask Bruno."

Chapter Forty-five

It was an interview McIntire did not intend to miss, even if it meant sharing the back seat of Koski's lethargic but loud Power Wagon with his two prisoners and the dog. It didn't. Koski had business with his nemesis, Myrtle Van Opelt, J. P. McIntire left him at the justice's house and drove the Power Wagon to collect the two youths himself. Mrs. Hofer chose not to come along, even with the large vehicle, and she also hadn't gotten hold of an attorney.

"I don't have a telephone."

"I understand, Mrs. Hofer. We'll get somebody."

"They shouldn't be going alone. I wish Jane was still here."

"Are you sure you don't want to change your mind? Come along?"

"No. No, I don't think so. Jake and Sam are almost grown men, and they've done nothing."

She wasn't however, able to tell him where Jake and Sam were at the moment. "Claire's in the garden. She'll know."

Claire wasn't in the garden. She was standing next to the Power Wagon, a pair of blue jeans three sizes too big belted around her middle, gingerly approaching Geronimo, who sat on the front seat with his head out the window.

"He's friendly," McIntire said.

She swung around, face frozen in fear and disappointment. Obviously the child hadn't expected the wagon to have brought John McIntire.

"Your mother says you can tell me where to find your brothers."

The outline of the earspool was plain under her thin dress, as she shrank back, pressing herself against the car door.

"No. They're not here. I think they went somewhere."

"Where?"

"I don't know. Maybe fishing. They probably won't be home until supper time. You can come back then."

She'd almost had him fooled into leaving, when Reuben Hofer's Allis Chalmers, pulling a wagon loaded with round bales of hay, pulled into the yard.

In twenty minutes, the boys were reasonably clean from the neck up and seated in the backseat of the wagon. They rumbled off to the Van Opelt's to retrieve the sheriff, at whose arrival Geronimo was consigned to the cargo space, an effrontery that left him growling under his canine breath every second of the interminable trip into Chandler.

Koski put his wife onto the job of securing a lawyer and seated the boys in the outer room of his office. In a few minutes they were enjoying a game of checkers accompanied by apple pie, also compliments of Marian Koski, whose cooking had been responsible for more than one minor crime wave.

McIntire took the opportunity to walk over to Paulson's Drugs to look for a card for Leonie. She'd still be away on her birthday. Maybe he should send a gift, but that would be trusting the mail to get it there before she was on her way back home. He took some time searching for a card that was romantic without being too flowery, big without being ostentatious, and tasteful without being exorbitantly expensive, finally settling for too flowery, ostentatious, and expensive.

When he got back to the sheriff's office, Attorney Solomon Scott was just entering the door. Even the multi-talented Marian obviously had her limits. Solomon was old enough to have been the original, but the similarity ended there. No doubt he was the best she could manage on such short notice, and would do as a temporary measure.

He nodded to Jake and Sam, and asked if they knew why they'd been brought in. They both said no, with shakes of the head and round innocent eyes. That seemed to be good enough for Solomon. He tugged at the shiny lapels of his black coat to pull it more snugly against the eighty degree temperatures, and preceded the sheriff into his private office.

Mrs. Koski also insisted on being present, to "take notes," which made for a crowd in the inner sanctum.

Koski started with the older boy, leaving his brother to stew himself into a state sufficient for a blubbering confession, McIntire guessed.

"State your full name and age."

"Jacob Reuben Hofer. I'm seventeen." He was relaxed, polite, and mature. "You can just call me Jake."

"Okay Jake. I'm not going to beat about the bush. Have you ever fired a gun?"

"Pardon?" He turned that innocent stare on the sheriff. "Do you think maybe you could shut the window? The waves...I can't quite hear."

Marian put down her notebook and closed the window, shutting out the sounds of the lake, and the cool air it generated.

"Thanks."

"Don't mention it." Koski replied, then after a period of silence, "Answer the question."

"What was it again?"

"Have you ever fired a gun?"

"Oh, that's right. Ya."

"Ya, you *have* fired a gun?"

"Sure."

The ready admission seemed to leave Koski temporarily disarmed, and McIntire asked, "Does anyone in your family own a gun?"

"My grandfather gave one to my mother."

"And have you ever fired that particular gun?"

"Ya. My grandpa showed us how. He made us practice."

Koski recovered, "Do you know where that gun is now?"

"In the house somewhere, I guess. My mother always hid it because my father doesn't believe in—"

"Right. We know about that."

There was nothing in the youth's demeanor to betray agitation, or any emotion at all. Was that an indication of innocence, or the mark of a cold-blooded killer? Despite their denials to Lawyer Scott, there was no doubt that both boys knew exactly why there were there, and that should have given even the most blameless of kids a bit of a sweat.

Although if sweat was an indicator, Solomon Scott was the only one in the suffocating cubicle with nothing on his conscience. He sat, dry-browed and stiffly upright, thin purple-veined hands folded. His gaze was focused unerringly on Pete Koski's face, except for those periods of time that the lids sagged, and his chin dropped to his chest

"When your father died," the sheriff continued, "where were you?"

"I was with my brother, hilling the potatoes."

"What time did you go out to the potato field?"

"I don't know. Sam did the milking first, and I cleaned the barn. I don't know what time it was."

"Make a guess. Early?"

"Oh ya. We hadn't been up all that long. Just long enough to eat and do the chores." The kid could use a radio.

"And how long did you stay in the potato field?"

"Until in the afternoon, when Father Doucet came out and said that my mother wanted us to come inside."

"Did you leave the field at any time before that?"

"No."

"Not even for a few minutes?"

He bit at his fingernail, but replied without a blink. "No."

"Did your sister, or your younger brother, bring your dinner out to you?"

"I—I don't remember, not for sure. We weren't all that far from the house."

"You didn't go inside to eat," Koski said. "I was there."

"Then Joey must have brought it to us."

Just when Jake was showing signs of weakening, the sheriff wiped his hands on his knees and said, "Marian would you escort this young man out and bring in his brother?"

It didn't seem like a sensible move, but Koski's earlier stratagy had worked. Samuel David Hofer entered the room shaking like a leaf.

Koski moved to open the window. "Unless you have a hearing problem like your brother?"

"No." Sam said. He'd picked up the sheriff's sarcasm. "He didn't make it up. Jake's ear makes noises by itself, so sometimes he can't hear other things very well. It got hurt."

"From what?"

Maybe the tremors stemmed from a source other than fear. He answered bitterly and without a pause. "From Pa knocking him in the head."

Marian Koski's breath whistled back into her lungs. Even Solomon opened his eyes a peek.

Sam glared at nobody in particular. "I don't care who knows. Jake was supposed to get gas for the tractor, but he went in the ditch, and the store was closed when he got there. So Pa hit him. Hard."

"When did this happen?"

His confidence faded. "I'm not so sure. A while ago. Maybe two or three weeks."

"Could it have been shortly before your father died?"

The tremor increased, and Sam clenched one black-knuckled hand with the other and moved them under the table. "It might have been. I don't remember exactly. You have to ask Jake."

"I will. He must have been pretty peeved about it."

"Who wouldn't be?"

"Did your father hit you and your brothers often?"

"No. We didn't give him any reason to. Jake got along with Pa the best of any of us, and Pa didn't need to hit him. It wasn't Jake's fault he fell asleep."

Scott snored in agreement.

"So when your father got mad, you just kept out of his way?"

"He hardly ever got mad. He was just plain mean. We stayed away from him as much as we could all the time."

A truck loaded with logs rumbled along the main street, putting a temporary halt to the questioning and giving Koski the opportunity to stand and stretch his back. He lit another cigarette before he continued, leaning against the window frame. "Jake says he knew how to use your grandfather's shotgun. What about you?"

"Grandpa showed us. He said every man should know how to handle a gun."

"Where is that gun now?"

"I guess it's in the house somewhere. I ain't sure where Ma keeps it."

"What about shells?"

"There might have been a few. Ma hid those, too."

"Slugs?"

The boy shrugged. "Maybe."

"You can go back with your brother. We'll get you home." Koski pushed back his chair. "Sol!"

Scott's head jerked up with whiplash force.

"We're done here."

McIntire put out his hand to keep Sam in his seat. "I talked to you the morning after your father died. Do you remember?"

"Ya."

"And do you remember what you were doing?"

"We were still hilling the spuds." He smiled for the first time. It was with the same sort of sarcasm the sheriff exhibited. "You said you'd help."

"Sorry. But you managed to finish up without my assistance. When?"

"That same day."

"When I was out there, talking to you, you weren't even half done."

"We're fast." Sam clearly began to see where this was heading. "When we want to be, that is."

"What kept you from wanting to be fast the day before? The day your father died?"

He gave a shrug. "It was hot."

"Yes, it was. So hot that maybe you didn't spend all day in that field."

"Well," he admitted., "maybe not the *whole* day."

"So where were you?"

"We might have gone off for a while. Maybe done some exploring. Just to cool off. It was boiling hot, and Jake's head hurt."

McIntire recalled the aroma of the previous night's meal that had lingered in the Hofer's kitchen the day after Reuben's death. "Might you have gone down to the river to do that cooling off?

"Could be."

"And possibly get some fish for supper?"

Homicide was one thing, but fish and game laws were serious business. Koski glowered. "That was your fish trap?"

"It was Grandpa's."

Koski shooed him back to his brother. When they were once again engrossed in their checker game, with Marian hustled off for a restorative snack, he uncased Greely's twenty gauge and carried it to the doorway of his office. "This look familiar?"

"Where'd you get it?" It burst out of Jake Hofer before his brother gave him a shove.

"That ain't ours, you moron!"

Koski closed the door, with a self-satisfied grin.

McIntire dropped back into his chair. "It doesn't tell us a whole hell of a lot. All shotguns probably look alike to a kid that age."

"It tells us Grandpappy's shotgun was in the ballpark, and that Jake, at least, expected it to be somewhere we wouldn't find it. I thought you were one hundred percent convinced those two are guilty as all hell."

"I was ninety percent convinced, and I still am. Might be down to around seventy-five now though. They just don't seem like murderers. Maybe with their old man gone, the kids are turning back into kids." That had certainly been true of young Joey.

"Well, I ain't ready to arrest them, by a long shot, but I'd sure as hell like to find out what happened to that shotgun."

"Talk to Bruno. It *could* have been stolen."

"That's right." He brightened up and patted the gunstock on his knee. "Ya. Maybe Wanda's been filling us full of shit, and this *is* the one!"

Chapter Forty-six

First that skinny jerk had come over and started picking on Joey, and the next thing Claire knew, he was back, taking Jake and Sam away. To jail. He had the sheriff's car so it had to be to jail.

It was horrible back in Iowa; everybody at school knew her father was in prison. The kids here didn't know. She could have started all over again. Now her father was murdered and her brothers were in jail. The chance for a new start was gone, and this time, it would be way, way worse. Claire didn't even try to stop the tears that ran down her face and dripped onto Spike's ears.

Joey came running out onto the porch and yelled. "Claire, come here! Hurry up!"

Ma's coffee cup was on the floor and she was standing up, leaning with both hands on the table. Her face was grey and sweat ran down her neck. She talked fast, in little spurts. "I don't feel very well. I'm going to lie down. I want you to run to the Thorsens' and get Mia to call Doctor Guibard. Tell her it's an emergency."

Claire was froze. Stuck to the spot.

"Go now!" Then her face tried to make a smile and she touched Claire's hair and said what she always said when there was a hurry, "Immediately, if not sooner!" She reached for the side of the door and started for the bedroom. "And take Joey with you."

Claire didn't wait another second before she was out the door and down the steps.

Joey wheezed behind her, "Don't go so fast. I can't keep up!"

"You can catch up!"

Claire had never run so fast in her life, or felt like she was going so slow. When she finally got there, Mia Thorsen was in her garden, and Claire's side was hurting so bad she couldn't hardly tell what she wanted. Mrs. Thorsen had long legs, and could walk almost as fast as Claire could run. When Claire got to the door, she heard, "Yes, I think an ambulance would be best." Then she came out the door and yelled for Nick.

She touched Claire's hair, too. "I'm going to go to your mother now. I want you to stay here with Joey 'til I get back." She moved her finger to under Claire's chin and stared hard like Pa used to do. "Promise."

Claire promised, and Nick and Mia Thorsen took off in the car. Even though he was sick, Nick Thorsen drove as fast as Father Doucet.

When she couldn't hear the car any more it got very quiet. Joey came along the path from behind the workshop. He had given up running, and so had Spike.

"Is it okay to go inside and get a drink?" His face was red as a beet, and Spike was panting.

It was probably okay.

Thorsens had running water. Claire opened the big cupboard and took out two glasses. Her hands were so sweaty she could hardly hold on to them. She had to stretch to reach the faucet. She held a glass under the spout and turned the handle. Water whooshed out and splashed back all over her face and down her front. The glass slipped out of her hand and crashed into a million pieces in the sink. She'd have cried if Joey hadn't started to.

"It's nothing to bawl about," she told him. "I'll clean it up in a minute." She dried her hands and held the other glass under the faucet. This time she turned the handle very slowly and let the water trickle in. "Be careful." She handed it to him. "Take it outside."

Cleaning up the broken glass took a long time. She picked it all out and put it in a brown bag. Some of it fell down into the sink drain. Nick would probably be mad, but she didn't know how she could get it out.

She put some water in a glass for herself and went out to sit on the steps next to Joey. After she drank some, she put the glass down and tipped it so Spike could have a drink.

"She'll go to heaven. If she dies, she'll—"

"Shut up, Joey."

In a while they heard a siren. They both knew what it was—an ambulance coming to get Ma. Claire kept her face aimed away from Joey so he wouldn't see how scared she was.

It wasn't how things went in books. In books there was some danger you had to fight, not just bad things happening that you couldn't do anything about. Maybe it was easier to be brave if you only have one danger or one enemy to worry about. You can fight it, and when you get it over with, everything is fine. You can go home and forget about it.

The sirens stopped. Joey looked up. "They're there now."

It seemed like a long time before they heard the sirens again, taking Ma away. So long that Claire was starting to be afraid they wouldn't ever hear them; that it was too late for Ma to go to the hospital. So hearing the ambulance was a good thing. Ma wasn't dead. But she might die. She was having a heart attack, Claire knew that. When people had heart attacks, they died.

When the Thorsens' car came back, it only had Nick in it. It took him a while to get out, and he walked slow.

"Your mother is on her way to the hospital." When he talked, he sounded almost as jerky as Ma had. "Mia went with her. Where are your brothers?"

"Jake and Sam are in jail," Claire said it as mad as she could. "John McIntire came, and he took them to jail."

Nick didn't say anything to that, then he asked, "You hungry?" Joey shook his head. Claire was sort of hungry, but it wouldn't be polite to say so.

Nick went inside, and Claire heard him on the telephone, but she didn't bother to try to listen to the words.

After a while he came back out and said, "I'm just going to start the sauna going." He gave Spike a dirty look and walked down the path with teensy baby steps.

Joey started to cry. Claire didn't know what to do, so she just sat.

Chapter Forty-seven

McIntire had no way out of driving the boys back home in the he-man Power Wagon. Off the hook for the time being, they sat in the back and blabbed all the way like two old biddies who were suspected of nothing more serious than cheating at bingo.

Their conversation mainly took the form of words spoken too low for McIntire to hear over the engine.

Sam leaned over the seat and shouted in his ear, "Hey, can't this wreck go any faster?"

"No, it can't."

"Doesn't it seem kind of funny that the sheriff's car will only do about twenty miles an hour, and the priest drives a hot-rod?"

"Yes, it does."

He was tempted to just drop them off at the end of the drive and be on his sluggish way, but he couldn't leave without letting Mary Frances know what had transpired. He got out and trailed the two toward the house.

Before he made it to the door, Sam was in and back out. "They're gone!"

"What's gone?"

"Everybody. Ma, Claire, Joey. Nobody's here!"

"Maybe they've gone to visit somebody." The kid's expression reflected the stupidity of McIntire's suggestion. Mary Frances Hofer was not out gallivanting around the neighborhood. Nine chances out of ten it was another medical situation. Having her sons hauled off to be questioned about their father's murder probably hadn't done much for her health.

"I'll go see what I can find out." McIntire headed back to the car. "You two stay put!"

If there'd been an emergency, they'd have gone to the nearest phone to call Guibard. That would be Mia's.

McIntire didn't want to go to the Thorsens' again. He wanted to go home, see if he had a letter from Leonie, put his feet up, have a bottle of beer, read the paper, sit and watch the sunset, and go to bed early. He was tired of it all. He was beginning to not give a damn who killed Reuben Hofer.

Maybe Reuben's sister was right. The important thing now was to take care of his wretched family, try to put some the pieces back together.

But somebody *had* done it. Somebody had stood at the edge of that field and, with absolute premeditated intent, had sent Reuben Hofer's brains, and his life, dripping onto his feet. Whoever had done it was walking around now; talking, laughing, eating, sleeping, like nothing had happened.

Nick was in back of the sauna, poking wood into the heater. He waved and started his awkward shuffle up the path. McIntire hurried to meet him.

He confirmed McIntire's guess. Mary Frances had suffered a major heart attack. They'd taken her to Ishpeming in an ambulance, and Mia had gone along.

"The two kids are in the house. Is it true what they say?" he asked. "Koski's arrested the older boys?"

"He took them in and gave them a feeble once-over. I just brought them home."

"Well, you'd better watch your back. The young lady's on the warpath. She thinks you've locked them up and thrown away the key."

"Well, you can set her mind at rest. Have you heard from Mia? What's the outlook?"

"Not good. She was after me to get hold of Father Doucet, but he's gone to see somebody in Au Train. She figured they wouldn't wait around, that they'd get the priest in Ishpeming to give the last rites, so I guess it's looking bad."

"Maybe it was just a precaution. If I run into the father, I'll let him know."

"Okay." He stared into the setting sun. "I guess I have to feed those kids." He spoke over his shoulder, "sauna'll be ready in an hour or so."

McIntire ran into Doucet sooner than he expected. The priest was just loading Sam and Jake Hofer into his car. Their cheerfulness of earlier was gone. Now they may well have been tried and convicted, and being transported to the gallows.

Doucet crossed the yard to lean against the side of the wagon. McIntire was glad to, for once, be able to speak to the man without getting a charley horse in his neck.

"I'm taking them to their mother."

"I figured that. Claire and Joey, too?"

"Not right now. They probably won't let the young ones into the hospital, and it might not be the best for them to see their mother in her present state. I'll be back for them soon as I can." He stood straight but didn't leave. "I take it Jake and Samuel were questioned today, about their father's death."

"Not precisely. They were questioned about their mother's shotgun."

"They shouldn't have been questioned at all. They've been through enough, all of them. Look what it's done to their mother, just at the time they need her most."

"I understand that," McIntire said, "but we're talking about pre-meditated murder here."

"Those boys didn't kill their father."

"Those boys hated their father, they had a shotgun, and it's gone now."

"Their house was burglarized. You might leave the Hofers' alone and go after the guy who did that."

"We have. The person who ransacked Hofer's house has confessed."

"Who?"

"They haven't been charged yet." McIntire invoked his own confidentiality standards. "But we're reasonably sure they didn't steal the shotgun. They'd have no reason to lie."

"Unless they shot Reuben with it."

It was a thought, but, according to Mary Frances, the gun had been in the house after her husband died. Of course Mary Frances hadn't been entirely truthful. It would be ironic if, in an attempt to protect her sons, she was unwittingly protecting Bruno Nickerson or her husband's former lover.

Doucet sped off in his customary cloud of dust, and McIntire lumbered along behind him, kicking up an equal amount, but without nearly the *panache*.

There should be something he could do, but he couldn't think what. That evening with the beer, watching the sun go down, held little attraction for him now. Those two kids were alone in the care of Nick Thorsen, of all people. They weren't stupid; they would know their mother might be dying. They needed somebody to take care of them. Given how they felt about McIntire, his presence would be worth less than nothing.

There was a letter from Leonie in the box. He propped it against the sugar cannister, while he opened a can of spam. He couldn't keep his eyes off it, her exuberant handwriting, so familiar in its illegibility, so reassuring.

He sliced off a hunk of the Spam and chopped it into Kelpie's dish. The remainder he sliced, fried, smothered in canned pork and beans, and heaped onto a plate. Only when he sat with the plate in front of him, did he open the letter.

Clear out the dancing girls, I'm on my way, and I'll be bringing impressionable children.

He place the paper face down on the table and ate. When he'd swallowed the last tepid bean, he picked it up again. The words "bringing" and "children" were still there, and still contained within the same sentence.

As she had suspected, Stevie and her husband, Angus, weren't getting on so well. It was a difficult time, and they all agreed that it would be better for Chuckie and the girls to take a trip to America with Grannie until things were sorted one way or the other. They'd sail from Southhampton on the twenty-seventh of July. She was excited about seeing her horses and garden—were the beans ready to pick?—and him, of course.

The beans might be ready, if you could find them amidst the tansy weed and thistles. How much time did he have?

The unreasonable belief that Leonie's return would put an end to the dismal happenings of recent days filled him to the tips of his fingers. He felt a sudden urge to do something—something to make it true.

He chucked Kelpie under the chin. "I think," he said, "that there's enough daylight left to cut the grass."

The spaniel made no move to join him, but wagged her moral support.

McIntire looked out at the ancient reel mower buried in shin-high grass, and wished he hadn't been such a cheapskate. After ten minutes searching the porch shelves for a whetstone and the can of oil, he headed out the door.

Chapter Forty-eight

Nick sat on the porch, feet on the railing, looking more like the pre-Parkinson's Nick than McIntire had seen in months. "You walk over?" he asked.

"It was that or the Koski Wagon, and I wanted to get here before morning. Battery's dead on the Nash."

Nick held the old familiar tumbler in his hand. The children had either given him a new lease on life, or driven him back to his old ways. He displayed the amber colored liquid. "Iced tea," he said. "Want some?"

"Hell, no. You teetotallers are a smug bunch of SOBs. Sauna still hot?"

"Hot enough for the likes of you. Help yourself. It looks like you could use it. What the hell you been up to? No, don't tell me. I'm off to bed, now I've got the little tykes all tucked in."

"Mia's not back yet, I take it."

"No. She's still at the hospital. I called a half hour ago to make sure she wasn't lying in the ditch somewhere."

McIntire bid his host goodnight and took the path to the sauna. Before he went inside, he stopped to throw a few more sticks of wood into the heater. When he looked back at the house, a light shone from the windows in his old bedroom. At least one of the little tykes wasn't completely tucked in.

He stripped himself of the oil stained trousers and the sweat stained shirt, and peeled off the grass stained socks. Maybe his washing would keep until Leonie got back. With Chuckie and the girls. Good lord.

He stepped into the steam room, filled the bucket from the barrel of water, threw a dipperful onto the rocks, and gasped. It was hot enough for the likes of him, all right, and probably ten degrees hotter at his level than at Nick's. He wet down the wall and turned sideways to lean against it, stretching his legs the length of the bench. That was better. Hot, but not boiling his brain. He splashed another dipper of water onto the stones and felt a trickle of sweat down his side.

What would it be like to have children in the house? He only knew two children, four if Sam and Jake counted, and they all couldn't stand the sight of him. Didn't like him much, anyway. What did Koski have that he didn't? Was cowboy boots all it took?

The warmth and the aroma of cedar lulled him into a doze that soon became solid sleep.

A noise roused him, a dull scraping sound followed by a rustle coming from the dressing room. Company? "Nick, that you?" There was no answer, but McIntire could sense a presence on the other side of the door. Mia? Oh, lord, it couldn't be. He held his breath. The outer door opened, then softly, gently, closed. She'd thought better of it. McIntire felt relief and a flood of guilt that accompanied his undeniable twinge of disappointment.

The next sound obliterated all thought of illicit romance— unmistakable, the scraping again, and this time he knew that it was the bolt to the outer door being slid into place.

"Hey, I'm in here!"

A scuffling, whispery as a mouse, and then, from over his head, a metallic thump against the stovepipe.

"Open up!" It was pointless; whoever had locked the doors was well aware that they'd trapped him inside.

Thin tendrils of smoke snaked out from the seams in the cast iron heater. The first thought that came was total disbelief. Someone had locked him in and stopped up the chimney. Someone who wanted to smoke him like a ham. The second thought aroused sheer terror. He knew how fast smoke could kill. Minutes, maybe even seconds. He was naked, armed with only an aluminum dipper to break his way out, and the place was built like Fort Knox.

One more sound assaulted his brain. The door of the stove creaked open. More wood thrown in. Stoking the fire to roast him.

"Are you crazy? Let me out of here!"

The room was already choked. McIntire flung himself onto the floor and pressed his mouth against the narrow crack under the door. Nothing ever tasted so good. Shouldn't there be a vent in the room somewhere? He sucked in a breath and twisted away. There it was, high above him, an eight inch opening in the wall—into the dressing room. It too would soon fill with smoke. Here on the floor he might have five minutes left.

The stove was cemented into the wall. It was the single vulnerable spot in the room. If he could knock the stove out...but it was red hot and piled with sizzling stones. He had water, a fifty-five gallon drum full to the brim. Could he somehow use it to put out the fire? If he could knock the stovepipe from its connection to the chimney maybe he could pour water into the heater, onto the fire. It would never work; the place would fill with smoke within seconds after the stovepipe fell, before the water did any good.

The water. A barrel filled by the recent rain with water that ran off the roof. It had to get in some way. McIntire twisted away from the air again. A copper pipe protruded through the logs and ran down the wall to drain into the drum. He could try to snap the pipe at its joint near the ceiling or to shove the barrel from under it to get at its open end. The second option seemed safest. He braced his feet against the barrel and pushed. The drum barely budged. He put his mouth back to the crack. He'd try again when he recovered some strength.

Chapter Forty-nine

Claire lay in bed, her heart beating like a hammer in her chest. She'd done something brave. John McIntire would be locked in the sauna house, with the pail over the chimney, until somebody went looking for him. And he'd be sick when they found him. Sick from the smoke, too sick to break down the door. Nobody would know it was her. And if they found out, how could they blame her? He took her brothers to jail, and he made her mother have a heart attack. She might not have saved her brothers, but she'd avenged them. John McIntire would regret what he'd done to them, and they'd owe it to her.

It was a long time before her heart beat slow enough so she could fall asleep, and then, before knew it, Joey was shaking her. The light was on, but it was still night outside.

"Wake up. Nick says we have to get up and come downstairs." He hurried out the door in just his undershorts, but Claire put on her jeans and blouse before she went down. Nick wasn't there, or Mia Thorsen either, only Father Doucet.

"Where's Nick?"

"He's gone back to bed." Father looked at Joey. "Get some clothes on. You need to come with me."

Joey went right back upstairs, but Claire asked, "Where to?"

"You'll see."

That didn't tell her anything, and she went to the bathroom. When she came out, Joey and Father Doucet were standing by the door.

"Shouldn't we tell Nick where we're going?"

Father Doucet put his hand on Claire's shoulder. "He knows. But I didn't mean you. It's Joey that needs to come."

Up until then, Joey had looked excited. Now he looked down. "I want Claire to come, too."

Claire wasn't sure she wanted to go anywhere, but Joey was scared to go by himself.

Father Doucet twisted his mouth, like he couldn't make up his mind. Joey started to sniffle, and finally Father looked at his watch and said, "Okay, then. Let's get going."

Spike was jumping around, all worked up, but Claire didn't even dare ask. She put on a sad face, so maybe Father would feel sorry for her, and for Spike, but he didn't seem to notice. She patted Spike and hugged him tight. "Sorry Boy, you have to stay." When she shut the door on him, he had a sad face, too.

The moon was big and bright, and there were a million stars. Another light twinkled through the bushes—the sauna. Claire wondered if she should tell that John McIntire was locked in. But then Father would wonder how she knew about it. She could pretend that they should go turn off the light, because somebody must have forgot. But as far as she was concerned John McIntire could suffer all night.

Claire would rather have sat in the front seat next to Father Doucet, but he made both her and Joey get in the back with a pillow and a scratchy army blanket. Father started the car. "Lie down and get under the blanket. It will be a long drive." It was warm enough; they didn't really need a blanket, but he waited until they were all tucked in before he took off.

"Are we going to see Ma?" Joey asked.

Father just said, "Not right now."

They drove for a long time. Joey fell fast asleep, snoring almost as loud as Jake did. Claire wished she'd begged harder about bringing Spike, but he might puke in the car.

It was strange, lying on her back, flying along through the dark, not being able to see a thing but shadowy tree branches and a moving glow now and then from Father's cigarette. Moving through the world, but not being in it. Like her real life was just a dream, and she was a ghost.

It was getting cooler. She put her feet on Joey to keep them warm and pulled the blanket up around her chin. Father Doucet started to sing. It wasn't very loud, and she didn't understand the words.

"Is that another language?" She asked.

"It's French." Father sounded like he was in a dream, too. "It's a song my mother used to sing when I was a little boy."

"Is your mother in France?"

"She was. She's passed away now."

Passed away. Maybe that's what Claire's would have to learn to say, *"My mother's passed away, and my father's passed away, too."*

Father's cigarette glowed again. "All of my family are dead."

She didn't ask, but he told her anyway, "They were killed in the war. By the Germans."

"You mean…? All of your relatives?"

"Yes, they lived in a small village. The German soldiers came and made all the people in the village go into the church. Then they locked the doors and set fire to the church, so everybody died."

Claire just plain didn't believe it. Soldiers fought the enemy, and the enemy was other soldiers. "Even the babies?" she asked. "Even the grandmothers?"

Father Doucet said, "Yes. Even *my* grandmother."

Claire still couldn't believe it, but Father wouldn't lie, and he was talking to her like she was grown up, so Claire asked, "How did you escape?"

"I wasn't in France then. I already lived here."

"So the Germans couldn't get you."

"No."

"My father wanted us to sing German songs sometimes, maybe they were songs his mother sang when he was a baby," she told him. "But we didn't know what the words meant, because we don't talk German." She added, "Sister does."

"Yes," he said, "I know."

Chapter Fifty

It was after one in the morning when Mary Frances Hofer died.
Mia had dozed off and wasn't aware when the woman stopped
breathing for good—forever. She leapt up at Guibard's hand on
her shoulder and his words, "Looks like it's over."

"How in God's name will we get a big enough casket?" Mia
heard the words as from a distance, but it wasn't like it was her
speaking. She must have been still asleep. She'd never have said
such a thing otherwise.

Mrs. Hofer was now only a gigantic sheet-covered mound
in the bed.

Guibard was gray; an exhausted old man. "We'd better go
tell the boys."

"Maybe the priest should do it."

"He left at least a couple of hours ago."

"Left?" Doucet had been in the room when Mia fell asleep,
talking to Mary Frances, listening to her. He'd even made her
laugh a few times. A real laugh, not just the nervous cackle.

"He was on the phone for a long time. I assume trying to
reach the aunt. Then I guess he went for the other kids."

"Probably."

It took three tries, but Mia managed to unbend her body
enough to stand up.

"I'll get you home. And the boys, too?"

Mia nodded. What would happen to them now? "They're orphans," Mia said. "Four orphans."

"We'll think about that in the morning."

Jake and Sam didn't start crying until they got into the dark of the coupe's back seat, and didn't stop until it came to a halt in the yard. They refused to leave the car, insisting that Guibard take them home. There was no point in arguing. They were hardly children anymore, not after tonight.

The light was on in the room where Claire should be sleeping. Otherwise everything was dark. Dark and clear and silent. Was the child awake, waiting? Mia couldn't bear to be the one to tell her. She watched the taillights disappear down the driveway and around the bend.

A faint pinpoint of light was visible beyond the garden. She could leave it on, it didn't matter all that much, but a short walk, some fresh air, would feel good. And give her time to think.

She let her memory and the moon, almost full, guide her along the path, past the gnarled remains of the pines, past the old root cellar, to the sauna.

The door was closed and latched, the single window was a hazily glowing rectangle. She pushed open the door and jumped back at the cloud of acrid smoke. What the devil had Nick done this time?

She waved away the smoke and fumbled to open the door to the steam room. A naked and retching John McIntire fell into her arms. His words as she cradled him were a painful croak. "I think I've had this dream before."

Four hours of sitting with his lips wrapped around the end of a blistering hot vertical copper pipe had given McIntire a sorer neck than he thought it was possible to survive. And the sorest back, and the sorest lips. He didn't allow Mia to summon the doctor back. "I'm alive. It's too late for it to kill me now. At least not tonight." Worrying about Black Lung could come later, as could dealing with the miscreant, the identity of whom he had no doubt whatsoever. She had other problems now. He asked, "Has anybody told the younger kids?"

Nick answered, "I suppose the priest did."

"I'm not sure he knows," Mia said. "He was with Mary Frances at the hospital, but he left before she died. She wasn't looking so bad then. The final heart attack happened later." She swept her fingertips across her eyelids. "Do you think I should wake them up? Would it be okay to wait until morning? Maybe we can get Father Doucet back before we tell them."

"They're not here," Nick sounded mystified. "I thought you'd have seen them. He came to get them a while ago. I'm not sure what time—I was asleep when he got here—but it must have been after midnight. I thought it was crazy getting them up. I couldn't see how it would be good for them to see her sick like that, and I didn't figure the hospital would let them in. But maybe priests have pull. I guess they didn't make it back in time, anyway. It would have been better to let the kids sleep."

"We must have crossed paths." Her reflection in the window showed the helplessness that McIntire felt. "The poor babies. It must have been awful. Getting there too late."

McIntire fell into a fit of coughing that sent him out the back door. When he returned, Nick handed him a glass of water, "Sorry. We seem to be forgetting that somebody tried to kill you."

Mia spoke through a yawn. "Tried to kill John? Why? Besides they must have thought it was you in there."

"I didn't take it quietly," McIntire said. "They knew who it was inside, and I know who it was outside."

Chapter Fifty-one

It was only a few minutes past eight when the phone rang, but McIntire was more or less up. He coughed into the mouthpiece to let his caller know they had reached a living body.

"John?" It was Ellie Wall.

McIntire choked out what he hoped sounded like an admission to being more or less himself.

"I've just come from getting ready for nine o'clock mass. Father Doucet isn't there, and he's not at his house."

The question of why he should care crossed McIntire's mind. "He's probably with the Hofer children. Mrs. Hofer died last night."

"Oh, no. How terrible. I had no idea." There was a pause, lengthy enough to lead McIntire to wonder if she'd fainted. No, not Ellie, but she might have simply rushed off, forgetting to hang up the phone. Finally she said, "But Father should be here. He wouldn't just forget about mass."

"Under the circumstances he might. Or he might have overslept, it was a long night. I'll go check."

"No, don't bother. Adam is here having breakfast. I'll send him over to Hofers'. You'd better take care of that cold."

McIntire stepped outdoors and spent a few minutes spitting disgusting black slime into his newly trimmed grass. He sank to the steps limp, depleted, physically and every other way. Kelpie turned bleary sympathetic eyes to his. He cupped her chin in his hand. "Brew a pot of joe will you?" When she made no move for the kitchen, he went on, "What the hell is the world coming to? I'm pretty damn sure that a little girl tried to kill me last night. Tried to roast me like a Fourth of July pig. I survived, but her mother is dead. She's an orphan. Is it divine punishment? What sort of God would punish four children for the act of one? Although the rest may not be so very innocent either. Did Reuben and Mary Frances Hofer spawn a family of homicidal psychotics do you suppose? Are *their* deaths the Vengeance of the Lord? The authority on the subject has gone AWOL."

The jangling phone cut his soliloquy short. This time McIntire managed hello on the second try. It was Adam Wall.

"He ain't here?"

"At Hofers'?"

"At anywhere. And he's got the kids with him."

McIntire tried to ignore his burning throat to focus his mind. "Maybe he went back to the church."

"I don't think you're listening. Last night he picked up those two kids. He told Nick he was taking them to the hospital. He never showed up. He didn't say that he was going somewhere else, and he hasn't come back."

Only one thought came into McIntire's head. "He drives like a maniac, and he must have been getting tired."

"That's what I'm guessing. Koski and Newman are on their way to Ishpeming. We can start from this end. We'll have to check the side roads in case he got groggy and took a wrong turn."

With luck maybe they were only lost. "What about the boys? Are they still around?"

"I doubt it like hell. They were at home when I got there. I told them to stay put, but they got a car, you know."

"And they got a head start on us," McIntire said. "I'll get moving."

It was bound to happen sooner or later. But you'd think with two kids in the car, a man purporting to be the agent of God could lighten up on the gas.

How much tragedy could one family take? Would it be capped by Sam and Jake Hofer discovering the bodies of their younger siblings in the twisted wreckage of a Maroon Buick Riveria?

Chapter Fifty-two

When Claire opened her eyes it was getting light, and the car was stopped at a filling station. Father Doucet said she could go to the bathroom, and he woke Joey up so he could go, too.

Father didn't look tired at all, even though he'd been up all night.

She was stiff from sleeping curled up, and it felt good to stand straight and stretch her legs, and good to be able to look at something but the sky and the back of Father's head.

They were in a town. The sun was only just coming up, but the sidewalk felt warm under her feet. It was a pretty filling station, made to look like a tiny white and pink castle. It even had a little bitty tower with a pointy roof. The sign on the door said, *MINNOWS AND WORMS* in big letters. Underneath it said, *We Get Up Before The Fish Do.*

The guy that put the gas in the car looked sort of like Sam. He filled up Father's two gas cans, too, and winked at her when he was washing the dirt off the windows. Sam was in jail now. Sleeping on a hard bunk in a cell. Claire wondered if they'd let him and Jake share a cell.

When they got back in the car, Father said Joey could sit in the front seat.

There was a bakery down the street, so the gas station people weren't the only ones up before the fish. Father went in and bought some rolls. Claire and Joey both had long johns, two each, and Father Doucet had a bismark.

"We'll stop for a real breakfast soon."

They went over a bridge across a wide, wide river. It had to be the Mississippi. They had crossed it when they moved from Iowa, so she knew they must be going west now. Where women are double breasted.

Joey hung his head out the window to look down at the water. After they were across he said, "Next week is when I make my First Communion."

"That's right."

"On Saturday, I make my first confession."

It was quiet for a while, then Father said, "You can make your first confession now."

"There's no church."

Father slowed the car down and drove onto the side of the road. He put his cigarette out in the ash tray, and opened the door. "This will do just fine." He looked around at Claire. "You can both make a confession."

It wasn't fair. Claire hadn't planned on going to confession. It was something she needed to get herself ready for, to think about for a while—for a long while. Going to confession always made her feel sick, but it felt good afterwards, to start all over with a clean soul. She hadn't been to confession with a priest that she knew, like she did Father Doucet, and she'd be humiliated for him to know all the bad things she'd done. You weren't supposed to keep anything back. That would be a worse sin. And the priest wasn't ever allowed to tell, no matter what you'd done. But he'd still *know*. It wasn't fair. If you lied to the priest, could you just go to confession again and confess that you'd told a lie? Maybe she should just say, "No, thank you. Some other time."

They all got out and Father took Joey a little ways down the road to a tree trunk that had fallen down. Claire waited.

Father Doucet sat on the log, and Joey got down on his knees beside him. Claire saw him make the sign of the cross and then felt ashamed for watching and turned her back.

They were on a high hill, and you could see way across a valley with a creek at the bottom. Some Holstein cows, like Grandpa's, stood in a group in the mist. It made a pretty picture, but Claire could only think about the butterflies in her stomach.

She didn't hear Joey coming until he tapped her on the shoulder and said it was her turn.

She settled for telling that she lied and had bad thoughts, but it was like Father wasn't even listening to her. He prayed under his breath, and then said that her penance was out of his hands, and she should go in peace.

Joey was waiting by the car. His eyes were red, but he wasn't crying. He looked at Claire like he was scared she'd whack him or something, and said she could have the front seat.

Chapter Fifty-three

By noon it was obvious that the Reverend Adrien Doucet and the two youngest Hofer children had effectively disappeared. The only automobile casualty on any roads between St. Adele and the hospital on the outskirts of Ishpeming was the older Hofer brothers' Oldsmobile, pulled off the road, out of gas. The two had made it almost back to Karvonen's store on foot, lugging a three gallon gas can. The dread in their eyes was agonizing.

"We haven't found anything," McIntire told them. "And the sheriff hasn't heard about any car accidents."

"I don't get it," Jake put down the can. "Has he kidnapped them?"

It was a bizarre idea, but it almost seemed as though he had. "They'll be okay."

"Do they know about Ma?"

"Probably not."

Sam gulped and turned his back. Jake wiped his nose on his sleeve. McIntire could think of nothing to say but, "Come on. I'll take you home. We can get the car later."

Ellie Wall was waiting for them. She'd milked the long-suffering Opal and baked a pan of biscuits. She had hardly set to work, frying eggs and potatoes, before her son showed up trailed by Pete Koski, come to reclaim his Power Wagon.

They ate in silence, not from awkwardnes; in a strange way it was a companionable concentration on satisfying hunger while united in tragedy and disbelief.

Koski pushed back his chair and shifted to face the youths, tapping his fork on the table. "Think," he said. "Think very, very hard. Yesterday when the priest drove you to the hospital, what did he talk about? I want to know every single solitary word you can remember."

Sam swallowed. "He said that our mother had a heart attack, and...he said it was possible that she wouldn't live."

Jake added, "And we should pray for her."

"That's it?"

Jake nodded. Sam said, "Mostly."

"He must have said something more. It's forty-five minutes from here to Ishpeming."

Sam observed, "Not the way Father drives."

Jake stared at his empty plate. "He said that nothing is more terrible than losing your entire family, and it would be especially hard for us, because we're young ."

"Are those the words he used? Your *entire* family?"

"I guess he meant if Ma died, that would be both her and Pa."

"And Grandpa," Sam put in.

"That's the grandfather that gave you the shotgun?"

"Ya."

"And he taught you how to use it?"

Jake took another biscuit from the pan. "He made us practice. Mostly by shooting gophers. Every morning he gave us each one shell and sent us out to get gophers. He expected us to come back with three gophers. Three shells, three gophers. If we didn't, he'd make us wash his truck, or cut the grass, something like that." He reached for the butter. "He wasn't mean about it. Not like Pa."

McIntire's gaze met Koski's over the stubbly heads. Koski cleared his throat. "Three?"

"Ya. One for each of us."

"Your sister learned how to handle the gun, too?"

"Are you kidding? No! Well, she wanted to, but Grandpa said it wasn't for girls."

"Joey?"

"He had to rest the gun on a fence or something, but the little guy's a good shot. Sometimes Jake and me just gave the shells to him and let him shoot all…." Sam's voice trailed into a dead, suffocating silence. Jake whispered, "Christ. Joey."

The screen door smashed against the side of the house. "Have they come back?" Mia Thorsen stood in the doorway, the eagerness fading. "What's happened? Please, are they…?"

Ellie Wall leapt up. "As far as we know they're fine. They're with Father. They'll be fine."

"With Father where?" The mongrel terrier bounded in behind her.

"That we don't know." Koski looked again to Jake. "Where the hell is that gun?"

He shook his head.

"Where was it kept? To hide it from your father?"

"In the chest of drawers. In the second drawer from the bottom." The reply was automatic. The boy might have been talking in his sleep.

"Ya, that's what your mother told us. She said she saw it there the day after your father died, when she was getting sheets to make a bed for your aunt."

Again Jake mouthed the soundless word, *Joey*, and it was left for Sam to respond, "So the burglars stole it."

"The burglars didn't steal it We know who it was that broke in, and they didn't take the gun, they claim they didn't see it, and I don't think they'd have any reason to lie about that. It was gone before they came." Koski leaned forward, "So that means it was there on Tuesday, the tenth, and gone by the evening of Thursday, the twelfth."

Mia inched around the room to stand behind McIntire's chair. When she put her hand on his shoulder, he continued to regard the two bewildered youths.

"We weren't here then," Jake came back to life. "We left for the funeral on Thursday, early in the morning."

"With your Aunt Jane."

"That's right. We went on the train."

"And your father's remains were brought here the day before." McIntire said.

"Ya. Ma couldn't go to the funeral."

"I suppose there were people in and out most of the day?" Koski waited for a confirming nod. "How hard would it have been to sneak a shotgun out the back door?"

"To where?"

Jake had hit the nail on the head. Getting it out without being noticed might not have been impossible—it had been taken out to commit the murder, after all—but it was almost certainly not hidden around the place somewhere. The only people who'd have had both the will and the means to get rid of it effectively, by taking it off in a car, were the two young men sitting at the table.

"Carried away somewhere on foot, not too far, but far enough?" The sheriff didn't ask, but the implication was there; how far could an eight year old boy have gotten with a shotgun without being noticed? He'd managed to make it to the hayfield and back when no one was expecting him to have it.

"It would have had to be at night." At Jake's words, Mia's hand tightened and McIntire reached to cover it with his.

"No," Sam said, "It couldn't have been. Sister stayed in the room all night, right next to the coffin."

"All night?"

"Ya. You can ask her."

"She sat with the casket? Not ten feet from where the gun was kept?"

Sam nodded.

McIntire said, "She might have fallen asleep."

"Not for long," Sam said. "Every time I woke up, I heard her singing, and then crying for a long time."

Koski looked up. "John, think you could dash off home and call Forrest Brothers? Ask them how the lid of Reuben Hofer's coffin was fastened."

Chapter Fifty-four

They drove again for a long time. All of them in the front seat, Joey in the middle. Father still hadn't said where it was they were going. It was like the Mystery Bus story in Claire's old reading book. The people were going on a trip, but they had to guess where. They were going to St. Ives. The driver whistled a song about St. Ives to give them a hint. Father Doucet was singing in the night, but it couldn't be a hint, because her and Joey couldn't understand French. Claire didn't think they were on their way to France!

Wherever it was, she hoped they'd get there soon. Although it wasn't so bad, being able to do nothing but sit and look out the window, not to have to think about Ma being sick or Sam and Jake being in jail.

Father slowed down when they went through a town, but most of the time they went like the wind. Joey gabbed away, about his model farm, and playing the fiddle, and not liking school, but Claire just looked out the window. It was the prettiest place Claire had ever seen; hilly, with open pastures and giant trees. Maybe she'd be an artist someday, and paint pictures that looked like this. She'd need a hundred different colors of green.

Father didn't say much. He smoked an awful lot. He had a thing under his dashboard to put cigarettes in, and when you wanted one, it just popped out and automatically lit itself, so you didn't have to take your hands off the wheel. He said it was a Prestalight.

They went down a long hill so steep that it made Claire dizzy. There was a town at the bottom. After a couple of wrong turns, they stopped next to the place Father was looking for. Thank goodness it was a café. Claire was starving even after both long johns.

The place was crowded, and Claire was embarrassed about her too-big shorts and her bare feet. She was still wearing what she had on when she went to Mia Thorsen's house to call the ambulance. It seemed like it was ages ago that Ma had said to go, "immediately if not sooner," and she'd taken off running, but it was only yesterday.

Most of the people in the café were dressed up, and that's when Claire remembered that today was Sunday. Father Doucet should be in church now. It seemed funny to be in a restaurant with a priest on Sunday morning. Father didn't have on his black outfit, so nobody would realize he was a priest and should be in church, unless he surprised them all and got up to preach a sermon!

They could have sat in a booth, but Father told the waitress he wanted a table by the window, so they had to wait for it to be cleaned off. Claire thought a booth would be more cozy, and people wouldn't be able to look at her, but Joey liked the table because there was a train depot across the street, and he hoped he'd see a train come in.

They ordered eggs and sausage and toast, and pancakes, too. The waitress brought a whole pot of coffee for Father Doucet, and he let Claire have some. They were just starting to eat, when Claire looked out and saw a lady come out of the train depot and start across the street. It was Sister Jane.

Chapter Fifty-five

"There's irony for you. Pacifist Reuben Hofer sharing his final earthly resting place with a shotgun." They were the first words Mia had spoken in the twenty minutes they'd been sitting on the front steps of the Black Creek Schoolhouse.

"The one that killed him." McIntire had to say it aloud once more, had to try to comprehend the preposterous. "The one that his youngest son used to kill him."

Mia leaned forward her head in her hands, and spoke to her knees. "My brain might know it's true, but that doesn't mean I'll ever really believe it."

"Joey. Why?"

"He spent all that time playing by the drain pipe. He heard every word that was said in that kitchen."

"But what could have been said that would lead a small child to kill his father? How could such a thing even enter his mind?"

McIntire had to lean close to catch the muffled reply. "Mary Frances Hofer was preparing to die. She said she'd told Father Doucet that she was tempted to do away with Reuben herself, that she was horrified at the idea of dying and leaving her children at his mercy. Of course she was exaggerating, and half joking—she said she'd do it by rolling on him in bed—but Joey couldn't have understood that. He knew his mother was going to die, and, if she squished his father, she'd go to hell."

"Did he think he was Hell-proof?"

"Yes. He was too little. Sin was for when he was more grown up. His mother wanted his father dead, and who knows what he might have heard from his brothers? The whole family hated Reuben, but Joey was the only one who could get rid of him, because he was too little for sin." She demanded, "Why do people tell kids things like that? If that's normal eight year old boy thinking, why aren't more parents dead?"

"Normal eight year old boys aren't sharpshooters."

"God."

"So Joey saved himself and his siblings from slavery, and his mother from eternal hell-fire, in one fell...shot."

Mia twisted her pigtail. "I don't think it wasn't so much the slavery, even if that was the core of it. Mrs. Hofer couldn't bear seeing what was happening to her children, the kind of people life with Reuben was turning them into. People who hated."

McIntire couldn't make sense of it. There was no point in trying. "What can we do now?"

"Wait."

They waited. It was growing dark when Father Adrien Doucet charged into the yard and stopped a few feet from the door.

Mia went down the steps with the leaping pup and opened the car door to escort the barefoot girl into the house.

McIntire repeated her action on the driver's side. He was less solicitous. "Get out of the car."

Doucet alighted with less than his customary flair, but hardly looked the worse for what must have been a mighty long thirty-six hours.

"Taking off with somebody else's children is known as abduction, and crossing a state line makes it a federal offense." McIntire wished more of the anger he felt showed in his voice.

"What makes you think I've crossed a state line?"

"Call it a hunch."

Doucet bent his head for a moment. Praying for deliverance? He didn't look that worried. "There's nothing criminal about fulfilling a sick woman's request that her child be taken to his grandmother to be cared for."

"Or to hide out?"

"He's an eight year old child."

"He's committed pre-meditated murder." Saying it aloud for the first time, McIntire still couldn't believe it.

"I know that."

Did the man's infuriating smugness ever stop? "Murder," McIntire repeated. "First degree homicide. He can't just get away with it."

Doucet shook the last of his ever-present cigarettes into his hand and crushed the pack. "If he was prosecuted, found guilty, what would happen to him?"

McIntire wasn't sure such a thing had ever happened before. "Reform school, I suppose. He'd be out in a few years. At least they'd let him go when he turns eighteen."

"He won't be getting out of Prairie Oak before he's eighteen, probably not ever."

The logic was ludicrous, but flawless. McIntire spouted the timeworn, "You're not a judge or a jury."

"No," the priest admitted, "and I'm damn glad of that."

That made a peculiar kind of sense, too. He owed nothing but to his own conscience, unlike McIntire, paid the odd fee by the citizens of St. Adele Township to do their dirty work. "Did his brothers put him up to it?" he asked.

Doucet put the unlighted cigarette in his shirt pocket. "I wouldn't go so far as to say that. They might have influenced him. Indirectly, I think we all put him up to it. He was too young to be punished for his sins, or his crimes. I led him to believe it. *I* believe it. How could any of us have known he had the capability of…How's Mrs. Hofer?"

"She died early this morning."

He looked toward the door the girl had disappeared through, but didn't move. "Am I going to be arrested?"

"Soon as Koski figures out what to charge you with."

"So I got time to get some sleep first?"

"Go ahead."

He slid into the car. "Where are the boys?"

"Gone with Ellie Wall, to start arranging their mother's funeral."

"Forrest Brothers?"

At McIntire's nod, the priest turned the key to his dusty Buick and sped off, not in the direction of his church and home in Aura, but on the road to Chandler.

Chapter Fifty-six

They'd been both sitting on the steps, blinking in the car head-lights, looking like twins, Mia Thorsen and John McIntire. They both got up and came to the car. Mrs. Thorsen opened the door before Claire had a chance to get out. The first thing she said was, "Do you have to go to the bathroom?"

Claire did, but she could wait. She shook her head and scooped Spike up in her arms.

John McIntire went to the other side of the car to talk to Father Doucet. He did look sort of sick, so her plan must have worked.

"Come inside then." Mrs. Thorsen wasn't smiling, and she didn't look happy to see her. Her hair was messy and she looked tired and gray like Ma did sometimes. It made her look more like a witch than ever. Thinking about Mrs. Thorsen being a witch made Claire remember about Joey, and she felt like she might start bawling again.

Father said it was the best thing for Joey, and she had to be brave enough to let him go. He said that Ma wanted him to go to Prairie Oak because she was too sick to take care of him, and that Joey would be happy there. He was probably right—at least he wouldn't have to go to school. But Joey didn't look happy when he walked away with Sister.

Mrs. Thorsen made her go into the living room and sit next to her on the davenport. First she asked if Claire was hungry, and then she told her that Ma died in the night. While her and Joey were driving away with Father Doucet, Ma died.

Everything was just too sad for Claire. She wanted to go to sleep and forget about it all. She ached from sitting in the car for a whole night and a day. She put her face on Spike's neck. He licked at her face, but then wiggled away and jumped onto the floor. She wanted to cry, but was ashamed with Mrs. Thorsen there. She stood up. "I do have to go to the bathroom."

She went out through the back door so she didn't have to pass by Father Doucet and John McIntire, but when she got out, Father's car was gone and John McIntire was sitting on the steps again.

She stayed in the can for a long time, but they didn't come to look for her. Maybe if she stayed there long enough they would forget where she was, and she could sneak out and run away.

But it was pitch dark, and she didn't have the energy for it.

She went back inside and straight up the stairs to her and Joey's bedroom. Somebody had shut the window; it was hot and didn't smell very good. Maybe she could sleep in Ma's room now.

Mrs. Thorsen came up the stairs. The room was too low for her to stand up in, so she sat down on the bed. "You can come home with me. I'll help you get your stuff together. Tomorrow we can decide what to do."

Claire didn't want to go. She wanted to crawl under the covers and stay there for a long long time. It wasn't going to do any good to argue, though, so she just said, "I'll get my clothes."

She waited to give Mia Thorsen time to go downstairs, but she just stayed on the bed, so Claire had to get out the box that her and Joey used the first time they went to Mia's, and put in her new socks and underpants. She opened the closet and took out the two dresses that Sister made. Joey's first communion suit was still hanging there, waiting for him. She touched the shiny white buttons.

Mrs. Thorsen said, "Maybe we could send it to him."

Claire shook her head. "He won't have first communion at Prairie Oak, so he wouldn't get to wear it."

"We could try dying it."

It was a good idea. Claire folded it down the middle and put it in the box.

"We can come back tomorrow," Mia Thorsen said. "We can pack up everything Joey might need and send it to him."

That was a good idea, too.

Claire wanted to get her treasure box from under the floor, but not with Mia Thorsen watching. It would have to wait until tomorrow, too.

Mia Thorsen was so tall she had to practically go on her hands and knees to make it to the stairs. Claire carried the box herself.

When they got downstairs, Claire put the box on the daven-port. She didn't know how they were going to get back to the Thorsen's house. She hoped not in John McIntire's car.

Mia Thorsen picked up the lamp, the one Pa made. "Maybe you'd like to take this with you."

Claire held it in both her hands. It was smooth under her fingers, and heavy. Pa had carved it long ago. It was a joke, Ma said. He chained it to his leg to pretend he was a convict. But he really did get to be a convict, and now he was dead and Ma was dead and Joey was far away and Sam and Jake were in jail.

Suddenly Claire had never been so mad. She heard a roar like a freight train in her head, and she felt like it would explode. She squeezed her eyes shut tight, and she howled, and she threw that lamp as hard as she could against the wall. The light bulb smashed and the wooden ball gave a thwack when it cracked in half, spurting sand out over the floor.

John McIntire came charging into the room. "What's hap-pened?"

"It's okay," Mia told him. "The lamp broke, that's all." She picked up the shade and squatted down and started gathering the pieces of wood. Then she did get on her hands and knees. "John," she said, "what do you suppose this could be?" She reached up and handed him something too small for Claire to see.

He held it up. "I'd say it's a fish hook. A two thousand year old fish hook."

Claire didn't know what he was talking about, but Mia Thorsen kept digging through the sand and picking our pieces of rocks and bent-up metal. Claire went to the kitchen for the broom.

The spilled coffee was cleaned up, and Ma's magazines were stacked up on the table. Claire grabbed the broom and went back out.

Mia said, "Look at this," and gave her something that looked like a little moon. "They're Indian relics, from hundreds of years ago. Can you find something to put them in?"

Claire went for her treasure box. Sheriff Koski had asked if Pa had Indian stuff, and it turned out that he did. Maybe Ma knew about it. Maybe that's why she kept the lamp, even when Pa was away in California and in prison, but Claire didn't think so. She probably kept the lamp because it was Pa's, and he made it. He might have told her, "This is just between you and me. Don't lose it," just like he'd said to Claire when he gave her the wheel.

Claire swept the sand, and Mia and John McIntire put the Indian things in her wooden box.

Then she sat on the davenport with it on her lap while John McIntire took the box with her clothes in it out to his car.

Mia Thorsen picked up the broken halves of the lamp and sat next to Claire on the davenport. "Claire, I think you need to talk to Mr. McIntire."

"Why?" He was the last person Claire wanted to talk to. Ever again in her life. She didn't want to ride in his car, and she didn't want to talk to him. She didn't want to ever see him again.

"In the sauna, the smoke could have killed him. If he hadn't found a pipe to breath through, he would have died."

"My mother died! He put Sam and Jake in jail and made my mother have a heart attack. He killed her!"

"Claire, I'm so…." Mrs. Thorsen didn't finish what she was saying. She had tears running down her cheeks, and Claire looked away. After a while she wiped her nose on her sleeve and said, "What made you think—? Claire, your brothers aren't in jail."

"Then where are they?"

"They went into town with Mrs. Wall. They're making plans for your mother's funeral."

Claire was tired, tired of having to think, tired of the way things were all scrambled in her brain. "He came and took them away. He had the sheriff's car and his police dog."

"Mr. Koski just talked to them. Mr. McIntire brought them home later." Mrs. Thorsen touched her hand. "You have to tell Mr. McIntire you're sorry."

Claire wasn't one darn bit sorry. Sam and Jake might not be in jail, but it was too late to take back Ma's heart attack. She was glad she'd made the man who did that sick. The sicker the better. But she didn't think the smoke would kill him.

"I thought it would just make him sick."

"Well," John McIntire came in the back door. "It did that."

He looked worn out and sad. He was Mia Thorsen's childhood sweetheart, and Mia Thorsen was an old woman, and she was crying. Claire was too tired. She lied again. She said, using a polite company voice, "I'm sorry, Mr. McIntire. I'm sorry I almost murdered you."

Chapter Fifty-seven

Leonie's telegram said they'd get to Chicago on Tuesday, spend the night, and take the overnight sleeper to Chandler, and he could pick them up at the station. McIntire wasn't prepared to wait that long.

He set out at five in the morning to catch the outbound Copper Country Limited, only slightly groggy from a late night scrubbing floors.

He paused at the end of the drive to look back. The lawn was neatly trimmed and the garden as free of weeds as a contrite Claire Hofer could make it. He'd felt guilty about taking advantage of child labor, but Mia insisted that it would make the girl feel better, and maybe she was right. It surely made the garden look better. The kid did a good job. But thank God, she was still enough of a kid to use her armloads of quack grass as an excuse to pay frequent visits to the horses. She'd come and gone without greeting or goodbye. It was going to be interesting to see what she and Leonie's grandchildren made of one another. Chuckie must be about her age.

It looked like the county would let her stay with Mia, for the time being, fulfilling a middle-aged woman's life-long dream. It was more responsibility than should ever be placed on scrawny eleven year old shoulders. When Nick's health got worse...Well, Claire would be no better off with her brothers. Legally, they were still residents of Iowa, and by the time county welfare got its rear in gear Jake would be eighteen and could conceivably be appointed Sam's legal guardian. Otherwise the two would have been prize catches for some farmer magnanimously offering a home to two foster children, and they'd start their life of servitude over again. Although with the question still officially out as to who had murdered their father, there might not be so many willing to take that chance.

Ironically, Joey might end up being the best off of the bunch.

The train was already at the depot when McIntire got there. He barely had time to buy a ticket—one way, trusting that Leonie had booked two sleeper compartments for the journey back. The kids would just have to squeeze into one. He hoped he wasn't being over optimistic. He didn't intend to spend the night sharing a berth with Chuckie.

It was the first train trip McIntire had taken since returning from Europe, and he'd missed it. Sitting with a book, no responsibilities, no ringing phones, no neighbors announcing deaths, watching the world passing by his window and pitying the people who weren't so lucky. He settled into his seat, his newspaper on his knees, and leaned back. When he opened his eyes the landscape hadn't changed, but his watch and his empty stomach said it was half-past noon.

The remainder of the day passed quickly enough with an extravagant lunch in the dining car, his newspaper, and another nap or two.

McIntire was not a connoisseur of train stations—bleak, cold spaces. They could have been made entirely more inviting by lowering the pretentiously high ceilings and limiting the icy marble.

The designers of Chicago's Union Station hadn't stinted on either ceiling height or marble, but the place was far from cold. It's soaring cavernous space was hot and still and infiltrated with all the odors associated with trains and the mass of people traveling on them.

The train would spend an hour in the station before heading back. That meant he could either run around looking for Leonie or hang around and wait until they showed up.

He didn't have to do either. The fair hair and pale British faces stood out in the sea of robust mid-westerners like lilies in a wheatfield. They sat straight-backed on the edge of the massive wood bench, presenting six white knees in a row—a serious-faced boy flanked by two thoroughly domesticated little girls in straw boaters, a separate species entirely from Claire Hofer.

Facing them, with her back to McIntire, was their grandmother.

McIntire crossed the pink marble expanse to approach from behind and put his hands over her eyes. "Guess who."

Her startled gasp was echoed by his own, as a spume of tepid water drenched his shirt. She turned, a cone-shaped paper cup in each hand, one empty. "John, you ninny! I've half a mind to throw the other one!"

"Welcome home."

"Thank you."

"Don't I get a kiss?"

She cocked her head, considering, her eyes locked on his. Then, without turning, she extended the cup behind her back to her grandson. "Here," she said, "Share this with your sisters."

To receive a free catalog of Poisoned Pen Press titles, please contact us in one of the following ways:

Phone: 1-800-421-3976
Facsimile: 1-480-949-1707
Email: info@poisonedpenpress.com
Website: www.poisonedpenpress.com

Poisoned Pen Press
6962 E. First Ave. Ste. 103
Scottsdale, AZ 85251